JAN - - 2019

Unmarriageable

BALLANTINE BOOKS

NEW YORK

Unmarriageable

A Novel

SONIAH KAMAL

Copyright © 2019 by Soniah Kamal

All rights reserved.

Published in the United States by Ballantine Books, an imprint of Random House, a division of Penguin Random House LLC, New York.

BALLANTINE and the HOUSE colophon are registered trademarks of Penguin Random House LLC.

LIBRARY OF CONGRESS CATALOGING-IN-PUBLICATION DATA
Names: Soniah Kamal, author.
Title: Unmarriageable: a novel / Soniah Kamal.
Description: New York: Ballantine Books, 2019.
Identifiers: LCCN 2018036398 | ISBN 9781524799717 (hardback) |
ISBN 9781524799724 (ebook)
Subjects: | BISAC: FICTION / Contemporary Women. |
FICTION / Family Life. | FICTION / Literary.
Classification: LCC PS3619.O533 U56 2019 | DDC 813/.6—dc23
LC record available at https://lccn.loc.gov/2018036398

Printed in the United States of America on acid-free paper

randomhousebooks.com

2 4 6 8 9 7 5 3 1

FIRST EDITION

Title-page, part-title, and chapter-opener art: © iStockphoto.com

Book design by Dana Leigh Blanchette

For Mansoor Wasti,
friend, love, partner,
and
Buraaq, Indus, Miraage,
heart, soul, life

Upon the whole, however, I am ... well satisfied enough. The work is rather too light, and bright, and sparkling; it wants shade; it wants to be stretched out here and there with a long chapter of sense, if it could be had; if not, of solemn specious nonsense, about something unconnected with the story; an essay on writing, a critique on Walter Scott, or the history of Buonaparte, or anything that would form a contrast, and bring the reader with increased delight to the playfulness and epigrammatism of the general style.

—Jane Austen on *Pride and Prejudice*
in a letter (1813) to her sister, Cassandra

I have no knowledge of either Sanscrit or Arabic. ... I have never found one among them [Orientalists] who could deny that a single shelf of a good European library was worth the whole native literature of India and Arabia. The intrinsic superiority of the Western Literature ... we are free to employ our funds as we choose, that we ought to employ them in teaching what is best worth knowing, that English is better worth knowing than Sanscrit or Arabic ... that it is possible to make natives of this country thoroughly good English scholars, and that to this end our efforts ought to be directed. ... We must at present do our best to form a class who may be interpreters between us and the millions whom we govern—a class of persons Indian in blood and colour, but English in tastes, in opinions, in morals and in intellect. To that class we may leave it to refine the vernacular dialects of the country.

—from Thomas Babington Macaulay's
"Minute on Education," 1835

Part One

DECEMBER 2000

Chapter 1

It is a truth universally acknowledged that a girl can go from pauper to princess or princess to pauper in the mere seconds it takes for her to accept a proposal.

When Alysba Binat began working at age twenty as the English-literature teacher at the British School of Dilipabad, she had thought it would be a temporary solution to the sudden turn of fortune that had seen Mr. Barkat "Bark" Binat and Mrs. Khushboo "Pinkie" Binat and their five daughters—Jenazba, Alysba, Marizba, Qittyara, and Lady—move from big-city Lahore to backwater Dilipabad. But here she was, ten years later, thirty years old, and still in the job she'd grown to love despite its challenges. Her new batch of ninth-graders was starting *Pride and Prejudice,* and their first homework had been to rewrite the opening sentence of Jane Austen's novel, always a fun activity and a good way for her to get to know her students better.

After Alys took attendance, she opened a fresh box of multicolored chalks and invited the girls to share their sentences on the blackboard. The first to jump up was Rose-Nama, a crusader for duty and decorum, and one of the more trying students. Rose-Nama deliberately bypassed the colored chalks for a plain white one, and Alys braced herself for a reimagined sentence exulting a traditional life—marriage, children, death. As soon as Rose-Nama ended with *mere seconds it takes for her to accept a proposal,* the class erupted into cheers, for it was true: A ring did possess magical powers to transform into pauper or princess. Rose-Nama gave a curtsy and, glancing defiantly at Alys, returned to her desk.

"Good job," Alys said. "Who wants to go next?"

As hands shot up, she looked affectionately at the girls at their wooden desks, their winter uniforms impeccably washed and pressed by *dhobis* and maids, their long braids (for good girls did not get a boyish cut like Alys's) draped over their books, and she wondered who they'd end up becoming by the end of high school. She recalled herself at their age—an eager-to-learn though ultimately naïve Ms. Know-It-All.

"Miss Alys, me me me," the class clown said, pumping her hand energetically.

Alys nodded, and the girl selected a blue chalk and began to write.

It is a truth universally acknowledged that a young girl in posses-sion of a pretty face, a fair complexion, a slim figure, and good height is not going to happily settle for a very ugly husband if he doesn't have enough money, unless she has the most incredible bad luck (which my cousin does).

The class exploded into laughter and Alys smiled too.

"My cousin's biggest complaint," the girl said, her eyes twinkling, "is that he's so hairy. Miss Alys, how is it fair that girls are expected to wax everywhere but boys can be as hairy as gorillas?"

"Double standards," Alys said.

"*Oof,*" Rose-Nama said. "Which girl wants a mustache and a hairy back? I don't."

A chorus of I don'ts filled the room, and Alys was glad to see all the class energized and participating.

"I don't either," Alys said complacently, "but the issue is that women don't seem to have a choice that is free from judgment."

"Miss Alys," called out a popular girl. "Can I go next?"

It is unfortunately not a truth universally acknowledged that it is better to be alone than to have fake friendships.

As soon as she finished the sentence, the popular girl tossed the pink chalk into the box and glared at another girl across the room. Great, Alys thought, as she told her to sit down; they'd still not made up. Alys was known as the teacher you could go to with any issue and not be busted, and both girls had come to her separately, having quarreled over whether one could have only one best friend. Ten years ago, Alys would have panicked at such disruptions. Now she barely blinked. Also, being one of five sisters had its perks, for it was good preparation for handling classes full of feisty girls.

Another student got up and wrote in red:

It is a truth universally acknowledged that every marriage, no matter how good, will have ups and downs.

"This class is a wise one," Alys said to the delighted girl.

The classroom door creaked open from the December wind, a soft whistling sound that Alys loved. The sky was darkening and rain dug into the school lawn, where, weather permitting, classes were conducted under the sprawling century-old banyan tree and the girls loved to let loose and play rowdy games of rounders and cricket. Cold air wafted into the room and Alys wrapped her shawl tightly around herself. She glanced at the clock on the mildewed wall.

"We have time for a couple more sentences," and she pointed to a shy girl at the back. The girl took a green chalk and, biting her lip, began to write:

It is a truth universally acknowledged that if you are the daughter of rich and generous parents, then you have the luxury to not get married just for security.

"Wonderful observation," Alys said kindly, for, according to Dilipabad's healthy rumor mill, the girl's father's business was currently facing setbacks. "But how about the daughter earn a *good* income of her own and secure this freedom for herself?"

"Yes, Miss," the girl said quietly as she scuttled back to her chair.

Rose-Nama said, "It's *Western* conditioning to think independent women are better than homemakers."

"No one said anything about East, West, better, or worse," Alys said. "Being financially independent is not a Western idea. The Prophet's wife, Hazrat Khadijah, ran her own successful business back in the day and he was, to begin with, her employee."

Rose-Nama frowned. "Have you ever reimagined the first sentence?"

Alys grabbed a yellow chalk and wrote her variation, as she inevitably did every year, ending with the biggest flourish of an exclamation point yet.

It is a truth universally acknowledged that a single woman in possession of a good fortune must be in want of a husband!

"How," Alys said, "does this gender-switch from the original sentence make you feel? Can it possibly be true or can you see the irony, the absurdity, more clearly now?"

The classroom door was flung open and Tahira, a student, burst in. She apologized for being late even as she held out her hand, her fingers splayed to display a magnificent four-carat marquis diamond ring.

"It happened last night! Complete surprise!" Tahira looked excited and nervous. "Ammi came into my bedroom and said, 'Put away your homework-shomework, you're getting engaged.' Miss Alys, they are our family friends and own a textile mill."

"Well," Alys said, "well, congratulations," and she rose to give her a hug, even as her heart sank. Girls from illustrious feudal families like sixteen-year-old Tahira married early, started families without delay, and had grandchildren of their own before they knew it. It was a lucky few who went to college while the rest got married, for this was the Tao of obedient girls in Dilipabad; Alys went so far as to say the Tao of good girls in Pakistan.

Yet it always upset her that young brilliant minds, instead of exploring the universe, were busy chiseling themselves to fit into the molds of Mrs. and Mom. It wasn't that she was averse to Mrs. Mom, only that none of the girls seemed to have ever considered traveling the world by themselves, let alone been encouraged to do so, or to shatter a glass ceiling, or laugh like a madwoman in public without a care for how it looked. At some point over the years, she'd made it her job to inject (or as some, like Rose-Nama's mother, would say, "infect") her students with possibility. And even if the girls in this small sleepy town refused to wake up, wasn't it her duty to try? How grateful she'd have been for such a teacher. Instead, she and her sisters had also been raised under their mother's motto to marry young and well, an expectation neither thirty-year-old Alys, nor her elder sister, thirty-two-year-old Jena, had fulfilled.

In the year 2000, in the lovely town of Dilipabad, in the lovelier state of Punjab, women like Alys and Jena were, as far as their countrymen and -women were concerned, certified Miss Havishams, Charles Dickens's famous spinster who'd wasted away her life. Actually, Alys and Jena were considered even worse off, for they had not enjoyed Miss Havisham's good luck of having at least once been engaged.

As Alys watched, the class swarmed around Tahira, wishing out loud that they too would be blessed with such a ring and begin their real lives.

"Okay, girls," she finally said. "Settle down. You can ogle the diamond after class. Tahira, you too. I hope you did your homework? Can you share your sentence on the board?"

Tahira began writing with an orange chalk, her ring flashing like a big bright light bulb at the blackboard—exactly the sort of ring, Alys knew, her own mother coveted for her daughters.

It is a truth universally acknowledged in this world and beyond that having an ignorant mother is worse than having no mother at all.

"There," Tahira said, carefully wiping chalk dust off her hands. "Is that okay, Miss?"

Alys smiled. "It's an opinion."

"It's rude and disrespectful," Rose-Nama called out. "Parents can never be ignorant."

"What does ignorant mean in this case, do you think?" Alys said. "At what age might one's own experiences outweigh a parent's?"

"Never," Rose-Nama said frostily. "Miss Alys, parents will always have more experience and know what is best for us."

"Well," Alys said, "we'll see in *Pride and Prejudice* how the main character and her mother start out with similar views, and where and why they begin to separate."

"Miss Alys," Tahira said, sliding into her seat, "my mother said I won't be attending school after my marriage, so I was wondering, do I still have to do assign—"

"Yes." Alys calmly cut her off, having heard this too many times. "I expect you to complete each and every assignment, and I also urge you to request that your parents and fiancé, and your mother-in-law, allow you to finish high school."

"I'd like to," Tahira said a little wistfully. "But my mother says there are more important things than fractions and ABCs."

Alys would have offered to speak to the girl's mother, but she knew from previous experiences that her recommendation carried no weight. An unmarried woman advocating pursuits outside the home might as well be a witch spreading anarchy and licentiousness.

"Just remember," Alys said quietly, "there *is* more to life than getting married and having children."

"But, Miss," Tahira said hesitantly, "what's the purpose of life without children?"

"The same purpose as there would be with children—to be a good human being and contribute to society. Look, plenty of women physically unable to have children still live perfectly meaningful lives, and there are as many women who remain childless by choice."

Rose-Nama glared. "That's just wrong."

"It's not wrong," Alys said gently. "It's relative. Not every woman wants to keep home and hearth, and I'm sure not every man wants to be the breadwinner."

"What does he want to do, then?" Rose-Nama said. "Knit?"

Alys painstakingly removed a fraying silver thread from her black shawl. Finally she said, in an even tone, "You'll all be pleased to see that there are plenty of marriages in *Pride and Prejudice*."

"Why do you like the book so much, then?" Rose-Nama asked disdainfully.

"Because," Alys said simply, "Jane Austen is ruthless when it comes to drawing-room hypocrisy. She's blunt, impolite, funny, and absolutely honest. She's Jane Khala, one of those honorary good aunts who tells it straight and looks out for you."

Alys erased the blackboard and wrote, *Elizabeth Bennet: First Impressions?*, then turned to lead the discussion among the already buzzing girls. None of them had previously read *Pride and Prejudice*, but many had watched the 1995 BBC drama and were swooning over the scene in which Mr. Darcy emerged from the lake on his Pemberley property in a wet white shirt. She informed them that this particular scene was not in the novel and that, in Austen's time, men actually swam naked. The girls burst into nervous giggles.

"Miss," a few of the girls, giddy, emboldened, piped up, "when are you getting married?"

"Never." Alys had been wondering when this class would finally get around to broaching the topic.

"But why not!" several distressed voices cried out. "You're not *that* old. And, if you grow your hair long again and start using bright lipstick, you will be so pret—"

"Girls, girls"—Alys raised her amused voice over the clamor— "unfortunately, I don't think any man I've met is my equal, and neither, I fear, is any man likely to think I'm his. So, no marriage for me."

"You think marriage is not important?" Rose-Nama said, squinting.

"I don't believe it's for everyone. Marriage should be a part of life and not *life*."

"You are a forever career woman?" Rose-Nama said.

Alys heard the mocking and the doubt in her tone: Who in their right mind would choose a teaching job in Dilipabad over marriage and children?

"Believe me, Rose-Nama," Alys said serenely, "life certainly does not end just because you choose to stay—"

"Unmarried?" Rose-Nama made a face as she uttered the word.

"Single," Alys said. "There is a vast difference between remaining unmarried and choosing to stay single. Jane Austen is a leading example. She didn't get married, but her paper children—six wonderful novels—keep her alive centuries later."

"You are also delivering a paper child?" Rose-Nama asked.

"But, Miss Alys," Tahira said resolutely, "there's no nobler career than that of being a wife and mother."

"That's fine." Alys shrugged. "As long as it's what you really want and not what you've been taught to want."

"But marriage and children *are* my dream, Miss!" Tahira gazed at Jane Austen's portrait on the book. "Did no one want to marry her?"

"Actually," Alys said, "a very wealthy man proposed to her one evening and she said yes, but the next morning she said no."

"Jane Austen must have been from a well-to-do family herself," said the shy girl, sighing.

Alys gave her a bright smile for speaking up. "No. Jane's mother came from nobility but her father was a clergyman. In their time, they were middle-class gentry, respectable but not rich, and women of their class could not work for a living except as governesses, so it must have taken a lot of courage for her to refuse."

"Jane Austen sounds very selfish," Rose-Nama said. "Imagine

how happy her mother must have been, only to find that overnight the good luck had been spurned."

"It could also be," Alys said softly, "that her mother was happy her daughter was different. Do any of you have the courage to live life as you want?"

"Miss Alys," Rose-Nama said, "marriage is a cornerstone of our culture."

"A truth universally acknowledged"—Alys cleared her throat— "because without marriage our culture and religion do not permit sexual intimacy."

All the girls tittered.

"Miss," Rose-Nama said, "everyone knows that abstinence until marriage is the secret to societies where nothing bad happens."

"That's not true." Alys looked pained. She thought back to the ten years her family had lived in Jeddah, Saudi Arabia, where she'd studied at a co-ed international school and made friends from all over the world, who'd lived all sorts of lifestyles. Though she'd been forbidden from befriending boys, many of the girls were allowed, and they were no worse off for it. Like her, they'd also been studious and just as keen to collect flavored lip balms, scratch-and-sniff stickers, and scented rubbers, which she'd learned, courtesy of her American classmates, were called erasers, while a rubber was a condom, which was something you put on a penis, which was pronounced "pee-nus" and not "pen-iz." Alys's best friend, Tana from Denmark, stated that her mother had given her condoms when she'd turned fifteen, because, in Scandinavia, intimacy came early and did not require marriage. Alys had shared the information with Jena, who was scandalized, but Alys had quickly accepted the proverb "Different strokes for different folks."

"Premarital sex is haram, a sin," Rose-Nama said, "and you shouldn't imply otherwise to us, Miss Alys." Her eyes widened. "Or do you believe it's not a sin?"

Before Alys could answer, the head peon, Bashir, knocked on the door.

"*Chalein jee,* Alysba *bibi,*" he said, "*phir bulawa aa gaya aap ka.* Principal Naheed requires your presence yet again."

Alys followed Bashir down the stairs, past classrooms, past the small canteen where the teachers' chai and snacks were prepared at a discount rate, past a stray cat huddled on the wide veranda that wrapped around the mansion-turned-school-building, past the accountant's nook, and toward the principal's office, a roomy den at the end of the front porch with bay windows overlooking the driveway for keeping an eye on all comings and goings.

The British School Group was founded twenty years ago by Begum Beena dey Bagh. The name was chosen for its suggested affiliation with Britain, although there was none. However, it was to be an English-medium establishment. Twelve years ago, Naheed, a well-heeled Dilipabadi housewife, decided to put to use a vacant property belonging to her. She sought permission from Beena dey Bagh to open a branch of the British School, and so was born the British School of Dilipabad.

Naheed had turned her institution into a finishing school of sorts for girls from Dilipabad's privileged. Accordingly, she was willing to pay well for teachers fluent in English with decent accents, and, just as she'd all but given up on proficient English-literature teachers, Alys and Jena Binat had entered her office a decade ago.

Alys entered the office now, settled in a chair facing Naheed's desk, and waited for her to get off the phone. She gazed at the bulletin boards plastering the walls and boasting photos where Naheed beamed with Dilipabad's VIPs. They were thumbtacked in place to allow easy removal if a VIP fell from financial grace or got involved in a particularly egregious scandal.

Naheed's mahogany desk held folders and forms and a framed picture of her precious twin daughters, Ginwa and Rumsha—Gin and Rum—born late, courtesy of IVF treatments. Gin and Rum posed in front of the Eiffel Tower with practiced pouts, blond-streaked brown hair, and skintight jeans. Naheed's daughters lived in Lahore with their grandparents; she'd opted to send them to the British School of Lahore rather than her own British School of Dilipabad because she wanted them to receive superior educations as well as better networking opportunities. Gin and Rum planned to be fashion designers, a newly lucrative entrepreneurial opportunity in Pakistan, and Naheed had no doubt her daughters would make a huge splash in the world of couture and an equally huge splash in the matrimonial bazaar by marrying no less than the Pakistani equivalents of Princes William and Harry.

Naheed hung up the phone and, clearly annoyed, shook her head at Alys.

"Rose-Nama's mother called. Again. Apparently you used the 'f' word in class."

"I did?"

"The 'f' word, Alys. Is this the language of dignified women, let alone teachers?"

Alys crossed her arms. Naheed would not have dared speak to her like this when she'd first joined the school. Ten years ago, when Naheed had realized that Alys and Jena were Binats, her tongue had been a never-ending red carpet, for the Binats were a highly respected and moneyed clan. However, once Dilipabad's VIPs realized that Bark Binat was now all but penniless—why he'd lost his money was no one's worry, that he had was everyone's favorite topic—they devalued Bark and his dependents. As soon as Principal Naheed gleaned that Alys and Jena were working in order to pay bills and not because they were bored upper-class girls, she began to belittle them.

"Alys, God knows," Naheed said, "I have yet again tried to calm Rose-Nama's mother, but give me one good reason why I shouldn't let you go."

Alys knew that Naheed had tried to hire other well-qualified English-speaking teachers but no one was willing to relocate to Dilipabad. The sole entertainment for most Pakistanis was to eat out, and the elite English-speaking gentry in particular believed they deserved dining finer than Dilipabad offered.

"Alys, am I or am I not," Naheed's voice boomed, "paying you a pretty penny? It is not as if good jobs are growing on trees."

The fact was, over the years Alys had been offered lucrative teaching positions in other cities, and then there was Dubai, where single Pakistani girls were increasingly fleeing to find their fortunes, but she was unwilling to leave her family, especially her father.

"It was a crow," Alys said. "Rose-Nama and her mother should educate themselves on context. A giant crow flew into the classroom and startled me and—"

"Alys," Naheed said, "I don't care if twenty giant crows fly into the classroom and start singing 'The hills are alive with the sound of music'; you absolutely may not curse in front of impressionable young ladies. Rose-Nama's mother is right—if it's not cursing, it's something else. Last year you told students that dowry was a 'demented' tradition. Could you not have used 'controversial' or 'divisive' or 'contentious'? You of all people should be sensitive to diction. Then you told them that divorce was not a big deal! Another year you told them that they should be reading Urdu and regional literature instead of English. An absurd statement from an English-literature teacher."

"Not 'instead.' I said 'side by side.'"

"Yet another time you decided to inform them that if Islam allowed polygamy, then it should allow polyandry. This is a school. Not a brothel."

Alys said, stiffly, "I want my girls to at least have a chance at being more than well-trained dolls. I want them to think critically."

Naheed pointed above Alys's head. "What is the school motto?"

Alys spoke it by rote. "'Excellence in Obedience. Obediently Excellent. Obey to Excel.'"

"Precisely," Naheed said. "The goal of the British School Group is for our girls to pass their exams with flying colors so that they become wives and mothers worthy of our nation's future VIPs. Please stick to the curriculum. I'm weary of apologizing to parents and making excuses for you. Also, I know you value your younger sisters studying here."

Alys gave a small smile. Qitty, in the eleventh grade, and Lady, in the ninth, attended BSD at the discount rate offered to faculty family, which, all the teachers agreed, was not as generous as it could be.

"I may not be able to protect you any longer," Naheed said. "Begum Beena dey Bagh's nephew is returning from completing his MBA in America, and things seem to be about to change. For one, the young man plans to abolish the uniform. Can you imagine our students turning up in whatever they choose to wear? Anarchy!"

Alys understood Naheed's concern. She and her husband had the monopoly over the British School of Dilipabad's uniform business—winter, spring, fall—and the loss would be an expensive hit to their income.

Principal Naheed's gaze fixed upon the driveway. Alys turned to see a Pajero with tinted windows and green government number plates driving in. The jeep stopped and the driver handed the gate guard a packet. Minutes later, Naheed tenderly opened a pearly oversize lavender envelope embossed with a golden palanquin. All smiles, she drew out equally pearly invites to Dilipabad's most coveted event: the NadirFiede wedding, the joining of Fiede Fecker, daughter of old-money VIPs, to Nadir Sheh, son of equally important VIPs, though rumor had it that drug-smuggling was responsible for the Shehs' fast accumulation of monies and rapid social climb and acceptance into the gentry.

"Such a classy invitation," Naheed said, tucking the invites back in.

Alys disliked the word "classy," a favorite of those who aimed to be arbiters of class. She knew that Naheed was hoping the Binats would not be invited, despite their pedigree, since Alys and Fiede Fecker, a graduate of the British School of Dilipabad, had been at loggerheads over incomplete assignments and projects never turned in.

"Alys, the *namigarami*—the elite of Dilipabad—have spoken,"

Naheed said, fingering her invite. "Our duty is to send their daughters home exactly as they were delivered to us each morning: obediently obeying their parents. We are to groom these girls into the best of marriageable material. That is all." Naheed signaled to Bashir, who had been dawdling by the threshold, to get her a fresh cup of lemongrass tea and, in doing so, dismissed Alys.

Alys rejoined her ninth-graders, bracing herself for Rose-Nama to demand her views on premarital intimacy. But Rose-Nama was busy scolding the class monitor, a timid girl Principal Naheed had appointed because her father had given a generous donation to renovate the science laboratory. Mercifully, the bell rang as soon as she stepped in, and Alys, gathering her folders and cloth handbag, headed to the tenth-grade classroom.

"Girls," Alys said to the tenth grade, "open up your *Romeo and Juliet*. Let me remind you that Juliet is thirteen years old and Romeo around fifteen or sixteen and that they could have surely experienced a happier fate had they refrained from romance at their ages, which may well have been Shakespeare's cautionary intent for writing this pathetically sad love story."

Chapter 2

*W*hen the final bell rang, Alys headed toward the staff room, nodding at girls giggling and gossiping around Tahira's engagement ring. In the staff room, teachers were enjoying the celebration cake from High Chai that Tahira's mother had sent. Alys beckoned to Jena, and both sisters headed toward the school van.

For a small fee, BSD provided conveyance to and from school for teachers and their relatives studying there. The Binats had an old Suzuki but Alys thought it wise to save on petrol, no matter how much more it embarrassed fifteen-year-old Lady to ride in the school van.

Lady and Qitty were inside the van, squabbling.

"Qitty, move over, you fat hippo," Lady said, elbowing the sketchbook her elder sister was drawing in.

"Shut up!" Qitty said. She was the only overweight Binat sister, a blow she could never forgive fate or God. "There's no such thing as a thin hippo, so fat is redundant, stupid."

"You're stupid, bulldozer," Lady said. "You always hog all the space, hog. And stop showing off your stupid drawings."

"You wish you could draw." Qitty flipped to a fresh page and within moments had outlined a caricature of Lady. "The only talent you have is big breasts."

"Thanks to which, thunder thighs," Lady said, "I'm going to make a brilliant marriage and only ride in the best of cars with a full-time chauffeur. And, Qitty, you will not be allowed in any of my Mercedes or Pajeros, because I'll be doing you a favor by making you walk."

Qitty drew two horns atop Lady's caricature.

"Lady!" Alys said, avoiding the torn vinyl as she settled into the seat beside her best friend, Sherry Looclus, who taught Urdu at BSD. "Apologize to Qitty. Why do you two sit together if you're going to fight?"

The van driver was, as usual, enjoying the skirmish. The rest of the teachers ignored it.

"I pray your dreams come true," Jena said to Lady, "but that doesn't mean you can be mean to Qitty or to anyone. We are all God's creatures and all beautiful."

"Those who can afford plastic surgery are even more beautiful," Lady said. "Qitty, you fatso, stop sniveling. You know I call you fat for your own good."

"I eat far less than you, Jena, Alys, and Mari all put together," Qitty said. Lady was willowy and seemingly able to eat whatever she wanted all day long without expanding an inch. "It's not fair."

"It's not fair," Alys agreed. "But, then, who said life is fair? Remember, though, that looks are immaterial."

"Alys, you are such an *aunty*," Lady said, taking out a lip gloss and applying it with her pinkie.

"You can call me an aunty all you want," Alys said, "but that doesn't change the fact that looks are not the be-all and end-all, no matter what our mother says. Qitty is a straight-A student, and I suggest, Lady, you pull up your grades and realize the importance of books over looks."

Lady stuck her tongue out at Alys, who shook her head in exasperation. Once all the teachers had climbed in, the van drove out of the gates and past young men on motorbikes ogling the departing schoolgirls. These lower-middle-class youths didn't have a prayer of romancing a BSD girl, Alys knew, despite the fantasies that films tried to sell them about wrong-side-of-the-tracks love stories ending in marriage, because there were few fates more petrifying to a Pakistani girl than downward mobility.

Alys watched Lady's reflection in the window. She was running her fingers through her wavy hair in a dramatic fashion. Lady was a bit boy crazy, but Alys also knew that her sisters were well aware that they couldn't afford a single misstep, since their aunt's slander had already resulted in the family's damaged reputation. She tapped her sister's shoulder, and Lady looked away as the van turned the corner.

Dilipabad glittered after the rainfall, its potholed roads and telephone wires overhead freshly washed and its dust settled. The manufacturing town claimed its beginnings as a sixteenth-century watering hole for horses and, after a national craze to discard British names for homegrown ones, Gorana was renamed Dilipabad after the actor Dilip Kumar. In more-recent times, Dilipabad had grown into a spiderweb of neighborhoods, its outskirts boasting the prestigious residences as well as the British School, the gymkhana, and upscale restaurants, while homes and eateries got shabbier closer to the town center. In the town center was a white elephant of a bazaar that was famous for bargains, a main petrol pump, and a small public park with a men-only outdoor gym. The elite, however, stuck to the gymkhana, with its spacious lawns, tennis and squash courts, golf course, boating on the lake, swimming pool, and indoor co-ed gym with ladies-only hours.

Mrs. Binat had insisted they apply for the Dilipabad Gymkhana membership despite the steep annual dues, and since the gymkhana functioned under an old amendment that once a member, always a member, the Binats were in for life. The amendment had been added on the demand of a nawab who, after gaining entry to the gymkhana once the British relaxed their strict rule of no-natives-allowed, had been terrified of expulsion.

Though Mr. Binat was seldom in the mood to attend the bridge and bingo evenings, Mrs. Binat made sure she and the girls put in an appearance every now and then. Once Alys had discovered the gymkhana library, she'd spent as much time there as she had in the school library in Jeddah, where she'd first fallen in love with books: Enid Blyton. Judy Blume. Shirley Jackson. Daphne du Maurier. Dorothy Parker. L. M. Montgomery's *Anne of Green Gables,* and S. E. Hinton's class-based novels, which mirrored Indian films and Pakistani dramas.

In the gymkhana library, Alys would choose a book from the beveled-glass-fronted bookcase and curl up in the chintz sofas. Over the years, the dim chinoiserie lamps had been replaced with overhead lighting, all the better to read Agatha Christie, Arthur Conan Doyle, Austen, the Brontës, Dickens, George Eliot, Mary Shelley, Thackeray, Hardy, Maugham, Elizabeth Gaskell, Tolstoy, Orwell, Bertrand Russell, Wilde, Woolf, Wodehouse, Shakespeare, more Shakespeare, even more Shakespeare.

Alys pressed her forehead against the van's window as they left behind the imposing gymkhana and passed the exalted Burger Palace, Pizza Palace, and the Chinese restaurant, Lotus, all three eateries shut until dinnertime. Only the recently launched High Chai was open and, going by the number of cars outside, doing brisk business—in local parlance, "minting money"—because Dilipabadis were entertainment-starved.

Alys gazed at the café's sign: HIGH CHAI in gold cursive atop pink and yellow frosted cupcakes. It took her back to a time when their mother would dress her and Jena in frilly frocks, a time before their father and his elder brother, Uncle Goga, were estranged, a time when they'd been one big happy joint family living in the colossal ancestral house in the best part of Lahore: her paternal grandparents, her parents and sisters, Uncle Goga and Aunty Tinkle and their four children.

They'd play with their cousins for hours on end. Hide-and-go-seek. *Baraf pani.* Cops and robbers. Jump rope and hopscotch. They'd fight over turns and exchange insults before making up. However, Tinkle always took her children's side during the quarrels.

"Why is Aunty Tinkle so rude to us?" Alys would ask her mother. "Why does she act as if they're better than us?"

Pinkie Binat replied hesitantly, "Her children are not better than any of you. You have the same history."

Pinkie Binat made sure her daughters knew where they came from. The British, during their reign over an undivided subcontinent, doled out small plots to day laborers as incentive to turn them into farmers, who, later, would be called agriculturists and feudal lords, which is what the Binat forefathers ultimately became. These men then turned their attentions to consolidating land and thereby power and influence through marriage, and even during the 1947 partition the Binats managed to retain hold over their land.

It was infighting that defeated some of the Binats. After the death of his wife, Goga's and Bark's ailing father had increasingly come to depend on Goga and his wife, first-cousin Tajwer "Tinkle" Binat, a woman who spent too much time praying for a nice nose, thicker hair, a slender waist, and dainty feet. When Binat Sr. passed away, he left his sons ample pockets of land as well as factories, but it was clear Goga was in charge and not impressed by his much younger brother's devotion to the Beatles, Elvis, and squash. He was even less impressed by Bark's obsession with a girl he'd glimpsed at a beauty parlor when he went to pick up Tinkle.

"Please, Tinkle," Bark had begged his cousin plus sister-in-law, "please find out who she is and take her my proposal. If I don't marry her, I will die."

Tinkle knew immediately which girl had smitten Bark. She herself had found it hard to not stare at the fawn-eyed beauty and, in a benevolent mood, she returned to the salon to make inquiries into her identity: Khushboo "Pinkie" Gardenaar, seventeen years old, high school graduate. The girl's mother was a housewife, overly fond

of candy-colored clothes. Her father was a bookkeeper in the rail-
ways. The girl's elder brother was studying at King Edward Medical
College. Her elder sister was a less attractive version of Bark's crush.

The girl's family claimed ancestry from royal Persian kitchens.
Nobodies, Tinkle informed Goga; basically cooks and waiters. After
the brothers fell out, Tinkle would discredit Pinkie's family by stress-
ing that there was zilch proof of any royal connection. At the time,
however, the Binats accepted the family's claims, and so it was with
fanfare that Barkat "Bark" Binat and Khushboo "Pinkie" Gardenaar
were wed.

On the day of the wedding, Tinkle lost control of her envy. Was it
fair that this chit of a girl, this nobody, should make such a stunning
bride?

"She is no *khushboo*, good smell, but a *badboo*, bad smell," Tinkle
railed at Goga as she mocked Khushboo's name. "I'm the one who
went to a Swiss finishing school. I'm the one who sits on the boards
of charities. But always it's her beauty everyone swoons over. She calls
a phone 'foon,' biscuit 'biscoot,' year 'ear,' measure 'meyer.' She does
not know salad fork from dinner fork. How could your brother have
married that lower-middle-class twit? Doesn't Bark care that they
are not our kind of people?"

Tinkle's jealousy grew as Bark and Pinkie delivered two peach-
fresh daughters in quick succession. Tinkle's own children barely
qualified for even *qabool shakal*, acceptable-looking. Goga tried to
ignore his wife's complaints. He had bigger matters to trouble him,
including the loss of the Binats' factories after a wave of nationaliza-
tion. Goga was doubly displeased over Bark's welcoming attitude
toward the government takeover. Could his bleeding-heart brother
not see that socialism meant less money for the Binats?

In order to diversify assets, Goga invested in a series of shops in
Saudi Arabia to capitalize on the newly burgeoning mall culture. He
informed Bark he was needed to supervise the investment, and Bark
and Pinkie dutifully packed up and, with their daughters, Alys and
Jena, headed off to Jeddah.

Even though Pinkie had been reluctant to leave her life in Lahore, once in Jeddah, frequent visits to the holy cities of Mecca and
Medina were a great spiritual consolation. Alys and Jena were enrolled in an international school, where their classes looked like a
mini–United Nations and the girls made friends from all over the
world. Pinkie's friends were other expatriate wives, with whom she
spent afternoons shopping in the souks and malls for gold and fabrics. The Binats resided in an upscale expat residential compound,
which had a swimming pool and a bowling alley, and Pinkie hired
help.

Life was good; Jeddah was home. Bark grumbled occasionally
about the hierarchy—Saudis first, then white people, no matter their
level of education or lineage, then everyone else. Still, they might
have remained in Jeddah forever were it not for a car accident in
which a Saudi prince rear-ended Bark's car. In Saudi Arabia, the law
sided with Saudis no matter who was at fault, and so Bark counted
his blessings for escaping with only a broken arm and, fearing that
he might be sent to jail for the scratch on the prince's forehead,
packed up his wife and their now five daughters and moved back
into their ancestral home in Lahore.

It took two years for Bark to unearth the rot. His elder brother
had bilked him out of business and inheritance. Bark proceeded to
have a heart attack, a mild one, but Tinkle made sure Goga remained
unmoved by his younger brother's plight.

Bark had nowhere to turn. His parents had passed away. Relatives
commiserated but had no interest in siding with Bark or helping
him money-wise. Alys, then nineteen, convinced her father to con-
sult a lawyer. They were the talk of the town as it was, she said, and
they needed to get back what was rightfully theirs. Too late, said the
lawyer. They could appeal, but it would take forever and Goga had
already transferred everything to himself. They would learn later that
the lawyer had accepted a decent bribe from Goga to dissuade them
from filing.

Tinkle wanted them gone from the Binat ancestral home, and

Bark shamefacedly accepted the property in Dilipabad that Tinkle didn't want because of its ominous location in front of a graveyard. Bark told Pinkie that *she* could no longer afford to be superstitious and that they had to move as soon as possible, and so Jena and Alys were disenrolled from Kinnaird College and Mari, Qitty, and Lady from the Convent of Jesus and Mary school.

The Binats arrived in Dilipabad one ordinary afternoon, the moving truck unceremoniously dumping them outside their new house with its cracked sign proclaiming: BINAT HOUSE. Binat House was an abundance of rooms spread over two stories, which looked out into a courtyard with ample lawn on all four sides, gone to jungle. The elderly caretaker was shocked to see the family. As he unlocked the front doors and led them into dust-ridden rooms with musty furniture covered by moth-eaten sheets, he grumbled about not having been informed of their coming. Had he known, of course the rooms would have been aired. Cobwebs removed from the ceiling. Rat droppings swept off the floors and a fumigator called. Electricity and boiler connections reinstalled. A hot meal.

The Binats stared at the caretaker. Finally, Hillima, the lone servant who had chosen to accompany the fallen Binats—despite bribes by Tinkle, Hillima was loyal to Pinkie, who'd taken her in after she'd left her physically abusive husband—told the caretaker to shut up. It was his job to have made sure the house remained in working order. Had he been receiving a salary all these years to sleep?

Hillima assembled an army of cleaners. A room was readied for Mr. Binat. The study emerged cozy, with a gorgeous rug of tangerine vines and blue flowers, leather sofas, and relatively mildew-free walls. Once the bewildered Mr. Binat was deposited inside, with a thermos full of chai and his three younger daughters, attention turned to the rest of the house.

Mrs. Binat and Alys and Jena decided to pitch in; better that than sitting around glum and gloomy. They coughed through dust and scrubbed at grime and shrieked at lizards and frogs in corners, though Alys would bravely gather them up in newspaper and deposit them outdoors. Dirt was no match for determined fists, and Alys and Jena were amazed at their own industriousness and surprised at their mother's. They'd only ever seen her in silks and stilettos, fussing if her hair was out of place or her makeup smudged. Grim-faced, Mrs. Binat snapped that before their father married her, she'd not exactly been living like a queen. Soon floors sparkled, windows gleamed, and, once the water taps began running from brown to clear, Binat House seemed not so dreadful after all.

Hillima was pleased with the servants' quarters behind the main house—four rooms with windows and attached toilet, all hers for now, since the caretaker had been fired for incompetence.

Bedrooms were chosen. Alys took the room overlooking the graveyard, for she was not scared of ghosts-djinns-*churails*, plus the room had a nice little balcony. In their large bedroom on the ground floor, Mrs. Binat brought up to Mr. Binat—as urgently as possible, without triggering another heart attack—the matter of expenses. Pedigree garnered respect but could not pay bills. There was the small shop in Lahore that Goga had missed in his usurpations, which they still owned and received rent on, but it wasn't enough to live on luxuriously. Gas bills. Electricity bills. Water bills. The younger girls had to go to school. Mr. Binat's heart medicines. Food. Clothes. Shoes. Toiletries. Sanitary napkins—dear God, the cost of sanitary napkins. Gymkhana dues. Hillima's salary, despite free housing, medical, and food. They also needed to hire the most basic of staff to help Hillima: a *dhobi* for clean, well-starched clothes, a gardener, a cook. How dare Mr. Binat suggest she and the girls cook! Were Tinkle Binat and her daughters chopping vegetables, kneading dough, and washing pans? No. Then neither would Pinkie Binat and her daughters.

It was Alys's decision to look for a teaching job. She and Jena had been in the midst of studying English literature, and their first stop was the British School of Dilipabad. Principal Naheed pounced on them, particulary thrilled with their accents: The soft-spoken Jena would teach English to the middle grades, and the bright-eyed Alys would teach the upper grades. Alys and Jena were giddy with

joy. Newly fallen from Olympus, they were inexperienced and nodded naïvely when Naheed told them their salary, too awestruck at
being paid at all to consider they were being underpaid. What had
they known about money? They'd only ever spent it.

Alys and Jena had returned home with the good news of their
employment only to have Mrs. Binat screech, "Teaching will ruin
your eyesight! Your hair will fall out marking papers! Who will marry
you then? Huh? Who will marry you?"

She'd turned to Mr. Binat to make Alys and Jena quit, but instead
he patted them on their heads. This was the first time he'd truly felt
that daughters were as good as sons, he attested. In fact, their pay-
checks were financial pressure off him, and he'd happily turned to
tending the overgrown garden.

Alys was always proud that her actions had led their father to
deem daughters equal to sons, for she had not realized, till then, that
he'd discriminated. However, looking back, she wished he'd at least
advised them to negotiate for a higher salary. She wished that her
mother had asked them even once what they wanted to be when
they grew up instead of insisting the entire focus of their lives be to
make good marriages.

Consequently, Alys always asked her younger sisters what they
wanted to be, especially now that there seemed a cornucopia of
choices for their generation. Qitty wanted to be a journalist and a
cartoonist and dreamed of writing a graphic novel, though she said
she wouldn't tell anyone the subject until done. Mari had wanted to
be a doctor. Unfortunately, her grades had not been good enough to
get into pre-med and she'd fallen into dejection. After copious pep
talks from Alys, as well as binging on the sports channel, Mari decided she wanted to join the fledging national women's cricket team.
But this was a desire thwarted by Mrs. Binat, who declared no one
wanted to marry a mannish sportswoman. Also, Mari suffered from
asthma and was prone to wheezing. Mari turned to God in despair,
only to conclude that all failures and obstacles served a higher pur-

pose and that God and good were her true calling. Lady dreamed of modeling after being discovered by a designer and offered an opportunity, but their father had absolutely forbidden it: Modeling was not respectable for girls from good families, especially not for a Binat.

Alys had fought for her sisters' dreams. But wheezing notwithstanding, Mari was a mediocre cricket player, and, as for Lady, no matter how much Alys argued on her sister's behalf, their father remained unmoved, for he hoped his estranged brother would reconcile with him and he dared not allow anything to interfere with that. Whatever the case, Alys was adamant that her sisters must end up earning well; now if only they'd listen to her and take their futures seriously.

The school van drove into a lower-middle-class ramshackle neighborhood with narrow lanes and small homes, where some of the teachers disembarked. Unable to afford much help, they shed their teacher skins and slipped into their housewife skins once they'd entered their houses. They would begin dinner, aid their children with homework, and, when their husbands returned from work, provide them chai as they unwound. They would return to the kitchen and pack the children's next-day school lunches, after which they would serve a hot dinner, clean up the kitchen, put the children to bed, and then finally shed their housewife skins and wriggle back into the authoritative teacher skins to grade papers well into the night.

Alys and Jena had heard the weariness in the staff room as teachers wondered how long they could keep up this superwoman act. Yet their jobs provided a necessary contribution to the family income—a fact their husbands and in-laws frequently chose to downplay, ignore, or simply not acknowledge—and afforded them a vital modicum of independence. The trick, the teachers sighed, was to marry a man who believed in sharing the housework, kids, and meal preparations without thinking he was doing a great and benevolent favor, but good luck with finding such a man, let alone in-laws who encouraged him to help.

The school van entered the Binats' more affluent leafy district and stopped at the entrance to the graveyard. The Binat sisters had only to cross the road to enter their wrought-iron gate and walk up the front lawn lined with evergreen bushes to their front door. They'd barely stepped into the foyer when Mrs. Binat flew out of the family room: "Guess what has happened?"

Chapter 3

Mrs. Binat was in the family room, praying the rosary for her daughters' futures, when the mail was delivered and in it the opportunity. Hearing their voices in the foyer, she rushed to them, asking them to guess what had happened as she waved a pearly lavender envelope like a victory flag.

Alys immediately recognized the invite to the NadirFiede wedding. Lady whooped as Mrs. Binat rattled off the names of all the old and new moneyed families who would be attending: Farishta Bank, Rani Raja Steels, the British School Group, Sundiful Fertilizers, Pappu Chemicals, Nangaparbat Textiles.

Mrs. Binat was still dropping names as her daughters followed her into the family room, where they settled around the electric fireplace. Alys climbed into the window seat that overlooked the back lawn. She tossed a throw over her legs, making sure to hide her feet before her mother noticed that she wasn't wearing any nail polish. Qitty and Lady sat on the floor, beside the wall decorated with photos of holidays the Binats had taken once upon a time: Jena and Alys at Disneyland, Mr. Binat holding toddler Mari's hand next to the

Acropolis, Qitty nibbling on corn on the cob in front of the Hagia Sophia, the whole family smiling into the camera in front of Harrods, a newborn Lady in a pram.

"Alys, Jena." Mr. Binat rose from his armchair. "Your mother has been eating my brains ever since that invite arrived. I'm going to the garden to—"

"Sit down, Barkat," Mrs. Binat said sharply. "We have to discuss the budget for the wedding."

Alys sighed as her father sat back down. She'd been looking forward to finishing her grading and then reading the risqué religious short story, "A Vision of Heaven" by Sajjad Zaheer from the collection *Angaaray*, which Sherry had translated for her from Urdu into English.

"Discuss it with Alys," Mr. Binat said. "She knows the costs of things better than I do."

"I'm sure Alys and everyone else knows everything better than you do," Mrs. Binat said. "But you are their father, and instead of worrying whether the succulents are thriving and the ficus is blooming, I need you to take an active interest in your daughters' futures."

"Futures?" Mr. Binat beamed as Hillima brought in chai and *keema samosas*.

"I want," Mrs. Binat announced, "the girls to fish for husbands at the NadirFiede wedding."

Alys gritted her teeth. She could see before her eyes a large aquarium of eligible bachelors dodging hooks cast by every single girl in the country.

"Aha!" Mr. Binat said, taking a *samosa*. "Nadir Sheh and Fiede Fecker are getting married so that *our* daughters get married. So kind of them. Very noble! I suggest you also line up, Pinkie, my love, because between you and the girls, you are still the most beautiful one."

"I know you are mocking me, Barkat, my love, but a compliment is a compliment! However, once a woman births daughters, her own looks must take a backseat."

Mrs. Binat gazed at each of her daughters. From birth, Jena was near perfect, a cross between an ivory rose and a Chughtai painting, her features delicate yet sharp, good hair, good height, slender, and the disposition of an angel. Lady was a bustier, hippier, pug-nosed version of Jena and towered over her sisters at five feet nine inches (thankfully height had gone from impediment to asset!). Mari was a poor imitation of Lady, with plain features, a smallish chest, and without Lady's spark. Qitty was exceptionally pretty, except her features were lost amid the double chins. And Alys. Oh, Alys. If only she wouldn't insist on ruining her complexion by sitting in the sun. If only she wouldn't butcher her silky curls. If only she'd wear some lipstick to outline those small but lush lips and apply a hint of bronzer to her natural cheekbones. What a waste on Alys those striking almond eyes. And such an argumentative girl that sometimes Mrs. Binat would cry with frustration.

She extracted the cards from the invitation. "We have been invited to the *mehndi* and *nikah* ceremonies at the Dilipabad Gymkhana and to the *walima* ceremony in Lahore. Jena, Alys, Qitty, Lady, you'll have to take days off from school."

"Don't worry," Alys said to her mother. "Principal Naheed has been invited too."

Mrs. Binat's nostrils fluttered. "That means those scaly daughters of hers, Gin and Rum, will also be fishing. No doubt they will be wearing the latest designer outfits and carrying brand-name bags. Everyone will. Alys, what is the budget for new clothes?"

"None," Alys said. "Anyway, tailor Shawkat overcharges us."

"How many times must I tell you that girls are only as good as their tailor, and Shawkat is worth every paisa he charges." Mrs. Binat glared, Alys's hair suddenly annoying her more than usual. "Honestly, if you wanted short hair, couldn't you have gotten a nice bob like a good girl?"

Alys ran her a hand over her cropped curls and exposed nape. "I like this. It saves me hours in the morning."

"I like it too," Mr. Binat said.

Alys smiled at her father. She'd grown up with her mother constantly telling her father what a *jhali*—a frump—she was, and over time Alys had realized that she was her father's favorite for that very reason. He loved that she'd always squat beside him in the garden and dig in the soil without a second thought to broken nails, dirty palms, or a deep tan.

"Barkat, you like everything this brainless girl does," Mrs. Binat said. "Thankfully Alys has a nice neck."

Mrs. Binat's ambitions for her daughters were fairly typical: groom them into marriageable material and wed them off to no less than princes and presidents. Before their fall, her husband had always assured her that, no matter what a mess Alys or any of the girls became, they would fare well because they were Binat girls. Indeed, stellar proposals for Jena and Alys had started to pour in as soon as they'd turned sixteen—scions of families with industrialist, business, and feudal backgrounds—but Mrs. Binat, herself married at seventeen, hadn't wanted to get her daughters married off so young, and also Alys refused to be a teenage bride. However, once their world turned upside down and they'd been banished to Dilipabad, the quality of proposals had shifted to Absurdities and Abroads.

Absurdities: men from humble middle-class backgrounds—restaurant managers, X-ray technicians, struggling professors and journalists, engineers and doctors posted in godforsaken locales, bumbling bureaucrats who didn't know how to work the system. Absurdities could hardly offer a comfortable living, let alone a lavish one, and Mrs. Binat had seen too many women, including her sister, melt from financial stress.

Abroads: middle-class men from foreign countries like America, England, Australia, Canada, et cetera, where the wife was no better than an unpaid multitasking menial, cooking, cleaning, driving, looking after children, and providing sex on demand with no salary or a single day off. An unpaid maid with benefits. Mrs. Binat had seen enough of the vagaries of life to know that getting married to a middle-class Western Abroad could mean exhaustion and home-sickness, and she would not allow her daughters a life of premature aging and loneliness. As such, she was unwilling to marry them off to frogs and toads, because she was too good a mother to plunge her girls into marriage simply for the sake of marriage. For that, she would wait until Jena and Alys turned thirty-five. There was also the small complication of the girls' reluctance to move abroad, since, for better or worse, they loved Pakistan. But, most important of all, if she sent her daughters abroad, *she* would miss them.

The plan was to remain in Pakistan and wed a Rich Man. Of course, Mrs. Binat knew through her own sad experience that even rich men could turn into poor nightmares, for had she not married a Rich Man? And now where were her holidays, designer brands, and financial security? In her milieu, sons had been coveted for their income and thereby the security blanket they afforded retired parents, but, having married into wealth, she'd never cared to even pray for a son. Mr. Binat too had stopped hoping for a boy after their fifth child was a girl. How she wished now she'd prayed for sons, and kept trying in order to spare herself the worry of a destitute old age. Being financially savvy and ambitious was a vital component of a successful man, and often Mrs. Binat wondered whether she was to blame for not having had the upbringing to distinguish, in Barkat "Bark" Binat, the real from the impostor.

She would not allow her daughters to make this mistake. She clutched the NadirFiede invitation. This was a real Rich Man fishing ground she was not going to waste.

"We must give a marriage present that rivals everyone else's. We must give thirty thousand rupees."

"Thirty thousand!" Mr. Binat glanced in alarm at Alys and Jena. "We are neither family nor close friends!"

"Thirty thou is petty cash for Fiede Fecker." Alys laughed. "Five thousand from us should suffice."

"We don't want to look like skinflints," Mrs. Binat said. "They are sure to tell the whole town who gave them what."

"Mummy," Jena said gently, "five thousand rupees is stretching it for us as it is."

Mrs. Binat sighed. "Okay. Gifit is done."

"Gift," Lady said. "Gift."

"That's what I'm saying. Gifit. Gifit." Mrs. Binat shook her head. "*Oof*, I'm so sick of the tyranny of English and accent in this country. Alys, Jena, go get the trunk."

Alys and Jena dragged in the metal trunk that housed the Binats' sartorial finery, collected over the years—*saris, ghararas, shararas, peshwas, lehengas, anarkalis, angrakhas, shalwar kurtas, thang pajama kameezs*. Most of the outfits had been tailored out of fabrics Mrs. Binat had purchased in Jeddah, aware that with five daughters to dress, they would come in handy. Thankfully she'd had the foresight to pick neutral colors that could be worn through any turn of fashion and brightened with accessories and jewelry. The smell of mothballs rose as she riffled through the trunk, only to announce that Jena and Alys were definitely getting new clothes.

"I want new clothes too," Lady wailed.

"After Jena and Alys are married," Mrs. Binat said firmly.

"Oh, hurry up and get married already, you two!" Lady said crossly. "And Alys, no one cares if you don't want to get married."

"I've been praying so hard for them," Mari said, looking up from her nebulizer. "Obviously God must have good reason for putting us in this predicament."

"I'm leaning toward new silk *saris*." Mrs. Binat looked Jena and Alys up and down. "The other guests can wear brand-name *chamak-dhamak* razzle-dazzle from head to foot, but you two will have an understated, classic Grace Kelly look."

"Everyone," Lady said, "knows people go classic when they can't afford brands."

"People who depend on brands," Mrs. Binat said resignedly, "have no style of their own."

"Silk *saris* are going to cost a lot, Mummy," Alys said as she tried to calculate exactly how much.

"Cost-effective in the long run. The money can come out of your father's gardening budget"—she ignored Mr. Binat's huge, shuddering sigh—"and we'll spice up the *saris* with a visit to our special jeweler."

Ganju *jee* specialized in artificial jewelry that could rival the real thing. He was located in Dilipabad's central bazaar, in a pokey little alley where Mrs. Binat had stumbled upon him. After she smiled at him a little too kindly, he'd always been excited to oblige with wares at excellent prices.

"I want to wear a *mohti*." Lady grabbed the current issue of *Social Lights* and flipped past the pictures of people who seemed to do nothing but brunch, lunch, and attend fashion shows. She stopped at the fashion shoot where her favorite model, Shosha Darling, was wearing the garment of the moment: *mohtis*—miniskirt *dhotis*.

"You can't wear that." Mrs. Binat peered at Shosha Darling's bare legs. "It must cost a fortune. Look at all the hand embroidery on the border."

"I don't have to buy it," Lady said. She turned the pages until she came to the weekly column "What Will People Say—*Log Kya Kahenge*." This week's celebrity quotes concerned fashion designer Qazi of QaziKreations—Qazi had once designed an Oscar dress for a very minor celebrity, which had, back home in Pakistan, turned him into a very major celebrity—and Qazi's latest creation, the *mohti*, for which he was taking orders.

Shosha Darling: I'm always given gifts! Believe and you will receive.

"That's what I plan to do," Lady said. "Believe and I will receive."

"Please, Lady!" Alys said, laughing. "These stupid skirts are severely overpriced and Shosha Darling is an idiot."

"You think everyone is an idiot except for yourself." Lady scowled. "If I can't wear a *mohti*, then I want *saris* with halter tops."

"I wouldn't wear a *sari* even if I was paid," Mari said. "*Saris* are for

Hindus. As Muslims, our ties lie in Arab culture. We should be attending this wedding in *burqas*."

"I'd rather die," Lady said, "than go in a *burqa* to any wedding, let alone NadirFiede."

"Me too," Qitty said.

"Mari, have you gone crazy?" Alys said placidly, for after Mari's dejection they were all quite cautious, and even Lady dared not bring up her poor grades or medical school. "Pakistani roots have nothing to do with Saudi *burqa*, or any Arab culture. Muslims have worn *saris* forever and Hindus have worn *shalwar kameez*."

"I despise it when you use that teacher's tone at home," Mari said.

"It's that stupid club of yours, Mari," Lady said. "Each time you return with some holier-than-thou gem."

"Shut up, Lady," Mari said. "Alys, you know the club is just a bunch of us girls who want to discuss *deen* and *dunya,* religion and its place in our lives and the world. The last topic was menstruation, and we concluded it was probably a blessing for overworked women to be considered impure and so banished from cooking and other duties long enough to get a rest. We're also starting good works, and the first good work is my idea." Mari beamed. "A food drive for Afghan refugees. After that we're going to campaign for the abolishment of men selling brassieres and bangles and other purely female wares to women. It's shameful the way the bra vendors openly assess our breasts and the bangle vendors hold our wrists as if to never let go."

"That's truly admirable," Alys said. "And I think it's time you also got an actual job. Come teach. Or look for an administrative position somewhere. We could do with the money, and you could do with getting out and meeting new people."

"We can certainly do with the money," Mrs. Binat said. "Free *kaa* food drive! You'd better not take anything from the pantry without telling me. Good deeds! All this girl does is watch tennis all day long and wheeze whenever it suits her purpose."

Mari glowered. How she wished yet again that she'd gotten into medical school or that some pious man would marry her and take her away from her family. The first sister married. Then her mother would surely think the world of her.

"Since we can't afford brand names," Lady said, "the next best thing is to become as skeletal as possible. Hillima, can you make sure the cook prepares diet foods for me for the next two weeks before NadirFiede?"

Hillima, sitting by them and gawking at European models on the fashion channel, nodded.

"I'm not going to NadirFiede." Qitty looked up from her sketchbook. "I'm sick of going to places surrounded by skinny girls fishing for compliments by complaining how fat they are."

"I'm not going either," Mari said. "I don't approve of these ostentatious weddings, when Islam requires a simple ceremony."

"I swear, Mari," Lady said, "no one is going to marry you except a gross mullah with a beard coming down to his toes, and once he finds out what a party pooper you are, you'll be the least favorite of his four wives."

"The only party worth worrying about," Mari said, "is the one after death, and if you don't change your ways, Lady, you're going to end up in hell."

Mrs. Binat slapped her forehead. "Mari and Qitty, you're attending NadirFiede, whether you like it or not. Qitty, lose five pounds and you will feel much better."

Qitty glared at her mother. She hadn't had a single *samosa* so far, but now she popped one whole into her mouth.

"See, Mummy!" Lady said. "She doesn't want to be thin."

"Shut up," Qitty said. "You've had six. Mari is right. You're going to go to hell, Bathool."

Lady had originally been named after Mr. Binat's mother, but after bullies at school rhymed "Bathool" with "stool," "cesspool," "drool," et cetera, Mrs. Binat insisted Mr. Binat allow her a legal name change. Bathool chose Lady, from the animated film *Lady and the Tramp*, even though her sisters cautioned against renaming herself after a cartoon dog, no matter how regal.

"Sticks and stones may break my bones," Lady said to Qitty, "but names, hippo, will never hurt me."

Mrs. Binat half-suppressed a smile.

Qitty was livid. "This is why she calls *me* names, Mummy. Because you favor her."

"God knows," Mrs. Binat said, "I never play favorites. Qitty, I'm your friend, not your enemy, and I'm simply saying what is best for you. These days, you girls are expected to be the complete package. Gone are the days when a woman could get away with a single asset like a pair of fine eyes or a tiny waist. Now you have to be a bumshell."

"Bombshell," Mr. Binat corrected her. "Bom, not bum."

Mrs. Binat flashed her eyes at her husband. "Please, Qitty, for my sake try to lose some weight before NadirFiede. No one wants to marry a fat girl."

"You wait, Mummy," Qitty said. "Bathool the Fool is going to do something so unforgivable one day that my being fat will be nothing in comparison. You should have seen the way she was making you-you eyes at the motorbike brigade outside of school today."

"Liar!" Lady said. "Why should I make you-you eyes at motorbike boys? Although some are so handsome, while too many Rich Men are ugly."

Mrs. Binat squinted. "The uglier and darker the Rich Men, all the better for you, because they are actively hunting for fair and lovely girls to balance out their genes."

"Mummy," Lady said, "would you have married Daddy if he was ugly?"

"Luckily for me," Mrs. Binat said, "your father was handsome as well as rich. Alas, he was also unwise and so I became a tale of rags to riches, riches to rags. He let the corrupt Goga and Tinkle completely dupe him. Anyway, God is watching, and it is said the children will suffer for the sins of their parents."

"Pinkie, please." Mr. Binat sat up. "How many times must I say, Goga's and Tinkle's children did nothing to us; leave them out of it."

"Daddy, calm down." Alys got up to kiss her father's cheek. "Shall I get you fresh chai?"

"Daddy's *chamchee,* his toady," Mrs. Binat said. "Run and get him a bucket of chai, so he can drown of shame in it."

"*Hai,* Mummy," Lady said, "how shameful it will be when we arrive at the events in our *saddha hua* Suzuki *dabba.* That car is so embarrassing."

"Can you please," Jena said, "be grateful for the fact that we at least have a car? Anyway, Lady, why would you want to marry someone who cares only about the make of your car or the size of your house?"

"How is that any different from marrying someone because they are smart or nice?" Lady said. "Criteria is criteria!"

"Too many people marry for the wrong reasons," Jena said. "They should be looking for kindness and intelligence."

"Jena, my sweet girl, you are too idealistic," Mrs. Binat said. "On that note, Jena, Alys, if anyone asks your age, just change the subject. I so wish you'd stop telling everyone your real ages, but it is the fashion to think your mother unwise and never listen to her."

"But you're always telling the girls to be fashionable," Mr. Binat said, winking at Alys.

"Wink at Alys!" Mrs. Binat threw a dagger of a look at her husband. "Please, Barkat, wink at her again. Keep teaching her to disrespect her mother. Keep teaching all your daughters to deride me. You used to do the same in front of Tinkle. That woman wished she had one percent of my looks, and yet you allowed her and your brother to treat me like nothing. And what did they do in turn! They treated you like nothing."

"I'm going to the garden," Mr. Binat said. "If I sit here any longer, I'll have another heart attack."

"Please, go," Mrs. Binat said to his retreating back. "One heart attack years ago and constantly we have to be on best behavior. Who thinks of my health? I get palpitations at the thought of you five girls languishing in this house, never knowing the joy of marriage and offspring. *Hai,*" she said, suddenly wistful, "can you imagine Tinkle's face if even one of you manages to snag an eligible bachelor at NadirFiede, let alone all of you."

"Maybe Qitty can snag an eligible bachelor by sitting on him," Lady said.

Qitty picked up her sketchbook and whacked Lady in the arm.

"Jena, Alys," Mrs. Binat said, "shame on both of you if this wedding ends and you remain unmarried. Cast your nets wide, reel it in, grab it, grab it. But do not come across as too fast or forward, for a girl with a loose reputation is one step away from being damaged goods and ending up a spinster. Keep your distance without keeping your distance. Let him caress you without coming anywhere near you. Coo sweet somethings into his ears without opening your mouth. Before he even realizes there is a trap, he will have proposed. Do you understand?"

Chapter 4

Ten years ago, the evening Hillima declared the cleanup of Binat House complete, the Binats gathered in the study, wondering how to occupy their time. Jena began reading a pop-up *Alice in Wonderland* to her younger sisters. Mr. and Mrs. Binat quarreled about finances. Mrs. Binat segued into how she wished she'd gotten Jena and Alys married off before their banishment.

Alys escaped her mother's dire predictions regarding her prospects by fleeing to her new bedroom. She sat on her bed, made cheery with a yellow chenille bedspread and crewelwork pillowcases, and thought about what the hell she was going to do with her life in this small town.

She stared at her bare walls, livened up with a Pisces poster and a photo of herself amid friends during a school trip to the Red Sea. She remembered treading the ocean bed with Tana, laughing as they looked out for sea urchins, snorkeling under the hot sun, returning to land and sand fights. The future had seemed so limitless and bright back then.

Alys stepped out onto her small balcony. Evening had descended on Dilipabad, and the sun was setting in a sky pollution had turned milky. She wasn't sure when she began to cry. She wiped her tears and told herself to stop. She was crying because ever since they'd returned to Pakistan two years ago, all she'd heard was how, if she did not conform to certain beauty standards and demure etiquette, she was going to die alone. She was crying because she missed her friends in Jeddah and wondered if she'd ever see them again. When Alys had left Jeddah, she and Tana sent each other letters but, slowly, they petered out. In her last letter, Tana mentioned that her family was returning to Denmark, after which Alys's letter was returned saying "no forwarding address."

In Lahore, Alys and Jena had met some friendly faces in college. But sitting in the canteen and sharing greasy *naan kebabs* with girls who'd known each other since kindergarten and accordingly cracked ancient jokes just made them feel lonelier. So it was that the two sisters had turned to each other: "Do you remember Radhika in the Brownie troop getting into trouble for demonstrating how to play spin the bottle?" "Do you remember when we watched Madonna's Virgin Tour at Sahara's house?" "Do you remember when Tana showed us a condom and we thought it was a balloon?"

They'd been too young to say goodbye forever to friends, home, familiarity, and now they'd even left big-city Lahore and come to Dilipabad, where life seemed to revolve around marrying well and eating well. There wasn't even a proper bookstore or library. Alys's eyes filled up again. Any minute now, she was certain, her mother would come barging in to tell her that if she cried, then she'd ruin her eyesight, and if she started to wear spectacles, then no one would marry her.

Across the road, at the graveyard's entrance, a flower-cart vendor was putting away the marigold garlands and loose rose petals he sold to mourners to commemorate their dead. Alys blinked. The graveyard was the one place no one would follow her, because her family was terrified of ghosts, djinns, *churails,* and, thanks to Michael Jackson's "Thriller" video, ghouls, zombies, and monsters.

Alys tiptoed down the stairs and out of the front door and across the street to the graveyard's entrance.

"*As-salaam-alaikum,*" the vendor said, looking up from his flowers. "You are the new people who've moved into the house?"

"We moved two weeks ago," Alys managed to reply in her heavily English-accented, stilted Urdu.

"*Chunga*—good," he said. "No place deserves to remain empty for too long. From Ingland or Amreeka?"

"Jeddah."

"*Mashallah.* You must have gone to Mecca and Medina?"

"All the time."

"*Mashallah.* My cousin is working in construction there. Building malls. He doesn't like it. He misses home. But the money he sends has already gotten two daughters married off with full dowry, *alhamdulillah.*"

Alys sighed. Did anyone talk about anything except marriage in this country?

"I want to go into the graveyard," Alys said. "There's no closing time, is there?"

"No. But most people are scared of the dead, and even more so at nighttime."

"If you ask me," Alys said, "it's the living who people should be scared of."

The vendor laughed. He handed her a plastic bag full of rose petals. When Alys protested that she had no money, he smiled and said, "Today free, but next time buy double flowers."

Alys stepped into the cemetery and onto a paved path that wound through graves, some with plain tombstones and others with elaborately filigreed ones. Many headstones had epitaphs in both Urdu and English, the scripts of both languages shining like ebony jewels against the gray-veined white marble. She read random epitaphs, placing petals on strangers' graves.

A row of ashoka trees, vibrant and healthy, created a man-planted border, their roots feeding from blood and bones on both sides, and

Alys slipped through the trunks and into, it seemed, another cemetery. Dirt paths wound through overgrown vegetation and eroded marble headstones with British names in faded lettering. She walked on, scared now that she was so deep inside the graveyard. Moonlight spread down her back like ice. All was quiet except for crickets and her footsteps, crunching twigs. She saw a form leaning against a wall, an unnatural fiery glow emanating from where a mouth should be.

Alys screamed. The form screamed.

A girl stepped out of the shadows, a lit cigarette dangling from bony fingers, a scrawny braid curling down one shoulder to her waist. She was wearing red sandals and a purple-and-green *shalwar kurta* topped with a red cardigan with white plastic buttons. Not someone, Alys instinctively knew, her mother was going to think very highly of, for, as was the case with too many people who'd jumped class, Mrs. Binat was often the harshest critic of the class she believed she'd left behind.

"You scared me." Alys put a hand on her beating heart. "I thought you were a ghost."

"Hel-lo. You scared me." The girl spoke in Urdu. "I thought you were a rabid dog. What are you doing here? Are you from the family that has moved into the ruins in front of the graveyard?"

Alys nodded. "Not ruins anymore. It's cleaned up quite well."

"Aren't you Pakistani?" the girl said. "Your Urdu is very poor, even for a Burger."

Alys rolled her eyes at the derogatory term used to describe Pakistanis who predominantly went about their lives in fluent English by Pakistanis who predominantly went about their lives in fluent Urdu or a regional dialect. In local parlance, Alys was an English-speaking Burger and this girl an Urdu-speaking Chapati. Usually the two groups did not reside in the same neighborhoods, but that seemed to be the case here.

"Do you know any local languages?" the girl asked.

"English is a local language," Alys said, switching to English completely.

The girl replied in a stilted English, "Did you people buy the ruins?"

"We own it," Alys said.

"You are a Binat?" The girl switched back to Urdu.

"Yes."

The girl's eyes widened. "And what has brought the Binats to live in Dilipabad?"

Mrs. Binat had forbidden any mention of the family feud, but Alys felt they had nothing to be ashamed about. Also, who cared if people talked? People were going to talk anyway. So she told the girl the truth.

"They took everything?" The girl's face softened.

"Pretty much."

"Kismet, wheel of fortune, luck, destiny, what can one do? By the way, my good name is Syeda Shireen Looclus, but everyone calls me Sherry. What is your good name?"

"Alysba. Everyone calls me Alys."

Sherry held out her hand. Alys shook it.

"Married?" Sherry asked.

"I would be if my mother had her way. You?"

"Still unmarried, much to my mother's distress," Sherry said. "I am an Urdu lang-lit teacher at the British School of Dilipabad."

"A career woman." Alys beamed. "Do you know if your school is looking for English teachers?"

"You want to teach?"

"It just occurred to me."

"BSD is the best school here, and Principal Naheed is very picky. Education level?"

"Second year of undergrad in English literature."

"How old you are?" Sherry asked.

"Twenty."

"You look much younger," Sherry said wistfully. "How old are you really?"

"Twenty." Alys frowned.

"*Chal yaar*—whatever, friend. No need to lie to me, I won't tell a soul."

"I'm not lying. In March, I'll turn twenty-one."

"Really? Hasn't your mother ever told you that you need to pretend to be at least four years younger than your real age? That way you'll age much slower publicly and can stretch out your marriageable years."

"She has, but I think hiding one's age is stupid, and the only way to defeat ageism is to not comply with it. How old are you?"

"Twenty-eight," Sherry said. "Forever twenty-eight."

"And your real age?" Alys asked wryly. "I won't tell anyone."

"I don't know you to trust you. And you'd better not tell a soul you saw me smoking."

Alys signaled for Sherry to hand over the cigarette pack. A smile spread over Sherry's face as Alys lit one and took a drag.

"There," Alys said. "Now you saw me smoking too."

"*Yeh hui na baat!* That's more like it!"

"Can you finish it?" Alys handed it back to Sherry. "I'm not really a smoker. Not fond of staining my teeth. Also, cancer."

"I'll risk that for now," Sherry said as she put out Alys's barely touched cigarette and returned it to the pack. "Do you want chewing gum?"

Alys took some cinnamon gum to freshen her breath. "I had a couple of friends in Jeddah who smoked—secretly, of course, like you—and I'd join occasionally."

"Will you join me occasionally? I come here every evening after the Maghrib prayers. My mother thinks I'm feeding birds."

"You're twenty-eight or something like that. You have a job. Your own income and therefore independence. Surely *you* can smoke if you want."

"Good girls don't smoke." Sherry eyed Alys curiously. "Anyway, these mothers only stop dictating your life once you get married."

"True," Alys said. "And then your husband dictates it."

"I'd love to get married!"

"You would?"

"I'm tired of my parents worrying about me," Sherry said, "not to mention that everywhere I go, the first question I'm asked is: 'When are you getting married?' Everyone promises to pray for me. So far no one's prayers have come true, so I'm wondering if they really are praying."

Sherry smiled. Alys smiled.

"Anyway," Sherry said, "I don't want to die without ever having had a husband. I want that phase of my life to begin, but it might never happen. You see, proper proposals for me have dried up." She squatted behind a wide headstone. Alys sat crossed-legged beside her.

"I was engaged twice before," Sherry said, relighting the cigarette Alys had barely puffed. "First to a cousin. I liked him. He liked me. Then he went to Germany on an engineering scholarship and married a German lady for citizenship after convincing his parents that she was a good career move. They have five children now. Boys. They visit off and on. I avoid them completely."

"You're better off without such a person," Alys said, and feeling the intensity of Sherry's disclosure, asked for a cigarette.

"I managed to get engaged a second time, this time to a nonrelative, at my insistence." Sherry handed Alys a cigarette and struck a match. "He wanted to marry immediately, but my mother was undergoing knee surgery and we had to wait. Shortly after our engagement, he passed away. Turned out he'd had kidney problems, which his family had kept from us. His parents were very aged and they wanted a widowed daughter-in-law who could earn as well as look after them. I tell you, God saved me from that terrible fate. But as far as everyone was concerned, I'd driven one man into the arms of a foreigner and another into the mouth of death, so obviously I was *manhoos*, an ill omen. Then we found out I couldn't have children. Useless Uterus, that's me."

"Don't say that," Alys said, flicking ash onto the path.

"Everyone else does. Basically, until I started teaching, I was

nanny to my sister and two brothers. They're much, much younger
than me. After having me—a girl, unfortunately—my mother suffered from years of miscarriages. If my paternal grandmother had
had her way, my father would have remarried for a son, but he refused to, and thankfully, through the miracle of praying and *manaats*,
my mother was able to produce live births again and, finally, my precious brothers." Sherry took a long drag and looked out into the
distance. "Anyway, I still pray that one day my *shehzada*, my Prince
Charming, will come. I still get the odd proposal, but they're from
either men who come with a dowry list as long as my arm, which
my family is in no position to fulfill, or widowers with children looking for a nurse-plus-nanny in the guise of a wife, or divorced men
known for domestic abuse or something similar. Listen, tell me,
Ms. Burger, what is the English word for a man who is divorced? I
know a woman is a 'divorcée,' because that's what everyone is calling
an aunt of mine who left her cheater husband."

Alys frowned. "Actually, there's no specific label for a man. In
English we apparently live in a world where we only keep track of
whether or not a woman is a pigeon."

"Pigeon?"

"Virgin." Alys glanced at Sherry to see how she'd taken the use of
the supposedly bawdy word. Sherry was chuckling. "Pigeon is my
and my elder sister's code word for virgin."

"I love it!" Sherry said. "Pigeon. Let us pray that one day my pi-
geonly feathers flutter and I fly the coop."

Sherry and Alys gave each other shy high fives.

"By the way," Sherry said, "my real age is thirty-one. I'm thirty-
one years old."

Ten years later, Sherry was forty-one, though as far as the rest of the
world was concerned she wasn't a day over thirty-five. Over the years
she'd begun dying her skinnier braid and plucking her chin and,
when she laughed, which was often, her laugh lines deepened. Yet

she still hoped her Prince Charming would come, if only because there was simply no other respectable way for a girl from her class in this country to have sex.

So Sherry reminded Alys as they slipped into the graveyard and headed toward the spot where they'd first met. Sherry cleared leaves off a stone slab and sat down. She lit a cigarette. Alys did too.

"I would," Sherry said, blowing a smoke ring, "like to experience sex before dying, and not just with my hand. *Rishta* Aunty—"

Alys groaned. *Rishta* aunties were the local matchmakers, a perfect job for professional busybodies. Paradoxically, the key to a *rishta* aunty's success was keeping the secrets she learned about prospective clients to herself. Her job was to get people married off, but she did not guarantee happiness or children and she was very clear about the fact that if marriages were decreed in heaven, divorces seemed to be too, and that even spouses in perfect health could die and she should not be made to give a refund for services rendered.

While *rishta* aunties were a regular fixture at Sherry's home, Looclus Lodge Bismillah, Mrs. Binat did not entertain them. Not because she cared that it embarrassed her daughters to be forced to parade the mandatory *rishta* trolleys, prepare cups of chai to display their domestication, or be picked apart by prospective mothers-in-law, but because Dilipabad's *rishta* aunties were not up to standard. To Mrs. Binat's disappointment, they did not have the network or connections to go beyond Absurdities and middle-class Abroads, categories that Sherry's parents—Bobia Looclus, a homemaker, and "Haji" Amjad Looclus, a supervisor in a factory—were in rapture over.

"*Rishta* Aunty," Sherry continued, "told us this prospective groom-to-be is on the lookout for a nubile virgin. Pigeon I am, nubile I'm not, but *Rishta* Aunty believes this one is my stud of a Prince Charming. He's sixty-one and, despite managing a grocery store, apparently does not possess too big of a potbelly."

"Better to die a pigeon than copulate with a potbelly," Alys said solemnly.

"Clearly," Sherry said, "you're enjoying your hand."

"That I am." Alys laughed.

"Anyway, this particular potbelly has never been married, because he was looking after two unmarried sisters. The sisters recently married two brothers working in Sharjah, and so now he's looking for a bride of his own. He's probably as eager a pigeon to fly the coop as I am. He's fond of massage and being read to, because his eyesight is weak but he doesn't like to wear spectacles. *Rishta* Aunty told him I was strong and I'm a teacher, so I can read very well and earn. Let's hope that incentive seals the deal."

"Can you please meet the man first," Alys said, rolling her eyes, "before agreeing to marry him?"

"Not up to me, is it," Sherry said. "I'll wheel out the *rishta* trolley with the expected cake, fruit *chaat,* and *shami kebabs.* I'll make chai for him and the rest of his relatives, who'll have accompanied him for free food. I'll confirm that I've cooked all the food from scratch, which, in my home"—Sherry looked archly at Alys—"*I* will have done. Unlike you Burger girls, I can actually cook and don't just bake for fun."

"Be quiet, Chapati," Alys said. "I don't even bake for fun."

"I'll sit there after having served chai to the potbelly and pretend to be a shy and opinion-less dummy. And on my wedding night I'll turn into a sex maniac, and then he'll divorce me on account of too much enthusiasm, since ardor will imply immorality."

"Or," Alys said, "maybe he'll appreciate that you can't get enough of flying the coop."

Sherry took a long drag. "I hope this prospect doesn't decide to poop in our toilet, like the last one did. Took forever to unclog that mess."

"Here's a mess of a different kind. We received the invite to the NadirFiede circus. I've wasted all afternoon listening to what gift will make us look rich enough and what we're going to wear in order to captivate eligible bachelors. You know how despicable I think this whole husband-hunting business is."

"Yes," Sherry said, "I'm well aware. *Chalo,* best of luck. Let us hope you and Jena hunt good husbands."

"I don't even want to go," Alys said. "A bunch of himbos and bimbos showing off to each other about who enjoyed the glitzier holiday this year."

"Have you any idea how many people would die to be invited?" Sherry said. "I'd love to just see who in the world is marrying that pain in the bum Fiede Fecker. Do you think Fiede is a pigeon or have she and Nadir Sheh flown the coop?"

"It is a truth universally acknowledged that a good girl ought to keep her mouth shut about whether she's been keeping her legs shut."

"I bet Fiede's been humping and pumping night and day," Sherry said. "But at the wedding, like all good pigeons, she'll pretend her feathers have never fluttered."

"Come with us to the NadirFiede *mehndi,*" Alys said. "Come!"

It was quite acceptable in Pakistan to bring an uninvited guest to a wedding, for in a gathering of hundreds, what was one more?

"Your mother," Sherry replied, smiling, "will not be happy to have me tag along."

"Mummy will be fine," Alys said, knowing full well that she'd be annoyed. "Please come. The NadirFiede spectacle will actually be fun with you there."

Sherry shrugged an okay.

"Yeah! You're coming with us! And who knows, you might very well meet your Prince Charming at the *mehndi.*"

The friends laughed. They ground out their cigarettes in the grass and popped chewing gum into their mouths. Then, linking arms, they strode out of the graveyard toward their homes.

Chapter 5

The Binats parked in the overflow lot and headed to the gymkhana gates for the NadirFiede *mehndi* ceremony. The security guard at the gate beamed when he saw Alys, Jena, Sherry, and Mari. The four women had long been tutoring low-income children for free, and Jena asked the guard how his son's exams had gone.

"Excellent," he said, blessing them with happiness and long lives as he let them in.

"Such a good omen," Mrs. Binat chirped, "to enter such an event with the blessings of a menial. You watch, Alys and Jena, this wedding will end well for both of you."

"Mummy, shh," Alys said, as they joined other guests walking up the candlelit driveway toward the vast grounds and into the wedding *shamiana*, the huge multicolored tent shot through with gold thread. The scent of perfumes and colognes mingled with that of beef *seekh kebabs* and chicken *tikkas* cooking on coal grills. Guests stood in clusters, chattering, and children ran underfoot followed by ayahs preening in last season's castoffs.

The groom and his entourage had yet to arrive. A gaggle of young girls—Fiede's cousins and close friends—sat on the makeshift dance floor in front of the bride-and-groom stage with a *dholak* between them, though clearly none of them knew how to properly play the double-sided drum. Lady was an expert; she elbowed her way into the group, and soon she was playing the drum and bellowing Punjabi wedding songs—"*lathe di chaddar, chitta kukkar banere, sadda chidiyan da*"—with such gusto and to such ear-shattering whistles that several guests asked if she was Fiede's best friend.

Mrs. Binat spied Fiede Fecker's parents—Mr. Fecker, in a navy raw-silk *kurta*, and Mrs. Fecker, in hideous tangerine organdy—and she and Mr. Binat proceeded to congratulate them. Mr. Fecker shook hands with Mr. Binat. Mrs. Fecker's gargantuan eyelashes, supposedly imported from Milan, were apparently weighing down her eyes, because it took her a moment to recognize Mr. and Mrs. Bark Binat, after which she thanked them for coming before moving on to the next guest.

Mrs. Binat glowed as moneyed folk flitted around. She recognized acquaintances from when she too had been moneyed folk, and she chose to overlook the women's cool greetings. Instead, she basked at the welcome their husbands were giving Barkat. They were embracing him and exclaiming that they hadn't seen Bark-Bark in years, which was true, for Mr. Binat had chosen to become something of a recluse since his elder brother's betrayal.

In fact, Mr. Binat had been reluctant to attend NadirFiede, for fear that his brother and sister-in-law might be there. It was only after Alys reminded him that it was the perpetrators who should be mortified and stay away and not the victim that Mr. Binat agreed to come. As their father stood among old friends, a little bit of his former self returned, and all the Binat girls stood taller as he introduced them to uncles who remarked how much they'd grown and how lovely they'd become. Soon the wives steered their husbands away from Mr. Binat's daughters, and Mrs. Binat, refusing to allow any slight to upset her this evening, proceeded to lead her brood to one of the fuchsia velvet sofa sets arranged around coal stoves.

She was pleased to note the number of eyes following Jena as they walked down the Afghan rugs covering the lawn and into the seating area. She'd dressed her daughter well. Jena was in a dove-gray silk sari, the muted color enhanced with a darker gray sequined blouse and a *kundan*-and-emerald choker set—the gems fake, of course, thanks to Ganju *jee,* but no one was the wiser. At an event where everyone was dressed like a Brazilian parrot, Jena's understated elegance as the African parrot stood out. If it weren't for the wretched Tinkle's smear campaign, Mrs. Binat knew, women seeking brides for their sons would have been coming up to her in order to make inquiries about Jena's age, occupation, and intentions for marriage.

Still, Mrs. Binat knew beauty had the potential to defeat the slurs of a jealous relative. Jena had only to sink her hooks into a prospective Rich Man, who would subsequently be so besotted by her looks that he would ignore rumors about her family. Alas, Mrs. Binat thought as she smoothed a wrinkle from Jena's *pallu,* none of her daughters were proficient in the art of hook, reel, grab. In fact, except for Lady, her daughters were discomfited by the very notion of catching a husband, despite the number of times she'd told them that one had to seek out a good proposal as one would a promotion or a comfortable shoe.

It was all this nonsense about falling in love that was making catching a husband unseemly. Of course one must fall in love, but let it initially be the man who falls and then, once his ring is on your finger, you too may allow yourself to fall in love—though within reason, Mrs. Binat always cautioned, for the best marriages were ones where the husband loved the wife more. She sighed. It was her full-time job as a good mother to get her daughters married well, and she was determined to do her duty regardless of all obstacles, even Alys's obstinacy.

Despite Mrs. Binat's copious pleas for Alys to wear a new sari like Jena's, the disobedient girl had dived into the trunk and picked out a lackluster outfit. Couple that disgrace with barely any makeup at an event where women were wearing so much they would have to use scalpels to scrape off the cosmetics. Not that any of her daughters required any makeup, Mrs. Binat thought with pride, but, still, didn't all girls like enhancing their assets? Sometimes she feared Alys was serious when she said she didn't want to get married. What sort of girl did not want to get married? What sort of girl did not want children?

Mrs. Binat had, a few years ago, made Jena, closest of Alys's confidantes, put her hand on the Quran and swear that Alys was not a lesbian. Asking Alys directly would have been useless; she would have defiantly said, "So what if I was?" and given her a lecture. Mrs. Binat had also considered asking Sherry, but she did not trust friends and so did not want to give Sherry any ammunition to start rumors about Alys.

Poor girl, Mrs. Binat thought, as Sherry settled on a sofa. Did she have no other wedding wear but nylon satin monstrosities? The only plus going for Sherry was her skinny body, luckily for her in vogue. But a side effect of being so thin was also to be completely flat-chested, a setback given that even the most *shareef*—pious—of men wanted a wife with some breasts.

Mrs. Binat was rescued from further rumination by Principal Naheed and her two daughters, who were making a beeline toward them. The principal had on a decent Chantilly lace *sari* in a tolerable puce, but those stubby daughters of hers—why in the world had she allowed them to wear *patiala shalwars* with crop-top tunics that made their limbs look like cocktail sausages?

Mrs. Binat rose to air-kiss Naheed, and she decided it was just as well that Gin and Rum displayed zero sartorial sense and sensibility, for that meant even more opportunity for JenaAlysMariQittyLady to shine.

"*Salaain-lai-kum*, Principal Naheed," Mrs. Binat said. "Gin and Rum are looking like visions of perfection."

"*As-salaam-alaikum*, Pinkie," Naheed said. "They're wearing the best of the best. QaziKreations' new line, QaziSensations." Naheed turned to Mr. Binat. "Bark, I see Pinkie continues to look just as dazzling as your daughters."

"Hello, Naheed, yes, Pinkie outshines us all. And how are you? How is Zaleel?" Mr. Binat asked, referring to Naheed's husband, Khaleel, by his nickname.

"Zaleel couldn't make it today," Naheed said. "He was lifting weights this morning and dropped a dumbbell on his foot."

"That's dumb." Mr. Binat guffawed at his own joke. "But let's hope for a quick recovery." Then he returned to surveying the tent for his brother and sister-in-law.

"I must say," Naheed said, "Fiede has outdone herself with the classy décor and arrangement. So striking, so *mashallah*."

"Striking, *mashallah*," Mrs. Binat agreed. Everything was very nice: the soft lighting in the tent, the fresh flowers, the low-backed sofas with faux pearl–encrusted sausage cushions, the heaters, the fairy lights looped around the tent poles, the arrangement of the buffet to be served in a separate tent.

Naheed said, "A friend of Fiede's has started event planning, and Fiede handed the wedding over to her—no charge, of course. But, then, this is how her friend will garner business in the future, for everyone will want Fiede Fecker's event planner to plan events for them. I have always said that the most troublesome students turn out to be the greatest assets, and Fiede Fecker is a true asset to the British School of Dilipabad. Hello, Alys, Jena. What an absolutely breathtaking sari, Jena, and such lovely jewelry."

Jena nodded thanks at the compliments.

"Qitty, have you lost weight? I was expecting a watermelon, but you look like a cantaloupe tonight. You have such a pretty face; why don't you try to lose some of your chunkiness? Look at Lady! Slim 'n' trim!" Naheed said approvingly as Lady rejoined her family. "But, Lady, aren't you cold in sleeveless? Mari, you look very un-fresh compared to your sisters. Sherry, oho"—Naheed gave Sherry a terribly sweet smile—"*tum bhi pahunch gayee* NadirFiede. You've also managed to make it to NadirFiede."

Sherry flushed, but before she could answer, Gin and Rum decided to greet everyone with air kisses and cries of "*Bon-joor, bon-joor, bon-joor.*"

"*Hain?* What?" Mrs. Binat said, air-kissing the fidgety girls. They had so much foundation on, she could smell the chemicals.

"I'm so sick of the girls' French!" Naheed said, clearly not sick of it at all. "Ever since they've earned their fluency certificates from the Alliance Française, it's *parlez vois* this and *parlez vois* that."

"Not *vois*, Ama, *vous, vous*," Gin and Rum said together. "*Vous. Vous.*"

Naheed swallowed a withering reprimand to her daughters. "I keep reminding these two future Dilipabad superstars to stop the French talk with me and wait until they go to fashion school in Gay Paree."

"Gaypari?" Mrs. Binat asked. "*O kee?* What is that?"

"Paris, Aunty, Paris," Rum said. "Paris is also called Gay Paree, because it's fun time all the time and not because of any gay thing, in case you were wondering. Not that there's anything wrong with anything gay. It's becoming very fashionable these days to have at least one gay friend, and we hope to make one once we get there."

Everyone tried their best to look impressed, except Lady, who was genuinely impressed.

"Paris!" Lady squealed. "*Hai*, lucky! *Acha*, you had better give me discounts, because I'm already booking you both for making my *shaadi-ka-jora*, my only stipulation being that I want *motay-motay*, fat-fat, diamantés on the bodice."

"*Ah oui!* Oh yes!" the twins said. "Though we still have to apply to fashion schools in Paris and get in."

"You'll both get in," Naheed said tersely. "Lady, aren't you in a bit of a premature rush to book your wedding outfit? You have four unmarried older sisters ahead of you. Let's hope the next wedding we attend will be Jena's, *inshallah*."

"*Inshallah,*" Mrs. Binat said. "God willing."

They were interrupted by the unmistakable *dhuk-dhuk-dhuk* of the hired drummers who always accompanied bride-and-groom parties and whose beating drums no one could resist, at the very least, tapping their feet to. Cries arose: "The boy's family is here!" Fiede Fecker's cousins and friends—including Lady, who merrily joined the bridal party—grabbed platters of rose petals and lined up by the entrance.

"Here come the eager pigeons," Sherry whispered to Alys as Nadir Sheh's family and friends entered, dancing to the drummers. Laughter broke loose as petals were showered left, right, and center. The drummers changed beat every few minutes as the family entered, some dancing, some carrying baskets of flowers and trays of mixed sweets, others candles in earthen *diyas,* the oil lamps illuminating excited faces. Nadir Sheh had invited a few of his London college friends, and all were keeping up well with the *dholak* beat.

The bridegroom's party was led to the reserved chairs with red bows in front of the stage, and Nadir Sheh climbed up the stage and settled on one of the two baroque armchairs as if it was a throne and this his coronation. He sat with arms akimbo and legs splayed in his dandy outfit: an orange silk *kurta* topped with a heavily embroidered red waistcoat above a starched-to-death cream *boski shalwar,* and his feet were clad in the pointiest golden wedding *khusse.*

The guests turned for Fiede Fecker's grand entry. Again the drummers drummed up a frenzy as the bride's cousins and friends came in with platters of *mehndi* embedded with bangles, candles, and flowers. They were followed by Fiede's male cousins carrying a palanquin, in which sat Fiede Fecker, peeping through a curtain of marigolds. They rested the palanquin at the side of the stage, and Fiede's father helped her out and led her to the armchair next to Nadir Sheh. Fiede was wearing a vermilion *shalwar kurta* and a yellow *dupatta* pinned strategically to accentuate her long, flat-ironed hair. Fresh rosebud and jasmine hoops dangled from her ears and matched her floral bracelets.

Once the groom and bride were seated side by side, their immediate family members proceeded with the *mehndi* rituals. Nadir Sheh's mother, aunts, and female cousins began to dance a *luddi* around the henna platters they'd brought, circling the platters to the drumbeat and changing their dance steps for each new circumambulation. The guests looked on politely, clapping and chatting among themselves and wondering when the synchronized dances would begin, after which dinner would be served.

There were quite a few BSD students with their families present at the wedding, and they kept passing shyly by Alys, Jena, and Sherry, giggling as students are apt to do when they see teachers out of context. The recently engaged Tahira introduced her fiancé to them. He had an open, honest face and duly informed them that they were all Tahira's favorite teachers. He looked like a nice person, Alys thought, and she hoped he was. She managed to slip in how nice it would be if Tahira might finish high school after marriage, perfectly doable, and she was glad to see that he did not dismiss the suggestion outright.

Rose-Nama, crusader for duty and tradition, was here too. She and her mother had taken one look at Alys, their faces going sour, and had begun to mutter among themselves, Alys was sure, about how the Feckers had invited every *aira gaira nathu khaira*—every Tom, Dick, and Harry—as if it was a *mela*, a funfair, and not the Dilipabad wedding of the year.

"If Fiede sits any closer to Nadir," Sherry whispered to Alys, "she's going to end up in his lap. Nadir's mother looks like she's going to faint over Fiede's lack of decorum."

"So does Fiede's mother," Alys said.

Fiede Fecker was clearly finding it hard to look down demurely, as befit a proper bride-to-be. She was whispering away to Nadir Sheh and boldly surveying the tent to check out who was in attendance. But, then, Sherry noted, she was Fiede Fecker, Dilipabad's honorary princess, and therefore whatever she did would be considered proper and, soon enough, fashionable.

"I hope," Alys said, "Lady doesn't get any ideas from Fiede Fecker. Do you remember how Fiede was supplying marijuana to those girls at school, and the only people who got in trouble were the girls, because Principal Naheed dared not cross Fiede's mother, who insisted Fiede was being framed?"

Sherry nodded. "Fiede's mother would let her get away with murder."

"The only thing they didn't let her get away with," Alys said, "was going to college."

Dilipabad did not have a quality girls' college, and Fiede's parents did not want to send her to a boarding college. Instead, after graduating high school, Fiede was sent on a consolation holiday to Amsterdam, to relatives who lived there. Out on the canal, Fiede's boat bumped into Nadir Sheh's boat. Nadir Sheh, attending college in London, was visiting Amsterdam on spring break. He was attracted to Fiede's long, bleached-blond hair falling prettily onto her big Chanel bag. That Fiede was not bothered about world affairs or feminist rhetoric was the clincher for him.

On her part, Fiede had been enjoying Amsterdam very much—although the Anne Frank museum had made her very sad—but she was also missing her tribe terribly. Nadir Sheh's upper-class Pakistani demeanor made her feel back home, and his genuine Hermès belt—Fiede had an eye for impostors—signaled to her that he would be someone her family would willingly accept. Though a love marriage, officially, the Feckers were telling everyone it was a purely arranged marriage so that no one could accuse Fiede of being "loose" or "fast."

"That we should all have such happy endings," Sherry said, sighing, "if our boat bumps into someone else's boat. I tell you, Fiede Fecker is not a pigeon, though she's probably done everything but *it*, which makes her a part-time pigeon."

"I agree," Alys said. "Part-time pigeon."

The dances began. Wedding dancing was the one avenue where girls from good families were allowed to publicly show off their moves. Lady, who loved to dance, was having a hard time remaining seated but, since she was neither family nor a close friend, she was not supposed to join in the revelry. As a guest, her role was that of spectator.

Nadir Sheh's friends and family performed a synchronized dance they'd been rehearsing for weeks to a Pakistani number, *"Ko Ko Korina,"* which many guests would deem too obscure a choice for such a high-class wedding but, sigh, Nadir Sheh's family was new money, after all.

Then it was Fiede Fecker's family and friends' turn to perform a dance. They'd chosen the double-entendre Indian song *"Choli Ke Peeche Kya Hai"*—"What Lies Behind Your Blouse"—and were greeted with enthusiastic applause. This was a siren song for Lady, and in a sudden frenzy she leapt onto the floor. Other dancers stopped to stare. Alys yanked Lady off the floor and looked at her sister so ferociously that Lady remained glued to her seat through the remaining dances.

Once the synchronized dances were over, the DJ played requests. Fiede Fecker's friends and cousins started dancing, and Fiede decided, conventions be damned, this was her wedding and she was going to dance too. Who cared *log kya kahenge*—what people said—including her in-laws? And so she made history as the first bride in Dilipabad to dance at her own *mehndi* ceremony. Soon Nadir Sheh and his friends joined the freestyle dancing too.

Mrs. Binat and the other Dilipabadi matrons looked on and tried to gauge if Nadir Sheh had delivered any fish worth hooking. Gyrating on the dance floor was a cement scion. An owner of a sanitary-napkin company. A hotelier heir. A sugar-mill proprietor—twice divorced, but so what? Money was money. Also dancing was the young owner of the British School Group, recently returned from America.

Naheed was dying to know who the BSG scion was, for Gin's and Rum's sake, but also because she planned to have a few words with him about the rumor that he was going to do away with school uniforms. Was the BSG scion the sweet-looking gangly fellow with a flop of sandy hair? Or the ballerina-looking guy dancing well enough to not be the laughingstock but awkwardly enough to draw chuckles? Who was the chap that looked like a cross-eyed polar bear and was jumping up and down as if he was at an aerobics class? And that elderly gentleman who kept shaking his bottom too close to the seated young girls—surely he had to be Uncle Sugar Mill. And who was that tall, good-looking boy with the fine eyes?

The food was finally served close to midnight. Ravenous guests rose en masse toward the food tent, where they would serve themselves from either side of the chafing dishes, creating ideal conditions for boys and girls who longed to accidentally flirt and fall in love, eyes meeting over sizzling entrees, fingers caressing fingers as serving spoons were exchanged. The Binats entered the tent, a smaller rainbow replica of the larger one. Lady and Mrs. Binat headed straight for the buffet serving Italian food and loaded their plates with lasagna localized with green chilies and garlic bread infused with cumin. Sherry and Qitty headed for the Chinese buffet, piling their plates with egg fried rice and sweet-and-sour chicken. Alys, Jena, Mari, and Mr. Binat helped themselves to the Pakistani buffet, their plates soon full of beef *biryani,* grilled *seekh kebabs, tikkas,* and buttered *naan.*

At the dessert table, Jena, Alys, and Sherry wished they'd eaten a little less dinner. Still, they managed to sample everything: *gulab jamuns* in sweet sticky syrup, *firni* gelled in clay ramekins and decorated with edible silver paper, snow-white *ras malai,* tiramisu cups and lemon custard tarts, *kulfi* ice cream and sweet *paans* from a kiosk preparing them fresh on the spot, the bright-green betel leaves stuffed with shredded coconut, betel nuts, fennel, rose-petal jam, sugar syrup, and then folded into perfect triangles.

Jena was taking a dainty bite of an unsweetened *paan* when she was approached by two girls with cascades of highlighted hair. Some extensions, for sure, she thought, and a healthy amount of makeup, just shy of too much. They were dressed exquisitely in heavily embroidered *lehenga cholis* with their flat midriffs bare, and diaphanous *dupattas,* clearly the work of an established designer. Jena noticed their single-strap matte-silver heels. She'd been searching for shoes like these, but all she'd been able to find were horrendous wide-strapped glittery platforms.

"Where did you get your shoes?" Jena asked, smiling her admiration.

"Italy," one of the girls said. "I love the detailing on your sari blouse and border. Whose is it?" She rattled off a few designer names.

Jena shook her head. "No designer. My tailor, Shawkat. He has a small shop in Dilipabad Bazaar."

"Oh, I see." The girl's face fell for a second. "I'm Humeria Bingla—Hammy."

"And I'm Sumeria Bingla—Sammy," said the other girl. "Actually, Sumeria Bingla Riyasat. I'm married. Happily married."

"Jena Binat," Jena said. She proceeded to introduce Alys, Mari, and Sherry. Hammy turned to Sherry with a huge smile.

"Are you Sherry Pupels from the Peshawar Pupels clan?" she asked. "The politician's wife?"

"No," Sherry said. "I am Sherry Looclus from Dilipabad, born and bred."

Alys would swear Hammy-Sammy's noses curled once they realized that Sherry was not the VIP they'd mistaken her for.

"Hi." It was the sweet-looking sandy-haired fellow.

"And this," Hammy said, turning as if the interruption was pre-planned, "is our baby brother, Bungles."

"Fahad Bingla," he said.

"Bungles," Hammy said firmly. "Because, when we were children, he kept bungling up every game we'd play, right, Sammy?"

"Right, Hammy," Sammy said.

"And," Hammy said, "he'd still keep bungling up if Sammy and I didn't keep him in check."

Bungles laughed and shook his head. He held his hand out to Jena. Jena shook it and Bungles held on for a second too long. Jena blushed. Bungles shook hands with Alys and Sherry, but Mari wouldn't shake his hand, because, she said, Islam forbade men and women touching.

"Are you *all* very Islamic?" Hammy said.

"Clearly not," Alys said, a little annoyed, though she wasn't sure whether it was at Mari's self-righteous piety or Hammy's supercilious tone. "Anyway, this is Pakistan. You've got very religious, religious, not so religious, and nonreligious, though no one will admit the last out loud, since atheism is a crime punishable by death."

"What a font of knowledge you are, babes!" Hammy said. "Isn't she, Sammy?"

"She is," Sammy said, as she turned to a stocky man lumbering toward her with a cup of chai. "All, this is my husband, Sultan 'Jaans' Riyasat. He's thinking about entering politics. Jaans, all."

Jaans gave a short wave before plopping into a nearby chair, his stiff *shalwar* puffing up around him. He patted the empty seat beside him. Sammy glided over, perching prettily, ignored the fact that Jaans was taking huge swigs from a pocket liquor flask. She proceeded to take elegant sips of her chai.

The out-of-town guests had come to Dilipabad to attend the *mehndi* ceremony tonight and the *nikah* ceremony the next day and were staying at the gymkhana.

"So basically, babes, we're bored," Hammy said. "We got into Dilipabad two days ago, because Nadir wanted to make sure everyone was here, but there's literally nothing to do. We went to that thing this town calls a zoo, with its goat, sheep, camel, and peacock. And we went to the alligator farm and stared at alligators, who stared back at us, and I told them you can't eat me but I'll see you in Birkin. And Nadir and Fiede arranged for a hot-air-balloon tour over what amounted to villages and fields."

"The hot-air balloon sounds like fun," Alys said. "A bit of Oz in Dilipabad. You know, *The Wizard of Oz*?"

"Babes, for real, it was all green and boring," Hammy said. "What do you locals do for fun in D-bad?"

"We have three restaurants," Jena said. "And a recently opened bakery-café, High Chai."

"Oh dear God!" Sammy said. "Fiede took us there yesterday."

"There was a hair in my cappuccino," Hammy said. "A long, disgusting hair."

"And the place smelled like wet dog," Sammy said.

"We've been multiple times and everything was quite lovely," Jena said. "Nothing but the scent of freshly baked banana bread. And the staff wore hairnets and gloves."

"Oh my goodness, Jena!" Hammy took Jena's hand and stroked it as if she was speaking to a child. "The hair was bad enough, but the Muzak was some crackly throwback tape that played 'Conga' and 'Girls Just Want to Have Fun' on repeat. Get with it, D-bad. It's the year 2000."

Alys was suddenly offended on behalf of "D-bad."

"I'm sure the hair was an aberration," she said. "And you should have asked them to change the songs."

"Oh," Hammy said. "We abhor being a bother!"

"Yes," Sammy said. "We're guests. Passers-through. If you locals are happy with the state of things, why should we try to change anything? We can live without fun for a few days. Right, Hammy?"

"Right, Sammy," Hammy said. "Boredom is a bore, not a killer."

"And what," Alys asked, "according to you constitutes fun?"

Before Hammy-Sammy could answer, Lady, Qitty, and the fine-eyed guy on the dance floor descended upon the group at the same time. Alys glanced at him. His eyes were intensely black, with thick lashes their mother always claimed were wasted on men, as was his jet-black hair, which fell neatly in a thick wave just below his ears. He was taller than Bungles and had broader shoulders. He frowned and glanced at his expensive watch, and Alys noted that he had sturdy forearms and nice strong hands. Lovely hands.

"Hello," Lady said. She was carrying a bowl full of golden fried *gulab jamuns*. "Have you tried these? To die for. Isn't this the best wedding ever? I have a good mind to tell Fiede to get married every year."

"Is that so?" Hammy said. "I'm sure Fiede will be thrilled at your suggestion. And who are you?"

"Aren't you," Sammy said, "the girl who crashed the dance floor?"

Lady nodded, unabashed, even though her sisters cringed.

"I'm Lady, their sister." Lady pointed to Jena, Alys, and Mari. "And this is our other sister, Qitty."

"I can speak for myself," Qitty said. "Hello."

"But a moment ago," Lady said, "you told me you'd eaten so much you could no longer speak."

"Because I didn't want to speak to you," Qitty said.

"Qitty!" Alys said. "Lady!"

"Ladies' Room," Jaans called from his chair. "Everyone wants to go to the Ladies' Room. Is it open?"

"Oh, you!" Sammy smacked her husband on his hand. "Such a joker."

The guy with the intense eyes and lovely hands, Alys noted, was watching as if he'd decided the entire world was a bad comedy and it was his punishment to witness every awful joke.

"Bungles," he said, "if you're done entertaining yourself, can we—"

Bungles interrupted him. "This is one of my best friends, Valentine Darsee."

"Valentine," Hammy said, "say a big hearty hello to the sisters Binat and their friend Cherry."

"Sherry," Sherry said, flushing.

"Sherry," Hammy said. "My sincere apologies."

Darsee seemed to be taking his time giving them a big hearty hello, Alys thought, but before he could get to it, Lady began to laugh uncontrollably.

"Valentine!" Lady doubled over. "Were you born on Valentine's Day?"

Spittle sprayed out of Lady's mouth, and Darsee and Hammy jumped out of the way, revulsion on their faces.

"Lady!" Jena said, mortified.

"Oops!" Lady wiped her mouth with the back of her hand. "Sorry. Sorry."

"I'm sure you are," Hammy said. "But I'm not sure I'm getting the joke. Valentine is such a romantic name."

Everyone waited for Darsee to say something, but after several moments Bungles spoke up.

"Valentine's late mother," Bungles said, "was a big fan of Rudolph Valentino, and she named him Valentino. The staff at the hospital mistook it for Valentine and, by the time anyone checked, the birth certificate was complete and so that was that, right, Val?"

Valentine Darsee gave a curt nod. It was unclear to Alys whether he couldn't care less if they knew the origin story of his name or whether Lady's spittle had caused him severe trauma.

"Same thing happened with Oprah," she offered in a conciliatory tone.

"Pardon me?" Darsee said, as if he was seeing her for the first time and not liking what he saw.

"Oprah. She was named Orpah, after a character in the Bible, but her name was mistakenly recorded as Oprah." Alys added, "I read it in *Reader's Digest*, I think, or *Good Housekeeping*."

Darsee turned to Bungles. "I'm going to check in with Nadir for the night and then head back to our room."

He left without a smile, without a "pleased to meet you," without even a cursory nod. Hammy at least nodded at the group before running after him. Lady decided to get more *gulab jamuns* and dragged Qitty with her. Sammy and Jaans turned to each other. Bungles explained, sheepishly, that Darsee had recently arrived from Atlanta, where he'd been studying for an MBA, and was still jet-lagged. Alys and Sherry exchanged a look: Valentine Darsee was the British School Group.

"Jena," Bungles said. "Can I get you some chai? Dessert? Anything?"

"Jena," Sherry said, "why don't you and Bungles Bhai go get chai together?"

Bungles thought this a fabulous idea, and Jena, with no reason to refuse, walked with him to the tea table, where teas, pink, green, and black, were being served.

"That was obvious," Alys said. "A great 'grab it' move. My mother will be so proud of you."

"You and Jena need to listen to your mother once in a while," Sherry said. "Clearly Bungles Bhai is interested in Jena, and she needs to show a strong interest in return."

"She just met him," Alys said. "Two minutes ago."

"So?" Sherry said. "If she doesn't show interest, a million other girls will."

"If he's going to lose interest because she's modest, then perhaps he's not worth it."

"Of course he's worth it. And aren't you the sly one to use the word 'modest.'"

"Huh?"

"'Modest sanitary napkins for your inner beauty, *aap ke mushkil dinon ka saathi,* the companion of your hard days,'" Sherry said, spouting the jingle that played during the animated advertisement for Modest sanitary products. "Bungles, Hammy, and Sammy are Modest. They own the company. I recognize them from interviews. And soon our Jena will be Mrs. Modest."

"You'll be naming their children next." Alys shook her head. "They barely know each other."

"Plenty of time for them to get to know each other once they're married."

"I think," Alys said, "better to get to know each other before deciding to get married."

"Big waste of time," Sherry said. "Trust me, everyone is on their best behavior until the actual marriage, and then claws emerge. From what I've gleaned, real happiness in marriage seems a matter of chance. You can marry a seemingly perfect person and they can transform before your eyes into imperfection, or you can marry a flawed person and they can become someone you actually like, and therefore flawless. The key point being that, for better or for worse, no one remains the same. One marries for security, children, and, if one is lucky, companionship. Although," Sherry laughed, "in Valentine Darsee's case, good luck on the last."

"I can't believe Lady!" Alys said. "No one deserves a spittle spray. Actually, I take that back. Hammy probably does deserve it."

Ten minutes later, Alys believed Darsee deserved it too. She'd gone to congratulate Fiede and was about to climb down off the stage when she heard Bungles's and Darsee's voices. Their backs were turned to her and, despite knowing it was a bad idea to eavesdrop, Alys bent down to fiddle with her shoe.

"*Reader's Digest?*" Darsee was saying. "*Good Housekeeping?* She is neither smart nor good-looking enough for me, my friend."

"I read *Reader's Digest,*" Bungles said, laughing.

"Yes," Darsee said, "sadly, I know."

"You have impossible standards in everything," Bungles said. "Alysba Binat is perfectly attractive. But you've got to admit, Val, her elder sister is gorgeous."

"She is good-looking. But, please, stop foisting stupid, average-looking women on me."

In the car on their way back home, Alys announced what she'd over-heard. She laughed as she recounted Valentine Darsee calling her "stupid," "average-looking," and "neither smart nor good-looking enough." However, Alys was not one to lie to herself: His words had stung. Valentine Darsee was handsome and he was wealthy, but ob-viously his upbringing had lacked classes on basic manners and eti-quette: He was rude, he was disdainful, and he thought altogether too much of himself.

Mrs. Binat agreed. She was most indignant. Never before had a single person doubted the beauty of her girls.

"I hate Valentine Darsee," Mrs. Binat declared, and proceeded to inform everyone of the Darsee family's less-than-stellar background. Valentine's mother was a dey Bagh, this was true, the crème de la crème. But his father's family was another story. Although the Darsee clan had accumulated an immense fortune via the army, they did not come from noble stock. They were neither royalty, nor nawabs, nor even feudal landowners like the Binats. The Darsees descended, Mrs. Binat announced, from *darzees*—tailors—and at some point their tradesman surname of Darzee had morphed into Darsee, or else, she suggested, squinting, an ancestor must have deliberately changed Darzee into Darsee on official certificates.

"I wish you wouldn't bring up everyone's lineage all the time," Alys said. "Who cares?"

"Good society cares," Mrs. Binat said. She turned from the passenger seat, where she sat in Qitty's lap, in order to glare at Alys. "Let this be a lesson to you to never attend another function not looking your absolute best. And don't you dare sit in the sun any longer."

"I like my complexion dark," Alys said decisively.

Mrs. Binat sighed. "Gone case."

"Oh God," Qitty groaned. "If Valentine Darsee thinks Alys is not pretty and a frump, he must think I'm ugly and a lump."

"I can assure you," Lady said, "Valentine Darsee was not looking at you. No one was."

"No one looked at you either," Qitty said, "except when you laughed like a hyena or embarrassed yourself by spitting or gallivanting onto the floor like a dancer-for-hire."

"Shut up, *behensa*—buffalo," Lady said.

"You shut up, '*Choli Ke Peeche*,'" Qitty said.

"Both of you, shut up," Mrs. Binat said. "For God's sake, is this why I went through pregnancies and labor pains and nursed you both and gave myself stretch marks and saggy breasts? So that you could grow up and be bad sisters? How many times must I tell you: Be nice to each other, love each other, for at the end of the day, siblings are all you have. Qitty, you are older than Lady. Can't you just learn to ignore her?"

"I'm barely two years older than her," Qitty sputtered. "We may as well be the same age."

"Stop laughing, Lady," Alys said. "Between spitting and dancing uninvited, what you did was unacceptable."

"But '*Choli*' is such a good song," Lady said.

"All it takes is a good song for you to lose self-control?" Alys asked.

"What about Fiede Fecker?" Lady demanded. "She crashed her own dance floor."

"She's Fiede Fecker," Sherry said. "She can do whatever she wants to do."

"I want to be Fiede Fecker too," Lady said, angry tears appearing in her eyes.

"Fiede Fecker's mother-in-law looked most unhappy," Sherry said.

"I was unhappy," Mari said, "at the dancing and singing, especially in an unsegregated gathering."

"Oh God!" Lady said. "The high priestess has begun!"

"Mari, if Allah forbade mixed company," Mr. Binat said, without taking his eyes off the road, "then holy pilgrimages would be segregated."

Mari decided to use her inhaler because she didn't know what to say.

"Live and let live, Mari," Alys said encouragingly.

"You're such a hypocrite, Alys," Lady said. "You don't let me 'live and let live.'"

"You humiliated us, Lady," Jena said quietly. "You humiliated me. What must Bungles and his sisters be saying about us."

"Jena, don't be angry with me," Lady said. "I apologized, didn't I? Which is more than that fat man, Jaans, did after calling me 'Ladies' Room.'"

"Jaans is hell-bound for sure," Mari muttered.

"So is that arrogant Darsee," Mrs. Binat said, "*darzee ka bacha,* son of a tailor."

"The truth is," Sherry said, balancing on Alys's knees in the cramped car as Mr. Binat swerved to avoid a donkey in the road, "whether Darsee descends from *darzees* or *dhobis* is immaterial because, at present, he is A list, and who can blame him for being proud and thinking no one is good enough for him?"

"I'd allow him a smidgeon of an ego," Alys said, "if he hadn't destroyed mine."

"He was having a private conversation, Alys," Jena said. "Not that any of what he said is true, but you weren't meant to hear it, and I'm sure he'd be upset to know that you had and were hurt by it."

"Jena," Alys said, "can you please stop supposing people are nicer than they are?"

"Our Jena is such a sweet soul," Mrs. Binat said.

"Doesn't Darsee know pride comes before a fall?" Alys asked. "Who the hell does he think he is!"

"Your boss's boss," Sherry said solemnly, "as it turns out."

"I'll resign," Alys said.

"You'll do no such thing," Mrs. Binat said sharply. "Barkat, tell your brainless daughter that she'd better not do anything impulsive. If anything, she should be asking for a raise."

Mr. Binat caught Alys's gaze in the rearview mirror.

"Alysba, my princess," he said, "why are you letting some spoiled rich boy cause you a single second's upset? You are not stupid. You are not unattractive. You are so smart. You are so beautiful. Let him look down on *Reader's Digest* and *Good Housekeeping.* You should be proud that you are an equal-opportunity reader and will read whatever you can get your hands on—highbrow, middlebrow, lowbrow."

"Prophet Muhammad, peace be upon him," Mari said, "is said to have said, 'He who has in his heart the weight of an atom of pride shall not enter paradise.' In my humble opinion, pride is a fairly common sin, because everyone thinks very highly of themselves.

And vanity is no different. We are vain because we want others to regard us as highly as we regard ourselves. He's hurt your pride, Alys, because you are vain. In that respect, you and Darsee are the same."

"Be quiet, Mari," Mrs. Binat said. "How can you compare your sister to that egotistical descendant of tailors, no matter how elite his schooling. But, his friend, Fahad Bingla—*ahahahaha*, perfection. All the girls were looking at him, and he was looking at you, Jena."

Jena blushed.

"Bungles seems very sweet," Alys said. "But his sisters are not as nice as they pretend to be."

"I disagree," Jena said. "I thought Hammy and Sammy were very nice."

"They were very nice to *you*," Alys said, "and when someone is nice to you, of course you are bound to think they are nice."

"Bungles's parents," Mrs. Binat said, having gotten the full story from gossiping matrons, "live in California. His mother is an anesthesiologist and very active in the Pakistani community, and his father made a fortune in start-ups. Fahad Bingla's elder brother, Mushtaq, works with their father and is married to a lawyer named Bonita-Hermosa."

Years ago, the Bingla family had made a trip to Lahore to get in touch with their roots, and the parents had decided to leave behind the eight-year-old Hammy-Sammy and seven-year-old Bungles, under their grandparents' tutelage. The siblings had returned to America for college, but after graduating they'd returned to Lahore, because that was home for them.

Hammy and Sammy had long noticed a need for affordable feminine hygiene products in Pakistan and, with Bungles on board, the three siblings "borrowed" money from their parents and set up Modest. The company soon outperformed their modest expectations, thanks to God's blessings, their hard work, and the demand for good-quality, reasonably priced sanitary napkins and adult diapers. Also, Mrs. Binat had been told, they regularly threw good parties and get-togethers and thus became popular on the social scene.

However, not hailing from a pedigreed background could have its drawbacks, no matter having attended the best of schools, and so Sammy had married Sultan "Jaans" Riyasat, a shabby-chic nawab—meaning he came with a coveted surname but zero money. The union turned Sammy and her future children into Riyasats and, thanks to her, Jaans came into money once again. Hammy was on the lookout for an equally illustrious catch.

"As for Fahad Bingla, he has chosen Jena." Mrs. Binat beamed. "And mark my words, by tomorrow, *inshallah*, she will be engaged to him. We'll throw a fancy func—"

"Pinkie," Mr. Binat said. "Can you please wait until this Bungles fellow proposes before planning functions."

"You proposed to me at first sight," Mrs. Binat said with quiet pride. She had lucked out on looks alone, and it was the defining moment of her life.

"That was a different era," Mr. Binat said. But he smiled blissfully, for he was forever tickled at having pulled off a love-at-first-sight marriage in a time where arranged marriage was the norm.

"You watch," Mrs. Binat said, with a knowing nod. "Fahad 'Bungles' Bingla will propose to Jena tomorrow during the *nikah* ceremony. I am certain of it—otherwise, I promise you, I will eat my shoe."

Chapter 6

The next day dawned sunny but cold. Mr. Binat decided that he needed to recover from the previous night's stimulations and was not going to attend the *nikah*. Mrs. Binat did not argue, for if she allowed him to miss this, then he would have to agree to attend the final ceremony, the *walima,* in Lahore. Mr. Binat, oblivious to his wife's calculations, happily went into the garden to inspect his spider plants, his fingers tenderly smoothing the variegated, long leaves as he wiped them free of debris.

The Binat girls spent the morning beautifying themselves in the courtyard. Mrs. Binat was very strict when it came to beauty regimens and only allowed homemade products. She'd risen early and whipped up face masks of rosewater and ground chickpeas for Jena, Alys, and Lady, who had oily skin, and for Mari and Qitty, who had dry skin, she added a drop of almond oil into the mixture.

Mrs. Binat sat her daughters before her and vigorously massaged their hair with organic cold-pressed mustard oil, on which she'd spent a pretty penny. Jena wordlessly took the special hand mask made for her from oatmeal and lemon juice, which would soften her hands since, her mother insisted, they were going to be the focal point tonight on account of the soon-to-be-acquired engagement ring. The waxing woman arrived and duly waxed each girl, gossiping the whole time, whether they cared for it or not. Tailor Shawkat arrived in case their outfits required last-minute alterations.

Mrs. Binat's choices for the girls' attire this evening were long flowy chiffon *anarkalis* with *mukesh-* and *zari*-embroidered bodice and hem, matching *dupattas* paired with matching silk *thang pajamas* and jewelry courtesy of Ganju *jee,* and topped with expensive shawls. Mrs. Binat wanted Jena to once again stand out as the epitome of purity and had picked for her white chiffon—paired, however, with a real diamond set. Hillima was handed the five outfits to iron and, because she wanted the girls to dazzle, she diligently pressed out each wrinkle.

After she was done, Hillima laid out each girl's outfit on her bed. Jena was finishing up her prayers, and after folding the prayer rug, she thanked Hillima. She was terrified, she said. She should be, Hillima replied; grabbing a man was much harder than it sounded, but all their combined prayers should deliver positive results, and, reciting a quick prayer, she blew it over Jena.

Closer to midafternoon, as the girls began to bathe, Mr. Binat scrubbed the soil off his hands and prepared to drive his daughters to Susan's Beauty Parlor for their hair appointments. Although Mrs. Binat had been willing to spend money on a driver's salary, she'd ultimately decided against the hire, because having Mr. Binat drive the girls around was one of the few ways she could compel him to leave the house. Alys was the only one not going to Susan's for a blow-dry. Anyway, Alys seldom went to Susan's for anything. In fact, Mrs. Binat was quite sure that her silly daughter would discard the teal chiffon she'd picked for her and instead choose something dowdy. Clothes were women's weapons, Mrs. Binat often told Alys, but God forbid that girl heeded her words. And so Mrs. Binat was enormously surprised and delighted when she saw Alys take an interest in her appearance for the first time in a long time and hand Hillima the teal chiffon to iron.

Alys found herself slipping into her mother's chosen outfit, jewelry, and black *pashmina* shawl, one of ten in various colors Mrs. Binat always thanked God she'd had the foresight to purchase when she'd had money to spend on pure *pashminas* and *shahtooshes*.

Alys sat before her dressing table and applied liquid cat-eye liner on her upper lids, a nice flick of mascara, and painted her lips with a red pencil that deepened her tan. Unlike her sisters, who were getting their long hair blow-dried into the desirable waves or straightened, Alys rubbed lavender-scented gel though her hair and finger-dried her tight curls. Lady, returning from the parlor in big hair, took one look at Alys and whistled, a compliment she usually reserved for Jena, who was looking ethereal in her white chiffon ensemble and diamonds.

Come evening, Alys drove them through a thick fog to the gymkhana. Since Mr. Binat and Sherry were not going—the potbellied suitor was scheduled for a look-see that evening—there was plenty of space in the car, which automatically quelled a few spats between Lady and Qitty. Also, the sisters had tacitly agreed to get along tonight on account of it being the night one of them was finally going to get engaged.

At the gymkhana, a red carpet led the Binats to the main entrance, where Mr. and Mrs. Fecker welcomed guests into the great hall. The hall was festooned with curtains of golden gauze and marigolds galore, and illuminated by bright yellow lighting. Round tables were topped with pleated cream cloths and crystal and yellow rose centerpieces. A perk of the Binats' punctuality was being able to choose a good table, and Mrs. Binat headed for one close to the wedding stage, where the nuptials would take place. Once her daughters were seated, she caressed Jena's cheek and declared that it wouldn't be long now and she was sure it would be a big and sparkling solitaire.

Waiters in white uniforms with gold buttons were serving fresh seasonal juices, and soon the Binats were sipping foamy pomegranate juice. Slowly, the hall began to fill up. Men arrived in suits and ties and women in multitudinous loud hues, their ears, necks, wrists, and fingers drowning in gold, diamonds, rubies, sapphires, and emeralds. As Mrs. Binat suspected, her daughters once again stood out, this time like graceful nymphs among the gaudy and the gauche.

"There should be a mandatory note," Mrs. Binat mumbled to her daughters, "on wedding invitations, saying: 'Please do not try to out-bride the bride.'"

"Mummy," Lady said, starting in on her third glass of juice, "you are always so right. We will put that note on Jena's wedding invite and also on mine."

A ripple went through the guests at the news that the governor, or at least one of his family members, was to make a special guest appearance, as was a general who might or might not be harboring dreams of coups and presidential palaces. But Mrs. Binat had eyes only for Bungles's arrival.

The groom and his retinue arrived respectably late, amid the customary fanfare of beating drums and rose-petal shower. Nadir Sheh, in a custom-made *sherwani* with a tall crimson turban, graced the stage and sat on a velvet sofa. Fiede Fecker, soon to be Fiede Sheh, had all this while been secreted away in a bridal waiting room with her excited friends, impatiently anticipating Nadir's arrival. When Fiede made her grand entrance, everyone fell silent.

"Someone must have had a few words with Fiede Fecker," Lady whispered to Qitty, because Fiede was walking with her head bowed like an obedient bride, or else the bulky crimson *dupatta* she had pinned to her bouffant was weighing her down.

Flanked by her parents, Fiede took her time walking down the red carpet all the way to the stage, because one only walked this walk once. The usual murmurs from the guests accompanied her: "beautiful bride," "stunning outfit." Though the truth was, Mrs. Binat muttered to Jena, Fiede's crimson-and-gold *gharara* was too ornate for her small frame. She looked like a child hiding in a pile of brocade curtains.

Fiede's mother picked up her daughter's voluminous skirt and helped her up the stage steps and seated her next to Nadir Sheh. It was announced that Fiede had not asked for the right of divorce on her marriage certificate, since to ask for this right was to begin one's marriage inauspiciously. It was also announced that Fiede had agreed to an amount of *haq mehr* equivalent to the sum given during the Holy Prophet's time by grooms to their brides and that she had agreed to this now-paltry figure because she was a pious woman and not at all money minded.

"Easy to accept pennies and not be money minded when you have money," Mrs. Binat snorted, "especially when you are the sole heir to your parents' fortune."

As soon as the bride and groom were seated and professional photographers began taking group shots, members of Nadir Sheh's entourage were free to do as they pleased, and Bungles's eyes sought out Jena.

"Here he comes," Mrs. Binat said, squeezing Jena's arm as she nodded at Bungles striding toward them with his sisters at his heels. "Here he comes with the ring."

Such was their level of expectation that all the Binats were shaken when Bungles did not drop to one knee and ask Jena to be his wife. Jena was so disoriented that it took Bungles saying hello thrice before she was able to respond.

Hammy and Sammy, looming behind their brother, took Jena's delayed response as an obvious lack of interest and hoped this would jolt Bungles out of his crush. Last night the sisters had made inquiries into Jena's family. Jena's own reputation was blemish-free, but unfortunately, thanks to her parents, she still came stained. Jena was a Binat from her father's side, but they were the penniless Binats of the clan; her father was ineffectual at business and estranged from his successful elder brother, which implied that Jena's family did not value family ties. As for Jena's mother's lineage: beyond disastrous.

"How was your day?" Alys asked Bungles and Hammy-Sammy in order to give Jena a moment to recover.

"Excellent," Bungles said. "Darsee and I played a game of squash, enjoyed a very nice Continental breakfast by the gymkhana lake, and I took a nap."

"Sammy and I," Hammy said, "were recommended some horrid beauty parlor, where the girl flat-ironing my hair didn't know what she was doing and nearly burned off my face."

"Where did you go?" Qitty looked up from the paper napkin she'd been doodling on.

"Best Salon."

Mrs. Binat made a face. "Whoever recommended Best Salon must be getting a commission."

"We had a good mind not to pay," Sammy said, "but that girl probably never received any training, so not her fault. But, still, you have to send a monetary message, and so we didn't leave a tip."

After a second of silence, Lady said, "Next time go to Susan's. She's the best."

Susan's was Dilipabad's premier beauty parlor, run by a family whose patriarch had fled to Pakistan during the Chinese Cultural Revolution and never returned.

"Thank God there'll be no next time," Hammy said. "We're out of D-bad first thing tomorrow morning. Bungles can't wait!"

"That's not true." Bungles gazed at Jena.

"That's what you said," Hammy said. She happily observed that Jena was playing with the beads on her handbag and seemed not at all bothered by who was going and who was coming.

"All I said was it will be nice to be home again," Bungles said.

"Tomorrow morning?" Mrs. Binat said very loudly, as if the decibels of her voice alone might compel Bungles to propose. She quieted at the announcement that it was *nikah* time.

Everyone in the hall hushed as the maulvi read out loud the relevant verses from the Quran. He turned to Nadir Sheh: "Do you accept Farhana Farzana Fecker for your wife?" Nadir said *qabool hai*—"I accept"—thrice and signed the marriage certificate. The maulvi turned to Fiede Fecker: "Do you accept Nadir Nauman Nazir Nizam Sheh for your husband?" Fiede Fecker said *qabool hai* thrice and signed the marriage certificate.

The Feckers and Shehs embraced to cheers of congratulations, and Nadir's mother and Fiede's mother hugged with tears in their eyes. Turning to the newlyweds, they immediately demanded a grandchild. Nadir said that could be arranged. Fiede blushed on cue. Everyone laughed. How cute!

"A few naughty uncles," Lady whispered to Qitty and Mari, "must surely be imagining Fiede in her wedding lingerie."

Qitty began to sketch a naughty uncle on a napkin.

"Disgusting!" Mari hissed at Lady and Qitty. "You both need to get your heads examined before you really head to hell."

Bungles returned from participating in the rituals of *doodh pilai*—in which Fiede took a ladylike sip from the glass of milk meant to give the couple fertility and strength on their wedding night and Nadir guzzled down the rest—and *jhootha chupai*—in which Nadir had ended up distributing a lot of money to Fiede's friends and cousins in order to get them to return his shoe, which they'd hidden—and dragged a chair as close as he could to Jena's. Hammy and Sammy also rushed to sit close to Bungles. And here came Jaans, who was regaling Darsee with tales of recent financial scandals that had befallen otherwise-upright Pakistanis.

"Valentine," Hammy said, jumping up, "take my seat."

Alys watched in amusement as Darsee took her seat. He did not say hello to anyone.

"You look dashing," Hammy said to Darsee, and he did, in a raw-silk ivory *shalwar kurta* with a teal mirrored waistcoat. "I swear, you should think about modeling just for fun. I can already see you on a Times Square billboard."

Alys longed to say that instead of modeling, it might be better if Darsee enrolled in an etiquette class or two.

Lady whispered to Qitty, "Hammy is making you-you eyes at Darsee."

"Gigantic you-you eyes," Qitty whispered back. "Her *dailay*— eyeballs—are going to pop out."

"Hammy is right, Valentine," Sammy said. "Times Square. Modeling a watch. Or underwear."

"*Oye, Begum,* Wife, stop talking about other men's underwear!" Jaans said. "I'd look dashing too if it wasn't for you."

Apparently Jaans was wearing ill-fitting attire because Sammy had packed his pre-weight-loss suit by mistake and, even worse, handed away his brand-new custom-made suit to their driver. Sammy had asked the driver to return it, except he'd already sent it to his village, to a cousin who was leaving for a job in Hong Kong.

"That will be one happy bastard strutting around in my suit," Jaans said. "Who can train my wife in housewife skills?"

"Not a housewife," Sammy said testily. "I run a company."

"Jaans, dude," Bungles said, "company or no company, pack your own clothes."

"Bungles *beta,*" Mrs. Binat said, "isn't Jena looking lovely tonight?"

"Yes." Bungles turned red. "She is."

"Mummy! Stop it!" Jena said.

"What stop it? If a mother cannot point out the obvious, then who can? Bungles, you must stay in Dilipabad for another few days. And if you need anything . . . but why should you need anything? God has blessed you with everything, except . . ." And she glanced at Jena.

If Jena wished to turn invisible, Alys did too.

Darsee's mouth fell open. Never in his life had he heard such a blatant hint. Neither had Hammy and Sammy. Darsee could tell the sisters were stunned. His eyes traveled across the table and connected with Alys's, who just happened to be looking in his direction at that very moment.

Now that Darsee had, for the first time, looked directly in Alys Binat's face, it occurred to him before he could stop it that she had luminous eyes. It occurred to him that even though she was the opposite of everything that was considered beautiful in these parts—an alabaster complexion, long hair, light eyes, a simpering femininity—she was uncommonly attractive. Alys held his gaze for a moment and then, blinking in obvious disinterest, turned away to talk to some girl.

Darsee was well aware of all the ruses gold diggers practiced these days. The most popular, Jujeena, his only sister, had informed him, was a pretense of disinterest. Although it seemed to Darsee that Alys Binat truly did not care. He found himself stepping a little closer to Bungles and, as it so happened, in eavesdropping range of Alys's conversation.

Alys was talking to an ex-student, Sarah, one of her pride and joys, who'd badly wanted to go to college abroad. Her parents had set the condition that she could go only if she got a full scholarship, and Alys had helped Sarah get one. Sarah was in her final year and diligently studying economics plus literature. At the moment she and Alys were discussing potential thesis topics.

"You can," Alys suggested, "ask if friendships in Austen are more complex between friends or sisters. Or explore who jumps class in Austen and whose class cannot be forgiven, overlooked, or worked around. Or compare colonizer Babington Macaulay and Kipling's 'England's Jane' with a 'World's Jane,' a 'Pakistani Jane,' a 'Post-Colonial Jane,' Edward Said's Jane. What might Jane make of all these Janes? Discuss empire writing back, weaving its own stories."

Alys could ignore it no more. She turned to Darsee. "You're clearly enjoying our conversation. Care to join in?"

"No," Darsee said, "but I would like to know, how do you know all this?"

"*Reader's Digest,*" Alys said, "and *Good Housekeeping.*"

Darsee stared at her. Principal Naheed had arrived to say hello in the last seconds and she said, "Alys, don't be silly! Valentine, have you met Alys and Jena yet? Jena teaches English to the middle grades at BSD and Alys the upper grades."

Gin and Rum, dressed again in QaziSensations and looking like disco balls, had been told by their mother to sound their most intelligent in front of Valentine Darsee, and so they proceeded to show off their knowledge of international books with titles they'd memorized.

"Miss Alys, do you remember," Gin said, "when you made us join that summer book club? I still recall Leslie Marmon Silko's story 'Lullaby' and Bi Shumin's 'Broken Transformers.'"

"You made us read,"—Rum squinted—"*The House on Mango Street* by Sandra Cisneros, 'Désirée's Baby' by Kate Chopin, and 'Everyday Use' by Alice Walker. And then you made us read that novel *The Blackest Eye.*"

"*The Bluest Eye,*" Gin said.

"Yes." Rum beamed. "*The Bluest Eye.* We were all so disturbed by the incest in it."

Naheed changed colors.

"What my brilliant daughters mean," she stuttered, "is that Alys is such a forward-thinking teacher who never shies away from any subject."

"I see," Darsee said.

Alys had no desire to know what Darsee saw. Taking the gift envelope from her mother, she strode to the stage. Horrid man! Listening to her with that mocking look. And thoughtless Gin and Rum for mentioning that particular novel, over which Naheed had very nearly been forced to fire her because so many parents had turned up at the school. Thankfully the author, Toni Morrison, had won a Nobel Prize in Literature, and that had calmed them down.

Darsee watched Alys leave, and he allowed Principal Naheed to distract him with her view on school uniforms. By the time dinner was served—a buffet to rival the fare at the *mehndi* ceremony the night before—Alys was barely on his mind. As he ladled a fragrant mutton *biryani* onto a plate, Hammy joined him.

"Babes, you must try the *rogan gosht*," she said, "before Lady and Qitty gobble it all up. I've never seen greedier creatures. Jaans thinks Alys is a lesbian. Agree?"

"*Why* would Jaans think that?"

"Her hair, babes, her hair."

"That's ridiculous," Darsee said. "I happen to think her cut accentuates her eyes."

Hammy's rather ordinary eyes grew wide. Darsee instantly realized his mistake and, nonchalantly popping a mutton *boti* into his mouth, waited for Hammy's response.

"My heartfelt congratulations," Hammy said, "on finding your soulmate in D-bad."

"So, so predictable," Darsee said, shaking his head.

Hammy gave a feeble laugh. "I'm beginning to wonder if the Binat girls really do practice magic. First my brother is bewitched. Now you."

"I'm not bewitched or any such thing."

"Your future mother-in-law," Hammy said, "the oh-so-charming Pinkie Binat, will be so thrilled to have not one but two sons-in-law to paw."

Darsee grimaced. "Not prime mother-in-law material."

"Nor are those creatures sister-in-law material!"

"Agreed," Darsee said.

Hammy was relieved not only that Darsee had not complimented Alys further but that he'd acknowledged the appalling nature of the Binat family.

"I wish Bungles would wake up from Jena's spell or whatever you want to call it."

"It'll pass," Darsee said. "His crushes, unlike mine, always do, which is why I've learned to not fall as easily as he does."

"And who is your current crush?" Hammy asked, a little too quickly.

"No one," Darsee said. "I'm too busy with Jujeena. I should not have gone to do my MBA. I neglected her."

"Don't be so hard on yourself," Hammy said. "I bumped into your sister a few times this last year and she seemed happy living with your aunty Beena.'"

"Beena Aunty took excellent care of her, but"—Darsee stopped— "she has her hands full with Annie."

"How is Annie's health?"

"So-so," Darsee said. "Anyway, I'm back now, and my top priority is my sister, as well as getting involved with the British Schools. No time for crushes."

"Please knock the same sense into Bungles, at least when it comes to Jena Binat."

"I'll try," Darsee said.

However, when it came time to leave the *nikah* ceremony, Bungles asked Jena if her family was planning to attend the *walima* ceremony in Lahore. When Jena nodded, Bungles instantly turned to Mrs. Binat: He, Hammy, and Sammy were going to a charity polo match for breast cancer at the Race Course Park, and could Jena accompany them as their guest?

Chapter 7

The next morning Sherry visited the Binats and, over chickpea *chaat* and chai, Lady and Qitty excitedly informed her of Jena's invitation to the polo match. They'd been discussing, nonstop, Bungles's failure to propose to Jena, juxtaposed with the fact that he must really like her to have invited her to the polo match, to which Mrs. Binat had so readily and graciously given her permission.

"Of course he likes Jena," Mrs. Binat said, fishing out a spicy potato from the *chaat*. "Likes, my foot. He loves her. He's just a shy boy, but, then, not everyone can be bold and daring the way your father was when he asked for my hand in a heartbeat."

Mr. Binat entered with one of his wife's shoes in hand.

"But, Pinkie," he said gaily, continuing a previous conversation, "you guaranteed this Bungles fellow would propose last night and that if he didn't you would eat your shoe. Come on now, eat up."

"*Oof.*" Mrs. Binat pushed away the shoe her husband was thrusting at her. "Barkat, you really must get out more. Your attempts at humor are becoming third-class. Put down that filthy shoe. He's taking her to the polo match in Lahore, where, I guarantee you, he will propose."

"Mummy," Jena said, "you led me to believe he was going propose yesterday, and I was so nervous I could barely look at him or speak to him properly. I'm going to go to the polo match with no expectations."

"You'll see," Mrs. Binat said. "You'll return from the polo match with a diamond ring so big your finger will fall off."

"*Tauba*," Mr. Binat said, helping himself to the *chaat*. "Dear God, what a thing to say."

"Look, Jena," Sherry said, pouring extra tamarind chutney into her bowl, "you need to steer Bungles Bhai."

"Steer him?" Jena said. "Is he a bull?"

"Jena, you need to do no such thing." Alys scowled.

"She does." Sherry looked from Jena to Alys. "Jena, trust me. You need to drop little hints such as 'I'm getting so many proposals' or 'I'm scheduled for a look-see and if it works out I'll be getting married.' You know, hints to hurry him along."

"Vomit, puke, *ulti*," Alys said.

"Alys is a fool," Mrs. Binat said. "Sherry, you are a girl after my own heart and know well the game of grab-it."

"Thank you, Khala," Sherry said. "Although if I knew how to grab it that well, wouldn't I have grabbed a husband by now?"

Everyone observed a moment of contemplation.

"Jena," Sherry said, sipping the last of her chai, "follow my advice and if Bungles Bhai has got any smarts, he'll realize that you are hint-dropping, and then he'll be in no doubt that you like him."

"How about *I* just propose to *him*?" Jena said, annoyed. "That should clear up any confusion."

"In Islam," Mari said, looking up from the tennis match on the sports channel, "women can propose, since Hazrat Khadijah proposed to the Prophet Muhammad, peace be upon him."

"*Hai!*" Mrs. Binat slapped her chest lightly. "No one follows religious example properly in this country. If only girls from good families could propose, how easy everything would become. Instead, we have to wait until the man decides it is time."

"May I remind everyone," Alys said, squashing a chickpea with her fork, "that Jena and Bungles literally met a day ago. They don't even know if they like each other, much less love."

"Love at first sight, followed by rest of life to sit around falling in like. That is the farmoola," Mrs. Binat said.

"Formula," Mr. Binat said. "Form-you-la."

"Far-moo-la. That's what I said." Mrs. Binat extracted a hairpin from her bun and used the looped end as a cotton swab. She ignored her daughters' aghast looks. "How long does it take to fall in love? Your father looked at me, instant love"—she snapped her fingers—"and immediately he sent Tinkle to find out who I was and, the very next day, proposal."

Mrs. Binat regaled them with a detailed account of their honeymoon in Chittagong Hills and Cox's Bazar beach in current-day Bangladesh. It had been her dream to go there, and their father had made it come true.

"He was such a hero," she preened. "Every day, flowers, frolic, and I love you, I love you."

"Daddy was a lover boy," Lady said, her eyes shining. "A romantic hero."

"I was indeed," Mr. Binat said bashfully, for he quite loved to hear what a hero he'd been.

"Times have changed," Alys said. "No one gets married like that anymore. Love doesn't work like that anymore, if it ever did."

"Love is love and will never change its nature," Mrs. Binat said. "One look is all love needs. One look."

"I can't wait to fall madly in love," Lady said. "*Acha*, Jena, do you love Bungles?"

Jena tossed a cushion at Lady. "Mind your own business. And forget love-shove—why aren't you studying your algebra? Your teacher at school told me you're very good with equations if only you'd apply yourself."

"Who cares about equations?" Lady said. "I don't need equations to be happy. I need love to be happy. I'm not going to marry anyone unless I fall in love, love, love. First comes love, then comes marriage."

"First comes marriage, *then* comes love," Mrs. Binat said sternly as she summoned the giggling, eye-rolling Lady to snuggle with her on the sofa, after which mother-daughter switched the TV channel from sports—despite Mari's outcry—to the Indian film channel, where Sridevi and Jeetendra were dancing-prancing-romancing around trees to the ludicrous love song "Mama Mia Pom Pom." After a few sullen minutes, Mari curled up on her mother's other side, even as she asked God's forgiveness at wasting her time over frivolous fare. Qitty joined at the far end of the sofa and opened up *Drawing on the Right Side of the Brain.* Jena took out some grading. Alys and Sherry murmured that they were going to feed birds and headed toward the graveyard.

In the graveyard, Alys and Sherry took a path that led to a cluster of family tombs in a roofed enclosure. They sat in a patch of late-afternoon sunlight on the cracked marble floor. Alys told Sherry she'd caught Darsee looking at her a few times.

"*Oof* Allah, he likes you," Sherry said, taking out her cigarettes. "He loves you. He wants to marry you. He yearns for you to have his arrogant babies."

"Ho ho ho. Ha ha ha. You should become a comedienne." Alys shook her head. "He was, no doubt, checking to see how crooked my nose is, how crossed my eyes are, and whether I have all thirty-two teeth intact. I was talking to Sarah—"

"How is she?"

"Good. Her mother is adamant that she drop future PhD plans, because, she insisted, no one wants to marry an overeducated girl in case she out-earns her husband, which will drive him to insecurity and subsequently divorcing her. I told Sarah to forget her *khayali* nonexistent husband's self-esteem and work toward her dreams. We were talking about thesis topics and Darsee asks me, 'How do you know all this?' Literally. As if I'm some ignoramus."

"What did you say?"

"*Reader's Digest* and *Good Housekeeping*."

Alys and Sherry exchanged high fives.

"How did it go with the potbellied Prince Charming?" Alys asked.

Sherry gave a small laugh. The potbellied prince had brought along sixteen family members, for whom Sherry and her younger sister, Mareea, had to scramble to fry up double, triple batches of kebabs. Then, after serving everyone chai, which took a good hour, Sherry was told she had to take a reading test. The potbellied prince produced a conduct book of Islamic etiquette, *Bahishti Zewar*—"Heavenly Ornaments"—and made her read out loud, in front of everyone, the section on how to keep oneself clean and pure before, during, and after sex.

"My father left the room, lucky him." Sherry exhaled a smoke ring. "But no one thought to stop the reading. I suppose they were picking up tips."

"You should have just stopped," Alys said.

"The reading was the easy part," Sherry said. "Next test was massage."

She'd had to massage his ropy, sweaty, oily neck for several minutes while he shouted, "Left, right, upper, lower."

"You should have pinched him," Alys said.

"I did," Sherry said. "I even dug my nails into him. But he seemed to enjoy both."

The real shock came when he was leaving. He'd looked straight at her, removed his dentures, which *Rishta* Aunty had neglected to inform them he wore, and wiggled his tongue in an obscene manner.

"Anyway, he rejected me." Sherry lit another cigarette with trembling fingers. "He telephoned to inform us that, although I'm a competent reader, my fingers do not possess the strength he, at age sixty-one, requires, and also I'm too thin and don't earn enough to compensate for my lack of a chest."

"Would you have married the potbellied pervert if he'd said yes?" Alys asked quietly.

Sherry sighed. "There's no dashing Bungles waiting to de-pigeon me. I'm down to either perverts fluttering my feathers or a lifetime of listening to my brothers groan and moan about having to look after me in my old age. These are the same brothers whose diapers I changed, snot I wiped, whom I taught to walk and talk. I'm tired of them treating me like a burden and I'm sick of my parents' morose faces, as if every day I remain unmarried is another day in hell *for them*. Honestly, Alys, Jena needs to *chup chaap*, without any frills, make her intentions clear to Bungles, before it's too late."

"It is a truth universally acknowledged," Alys said, "that hasty marriages are nightmares of *bardasht karo*, the gospel of tolerance and compromise, and that it's always us females who are given this despicable advice and told to shut up and put up with everything. I despise it."

"Me too," Sherry said. "But I'd rather *bardasht karo* the whims of a husband than the scorn of my brothers. Not that I blame my brothers. It's my duty to get married and I'm failing. I'm a failure."

"It's not your duty and you're not a failure." Alys planted a kiss on Sherry's cheek. "You and I will live together in our old age, on a beach, eat *samosas* and scones, and feast on the sunsets. We won't need anyone to support us or feel sorry for us. Your brothers and everyone else will instead envy our forever friendship."

"Outstanding fantasy." Sherry inhaled the last of her cigarette. "You won't believe what my mother did after the potbellied pervert telephoned. Instead of thanking God that I'd escaped a fate of being reader and massager in chief, she starts berating me for not massaging him properly and so losing another proposal. I swear, I wish my mother would just disappear for a while."

"Better yet, I know how to make you disappear." Alys put her arm around Sherry. "We're going to Lahore for the NadirFiede *walima*, and you're coming with us."

Chapter 8

$\mathcal{M}$rs. Binat would have been utterly displeased about Sherry's inclusion in the Suzuki for the two-hour trip to her elder brother's home in Lahore, but she was so excited about Jena's and Bungles's future nuptials that she did not complain too much. Before they knew it, they were parking in the driveway of the six-bedroom house located in Jamshed Colony—unfortunately no longer a fashionable part of town, much to Mrs. Binat's chagrin, but thankfully not one of the truly cringeworthy areas either.

When they heard the Binat car honking at their gate, Nisar and Nona Gardenaar came rushing out to the driveway with their four young children—a daughter, Indus, and sons, Buraaq, Miraage, and Khyber.

"Now, this family," Alys said to her mother, "is what liking your spouse and compatibility look like."

"It was love at first sight, is what it was," Mrs. Binat said.

Years ago, Nona's older brother, Samir, had been cohorts with Nisar during their medical residencies. Nona had been studying at the National College of Arts, and one day Samir's motorbike broke down and he borrowed Nisar's to pick her up from college. As thanks for lending his bike, Nisar was invited to their house for dinner. The somber boy with a shy smile found Nona's family—her parents, her brother, and Nona herself, with her freckles and sugar smile—a very pleasing contrast to his younger sisters, Falak and Pinkie, who seemed obsessed with fashion, celebrity gossip, and who's who.

Under one pretext or another, Nisar began to frequent Nona's home. He wanted to be a doctor. She wanted to be an artist. Her father worked at a travel agency, and her mother was an art teacher in a government school, and Nona wanted to teach art too. Her goals were to earn enough for art supplies and, once in a while, to go out for a nice meal. Nisar warned his sisters that they may not be impressed by Nona, but, to his pleasant surprise, Falak and Pinkie fell in love with Nona and her total disinterest in where they came from and who they were now.

By then Falak was struggling to find some happiness with the bad-tempered underachiever she'd married, who was very proud at having no ambition other than playing cards and carrom and smoking charas and who knew what else with his equally feckless friends, and finally she'd been forced to look for a job. Through a friend's recommendation, she joined a bank as a teller and felt forever guilty at not being a stay-at-home mother to her only child, Babur.

In turn, Pinkie died a million deaths whenever Tinkle and her friends openly mocked her name, Khushboo, by calling her "Badboo" and laughed at her mispronunciation of words or brands—"Not paaanda, darling, pan-da." "Not Luv-is, dear, Lee-vize." "Goga, you must hear Pinkie's latest gaffe. Pinkie, say 'Tetley' again. What did I tell you, Goga, 'Tut-lee!'" How utterly lost and stupid Pinkie would feel as Tinkle and clique conversed about Sotheby's and Ascot and the Royal Family and "oh, how very mundane it all was at the end of the day." Pinkie derisively referred to her in-laws as *Angrez ki aulad*—Children of the English—even as she envied them their *furfur* fluency in English and swore to herself that her children would also master the language and customs and never be mocked on that score.

"Both my poor sister and my rich sister are unhappy in their own ways," Nisar had told Nona one evening as they sat on the metal swing in her parents' garden. "After our parents passed away, as their brother, I vowed to take care of them whenever needed, and, Nona, I want to continue with that vow once married."

That had been the beginning of Nisar's proposal to Nona, and she said yes. Nona's parents cautioned her that marrying out of one's religion could be extra-challenging, but having had their say they welcomed the Muslim Nisar. Falak and Pinkie did not care that Nona was Christian. They did care that she adored their brother and was kind to them.

It was Nona who babysat Falak's son until she was promoted to bank assistant manager and was able to hire a reliable woman to look after Babur during the day. It was Nona who dropped the high-end fashion magazines into Pinkie's lap and told her to study them, until Pinkie, with her killer figure, could confidently out-style anyone—especially Tinkle, who Nona had disliked on sight, what with her ample art collection but scant knowledge of who she'd had the disposable income to collect.

Over the years, Nona would get annoyed over Falak's lack of pride in being a working woman and her rants against her husband but refusal to subject Babur to a "broken home," as well as over Pinkie's obsession with marrying her daughters into great wealth, but overall she loved her sisters-in-law and all their children.

Nona hugged the Binats and Sherry, then put her arms around Jena and Alys, and they all headed into the living room. The house smelled of vanilla and chocolate. The maid, Razia, brought in tea and the mini-cupcakes Indus had made especially for them.

"Your daughter is going to outdo you one day, Nona," Mr. Binat said, wagging his finger before following Nisar into the garden to take a look at a guava tree.

"She must!" Nona proclaimed. "That's what children are for, aren't they? To become better versions of their parents. Girls, what news?"

"*Hai,* Nona *jee!*" Mrs. Binat said, shaking with excitement. "We have struck gold. Gold! Such a good boy! And sisters are also mod-run, but in a good way."

"Not mod-run, Mummy," Lady said. "Mod-ern."

"Modrun. Modrun. That's what I'm saying," Mrs. Binat said. She proceeded to inform Nona that she was sure Bungles had chosen the upcoming polo match as the proposal venue so that he could ride up to Jena on a horse, just like a prince in olden-day films.

"*Hai*, Mummy," Lady said, as she took the hairbrush Indus brought her and began to French-braid her young cousin's hair. "I also want someone to propose to me astride a horse."

"Me too," Qitty said as Khyber dropped crayons into her lap.

"Not me," Mari said as she, Buraaq, and Miraage opened up the Snakes and Ladders board game. "Imagine the man is proposing while the horse is pooping away."

The kids started to giggle at the thought of a poopy horse.

"Jena," Nona asked gently, "are *you* expecting a proposal?"

Jena glanced at her mother. "I know he likes me."

"Likes you!" Mrs. Binat said. "Any sane person can see he is badly in love with you."

"And his family?" Nona said. "Are they also badly in love or might they have some other girl in mind?"

"If they have some other girl in mind," Mrs. Binat said indignantly, "then Bungles will be no better than that hoity-toity Darsee, who insulted Alys's looks."

"And intelligence," Sherry said, adding five spoons of sugar to her milky tea.

"But," Mrs. Binat said, "Bungles is not like Darsee. Girls, tell Nona how Bungles is one in a million."

The girls proceeded to tell her.

"*Chalo*, okay, Jena, good for you," Nona said after she heard them out. "If I could bake a magic cake that would make him propose this very minute, I would."

Three years ago Nona had baked an Arabian Nights cake for her daughter's birthday at school. The children had fallen silent at the

sight of the fondant bed with yellow marzipan pillows, the straw-
berry pantaloons–clad storyteller, Scheherazade, and her blueberry
pantaloons–clad sister, Dunyazade, on the bed, surrounded by
crystal-sugar characters from the stories: Aladdin, Sinbad, Ali Baba,
and Prince Shahryar turned chocolate giant with licorice whiskers.
The teachers cut the cake carefully, a little apprehensive that, like
many things in life, it would look beautiful from the outside but
would turn out to be tasteless from the inside. It was delicious. Word
of mouth spread so fast that Nona was soon inundated with orders.

"You need to charge," Falak and Pinkie urged Nona. Soon, white
boxes with lace calligraphy saying NONA'S NICES were being sold to
weddings, birthdays, graduations, anniversaries, Quran starts and
finishes, Eids, Iftars, Christmases, Holis, lawn launches, fundraisers,
et cetera. Nona and Nisar were, Falak and Pinkie often marveled
with dazed pride, minting money.

"I'm doing more charity cakes," Nona said. "Birthday cakes for
orphans at the Edhi Foundation, at Dar-ul-Sukun for the disabled,
and I've added Smileagain Foundation for acid-attack survivors."

"Aunty Nona," Mari said as she rolled the dice, "you are surely
going to heaven."

"Truly," Sherry agreed. "You are."

"You live the life I'd like to lead," Jena said softly. "To be able to
contribute happiness to the less fortunate."

"Jena," Mrs. Binat said, "concentrate on grabbing Bungles, and,
once you're married, you can do whatever you want."

"That's a lie." Alys gave a derisive laugh. "The dangling carrot to
lure us into marriage."

"Lost cause," Mrs. Binat muttered, gazing sorrowfully at Alys.
"You will die of loneliness if you don't get married."

"I'll never be lonely,"—Alys gave a satisfied sigh— "because I'll
always have books."

Nona smiled.

"Nona *jee*, don't encourage this *pagal larki*, mad girl," Mrs. Binat said, and she turned to Jena. "Jena, *beta,* I'm sure Bungles will allow you to—"

"Allow!" Alys shrieked. "Vomit, puke, *ulti.*"

"Yes, allow," Mrs. Binat said firmly. "And don't you dare ever encourage your sisters to disobey their husbands. You want them divorced and also relying on books for companionship and God knows what else! Jena, as I was saying, Bungles will *allow* you to aid every charity under the sun, because that's what begums do in order to keep themselves busy and give purpose to their lives. Do not scoff, Alys! Their need to keep busy is what helps those in need. I too was going to be a busy begum, devoting my life to good causes; instead, here I am, a nobody."

"Pinkie," Nona said, exchanging a glance with Alys, "even nobodies can devote their lives to charity."

"Yes, but when you are somebody, then you have the satisfaction of being told how wonderful you are," Mrs. Binat said, longingly. "Look at that *kameeni,* horrible Tinkle. People think Tinkle is such a great humanitarian, but I know what she really is—fame hungry, her road to importance paved with carefully calculated good deeds. Nona *jee,* the polo match Jena is invited to is tomorrow afternoon, and I'd rather she arrive in your good car than in our crap car. Will yours be available?"

The next morning a winter sun shone down on Lahore as Jena and Alys climbed into the good car and Ajmer, the driver, backed out of the driveway. He was a sweet man with a weak memory for addresses, but Nona and Nisar could not muster the heart to replace him.

"*Aur,* Ajmer," Alys said, sitting back in the car, "how are you?"

"Very good, *baji*!" Ajmer smiled, his henna-dyed red mustache swallowing his upper lip.

"Your children?" Jena asked.

"My son is beginning his medical degree in Quetta and my daughter is finishing up tenth grade. Her dream," Ajmer said proudly, "is to become a doctor like her brother, and Nisar Sahib promised to help her get into medical school too."

"Every girl should have a father like you," Alys said. But she also wondered how benevolent Ajmer would have been had his daughter wanted to be an actress or singer or model. She sighed as she recalled how bitterly Lady had cried at their father forbidding her to model. For the truth was that behind every successful Pakistani girl who fulfilled a dream stood a father who allowed her to soar instead of clipping her wings, throwing her into a cage, and passing the keys from himself to brother, husband, son, grandson, and so on. Alys felt a headache coming on.

"Ajmer, turn the music on please," she said, and within seconds the car filled with an exuberant "Dama Dam Mast Qalander."

As they entered a busy thoroughfare full of cars, rickshaws, motorbikes, bicycles, everyone honking madly, Alys straightened Jena's hoop earring. Since Bungles, Hammy, and Sammy had already seen Jena in plenty of Eastern wear, thanks to NadirFiede, Mrs. Binat had declared it was time for some Western wear. They'd settled on boot-cut dark-denim jeans, a black-and-white striped turtleneck, and a chocolate leather jacket, which Jena had seen in *Vogue* and had tailor Shawkat replicate. Jena wanted to wear sneakers, but Mrs. Binat had handed her a pair of chocolate pumps originally brought for Qitty and so slightly large for Jena but still a decent-enough fit.

"I'm nervous," Jena said to Alys as the car inched closer to the Race Course Park. "I wish you were coming with me."

"You'll be fine," Alys said. "I plan to walk for an hour or so before returning home. Do you want me to send Ajmer to you before I head home? That way, if you want to return, just make an excuse that an emergency has come up and he's come to get you."

"Yes!" Jena said. "I'd rather face Mummy's wrath than sit there if I'm feeling awkward."

The car glided through leafy suburbs before turning in to one of the park's back lots and, from there, taking another turn onto a wide dirt road. The dirt road led up to Aibak Polo Ground, where privileged children learned to horse ride and some of them grew up to play polo on the impeccably mowed green ground.

The polo match had begun, and Alys and Jena could see majestic horses galloping at full speed toward goals, their coats polished by the sun, their riders in crisp whites wielding their mallets as they went after the wooden ball. Jena got out of the car and teetered for a moment on her shoes before turning resolutely toward the polo ground and clubhouse.

Ajmer drove back down the dirt road and parked amid a row of other good cars. Alys got out and told him she'd be back soon. Ajmer nodded. Pressing PLAY on her Walkman—she and Jena had recorded English songs on one side of the tape and Pakistani songs on the other—she hummed to "Material Girl" and jogged to the clay track that ran around the periphery of the Race Course Park. Once an actual racecourse, until betting on horses was banned for political expediency in the name of Islam, the course had been converted into a sprawling public park.

Alys passed the Japanese garden and pagoda. Every few steps the park gardeners pruned leaves and deposited seeds, their *shalwars* pulled up over ashy knees, their sun-wrinkled legs planted firmly on the earth. She nodded a greeting as she walked by, and they nodded back. She thought of her father and the calm and refuge he'd found among flora and fauna. She passed by a couple seated on a bench, eating oranges in front of impeccably manicured flower beds. The veiled woman was feeding the bearded man with her fingers, and a citrus scent floated over the jogging track from the orange peels gathered in her lap.

Stopping to stretch her calves, Alys gazed at some boys playing cricket. The wickets were red bricks set upright on their narrow ends. The fielders stood waiting in their jeans and knockoff T-shirts. The bowler was good; the batsman was nervous; the rest was history. She switched the tape to side B, and Nazia Hassan's seductive "Aap Jaisa

Koi" came on, followed by "Disco Deewane." Nazia and her brother, Zoheb, were the first Pakistani pop singers Alys and Jena had heard and loved in Jeddah. Nazia had died earlier that year, and the sisters had mourned her passing.

Alys jogged by the artificial lake with paddleboats chained to one end for the winter and climbed up the steep man-made hill. Standing at the summit, she caught her breath as she looked out at the landscaped park, at the children in the playground, at groups of young men studying or napping, at the flock of sparrows in the blue-gray sky.

A little over an hour later, as she neared the polo ground, Alys hoped Jena was having a good time. She wiped sweat off her forehead and stepped into the parking lot. Where was the car? Her eyes swept over the rows. Ajmer had parked by the turnstile entrance. She was sure of it.

"*Suno*, bhai—listen, brother," she asked a driver leaning against a Civic, "have you seen a black Accord? A driver with a red mustache?"

The man shook his head. He called out to another driver, who informed Alys that the man she was referring to had driven away ages ago. In fact, right after she'd gotten out.

Alys stared. "Did he say where he was going?"

"Not to me."

"Oh my God," Alys said to no one in particular. Hadn't she told Ajmer to remain here? She had. Didn't he know he was supposed to wait for her to return from her walk? He did. Maybe he went to buy some cigarettes. Or to the toilet. But why would he take the car to drive to a toilet when the park had public toilets?

Alys bit her thumb. Even if she caught a rickshaw and went home, she could hardly leave Jena stranded and frantic when she wouldn't be able to find the car, or Ajmer. And Alys couldn't call Jena once she got home, because she didn't have the polo club's phone number. She shook her head in frustration as she marched up the dust road toward the polo ground. She knew she looked a sight, with her hair plastered to her face, her sneakers caked with mud, armpit sweat stains, and no *dupatta*, because she didn't believe in wearing one—men should avert their eyes from women, rather than women being forced to cover themselves—and oh, she must stink.

Still, Alys was taken aback at the degree of hush that fell over the polo-match spectators when she appeared. A solid block of designer sunglasses looked her up and down, saw she was not one of them, and turned back to the field.

Alys scanned the bleachers.

"Excuse me," she finally said loudly, "I'm looking for Fahad, Humeria, and Sumeria Bingla."

And who should rise, in culottes and a Swarovski-embellished cardigan, but Mrs. Nadir Sheh—aka Fiede Fecker.

"They're in the clubhouse," Fiede said like a queen addressing a peasant. "You may enter from the back, or the front."

Alys chose the front entrance. If the spectators wanted to gawk at her, then she would give them ample opportunity to do so. Past the bleachers, past the chairs, past sponsors' banners, past overdressed youth, past oily uncles and grande dames with facelifts, until she arrived at the front entrance and went down the steps into a hall.

She immediately saw Jena. She was perched on a sofa, her bare foot resting on a stool. Bungles squatted beside her, holding an ice pack to her ankle. Hammy and Sammy hovered over them. Jaans was sipping from his liquor flask. Darsee towered over them all.

"What happened?" Alys said, hurrying to her sister.

Everyone turned at her voice. Relief flooded Jena's face.

"Alys! Babes! Oh my goodness," Hammy said, "are you all right? You look like a horse dragged you through a swamp."

"I was walking," Alys said. "In the park."

"Walking?" Sammy said. "In the park? Without a *dupatta*?"

"Jena," Alys said, ignoring them, "what happened to your ankle?"

As it turned out, a divot-stomping session and Jena in Qitty's heels.

"Her entire ankle turned," Bungles said, worry etched on his face. "She needs an X-ray. I went out a couple of times to look for your car in the parking lot but couldn't find—"

"Alys, where is our car?" Jena managed to ask through her pain.

"I don't know," Alys said, baffled. "Ajmer is MIA. I hope he's okay. Is there a phone here?"

"I've been trying to call Uncle's," Jena said. "Busy signal."

Darsee took a flip phone out of his pocket and held it out to Alys. "Use this. Everyone should get one. Very convenient, especially in emergencies."

Alys had seen a few people carrying them. Principal Naheed had one. Alys had not used one before and looked at it for a moment.

"Dial zero-four-two," Hammy said, "and then your home number."

"Hammy doesn't have one yet," Jaans said, "but she knows all about it."

"You don't have one either," Hammy snapped back.

"I'm waiting for Sammy to buy me one."

Sammy said, "Why don't you go to work and earn it yourself?"

"*Oye,*" Jaans said, "don't get too uppity or I'll spank you."

"And I," Sammy said, "will withhold your pocket money."

"Anyone can make money," Jaans said. "Your company could go down the drain, baby, but my lineage will always remain. In this marriage, I contribute everlasting gains."

"You can take your lineage," Sammy said, "and shove it up your rear end."

Jaans flushed. "You better not get fat. Ever."

"Fuck off, Mr. Potato," Sammy said, jabbing her husband in his spare tire.

"If I'd known you were capable of such vulgarity, I would've never married you."

"You knew," Sammy said. "You need to stop drinking for two minutes in order to realize how lucky you are I married you."

"It's bad wives like you who cause good men like me to turn to drink. I know it's Hammy who's been poisoning you with all this women's rights crap."

Hammy hissed, "Sammy has a mind of her own, you know."

"Oh, shut up, Jaans," Sammy said. "I was no different when we were dating."

"Quit it," Bungles said. "Both of you. Jaans, don't speak to my sisters like that."

Alys returned Jena's quick pleased look. She too was heartened to see that Bungles had defended his sisters.

"Dating is different, Sammy." Jaans scowled. "Once you are lucky enough to become a wife, the rules change."

"Oh, come on, Jaans!" Darsee said. "That mentality really needs to change."

"It does," Bungles said, "and in the meantime, Jena is in pain and does not need to be subjected to you two fighting. Alys, please call your home."

Alys took Darsee's flip phone as fast as she could, making sure to not accidentally touch him. Stepping outside, she was relieved when her mother answered on the first ring.

"Thank God you picked up. Jena has been trying to call for ages."

"Why?" Mrs. Binat said. "Has he proposed?"

"No! And Ajmer has disappeared."

"I know," Mrs. Binat said gleefully. "I told him to drop you both off and come back home so that Bungles has ample time to propose."

"What!"

"And, Alys, you too are aging by the day. You also need to get married, and plenty of eligible bachelors must be at the polo match to come to your rescue when they find out you need a ride home."

"For your information, Mummy, Jena has twisted her ankle and is in a lot of pain. We need to come home immediately. Send the car back."

"Tell Bungles to drop you. *Allah keray*, God willing, he proposes in the car."

"If he proposes while she's in extreme pain, then he's a sadist."

"Who cares when and how a proposal comes. Foolish girl. Sit there and make sure that he asks her to marry him," Mrs. Binat said, and hung up.

Alys returned indoors. Jena was looking paler and her foot more swollen.

"Thank you," Alys said, returning the phone to Darsee. Why was he staring at her so intently? If he'd deemed her not good-looking when she was dressed up for a wedding, he was probably having conniptions at how she looked after a strenuous walk.

"My pleasure," Darsee said, slipping the phone back into his pocket.

"Valentine always comes to the rescue," Hammy said, not pleased with the way Darsee was looking at Alys. "Don't you, Valentine?"

"No, I don't." Darsee turned to Alys. "Were you able to get through?"

"Yes," Alys said, and murmured that Ajmer had misunderstood her directions and gone home. "Bungles, could you please drop us? Our uncle lives in Jamshed Colony."

She ignored the look Hammy-Sammy shared. Jamshed Colony had once been a very prestigious residential area of Lahore and had only seen a sharp decline in the last fifteen years, as commercial enterprises turned it into one big shopping center.

"I think we should take Jena straight for an X-ray," Bungles said. "There's a first-rate private clinic ten minutes away."

"It's a good facility," Darsee said.

"Thank you for the offer," Alys said to Bungles, even as she stopped herself from informing Darsee that no one had asked his opinion. "But I think we should go home."

"Look," Bungles said, "the swelling is getting worse even as we speak."

"I want to go home," Jena said. "My uncle is a doctor—"

"Doctor of?" Darsee said.

"Pulmonology," Alys said.

"Your sister doesn't need her lungs heard," Darsee said. "She needs her ankle X-rayed."

Alys said coldly, "My uncle knows the best doctors for every ailment."

"Jena," Bungles said, pleading, "what if something is broken? You'll just be wasting time going home. Let the clinic take a look. Clearly your pain is unbearable."

"It's not that bad," Jena said, even as she groaned.

"Okay," Alys said. "Clinic."

She stared as Bungles proceeded to lift Jena in his arms and carry her out of the clubhouse. It was like the scene in Jane Austen's *Sense and Sensibility* when Marianne Dashwood slipped in the rain and Willoughby carried her home in his arms. It was not a good omen, Alys thought, as she snatched her sister's shoe off the floor and hurried after them. Marianne and Willoughby did not enjoy a happy ending, no matter how promising their start. Worse, everyone outside was now going to witness Bungles being a gallant knight, and Jena, who had not asked to be swept up in his arms, was going to be the talk of the town.

Hammy waited until the club door shut behind Alys before saying, "What did Bungles just do? Jena could easily have walked. It's all a big act."

"I did see her ankle twist," Jaans said. "I think she's really hurt."

"It's a ploy," Hammy said firmly. "What do girls like this call it—catching a man, trapping a man, grabbing a man. Right, Sammy?"

"Right, Hammy," Sammy said. "In the olden days they'd get pregnant. These days they sprain their ankles."

"Everyone must have seen him carry her," Hammy said.

"So?" Jaans said.

"So," Sammy said, "they'll think something is going on."

"Something is going on," Jaans said.

"Nothing," Hammy said, "had better be going on unless Sammy and I approve. And, in this case, we disapprove. There's the cheapster mother's family reputation to consider and the family itself. A loser father. A fundamentalist sister. A fat sister. A spitting sister. A decorum-less sister. I thought I was going to die when Alys appeared looking like a swamp creature. Can't they afford private gym memberships?"

"Lots of people exercise in public parks," Darsee said. "The Race Course Park was one of my mother's favorite places to walk."

"Of course," Hammy said. "It's a very respectable park, and I'd surely love to walk here too. But I'd wear a *dupatta,* and I'm quite sure, Val, your mother did too. Being modern does not mean being inappropriate."

"Jaans," Sammy said, "would you let your sister gallivant half-undressed in a public place?"

"My sister," Jaans said, scowling, "has a treadmill in her bedroom. No need to even leave the house."

"And you, Valentine?" Hammy said. "Would you want Jujeena going around like that?"

"Up to Juju," Darsee said.

"Juju would never do that," Hammy said. "I bet Alys Binat's eyes weren't so great today in that sweaty, blotchy face."

"Actually," Darsee said, "I think the fresh air made them even more luminous."

Hammy pouted and headed outside the clubhouse, where a million amused voices rushed to inform them that Bungles had left with his damsel in distress and her disheveled sister and that they were instructed to follow. Darsee, bothered by exactly how radiant he'd found Alys's eyes, had planned to go home. Instead, Hammy, Sammy, and Jaans climbed into his Mercedes and he headed toward the clinic.

Chapter 9

The clinic was an excellent facility, as all facilities that cater to excellent people tend to be, because excellent people demand excellence, unlike those who are grateful for what they receive. A nurse flipped Jena into a wheelchair and took her for an X-ray. The verdict: a mild ankle sprain. Even though the nurse said that an overnight stay was unnecessary and Jena agreed, Bungles immediately booked her into a VIP suite. Alys wondered how much the room was going to cost as Jena was lifted into a plush bed, where she lay elegant in her jeans and turtleneck, fiddling with the controls to elevate her foot. She'd been given a nice painkiller and was beginning to look relaxed.

Hammy and Sammy arrived. Their faces grew pinched at Bungles's insistence that an overnight stay was vital, no matter who said what.

"I'm not budging till Jena is discharged," he said, gazing at her with overwhelming concern.

"You have to budge," Hammy and Sammy said simultaneously.

Alys was enjoying the show that was the sisters trying to separate their brother from Jena, until she realized that Bungles intended to spend the night. Did he mean to completely obliterate Jena's reputation? As it was, there were already going to be vicious rumors over Jena *allowing herself* to be carried by him.

"Only I'll be staying with Jena," Alys said firmly. She went to the reception to call home and give her mother the news that Jena had been admitted for the night.

"Good girls!" Mrs. Binat said. "Jena immobile in bed. Bungles by her side. If this isn't a recipe for a proposal, I don't know what is."

"Jena is in no state of mind to receive a proposal," Alys whispered furiously into the phone. "And if Bungles proposes while she's drugged up, I'll doubt his state of mind. Now, please ask Qitty and Mari to prepare an overnight bag with a change of clothes for me and also pack the books on my nightstand."

A little later, Mrs. Binat breezed into the clinic with a bag for Alys and pillows galore, as if Jena had been admitted for the next month. Mari, Qitty, and Lady were right behind her. Lady was declaring it most unfair that nothing fun ever happened to her. Mrs. Binat kissed Jena, all the while exclaiming what a first-class champion Bungles was to be "taking such wonderful care of my terribly injured daughter."

"It's a mild sprain," Alys said, drowning out her mother. "We wouldn't even be here if Bungles had not insisted Jena be kept for observation."

"*Chup ker,* be quiet," Mrs. Binat said. "Oh, Bungles, look at my poor daughter, how frail, how helpless—" She stopped abruptly. Perhaps Jena as Invalid Supreme might turn Bungles off. "But my Jena is a fighter. When my daughters were little they got malaria, vomit everywhere, though Jena's vomit was of a very dignified hue, and within days she was up and back to normal. *Haan, jee!* Yes, sir! My womb has produced those rare creatures: girls who are dainty but also tough. And their wombs will produce just as well. Not to worry! Even Qitty's womb is in tip-top shape; all she needs is a bit of dieting."

Alys braved a peek at the company. Bungles was smiling awkwardly. Hammy-Sammy and Jaans snickered behind their hands. Darsee was simply staring with terrible fascination.

"Oh, but," Mrs. Binat said, "if one is going to get infected and die, it should be in a facility such as this—"

"Mummy," Alys said, interrupting her, "why don't you go to reception and settle the bill?"

"I've taken care of it," Bungles said.

"First-class gentleman," Mrs. Binat said.

"But you can't," Alys said to Bungles. "Absolutely not."

"Please," Bungles said. "Jena was our guest at the polo match, and my sisters and I insist that we take care of this."

Alys glanced at Hammy and Sammy. They were insisting no such thing.

"No," Alys said.

"Aunty"—Bungles turned to Mrs. Binat—"I will take it as a personal insult if you do not let me foot the bill."

"*Hai,*" Mrs. Binat said, "that we should die before insulting you. May Allah grant you the pocket and power to foot a million such bills."

"Jena," Lady said, "you should stay a whole month now that we are not paying."

"Lady!" Alys glanced at a tight-faced Darsee.

"It's a joke!" Lady said. "Alys, you have no sense of humor. So boring all the time."

"Alys is not boring," Mrs. Binat said. "Not all the time." She dug her eyes into Darsee, who was looking sullenly at the black-and-white-tiled floor. "She is also very attractive, and anyone who can't see that should get their eyes examined. Smart too, in her own way. At her school debate club, Alys was two-time gold medalist, and she was also backstroke champion, though I'm not in favor of girls playing sports. Take swimming. It makes the girls' necks very beefy, and goodbye to wearing necklaces. Bungles, are you in favor of girls swimming-shimming? You watch Olympics?"

"I do." Bungles nodded even as he made eyes at his sisters and Jaans to stop laughing.

"You must come watch Olympics with us in Dilipabad," Mrs. Binat said. "Our cook makes the best Chinese food. Humeria-Sumeria, Jaans, you must also come." She smiled at Jaans, who gave her two thumbs-up and said, "Go D-bad," and then she said curtly to Darsee, "You also come."

"Mummy," Alys said, standing up, "Jena needs to nap."

After managing to send her mother and sisters home, Alys disappeared into the attached bathroom to shower and change. As she slipped out of her T-shirt and track pants and shoved them into the bag, she hoped that everyone else would leave too. She'd love an evening alone with Jena, the two of them discussing Bungles at the match, and everything else. She emerged a half hour later, after a hot shower, smelling of gardenia-scented shampoo, water dripping off her curls and onto her red V-necked sweater and jeans, delighted to find that Sammy and Jaans had left in her absence after, apparently, quarreling yet again over whose contribution to their marriage was more vital: her money or his pedigree.

Alys took her *Kolhapuri chappals* out of her bag and slid her feet into them. She hoped that Bungles, Hammy, and Darsee would leave too. She did not relish the idea of having to endure Darsee's and Hammy's company, and she wished that Bungles, sitting beside Jena and looking as if he was going to burst into poetry, would propose soon so that Jena would no longer require chaperoning. Why was Darsee looking at her? Hadn't he seen a girl with messy hair and no makeup before? She flushed and ran her fingers through her tangles.

Bungles declared Jena was craving Chinese food, and he proceeded to place a dinner order for everyone.

"Jena," Bungles said when he hung up the phone, "do you want anything else? Shall I turn the TV on?"

Jena shrugged. Alys could tell she was being extra-cautious and acting all the more aloof. Good. Until she and Bungles were officially engaged, Jena's reserve was smart.

Hammy took the remote control from Bungles and switched on the TV. The clinic's movie channel came on. "Ooh! *Pretty Woman*." She gazed at Darsee, who stood by the window, gazing at the moon. "Val, I love this film."

"Every woman does," Darsee said in a not-too-kind tone.

"How presumptuous." Alys matched the snooty look Darsee gave her. "I don't. It sets up unrealistic expectations."

Alys was not a fan of updated Cinderella stories, *Pretty Woman* being a version in which a prostitute cleans up well and ends up earning herself a rich *roti*—a rich meal ticket—because she has a great figure and a heart of gold. Another version, readily available via Pakistani dramas, was a girl from the lower middle class who earns the respect and love of a rich *roti* because she's virginal and, no matter how smart or accomplished she is, allows her husband to put her in her place. Mari approved of these silly dramas, for she believed they were excellent propaganda for teaching women their role in society. Lady and Mrs. Binat were big fans too but more for the romance and fashion than the lessons espoused. Qitty watched them in order to people her caricatures.

"Unrealistic expectations!" Hammy frowned. "I'm surprised you don't like rags-to-riches stories."

"I don't like rags-to-riches *love* stories."

"Where did you learn to dismiss romance?" Hammy scoffed. "Jeddah?"

"Jeddah?" Darsee said.

"You don't know," Hammy said. "The Binats lived in Saudi Arabia for a while, where they attended, I believe, the Pakistan Embassy School."

Alys glanced at Jena. Surely she'd caught Hammy's scorn. But Jena was too busy assuring Bungles her ankle was in a comfortable position.

"The Pakistan Embassy School was quite all right," Alys said. "However, we attended an international school."

"I went to an international school too," Darsee said. "In Bangkok."

Alys feigned disinterest, though she wanted to ask him about his experiences.

"How was your experience?" Darsee said. "Do you miss it?"

"I miss California," Hammy said.

"Your parents still live there," Darsee said. "Going to school-in-transit, so to speak, is different. Would you agree, Alys?"

"Yes," Alys said. "I've lost touch with all my friends."

"I wish," Darsee said, "there had been a better way of staying connected back then, instead of just letters."

"Technology makes it easier these days," Alys said. "There is the email thingy."

"The email thingy?" Darsee smiled.

Alys gave him a cold stare. "You should read *Reader's Digest* and *Good Housekeeping*. Keep you updated on technology."

"Babes," Hammy said, "Val is a tech genius."

"I take it, Alys," Darsee said, "you believe I'm not impressed by these two publications that have impressed you."

"Have you ever read either one?"

"Nope," Darsee said. "The covers—"

"The covers!"

"Covers don't lie," Darsee said.

"That's not true."

"A risk I'm willing to take," Darsee said.

"Of course you are," Alys said, and seeing Bungles rip himself away from Jena in order to send his driver to pick up the Chinese takeaway, she took the moment to flee Darsee for her sister's bedside.

When Bungles returned to the room, he was carrying a bouquet of narcissuses sold by flower hawkers outside the clinic. A nurse followed him with a glass of water. Bungles put the flowers in and placed them by Jena's side. A delicious scent pervaded the room.

"My favorite flowers," Jena said, caressing a yellow center surrounded by cream petals.

"I know," Bungles said. "You mentioned it at NadirFiede's wedding."

"Bungles is so thoughtful to everyone," Hammy said, an exasperated smile on her face as she turned up the volume to *Pretty Woman*.

In ten minutes, the driver was back with the food. Alys and Bungles took out the containers and paper ware. Bungles leapt to fix Jena a plate. Hammy was eager to serve Darsee, except he dashed her desires by helping himself. Alys took a bowl of chicken corn soup.

Everyone ate in silence— except for Bungles, who kept asking Jena if she needed anything. Finally Hammy said, in a saccharine tone, that Jena had sprained her ankle and not her mouth and that if she required his services, she would no doubt ask him. Bungles sheepishly distributed the fortune cookies.

"Jena," he said, "what does yours say?"

"A new beginning is on the horizon."

"Mine is so stupid," Hammy said. *"Karma is a witch."*

"You don't believe in karma?" Alys asked. She put her fortune cookie into her bag to give to Qitty, who was creating a food-and-word sculpture.

"If you don't remember anything from a past life," Darsee said, "then how can you avoid making the same mistakes in your present life?"

"I don't know," Alys said, taking some lo mein. "I suppose some people will be born with the same flaws, such as pride, and therefore be prone to repeating history."

"Pride isn't a flaw," Darsee said.

"It's just another word for smug," Alys said.

"Pride is a strength. Smugness opens one to mockery."

"Sometimes," Alys said, "one can be mocked through no fault of one's own."

"If you don't give cause, you will never be mocked," Darsee said.

"Let me guess—you've never given cause!" Alys turned to Hammy and Bungles. "You need to mock him; otherwise, he really will think he's perfect."

"Oh my God, babes," Hammy said, "Valentine *is* perfect."

"I'm not perfect," Darsee said to Alys. "Far from. My biggest flaw in this day and age is that I don't suffer fools gladly. I hate sycophancy, nepotism, cronyism. I don't care to be diplomatic."

"You can afford to be undiplomatic," Alys said. "People let people like you get away with anything."

"You know what your glaring fault is?" Darsee said.

Alys glared at him. "Do tell."

"You take great pride in hearing only what you want to hear, and then you're smug about your interpretation." Darsee scowled at his watch. "We should leave."

"Yes," Hammy said eagerly. "Jena's been yawning away."

"Jena, are you sleepy?" Bungles asked. "Should I go?"

Jena, far from being rude enough to say yes, hesitated, and Bungles beamed.

"Val, you and Hammy go," he said.

Hammy flopped back onto the loveseat, and it was clear to Alys that she had no intention of leaving Bungles alone. Alys dragged a chair close to Jena. Darsee offered to help, but Alys said she could manage by herself, thank you. Curling up in the chair, she took out several books from her bag.

"I see you read more than *Reader's Digest* and *Good Housekeeping*," Darsee said. "My mother read books one after the other, as if they were potato chips."

"Alys reads like that," Jena said, as she took the water Bungles insisted she drink.

"I love to read, Valentine." Hammy rose to hover between Darsee and Alys. "I'm the world's biggest bookworm!"

Alys began to separate the books into two groups. Darsee glanced at the titles.

"For class?" he asked.

"Analogous Literatures. I'm pairing Rokeya Sakhawat Hossain's *Sultana's Dream* with Charlotte Perkins Gilman's *Herland* for utopias. Khushwant Singh's *Train to Pakistan* with John Steinbeck's *The Grapes of Wrath* for family stories alternating with socio-pastoral chapters. Gloria Naylor's *The Women of Brewster Place* with Krishan Chander's short story "Mahalaxmi Ka Pul," comparing women's lives. And E. M. Forster's *A Passage to India* with Harper Lee's *To Kill a Mockingbird* for similar racial issues and court cases."

"I've read *Wrath* and *Mockingbird*," Darsee said. He skimmed *A Passage to India*. "I haven't read much local literature, not that *Passage* is local per se, though it's up for debate whether it's the nationality of the author or the geography of the book that determines its place in a country's canon."

"Val"—Hammy gave him her most dazzling smile—"have you read *Love Story*? It's really short and belongs everywhere, for love knows no boundaries." She sighed theatrically. "Love transcends country and geography."

Alys and Darsee both gave Hammy equally amused glances.

"I believe," Alys said to Darsee, "a book and an author can belong to more than one country or culture. English came with the colonizers, but its literature is part of our heritage too, as is pre-partition writing."

Darsee said, "My favorite partition novel is Attia Hosain's *Sunlight on a Broken Column*. Have you read it, Alys?"

Alys shook her head.

"That book made me believe I could have a Pakistani identity inclusive of an English-speaking tongue. We've been forced to seek ourselves in the literature of others for too long."

Alys nodded, adding, "But reading widely can lead to an appreciation of the universalities across cultures."

"Sure," Darsee said. "But it shouldn't just be a one-sided appreciation."

"I know what you mean," Alys said. "Ginger ale and apple pie have become second nature to us here, while our culture is viewed as exotic."

"Precisely," Darsee said. "At the wedding, you talked of a Pakistani Jane Austen. But will we ever hear the English or Americans talk of an equivalent?"

"Let's hope so," Alys said.

"You teach Austen, right?" Darsee said. "My mother adored Darcy."

"Oh my God, babes, I love Mr. Darcy," Hammy squealed. "Especially the part with his wet shirt. I could read that scene all day."

Alys's and Darsee's eyes met.

"Darcy is overrated," Alys said. "Mr. Knightley from *Emma* won my heart when he defended Miss Bates from Emma's mockery."

"I see." Darsee pointed to a bookmarked book. "What are you reading?"

"Virginia Woolf's *To the Lighthouse*."

"According to my mother, Woolf captured the essence of time plus memory."

"She does," Alys said. "I discovered her in the British Council library. She has an essay on Jane Austen."

"You mean Shakespeare in *A Room of One's Own*?" Darsee said.

His supercilious tone cut Alys. Instantly, she recalled that she wasn't talking to a fellow bibliophile but to Valentine Darsee.

"Just because," she said sharply, "you are ignorant about something does not mean that I'm wrong."

Darsee looked at Alys. He stood up. They were leaving. Yes, Bungles, right now! As Hammy and a reluctant Bungles followed him out, Darsee resolved not to say a single word to Alys the next day. In fact, he wouldn't show up.

The next morning, Bungles arrived alone, and despite his pleas that she needed to stay on, Jena was adamant that she was absolutely fine. Would Bungles please drop them to their uncle's house?

Mrs. Binat was devastated when Alys and Jena returned home without an engagement ring. Mr. Binat was delighted his daughters were back. He, Nona, and Nisar were longing to talk about something other than who had dressed like a complete clown at NadirFiede, who like a partial clown, and how massive a ring Jena should expect from Bungles.

"Jena, Alys!" Mrs. Binat said. "You barely gave Bungles a chance to propose. Nona, have you seen any more dim-witted girls than these two? Instead of practicing grab-it, they are mastering push-it-away. Even the likes of Benazir Bhutto and Lady Dayna did not push it away."

Nona, knowing it was no use refuting Pinkie Binat when she was in this mood, did not answer.

"Not Dayna, Mummy, Diana, Lady Diana," Lady said. "Had I stayed with Alys and Jena, I would have made sure Jena did not leave without a ring."

"I should have left you there," Mrs. Binat said. "You are the most sensible of the lot. Don't you dare serve me a shoe, Barkat! If these two nitwits would have stayed, that boy would have proposed, I guarantee."

"Mummy," Qitty said, looking up from pencils she was sharpening. "There's still the *walima*."

"*Chup ker*. Be quiet," Mrs. Binat said. "*Beheno ki chumchee*. Defending her disobedient sisters."

"We couldn't stay there forever," Jena said quietly, "waiting for him to propose."

Mrs. Binat was about to correct her on that score when Sherry returned from her overnight visit to her aunt—the divorcée, who'd thrived despite social stigma, thanks to a very well-paying job—and offered a sympathetic ear.

"Of course you are one hundred percent right, Pinkie Khala," Sherry agreed. "Jena should never have left."

Mrs. Binat was so gratified, she declared they would order Sherry's favorite meal for dinner: mutton *tikkas, keema naan,* and *bhindi* fry.

"Qitty," Mrs. Binat added, "don't you even look at the *naan*."

By meal's end, during which Qitty defiantly ate half a *naan*, Mrs.

Binat had calmed down enough to start preparing Jena for the NadirFiede *walima,* where, she guaranteed everyone, Bungles would propose. Mr. Binat pulled Alys aside and reminded her of her meeting with the lawyer the next day to sort out the matter of the land fraud.

Chapter 10

*A*lys parked her car and stepped out into bustling Mall Road, ignoring the whistles and catcalls of loitering men. She hurried past Ferozsons bookstore, glancing at the window display, past Singhar, the beauty shop fragrant with sandalwood, and, turning into an alley, arrived at the law offices of Musarrat Sr. & Sons Advocates.

Once upon a time, Bark Binat had purchased an acre of land. When he was forced out of the ancestral home, he'd turned to the acre, only to discover that he, along with others, had been conned. The acres sold to them were government land, and the government refused to compensate anyone for being gullible. Mr. Binat had been hesitant to hire a lawyer yet again—after his brother's betrayal, he had no gumption to bring strangers to task—but Alys had not let it go. Even if they never saw a penny returned, they had to at least try, and she'd hired Musarrat Jr. on a friend's assurance that he was honest and trustworthy. The Binats' initial petition concerning the Fraudia Acre case had been filed a decade ago and, since then, there'd been no real progress.

Alys stepped into the tube-lit office. She could hear Musarrat Jr.'s booming voice from inside his office, saying, "Trust in God." The receptionist looked at the recent letter Alys had received from them and told her to proceed into the office.

Musarrat Jr. was hanging up the phone, and he beamed when he saw Alys.

"Alysba Sahiba, it's been a while! Please sit!" He settled his paunchy self into his swivel chair. "Mr. Binat is hale and hearty, I hope?"

Alys assured him he was. She wished her father had not begged off coming just because money matters gave him palpitations.

"Alysba Sahiba," Musarrat Jr. said, "as it says in the letter, the con man has reentered the country and, because one of the claimants' sons is a police officer, he is being questioned aggressively. *Inshallah,* soon there will be some resolution." He pressed a buzzer. A peon entered. "Check if Jeorgeullah Wickaam Sahib is back from court."

A few minutes later a young man entered. Alys blinked. He was movie-star gorgeous, with chiseled features, dark-brown hair, and sleepy eyes the color of rich chai. His white shirt tucked into gray pants perfectly fit his well-muscled build. What good fortune, Alys thought as she sat up straighter and smoothed her floral sky-blue *kurta* over her scruffy jeans, that she wasn't the sort of person who would be taken by looks alone.

Musarrat Jr. introduced Alys and, with a proud smile, turned to the man.

"Alysba Sahiba, Mr. Jeorgeullah Wickaam, the lawyer newly as-signed to your case and a rising star among youngsters."

Alys gave a polite, shy smile.

"Wickaam grew up in Lahore, did a stint at a military academy, realized it was not for him, went to New York for studies, returned, and here is he willing and ready to serve the wronged citizens of his country."

Jeorgeullah Wickaam gave Alys a courteous nod, which also seemed to imply that while he perhaps deserved this flattery, it was nevertheless embarrassing.

"First steps first," Musarrat Jr. said. "I suggest, Alysba Sahiba, you show Wickaam Sahib your disputed acre."

When they reached the Suzuki, Alys took out her keys from her bag and Jeorgeullah Wickaam sprang to open the driver's-side door for her before he headed to the passenger side. Alys smiled to herself. Handsome, a rising star, polite. She could think of worse ways to spend an afternoon.

As she expertly reversed the car into an onslaught of traffic, he turned toward her with a friendly smile and informed her that though the arrested man was being questioned thoroughly, the chances of monetary recompense were bleak.

"Honestly," Alys said, stepping on the accelerator, "at this point a heartfelt admittance of guilt and a sorry would be very nice."

"Knowing how these rascals operate, I wouldn't bank on heartfelt anything." He shrugged regretfully. "By the way, please call me Wickaam."

"Call me Alys."

"A-L-I-C-E?"

"Pronounced the same but spelled A-L-Y-S."

"I had a *kebab* roll recently," Wickaam said. "It came wrapped in a magazine page with the photo of an elderly woman, and her name was A-L-Y-S. . . ."

"That's Faiz Ahmed Faiz's wife." Alys stopped at a light and glanced at him. He gave her a blank look. "Faiz? Poet, leader, communist, agnostic. His wife, Alys, was from England but she became a Pakistani citizen. Your meal came wrapped in her column."

"My apologies," Wickaam said.

"No need to apologize," Alys said as the traffic light turned green.

"True! It was a very good *kebab* roll."

Alys laughed.

"*Bol ke lab azad hain tere:* Speak, your mouth is unshackled,"

Wickaam said, quoting Faiz. "Of course I know who Faiz is. I was just playing with you."

"Thank God," Alys said. "I was like, oh no, a lawyer ignorant of his country's heritage."

"I think," Wickaam said, "you'll be pleased to know that historical preservation is one of my great passions. Have you been to England?"

"When I was much younger."

"With every step one is met by monuments to scientists, artists, thinkers. We Pakistanis have zero appreciation for anything except bargains and deals."

"Easier to commemorate history when you've been the colonizer and not the colonized."

"Whoa. I just meant history, not our purchases, should define us."

Alys gave a small smile. "I wrestle with how to incorporate history. Can any amount of good ever merit the interference of empire? Do we never speak English again? Not read the literature? Erasing history is not the answer, so how does a country put the lasting effects of empire in proper context? Not deny it, but not unnecessarily celebrate it."

Wickaam shrugged. "Best to concentrate on the future."

"But the future is built on a past, good *and* bad. It's troubling when someone takes a book and makes a shoddy film out of it and then comes the day when no one has read the book and everyone thinks the shoddy film is the original."

"Come now." Wickaam winked. "You have to admit that films are better than books."

"Never!" Alys said fiercely.

Wickaam raised his hands, surrendering. "Tell me about yourself, A-L-Y-S. What is your great passion? Are you single? Married? Children? Am I getting too personal?"

"It's all right. Single. Happily single, much to the disappointment of many who prefer that single women be miserable. And I don't know if it qualifies as a great passion, but I teach English literature."

"I knew I should have said I loved books! Now you'll hate me!"

"I won't hate you!" Alys exclaimed. "You were honest when most people would just say what's expedient."

They arrived at the acre. Alys parked by a ditch next to a meadow. The late afternoon had grown chilly, and she took her black shawl with silver lining, which she'd flung onto the back seat, and wrapped it around herself. She and Wickaam walked onto the land, an expanse of grass with the scent of fresh earth.

"What did you plan to do with this?" Wickaam said.

"My father was going to build his retirement home and homes for me and my four sisters. One big happy family till death do us part sort of a thing."

"That sounds so nice," Wickaam said. "It is a blessing to belong to a loving family."

"Happy families are all alike; every unhappy family is unhappy in its own way."

"*Zaberdast!* Wow!" Wickaam said.

"It's from *Anna Karenina*. Tolstoy's novel? Russian author?" Alys smiled. "There is a movie, I believe."

"I will watch it."

Laughing, they walked on, stopping at a small pond. A couple of boys were scrubbing buffaloes deep in muddy waters, shrieking as they flicked water at each other.

"Photo op," Wickaam said. "Poor little naked brown children bathing with domesticated beasts of burden in beatific nature: an authentic exotic snapshot of rural health and happiness. I should sell such pictures abroad to make my fortune."

"I'm sure the idea has already been signed, sealed, and delivered," Alys said. "And won the Pulitzer."

"Oh well," Wickaam said, "I'm too late to every party. Mediocre luck."

"Mediocre luck is what I have too and I'm quite happy." Alys's gaze followed a flame of a butterfly as it settled on a buffalo. "I mean, you might not be able to fly to London and Dubai for healthcare, but at least you're not suffering because you can't afford any."

"A-L-Y-S glass half-full. I like that you're content. Very lucky."

Alys blushed. "As content as a single girl in this country can be when all anyone ever asks her is why she isn't married yet, and they tell her she better hurry up before her ovaries die. It's you men who are lucky. You might be asked about your marriage plans, but everyone leaves you alone the second you mention career. If we women mention career, we're considered aberrations of nature or barren."

"That's because we bring home the bread and you bring home the baby and there's no biological clock on bread and there is one on baby."

"We can do bread too," Alys said. "And as for baby, science allows for babies at any age now."

"A-L-Y-S, surely you don't have to worry for a long time about any such thing."

"Flatterer!" Alys laughed. "I'm thirty, soon to be thirty-one."

"You are not."

"I am!"

"You don't look it."

"Good, but I don't really care. Age is just a number."

"That it is. I'm twenty-six."

They were quiet for a moment as they registered that he was younger than she.

"Well," Alys said, "now that you've seen the acre, I guess we should head back."

As they walked to the car, Wickaam said, "If you're free, Wagah border is not far from here, and if you haven't had the pleasure yet of witnessing the Pakistani–Indian closing-of-the-border-gates ceremony, it's truly an experience I recommend."

"My father took me as a birthday present ages ago," Alys said, "but I'd love to go again."

———

Alys and Wickaam chatted amiably about films and foods as she drove out of Lahore and entered the border village of Wagah, where the ceremony took place on the Pakistani side. On the Indian side, it took place in Attari village, which connected to the bigger city of Amritsar, home of the Sikh Golden Temple. Alys drove past sun-wrinkled women slapping dung patties to dry onto the outer walls of their mud huts, and she and Wickaam waved back at matte-haired children in bright sweaters who paused their play to wave at them.

At the venue, Alys parked outside the red-brick amphitheater overlooking the border gates. Last time she'd come, the bleachers had not been segregated, but now Wickaam entered the men's enclosure and she the women's. Climbing the stairs to the backmost row, she sat down at the end of an aisle beside a woman whose elaborate *mehndi* patterns on her palms and up her gold-bangled wrists indicated that she was a newlywed. A crow swooped over their heads, startling them. Together they watched it fly between the trees on the Indian side and the trees on the Pakistani side, its guttural *caw-caw-caw* reverberating freely in the open air.

The Pakistani and Indian spectators were sitting a stone's throw away from each other—or a flower's toss away, depending on international relations between the two countries on any particular day. The ceremony began. On the Pakistani side, a soldier beating a drum walked from the gates toward the audience. He was followed by mascot Chacha Pakistani, with his pristine white beard, holding aloft a Pakistani flag, the green representing the Muslim majority in the country and the white stripe the minorities. On this side, handheld flags fluttered green and white. On that side fluttered the tricolored green, white, and saffron flags. The crowds on both sides cheered and roared their patriotism.

"*Pakistan Zindabad!*"

"*Jai Hind!*"

Two giant soldiers from either side, rendered taller by their plumed turbans, stamped past each other in a mutual display of power. The two countries' flags, hoisted over their respective gates, were rolled down in unison, until the next morning, and, with that, the gates to the Wagah–Attari border crossing closed for the evening.

After more cheering and slogans, the audience headed out of the amphitheaters. Alys was milling outside the men's enclosure, on the lookout for Wickaam, with a crowd swarming around her, when she bumped into somebody.

"Oh, hello," Darsee said, his momentary confusion replaced by a quick smile. "What a surprise."

"I happened to be in the vicinity, believe it or not," Alys said, also flustered for a second, "and decided to see the ceremony."

"Bungles and I," Darsee said, nodding at Bungles, who appeared beside him, "are in charge of sightseeing for Nadir's wedding guests from abroad."

Alys exchanged congenial hellos with the guests: Thomas Fowle, Harris Bigg-Wither, and his girlfriend, Soniah. She asked them if they were enjoying Pakistan, and they assured her that they were loving it. Pakistan was beautiful, Thomas Fowle said. The people were so friendly, Harris Bigg-Wither said. It was far from the mess they saw on the news, Soniah said. Alys smiled. She pointed to the shopping bags in Soniah's hand.

"I see you managed to squeeze in my mother's favorite activity."

"Yes! We went to handicraft stores and open-air shops in A-naar-kaa-lee Bazaar. Darsee and Bungles were very helpful with the bargaining, they tell me. I got *choo-naa-ree doo-pa-tuss*, embroidered wallets, velvet-coated glass bangles, and some pure henna, different from the one I get back home in Addis."

"We've been to the Badshahi Mosque and the Sikh Temple," Bungles said. "Shalimar Gardens, the Wazir Khan Mosque, and now here."

"All in one day! I'm impressed!" Alys said. "But you must be exhausted."

"Our feet," Soniah said, pointing to her sneakers, "are killing us, but so worth it."

Bungles peered over Alys's shoulder. "Are your sisters with you?"

"No," Alys said, grinning at his supposedly subtle inquiry about Jena.

"There you are, Alys." Wickaam appeared, holding two bottles of chilled Pakola. "I was looking for you outside the women's section."

Darsee and Wickaam set eyes on each other. Darsee blanched. He looked as if he'd been kicked in the stomach. Wickaam turned red. He squawked a hello. Darsee turned and marched away. Bungles mumbled a weak hello in response to Wickaam's greeting and then, telling Alys he was looking forward to seeing her sisters at the NadirFiede *walima,* he hurried after Darsee, the visitors in tow.

Alys took her Pakola and sipped slowly from the neon-green soft drink. Clearly something was amiss. Should she ask Wickaam directly? But how to ask without being intrusive?

"Out of all the places to meet my dear cousin."

Alys nearly choked on her Pakola. "Valentine Darsee is your cousin?"

"My first cousin. Our mothers are sisters. How do you know him?"

Alys told Wickaam about meeting Darsee recently in Dilipabad at the NadirFiede wedding.

"I see," Wickaam said. "I went to school with Nadir too, you know. I'm invited to the *walima,* but I'm not sure I'll attend what with Darsee being there. There's the myth of close cousins and then there's Darsee and me. I bet you found him wonderful at the wedding."

"I certainly did not," Alys said. "No one did."

Wickaam brightened. "I'm not surprised. Darsee is a dreadful person who pretends to be a saint. He betrayed me. The betrayal is hard to talk about, though I'm perfectly happy to tell you."

"It would be my honor," Alys said, "to hear your story."

"Are you hungry?" Wickaam said. "Pak Tea House café is close to the law offices on our way back. Have you ever been there?"

———

Alys had always wanted to go to the illustrious Pak Tea House, established in 1940, and she eagerly followed Wickaam through the doors and into a snug hall. Men were seated at a few of the wooden tables. One was reading a newspaper, a cigarette smoldering in a glass ashtray. Another two were playing chess. Alys and Wickaam settled in a corner and Wickaam ordered chai and chicken patties. Alys gazed at the walls lined with photos of famous male novelists, poets, and revolutionaries who had once congregated here.

"Where are the women writers?" she asked.

"Upstairs, I think," Wickaam said. "So, how does it feel, Miss English Literature, to be sitting here surrounded by Local Literati Legends?"

"A little sad that they might have as much, if not more, to say to me than Baldwin or Austen, Gibran or Anzaldúa, but since I can't read Urdu fluently, though I do try, that's that. Anyway, hurrah for translations."

"Too much is lost in translation," Wickaam said. "I used to have an ayah, Ayah Haseena, whom I affectionately called Ayah Paseena. But while in Urdu the riff on Haseena/Paseena made perfect sense, in English trying to rhyme 'Beautiful' with 'Perspiration' was nonsense."

"You gain in translation by opening up a new world unto others," Alys said. "Anyway, a translation is better than nothing. We ourselves are works in translation, in a way."

"You sound like Valentine Darsee."

"Do not insult me." Alys frowned.

"My cousin *is* an insult!" Wickaam grinned. "I'm planning to write a novel to expose him, and not because it's fashionable these days to be a writer, ever since that Indian woman won the Booker Prize for the *Small Thing* something—"

"*The God of Small Things.*"

"Yes, that one," Wickaam said. "I haven't read it. I don't think I've read a novel since, oh, I don't know, years."

"You're planning to write a novel but you don't read them?"

"How hard can it be?" Wickaam said. "We all jot down words. Just a matter of finding time."

"Since we all have a brain, I plan to perform brain surgery as soon as I have a spare moment."

"You're funny," Wickaam said.

The waiter arrived with their order. Wickaam poured chai into their cups and Alys added a splash of milk to hers. She bit into the rich flaky pastry with the spicy chicken filling.

"Delicious! Listen, Wickaam, if you'd rather not tell me about Darsee—"

"I have nothing to hide. I'm an open book. In fact, I believe it's my duty to tell everyone what my cousin has done to me." He took a deep breath. "My maternal grandparents, as you know, are dey Baghs, descendants of royal gardeners and luminaries of this land. They had three daughters. The eldest is Beena, then Deena, and lastly Weena.

"BeenaDeenaWeena attended Murree Convent School, followed by a year of finishing school in Paris and then a year in London. When they returned to Pakistan, they married within months of each other. Beena married a first cousin, Luqman 'Lolly' dey Bagh, whom she'd always had her eye on. Deena married the son of a family friend her father held in great regard, Fauji Darsee, an army officer in the intelligence. And my mother, Weena, married a Pakistani-British man she'd met in London during an exhibition at the Serpentine Gallery. My father was not wealthy, but he'd studied philosophy and dreamed of becoming a great playwright, and my mother was happy to support him.

"BeenaDeenaWeena got pregnant within months of each other, and soon Weena had me, Deena had Valentine, and Beena had Annie. I have pictures of the three of us cousins in identical tartan dungarees, in a tree house, playing the piano, riding horses, that sort of thing. Our life was so nice; we used to say we never wanted to grow up. BeenaDeenaWeena were also happy, and they decided to fulfill a dream they shared—of being educators—and so they established a private school for girls, British School Group. Now it has branches all over the country. What! You teach in a British School branch! Small, small world.

"Do you remember the Ojhri arms-depot explosion in 1988, which killed and injured scores of civilians?" Wickaam blinked. "Both my parents and Valentine's father had been in the vicinity together. They all died.

"Valentine and I were fourteen years old. Deena Khala kept insisting she was my mother now, but no one can replace a mother. Beena Khala comforted Valentine and me as if our losses were equal. But Valentine had his mother and his four-year-old sister, Jujeena. I was the full orphan. Still, Valentine and I found ourselves crying shamelessly together and wishing revenge on everyone who told us boys don't cry and certainly not in public.

"Deena Khala was going mad with grief, just weeping all the time. She decided Pakistan reminded her of loss, and that a change of scenery would benefit us, and so we all moved to London. London was nice, except Valentine was growing sickeningly jealous of both his sister and me, for he couldn't bear to share his one remaining parent's love with anyone. Adding to Valentine's rage was his mother's frenetic dating, if 'dating' is what you'd call Deena Khala's revolving list of lovers. Darsee calls them 'unsuccessful relationships.' One day, Deena Khala declared she was in love with Ricky from Thailand and married him. They moved to Bangkok, and Deena Khala decided to take only Jujeena and Valentine with her.

"I was hurt, but I'd survived the death of both parents on the same day so this was nothing. I was sent to Bradford to live with my father's family. Everyone was very kind, but it was more out of duty than love.

"After three years, Deena Khala divorced Ricky because he wanted a second wife, and she came back to Pakistan. I also returned to live with them. But it was not the same. The closeness Valentine and I had once shared was gone. And Jujeena barely remembered me. Then we found out that Deena Khala had an advanced stage of cancer and had months to live. I was so sad. I thought this would bring us all closer. Instead, for all of their supposed love for my mother, both Beena Khala and Deena Khala tampered with my mother's will. I received no share in the British School Group, or anything. God only knows why they did this; I believe this question will haunt me forever. I am not materialistic, Alys, but to be cheated out of one's inheritance is a hard thing to bear. It's why I decided to be a lawyer. To make sure that others are treated fairly.

"My father's family had no clout compared to the dey Baghs, and everyone on my mother's side preferred to remain in Beena Khala's good books. I'll never forget one moment: I'd come to pay my last respects to Deena Khala on her deathbed. Beena Khala was there too when Deena Khala said, 'Jeorgeullah is our sister Weena's son. Let us give him his due.' But Valentine roared, 'Never!' And that was that. My own cousin, my buddy, my brother, if you will, betrayed me."

"I'm so sorry," Alys said, mortified. "I'm so sorry about the loss of your parents. Everything. I don't know what to say. My father went through a similar betrayal with his elder brother, and I understand your devastation."

"Thank you. Thank you very much. Your sympathy means so much to me."

"Darsee is even worse than I imagined," Alys said. "I can't believe he thwarted his mother's wish on her deathbed!"

"Believe it," Wickaam said, gazing into her eyes.

"I do!" Alys said, earnestly. "I most certainly do. But doesn't Darsee realize that money, power, prestige, it's all ephemeral, and that eventually we go to our graves with nothing and leave behind only memories?"

Chapter 11

*A*lys returned from her day with Wickaam in time to hear Nona sighing about having to make a night delivery and Ajmer being unwell. Alys volunteered to deliver the cake with Jena. Jena was making origami ornaments for the Christmas tree with the children, but she took one look at Alys and rose.

Alys backed the car out of the driveway and took a turn into the main street. She filled Jena in as fast as possible. Jena was thrilled that Alys had met Bungles and that he'd asked about her, but she was troubled at the report Jeorgeullah Wickaam had given of Darsee. If Darsee was as vile as his cousin claimed, then why was Bungles friends with him? Surely he must know about Darsee usurping Wickaam's inheritance.

"Perhaps," Alys said as she glanced at the address Jena was holding, "all decent people think Darsee is a decent person because he chooses to treat them decently."

"But, Alys," Jena said hesitantly, "just because a relative says something doesn't make it true. We know that!" A beggar tapped on her window and she rolled it down and handed him money. "I don't want to believe that Darsee is devious *or* that Wickaam has some ulterior motive for maligning him."

"You never want to believe ill of anyone," Alys said, driving around a bullock cart. "In a country where the national sport is backstabbing and one-upmanship, I don't know whether to hand you a trophy for sainthood or for stupidity."

"I don't want trophies," Jena said. "Take a right from here. All I'm saying is that we have no proof to back Wickaam's accusations and that a person should be innocent until proven guilty."

Alys rolled her eyes. "What was the house number again?"

At the house, Alys delivered the solar-system cake to the kitchen and took the remaining payment. She returned to the car and turned back onto the main road. A car cut in front of her. She honked. The man inside yelled, "Bloody lady drivers!"

Alys gave him the finger. "Jena, Wickaam has nothing to gain by lying to me about Darsee. And I trust him."

"How can you trust him? You just met him," Jena said, puzzled. "That's very unlike you, Alys."

"Wait till you meet him," Alys said, blushing. "You'll see."

Alys invited Wickaam to Nona and Nisar's Christmas party on the pretext that her father wanted to meet the man representing their Fraudia Acre case, but in her heart she wanted Jena to vet him. Wickaam accepted the invitation with an enthusiasm that surpassed mere lawyer-client relations, and Alys eagerly awaited his arrival.

On the morning of the party, the Gardenaars opened their Christmas gifts, attended church service, and returned to a festive house. A regal Christmas tree graced the drawing room, its boughs cheery with homemade baubles and store-bought trinkets, its fresh pine fragrance competing with the scents of roast lamb, leg of mutton, chicken *pulao,* mixed-vegetable *bhujia, aloo gosht, nargisi kofta,* shepherd's pie, and macaroni salad. Dessert was *seviyan,* vermicelli in sweet milk, and *zarda,* the saffron-yellow rice bursting with nuts, raisins, and orange peel, and, of course, Nona's Christmas cake, with the three wise men on caramel camels bearing their gold, frankincense, and myrrh, and pointing to an edible silver star, which would take them to baby Isa and his mother, Maryam.

At the party, Alys kept an eye on the door even as she and the children belted out "The Twelve Days of Christmas," followed by an improvised "The Twelve Days of Eid." A petite man entered. He stood at the threshold, one hand behind his back like a picture of Napoleon Bonaparte in a textbook. The man's dinner jacket hung off sloping shoulders, and his checkered tie lay lopsided over a satiny shirt. He scanned the room, his soft hooded eyes resting on teenage girls preparing a synchronized dance. He frowned before quickly composing his face into a benign smile and heading toward Nisar.

Nisar greeted the man, embraced the three children tagging behind him, and led them to his sisters for an introduction: Farhat Kaleen and his children—eighteen-year-old Fatima, fifteen-year-old Musa, and seven-year-old Isa.

Mrs. Binat and Falak were seated in front of a coffee table, and they paused their merry munching on dry fruit in order to smile benevolently at the man and his children. Mrs. Binat squinted. What in the world was he wearing? Polyester, if the patina on that shirt was anything to go by. The children were better dressed and greeted her and Falak politely.

"Pinkie, Falak," Nisar said, "surely you remember Farhat Kaleen, our cousin nine times removed from the branch of the family that moved to England so many moons ago."

Kaleen beamed brightly. Upon returning to Lahore, he'd made it a point to reconnect with relatives and so had begun the arduous process of winnowing out the worthy from the worthier. He was very pleased with Nisar Gardenaar's worth, and because Nisar was worthy, Kaleen was willing to overlook Nisar's sisters' unworthiness for having married losers. Still, better to be safe rather than sorry, for fortunes could literally change overnight. Apparently Falak's son,

Babur, was intelligent and had applied to prestigious colleges abroad, albeit as an agriculture major. His plan was to get in as a farmer and then switch majors.

Since Kaleen deemed it religiously inappropriate to shake hands with let alone hug women, even if they were his relatives, he proceeded to give Pinkie and Falak the most congenial of nods. He was, he told them, overjoyed to be reunited with them. He had a few memories from childhood, in particular visiting Lahore one summer when he was a young boy of ten and Pinkie sixteen and Falak seventeen. Did Pinkie and Falak remember being put in charge of baby-sitting him while his mother went to Ichhra Bazaar? Did they remember he found their lipstick-kissed posters of film stars and he'd threatened to tell their mother unless! "Unless what?" both sisters had cried. Unless, he'd replied, they let him tear out the picture of the girl in the red bikini in the lewd Western fashion magazine he'd also found tucked away in the drawer.

"That picture," Kaleen said, "allowed me an early window into the different types of women available in the world, and so I was able to see clearly at a young age which women were worthy of my time, attention, and earnings."

Mrs. Binat and Falak exchanged looks. So this is what had become of that snooping tattletale! Mrs. Binat vividly recalled his drawing-room preacher of a mother repeatedly proclaiming that if only Kaleen were a few years older than ten and Pinkie a few years younger than sixteen, then she would have gotten them engaged.

Kaleen, as if reading her mind, reminded Mrs. Binat of the same, and she giggled in embarrassed horror at the thought of ending up the wife of this balding, sartorially dismal man. Catching Mr. Binat's eye, Mrs. Binat shrugged coyly, for it was hardly her fault if admirers from the past popped up to remind her that she may very well have been their wife.

"And your wife is where?" Mr. Binat said, taking a step closer to Mrs. Binat even as he exchanged a bemused look with Alys. Alys and her sisters and Sherry had joined the circle around Kaleen, who seemed to be basking in the role of pistil to their petals. Mari, recognizing a kindred spirit with his talk of lewd magazines, was, for perhaps the first time in her life, experiencing the urge to make you-you eyes.

"Alas, my wife!" Kaleen put a hand on his heart. "My pious wife, Roohi, the good mother of my three children, passed away last year. She and I had gone for our evening stroll and she stopped to smell the flowers, and we suspect some insect entered her nose and from there her brain. Three days sick and on the fourth, poof, gone."

Amid a chorus of commiserations, Sherry's condolence rang out. She ruffled the seven-year-old motherless Isa's hair, smiling at him with all the kindness she contained.

"*Inna lillahi wa inna ilayhi rajioon.* From God we come and to God we return." Kaleen glanced resignedly at his daughter and sons. "But we miss her, and my poor children are left bereft of a most splendid mum."

He explained that he'd returned to Pakistan because it was difficult to raise obedient and virginal children in the promiscuous English *mohol,* atmosphere, with no motherly guiding light among the temptations of pubs and clubs. Also, he'd received a job opportunity too incredible not to accept, from a big-name patroness. She'd even introduced him to the most select of the select crowd, who in turn, all, by the grace of God, required his services in one capacity or another. Kaleen stood erect, hands clasped behind his back, and it was clear from his expectant expression he was waiting to be asked what he did.

Mr. Binat obliged. "What do you do?"

"I am," Kaleen stood tall on his tippy-toes for a second, "a physiatrist."

"A psychiatrist?" Lady said. "You'll have lots of business in this town, though no one will admit coming to you."

"Not psychiatrist!" Kaleen snapped. "Physiatrist. It is not the soul's trials I fix but the body's tribulations. Don't ask how much I make, because you will all faint."

"Faint in a bad way?" Alys half-smiled as she looked at her father, then glanced at the door. Where was Wickaam? He was quite late.

"In a good way." Kaleen frowned. "In a very good way. Is that not true, Nisar?"

"It is." Nisar nodded. "There is such high demand for physiatrists and pain management that Kaleen is setting up his private practice."

"Oh," Mrs. Binat said. She and Falak exchanged glances, acknowledging that if Farhat Kaleen was going to be an important member of society and mint money, then it was unwise to dismiss him. Mrs. Binat and Falak simultaneously moved to the edges of the sofa, and Mrs. Binat patted the center.

"Kaleen, you sit here and tell us all about your dearly departed wife, God rest her soul."

Kaleen perched between the two sisters; Mrs. Binat ordered Lady to introduce his daughter to the other teenage girls in the room, and she urged his sons to enjoy the appetizers, as long as they left plenty of room for the scrumptious dinner Nona had planned. The elder son settled on the edge of the couch and took a handful of pistachios. Sherry marched the younger son over to the children rehearsing carols for the show they planned to perform.

A sudden hush came over the room as all eyes turned to the entrance, where a dashing man stood with a bouquet of glitter-sprinkled red roses.

"Is that him?" Jena's eyes widened at Alys. "You told me he was decent, nice, and trustworthy, but I suppose you forgot to mention that he looks like a film star."

"I didn't forget," Alys said. "I just didn't see how it was relevant."

Alys hurried to greet Wickaam. He apologized profusely for being late—friends had coerced him into accompanying them to see the fairy lights strung all over town. Nona assured Wickaam he was not late at all, and Nisar added that he'd taken his own kids to see the city dolled up, although the decorations were for Pakistan's founding father, whose birthday fell on the same date as Christmas, a happy coincidence.

Wickaam complimented Nona on her bungalow, the Christmas décor, the tree, the lovely color of her walls and even lovelier shade of her burgundy lipstick, and, upon gleaning that the art on the walls was her own, he complimented Nisar on being the luckiest of husbands to have secured such a multitalented wife.

Alys introduced Jeorgeullah Wickaam to everyone. Wickaam could tell a good joke, and soon Nisar and the menfolk were slapping him on his back as if they were all old friends. Wickaam watched the children's Christmas show attentively. Afterward, to their delight, he mesmerized them with coin tricks. He helped the cook bring out dishes from the kitchen and arrange them on the dinner table around the green-and-gold-candle centerpiece. He praised Nona's menu, praised the cook's cooking, praised even the grocery stores from where the ingredients had been purchased. He was full of compliments for all the women. Someone's voice was angelic. Someone's hairstyle perfectly framed her face. Someone's shoes reminded him of royalty. He told Mrs. Binat that she was a stunner.

Mrs. Binat's heart fluttered. What a handsome man! What a solicitous man! What a gracious man! So conscientious of Alys! Thank God Alys had started to take a little more care of her looks. Bronzer dusted her cheeks and eyelids, and she was wearing a fitted embroidered *kurta* with bell sleeves that accentuated her bonny shoulders and waist. And, miracle of miracles, high heels.

When Lady put on film songs, every young person rose to dance. Mrs. Binat noticed that Kaleen did not look pleased at his daughter's participation. Mrs. Binat, in turn, was most gratified to see Wickaam force Qitty up. Considerate man! Amazing human being! True hero! In any case, Wickaam was paying special attention to each of her daughters, and Mrs. Binat prayed fervently that one of them would win the lottery of becoming Mrs. Jeorgeullah Wickaam.

Kaleen was feeling a bit green over having his thunder stolen by

this smooth-talking fine-looking devil. It occurred to him that perhaps the devil might be a suitable match for his daughter. He asked
Wickaam where he worked and how much he made. Wickaam informed everyone that he'd studied in New York, that he was back in
Pakistan and was working as a junior lawyer, and that he was just
starting out but he hoped, prayed, and planned to go places.

Hoping, praying, and planning to go places did not guarantee
getting anywhere, and Kaleen immediately lost interest. He wanted
to see his daughter married off as soon as possible, as per her dying
mother's final wishes, but he had standards, which did not include
struggling, penniless lawyers no matter how charismatic.

In her turn, Mrs. Binat tried to calculate how many years before
Wickaam would become a bigshot lawyer and which daughter of
hers might be able to wait for this inevitability. Such a beautiful man
was sure to ascend in the ranks based on looks alone. She concluded
Qitty was the perfect age and that Wickaam needed to stop hover-
ing over Alys and return to dancing with Qitty. Mrs. Binat's machi-
nations were interrupted by Kaleen's whispered disclosure that he
was on the lookout for a wife. He chucked his head diffidently and
informed her that he found her daughters bedazzling.

Kaleen had privately pondered why the Binat girls were still unmarried and concluded it must be because, given their great good
looks, they would only deign to entertain the most stellar of matches.
Rocking himself to his full height of five foot six, he believed that
with his promise of a thriving medical practice and immediate access
to the best of society, courtesy of his benefactress, he was on par as a
match with the best of the best.

"Your eldest daughter," Kaleen said, "is a vision of the houris in
heaven promised to men after death."

"My Jena," Mrs. Binat said proudly, "is getting engaged any day
now to Modest. You know, Modest *wallay*. The owners of Modest
Sanitary Company. Surely your daughter must be using their products? But . . ." Her hungry gaze settled on Alys. It would not be a
match to crow about, given that Kaleen was neither prince nor pres-

ident; however, getting this daughter married off to a future VIP
would be nothing to scoff at.

"My second daughter, Alys"—Mrs. Binat gave Kaleen a congenial smile as he rapidly morphed from nuisance into prospective
son-in-law—"is free for the plucking. Let me assure you she loves
children and will treat yours as if they dropped out of her own womb.
Frankly, you would be hard-pressed to find a more timid girl in all of
Pakistan. Also, she's a schoolteacher with excellent earning potential."

"No need for a wage-earning wife." Kaleen waved his fists. "A
woman's duty is to look after the children and run the household.
The only drawback to my success is that I am too busy and so require
a mother for my children. But, you see, I must marry someone who
will be kind to my children not just in front of me but also behind
my back. My children have grown up in an English atmosphere and
so they only know stepmothers from 'Cinderella,' 'Snow White,'
'Sleeping Beauty,' and other rubbish fairy tales in which stepmothers
want to murder the children. I tell them not to fear, for I will only
marry a quality Pakistani girl. Also," Kaleen confided, grinning rue-
fully, "between you and me, we know men have needs that good
women simply do not, and I am but a man."

"I believe Alys will prove to be exceptional with manly needs as
well as motherhood," Mrs. Binat said. "But, Kaleen, you know how
even in arranged marriages these days, young girls first want to get
to know the boy. Therefore, I suggest that for the time being we hold
off mentioning marriage to Alys. Instead, I recommend you endear
your good self to her. In fact, if you have no New Year's plans, you
must accompany us to a most coveted *walima*."

"New Year's!" Kaleen's toothbrush brows bristled. "You mean Sa-
tan's special holiday, barring Halloween. New Year's is a festivity that
encourages the triumvirate of 'B's: *Beygarithi, Behayai, Besharmi,* Im-
modesty, Indecency, Shamelessness."

"True," Mrs. Binat said, blinking, for she quite enjoyed a New
Year's get-together and the subsequent welcoming in of the new

year. Alys had lectured her one year about how time was a man-made concept and that no miracles were going to occur simply because a clock announced that December 31 had turned into January 1. Mrs. Binat prayed that, once wedded and bedded, her daughter would turn into a less opinionated and more cheerful person.

"Oho! Not a New Year's party but a *walima* on New Year's Eve," Mrs. Binat stressed. "After that we will be returning to Dilipabad, and you must visit us at your earliest convenience and stay with us."

"Done deal," Kaleen said, pleased.

"Also, my daughter, Mari, suffers from asthma, and I would be so obliged if you would check her."

"My pleasure," Kaleen said. Occupational hazard, and she'd not even cursorily mentioned payment, but then that was relatives for you.

"Oh, but Alys's health is superb. Do look at her." Mrs. Binat settled her eyes on Alys, and so did Kaleen. "How decorously she laughs. How daintily she crosses her legs. Such a meek creature, my little Alys, no one meeker to be found in Pakistan—therefore, I urge you again that until I give you the green light, not a word about your intentions."

"Of course," Kaleen said, proceeding to the dinner table with sudden gusto. "I understand and I approve of Alys's shyness, as well as the fact that in today's world it is right and fitting that she must get to know me before marriage. But for me, Pinkie, your assurance that Alys is demure and decent is enough of a guarantee that she will make a righteous wife and mother."

After the guests departed, the family settled down over fresh cups of chai to subject the evening to a postmortem. It was decided that Wickaam was the great hit of the evening—a pity about his lack of wealth but, oh, those dashing looks—and Kaleen was the great miss of the evening, income galore but a dud looks-wise.

"Farhat Kaleen has his own appeal," Mrs. Binat stressed to Nona and Nisar until they deigned to nod. Mari agreed with her mother, but she kept quiet.

"Mummy!" Lady said, "he's yuck-*thoo*! His nose looks like a popcorn! And he's so unstylish. Why did his kids let him dress like a clown?"

Mrs. Binat reminded Lady that sometimes parents did not listen to children and—she looked sharply at Alys—children also refused to benefit from their parents' wisdom.

"Qitty," Mrs. Binat said, "did you see how much attention Wickaam paid to you?"

Qitty nodded shyly.

Lady snorted. "He told me that I was a glamour queen destined for tremendous things."

Hopefully, Mrs. Binat thought as she rose to go to bed, the wait for Wickaam to become a Rich Man and propose to Qitty would not be too long, and at least Alys would not die in waiting for her Prince Charming, because Farhat Kaleen was truly eager to make her his blushing bride-to-be sooner rather than later.

Chapter 12

On the evening of the NadirFiede *walima,* Mrs. Binat opened the door to Farhat Kaleen arriving a full hour earlier than departure time. He was ablaze in sickeningly sweet cologne and looking, he believed, very sexy in a khaki suit, fuchsia shirt, and a white-and-fuchsia-striped tie.

Alys had chosen to wear the sari she'd refused at the *mehndi* ceremony. It was the color of Kashmiri pink tea, and Mrs. Binat couldn't help but conclude that the coincidence of Farhat and Alys both wearing shades of pink was a sign from God that they were a match made in heaven.

Jena looked striking in a peach *zardozi kameez* and seed pearl embroidered open front gown paired with a white silk *thang pajama,* a *shahtoosh* shawl, and Ganju *jee's* rubies. The rest of the girls looked their best in lavenders, yellows, and greens, though, on second thought, Mrs. Binat decided she was never going to dress Qitty in green again. She looked like a raw mango.

So it was just as well that Wickaam had sent Nona a thank-you note for the Christmas party with the message that, unfortunately, he would be unable to attend NadirFiede's *walima*. Qitty was understandably upset, and all the girls were miffed. Mrs. Binat herself was quite peeved at being deprived of his company, and she kept snapping at Mr. Binat to stop whining about not wanting to go: Even if his brother and sister-in-law were at the *walima*, he was to merely nod at them and move on.

When it was time to leave, Mrs. Binat put the Quran on Jena's head and read the Ayatul Kursi—not that there was doubt in anyone's mind that tonight, at NadirFiede's final event, Bungles must propose. Since Kaleen had his driver and car—the latest model of an excellent make, Mrs. Binat was gratified to see—she instructed Jena and Alys to ride with him. To her annoyance, Sherry climbed in with them—not that it really mattered, because no one in their right mind was going to give Sherry Looclus a second look, despite the poor thing having dressed up as best as she could in those tacky puffed sleeves and that greasy lipstick.

Mr. and Mrs. Binat, Lady, Qitty, and Mari got into Nisar's car with Ajmer, directions in hand, and they set off for the *walima*, which was to be held at Nadir Sheh's family's farmhouse. In this case, "farmhouse" meant a country villa surrounded by meadows without a single animal, barnyard or otherwise, to speak of. Since the Binats were arriving in good cars, Mrs. Binat insisted on idling at the gate in order to be noticed. Alys finally got out of Kaleen's car, grateful that the ride was over. Kaleen had talked at her the whole forty-five minutes about how many lives he'd saved, when all she'd wanted to do was mourn Wickaam's decision to stay away on account, no doubt, of horrid Darsee.

As soon as they entered the gates, Mrs. Binat saw Principal Naheed on the red carpet leading up to the farmhouse, with her husband, Zaleel, and Gin and Rum dressed in flapper-style long frocks. Dear God, Mrs. Binat thought, the twins looked like shredded streamers.

"Girls look great!" she said, greeting Naheed. "QaziKreations?"

Naheed nodded and complimented the Binat girls' attire. Formalities complete, everyone marveled at the abundance of flowers wherever they looked. The villa's main gate and boundary walls were strung with thick floral ropes. A tunnel of candlelit flowers engulfed the brick path from the gate leading to the driveway and a mini-fountain awash in petals. Guests turned from the mini-fountain into a dazzling floral pergola, which took them to the garden and into a tent of flowers, an Eden within an Eden, which meant, Alys couldn't help but think, there must be snakes too.

"This is what being in a bouquet must smell like," Mrs. Binat said as she made her way under the floral canopy toward forest-green velvet sofas.

Nadir and Fiede were wearing matching yellow-and-black ensembles designed by Qazi, for which, it was rumored, the designer had charged enough to enjoy at least five sumptuous holidays.

"Are NadirFiede supposed to be bumblebees?" Lady asked as she took an effervescent mint drink from a floral tray.

"I think," Mrs. Binat replied, squinting, "the newlyweds are sunflowers."

"Mummy," Alys said, "I think you just might be right."

"I'm always right," Mrs. Binat said, "even if you and your father seldom acknowledge it."

Mr. Binat barely registered his wife's complaint, on the lookout as he was for Goga and Tinkle, his ears buzzing so badly he could barely hear Kaleen's prattle.

Kaleen was admiring the fortune the Shehs must have spent to create this plucked paradise. That the Binats were invited to this VIP to-do had duly raised Barkat "Bark" Binat in his esteem. This was proof that Pinkie's family were not absolute nobodies, and Kaleen shed any doubts over his upcoming nuptials to Alysba Binat. He glanced at Alys. His bride-to-be looked like a rosebud tonight, one he could not wait to have and to hold. She was a little on the dusky side, but no matter; secretly he thought wheatish women equally as attractive as whitish ones. He wished he hadn't promised Pinkie Binat to keep his betrothal to Alys a secret, for he wanted this illustrious gathering to know that she belonged to him. He wondered what sweet nothings Alys was whispering into her friend's ear—what was her name?

Alys noticed Farhat Kaleen giving her another syrupy smile. The thought alone that he may have a crush on her was disturbing, and she focused on the stage. It was fashioned like a bower, on which Nadir and Fiede sat enthroned as if they were Shakespeare's fairy royalty, King Oberon and Queen Titania, greeting their florally smitten guests. Alys looked around for other characters from *A Midsummer Night's Dream*. There were Bottoms galore, wearing ass heads, a category into which she dropped Kaleen. Pucks abounded too, looking for mischief to spread between married couples, be they happy or unhappy, simply for their own amusement. Alys was sure she spied a couple of Helenas, the plain young girl who longs for love but can't find anyone to woo her. She pointed them out to Sherry, who was quick to remark that she was a Helena and she was sure Qitty felt like one too.

"I wonder," Alys sighed, "how many Emma Bovarys are here, sick of their rash marriages, and how many of Wharton's May Wellands, guarding their 'property.' And how many girls here are tomboys like Jo March in *Little Women* and what will happen to make them realize they are only women in a man's world. And how many of those women will then seek justice for that unfairness in the occult, like the mother in Zora Neale Hurston's story 'Black Death.'"

Alys pointed to the gathering of Daisy Buchanans, that spoiled little rich girl from *The Great Gatsby*. How many Myrtle Wilsons were here, nursing the wounds left from a Daisy Buchanan's emotional hit-and-run? Alys remarked that too many of the men in this room were Tom Buchanans and Meyer Wolfsheims, who believed they owned the women and most of the men, and ruled the world.

"As for Jay Gatsby," Alys said, "he's obviously a Wickaam."

"Jay Gatsby is a crook," Sherry said.

"He is a man turned crooked by society."

"And who are you?" Sherry asked as they made their way on the red carpet–covered lawn to congratulate the bride and the groom.

"I'm the omniscient narrator and observer in Austen's novels."

"I think," Sherry said, smiling mischievously, "you're that character who says no but ends up falling into a yes despite herself: You are Elizabeth Bennet."

"Elizabeth Bennet," Alys said, "had to marry Fitzwilliam Darcy, and he her, because Jane Austen, their creator-god, orchestrated it so. And there would be no Charlotte Lucas today because marrying for financial security is no longer the only choice she'd have. Thankfully we don't live in a novel, and in real life if I met someone as stuck-up as Mr. Darcy, I'd tell him to pack his bags, because there would be nothing that could endear me to such a snob, least of all the size of his estate. My views would frighten away a man like Mr. Darcy, who ultimately wants a feisty wife but also one who knows her place—"

"Excuse me—"

Alys stilled at the voice. Turning, she came face-to-face with Valentine Darsee. She reddened. Had he heard her? Not that she cared.

"May I help you?" she asked.

"You certainly may," Darsee said, nodding a polite hello at Sherry. "I wanted to give you this," and Alys, momentarily flustered, accepted the book he handed her, his fingertips brushing hers.

"*Sunlight on a Broken Column*," he was saying. "You said you hadn't read it, remember?"

"I don't remember," Alys said, though she remembered very well.

"I'd like to know what you think about it," Darsee said.

"I don't know when I'll be able to get to it," Alys said, and then added stiffly, "Thank you."

The girls walked on and, as soon as they were out of earshot, Sherry propelled Alys toward a secluded spot under a lantern fashioned of flowers.

"That man is definitely interested in you," Sherry said.

"Oh please." Alys was thankful Sherry hadn't caught their accidental touch. "Who cares."

"If you play your cards right, and he marries you, that would be the greatest coup."

"*I* wouldn't marry him. He's unmarriageable."

"You'd become the owner of the British School Group, and instead of Principal Naheed hauling you into her office, you'd get to tell her to behave."

"Even vengeance could not entice me to marry that man. Were Darsee to suddenly declare I was the most attractive woman in the world and not stupid, I would still not marry him."

"You've really got to get over that. He's a *real* catch and Jena is right, you weren't meant to hear what he said about you. Had you not heard it, you'd be delirious with joy that a fish like him is swimming toward your hook."

"I would not," Alys said. "You didn't see the way he cold-shouldered Wickaam at the border ceremony. For all Darsee's assets, he's still a jerk."

"I wish a jerk like that would fall in love with me." Sherry sighed. "You and Jena are so lucky. She'll marry Bungles and you'll marry Darsee. Your mother is right: All you need is one rich man to become besotted with your looks and, *jantar mantar,* abracadabra, your destiny is changed. Takes so much more for those of us without looks. So unfair."

"It is unfair. Especially when good-looking people complain how unfair it is that no one sees beyond their looks." Alys laughed dryly. "*Inshallah,* Jena will certainly marry Bungles. But there will be no such ending for me."

"I know why you are saying that," Sherry said. "It's that Wickaam. *You* are besotted by *his* looks."

"I don't get besotted by looks," Alys said. "You should know that much about me after ten years of friendship, Sherry."

"I know that you are human. But as your friend and well-wisher, let me advise you to put Wickaam aside and focus on grabbing Darsee."

"Will you please not use that disgusting word? You sound just like my mother."

"Grab it, grab it," Sherry joked, half seriously. "Grab Valentine Darsee because, trust me, he wants to be grabbed by you. Alys, listen to me: Wickaam seems nice, but Darsee has a lifestyle that only real money can buy."

"Money is not everything. And too many rich men have a tendency to be horrid because they think money stands in for character, decency, and smarts."

"Money is a safety net for everything that may not work out in life."

"Not if your husband is a control freak or a stingy hoarder."

"I really don't think Darsee is either. You two even share a love of reading."

"I don't want to share a love of anything with him, thank you," Alys said. "And luckily for both Wickaam and Darsee, I'm not a gold digger. I refuse to seek a rich *roti*. I'm going to make my own money and live happily ever after on my own terms."

"Tch," Sherry said. "I can understand why your mother is always so irritated by you. You're a teacher. In Dilipabad. And I know you don't look it or care, but you are getting older by the day."

"Would singledom be acceptable if I were still twenty and owned my own thriving business?"

"No."

"Thought so." Alys dropped *Sunlight* into the large cloth bag she was carrying instead of a delicate evening purse, much to her mother's exasperation.

Dinner was announced and the two friends joined the surge of guests going toward the buffet in the garden. It was a feast of prawns, by far the most expensive delicacy in Pakistan at the moment. *Tan-*

doori prawn. Prawn skewer kebabs. Grilled prawns. Prawn *pulao*. Penne prawns. Deep-fried prawns. Prawn *jalfrezi*. Prawn *korma*. Sweet-and-sour prawns. Butterfly prawns. Prawn fried rice. Prawn-stuffed *paratha*. Prawn cutlets. Prawn salad.

"Okay, Nadir Sheh, we get it!" Alys said as she and Sherry joined the buffet line. "You can afford all the prawns in the ocean. And I'd thought the flowers ostentatious."

"I love prawns," Sherry said, taking heaping spoonfuls of each entrée. "I've only ever eaten them once, and even then we only got four each. This is why you marry rich: an endless array of prawns whenever you want and prepared however you want."

"I think it's selfish!" Alys spooned a small serving of prawn salad onto her plate. "What about the people who don't like prawns? Or have allergies?"

"How sad to be allergic to prawns," Sherry said, as she followed Alys to the seating area, where guests were having trouble setting their plates down among the floral table décor.

Kaleen came to their rescue and led them to a table he'd already cleared of flowers as best as he could.

"Aha," Kaleen said, pointing to Sherry's full plate and then to his own, "I see we have prawns in common."

"Yes," Sherry said, "we do."

"Dear sweet Alys," Kaleen said, "your plate is shamefully empty. Allow me to pick prawns for you in the hope that my choice will please your palate."

"Oh!" Alys stood up abruptly. "Many thanks for your offer, Kaleen Sahib, but I see a friend I must talk to. Sherry here will be more than happy to keep you company." Alys smiled wickedly at Sherry. "Please do discuss all the prawns you have in common."

Valentine Darsee, in the buffet line, choosing a single prawn from each entrée, watched Alys rise from a table and stride across the tent.

How gracefully she walks in her sari, he thought, and balances her plate at the same time.

"What are you thinking, babes?" Hammy said, appearing by Darsee's side as she and Sammy and Jaans cut the buffet line to stand with him. There were a few murmurs but, since everyone hopes to cut some line sometime in life, no one made much of a fuss.

"Not thinking anything," Darsee said.

"I love prawns," Hammy said, happily ladling penne prawns onto her plate.

"I'm quite partial to prawns myself," Darsee said, "but what about the people who are allergic or don't like them?"

"Sammy doesn't like prawns," Hammy said.

"Shame on you, Sammy-whammy," Jaans said to Sammy, "to dislike prawns in the face of such abundance. Darsee, did you hear Nadir's honeymoon plans? I told him, '*Cheethay*, leave some countries for another time,' but, no, he wants to take Fiede on a world tour she'll never forget. Wife, when are you taking me on a tour I'll never forget?"

"When you deserve it." Sammy glared at Jaans. "I hate seafood."

"Eat the *naan*." Jaans shoved bread at her. "Since you're being ungrateful, it's all you deserve."

"I'm getting dessert." Sammy flung the bread onto Jaan's full plate. "Thankfully, you can't force prawns into desserts."

"Let's check on Bungles first," Hammy said. "The mother might have devoured him by now. Fortunately, Jena herself is standoffish; otherwise that brother of ours seems ready to be a doormat."

"Jena is just shy," Jaans said. "I've known girls like her. Too scared they might say something wrong and end up losing the proposal."

"There is no proposal," Hammy said.

"And," Sammy added, "don't you dare put such a notion into Bungles's head, Jaans."

"I don't have to," Jaans said. "He's not a child. What Brother Bungles is, though," Jaans made a rude face, "is a doormat, a *zun mureed*, a woman worshipper who will be perfectly happy to be a *joru ka ghulam,* a slave to his wife. He'll put her on a pedestal and expect them to be best friends."

Sammy made a wistful face; she wouldn't mind an uxorious husband for herself.

"So what?" Darsee asked Jaans.

"So," Hammy said grimly, "all the more reason Bungles needs to marry someone we can mold to our liking."

"That's disgusting," Darsee said. "Would you like to be molded?"

"I'd like to see someone try," Hammy said, gazing into Darsee's eyes.

"Brother Bungles," Jaans said, "is fully aware how lucky he is to have found a girl as beautiful as Jena Binat still single."

"Have you ever wondered," Sammy sneered, "why Jena the Beautiful is unmarried?"

"Why?" Jaans asked.

"Yes, why exactly?" Darsee said.

"Far be it for me to indulge in gossip," Hammy said, looking up at Darsee, "but Sammy and I have it on excellent authority that her mother belongs to a very bad family."

"What are you talking about, Hammy?" Darsee frowned.

"They say," Sammy said, "Pinkie Binat's ancestors come from a background of prostitution. Pre-partition, but still."

"Who says?" Darsee said.

"Everyone," Hammy said. "They say it wasn't even at the level of a courtesan but, rather, a cheap back-alley tart. Honestly, before I began investigations into the mother's family for Bungles's sake, I didn't even know there was a hierarchy of prostitutes. I thought they were all equal."

"Where's the proof they come from that?" Darsee said.

"Tinkle Binat told me. Why would she malign her own family?"

"Because," Darsee said, "the Binat brothers are estranged."

"Estrangement," Sammy said, "doesn't mean you concoct dirty ruinous rumors about your relatives."

"Where's concrete proof," Darsee said, "that any of us truly descends from our claims?"

"I'll give you proof in the Binats' case," Hammy said. "That mother of theirs might dress well, but the second she opens her mouth her style of talking, her demeanor, everything, speaks of an unsavory ancestry. She's all raspy and graspy like vamps and prostitutes in films. Like mother like daughters, I say, though you can detect the lack of breeding the most in Lady."

"Tone of voice is hardly proof," Darsee said. He put down his plate.

"It's not *not* proof," Hammy said. "There's nothing to disprove they aren't slut spawn."

"What a pleasant phrase," Darsee said. "Is it original?"

"Thank you! Yes!" Hammy said. "Now you'll understand why Sammy and I have always felt so sorry for the Binat sisters. They can dress like Audrey Hepburn as much as they want, but it's not going to confer class on them. Tinkle Binat told me"—Hammy lowered her voice for effect—"that Pinkie's lineage was the real reason for the brothers' rift. Goga Binat demanded his brother divorce her, but Bark Binat refused on account of his five daughters, and so what choice did Goga and Tinkle have but to disinherit them and banish them to D-bad."

"Honestly," Sammy said, "you should always tell the truth about your origins, especially in matters matrimonial, or be ready to face the consequences."

"If this is true," Darsee said, "then it was good of Bark Binat to stick by his wife and daughters even if it meant losing his inheritance. They're not her daughters alone. They're his too."

Hammy and Sammy exchanged a look.

"That puts a nice spin on the whole wretched business," Sammy said.

"Look, Val," Hammy said, "you have to knock some sense into Bungles's head. Jena will not do. Even if my entire family was willing to overlook Jena's hailing from a low-class prostitute, which we aren't, her family has issues. They are unsuitable girls from an unsuitable family."

"True." Darsee pursed his lips. "True."

Alys fled Kaleen's cloying overtures, only to find him following her and Sherry following him. Before she'd even set her plate down at her family's table, he was inquiring yet again if he could select her prawns. Alys's annoyed gaze met Jena's beseeching one: Bungles was sitting next to her. He was talking about whale-watching off the California coast and the aurora borealis in Alaska, two destinations on the NadirFiede honeymoon itinerary, which was available at each table in lamination for everyone's viewing pleasure. It was clear from Jena's face that he had yet to propose and that she was beginning to panic.

Dinner was fast coming to an end and the *walima* ceremony to a close; if he did not propose soon, there would be no more events at which he could do so. Yet Bungles did not seem like a man about to propose. He was busy eating *falooda,* taking dainty bites of the vermicelli in rose syrup and milk, all the while smiling at Jena with what anyone would only describe as utter devotion. No wonder Jena was losing her mind. Their mother was frantic, Alys could tell, from the way her eyes were darting all over Bungles, as if darts could prick him into action.

And then there was her father. Goga and Tinkle Binat had indeed arrived with great pomp and show but, luckily, boasting to all of the million weddings at which their appearance was vital, had left early. Mr. Binat had been terrified at encountering them and yet, when they'd completely ignored him, he'd become despondent. He sat now, his hand cupping his chin, utterly dejected and asking, every so often, what he could possibly have ever done to deserve his brother's conduct.

Alys would have ignored her family's behavior as usual were it not for Darsee, who kept walking by them to get to the buffet. Each time she saw him, she thought of the book in her bag, his fingers on hers. Why did he keep coming this way? The one time Bungles had gone to the toilet, Mrs. Binat loudly instructed Jena that, the second she became Mrs. Bungles, she was to search for equally suitable boys for her sisters. Another time Darsee passed them, Lady's soda spilled down her bosom, which she'd patted dry most indecorously. The last time Darsee had descended on the buffet, Mari was giving yet another female guest with a bare midriff a lecture on how women should not be upset over Islam's injunction to dress chastely, because the same was commanded of men.

From the corner of her eye, Alys spied Darsee coming their way again, this time with Hammy, Sammy, and Jaans.

"Hello, all." Jaans waved at the Binats. "How is everyone? Enjoying the prawns?"

Kaleen turned to the new arrivals. "My good name is Farhat Kaleen. I am a recent England return. I am a physiatrist."

"Psychiatrists are more than welcome in this loony bin of a Lahore," Jaans said.

"Physiatrist," Kaleen stressed. "Physiatrist. I deal with rehabilitation of the body in the event of accidents and chronic pain, and I am setting up private practice."

There was a lull before Bungles took it upon himself to introduce his group.

"Valentine Darsee?" Kaleen's eyes grew huge. "Nephew of Begum Beena dey Bagh?"

"Guilty as charged," Darsee said.

"I have been longing to meet you, sir!" Kaleen grabbed Darsee's hand and swung it vigorously. "Your 'unty Beena is my great benefactress. Have you guessed who I am? I am your cousin Annie's doctor! Dr. Farhat Kaleen. It is thanks to me that she has made startling improvements. By God, when I first saw her I thought she would not last the night, and now she sits upright and is showing an interest in fashion shows again. I've been encouraging her to return to modeling—why not, why should a cane stop her or anybody? Your

dear cousin Annie calls me her miracle worker. Though I must say I
have a model patient in Annie. Ha-ha. Model patient, no pun intended. Valentine Darsee! Such a pleasure to meet you! Had I known
I was going to meet you here, I would have . . ." Kaleen stopped for a
second, unsure of what he would have done differently. "I trust we
will be seeing much of each other, for, given Annie's health, I am
frequently at your 'unty's most grand estate, the Versailles of Pakistan."

Darsee extracted his hand from Farhat Kaleen's grip and perfunc-
torily announced, "It's time to go."

"Say goodbye to your friends, baby bro," Hammy said. "Up. Now."

"What's the rush?" Bungles said, gazing at Jena, who was staring
dully into her lap.

"The rush," Sammy said, "is we have to get ready for Fazool and
Moolee's New Year's party."

Bungles rose, but before relief could settle permanently on
Hammy and Sammy's faces, he invited Jena to the New Year's party:
Could she go?

Chapter 13

Hammy smacked Bungles's shoulder once again for good measure and mimicked Mrs. Binat, who'd risen like a peacock spreading its fan: "'Of course Jena may go; she's all yours. But surely you cannot expect young Jena to go without a chaperone, so she will be happy to be accompanied by all her sisters.'" And then she imitated Bungles's response to Mrs. Binat: "'But of course, I meant to invite them all.'"

"Why the hell did you invite Jena to begin with?" Sammy snarled. They were in Darsee's car on their way to the New Year's party, having gone to their homes to change out of their wedding finery and into party clothes, which, for Hammy and Sammy, meant the skimpiest outfits the current state of their slim figures would allow.

"Your puppy-like behavior is bad enough," Hammy said, "but that mother has apparently been informing the world that there is soon to be a wedding."

"You're stringing Jena along, Bungles," Sammy said, "and that's not very nice."

"Let Brother Bungles have his fun," Jaans said. "Jena's an adult!"

"Jena *is* an adult!" Hammy said to Bungles. "She's thirty-two years old to your twenty-five. Seven years' age difference."

"She could be a hundred years older than me for all I care," Bungles said, a bit cowed by the glares his sisters and even Darsee were giving him, though he glared back. "And I certainly don't care who her mother is or where she comes from."

"We care," Hammy said, "so that's that."

"It's not just the mother factor," Darsee said. "I don't believe Jena Binat is interested in you. She sits there without a smile. She barely says two words when you ask her a question. If she's a gold digger, she's not a very good one."

"Perhaps," Bungles said in a hesitant voice, "she's not a gold digger at all."

"Her mother is a gold digger!" Hammy said. "'Like mother, like daughter,' they say."

"Why should I listen to 'they'?" Bungles asked. "Who is 'they'?"

"*We* are they," Hammy and Sammy thundered simultaneously.

"But I like Jena," Bungles said. "I like her very much."

"That's because the mother has put a hex on you," Hammy said. "I can't believe you invited Jena and her sisters to the party. Fazool is going to freak. You know how exclusive and classy she keeps her parties. The Binat sisters probably can't believe their lucky stars. Let's hope their car gets a flat tire and we are spared all five frights."

For perhaps the first time in his life, Ajmer did not get lost on the way to an address, and so it happened that the Binat sisters arrived at the party at the same time that Darsee's car did. As Bungles's and Jena's eyes met, Alys was finally convinced that her mother was right: Bungles meant to propose at the stroke of midnight. There could be no other meaning behind the tender look he was giving Jena, who, in her turn, looked away from him, clearly overcome.

The group entered the gate to the mansion and walked to the front door, behind which music was playing. The door opened and

Hammy and Sammy were air-kissed by a slinky woman in a silver halter top and QaziKreations' most expensive *mohti*, the miniskirt *dhoti* shimmering with semiprecious stones; a man beside her grinned toothily when he saw them all.

"Amazing outfits! Love the shoes!" the woman said, looking Hammy and Sammy up and down as they tottered in red-soled black platforms. Hammy was in black leather biker shorts, a red lace bustier, and a black mesh bolero, and Sammy was in red leather biker shorts, a black lace bustier, and a red mesh bolero.

"Thank yous, thank yous," Hammy-Sammy said, complimenting Fazool's *mohti* and her red-soled nude Louboutins in return. Hammy introduced her to the Binats.

"Sisters Binat, these are our darling friends, Fauzia 'Fazool' Fazal and her husband, Hamid 'the Moolee' Fazal," Hammy said. "Friends, these are the five Binat sisters. Bungles graciously invited them. I hope you don't mind."

Fazool's eyes narrowed as she took in Mari's local garb, so out of place at such a happening event as her New Year's bash, at Qitty in a crushed-velvet black tent, at Lady in white jeans and a T-shirt that said UNMARRIAGEABLE in glitter and showed off her ample cleavage. Fazool glanced at Alys, whose chest also caused her envy. As for Jena—why did God bless some girls with so much beauty? Oh well, Fazool was rich and up there in the social register and clearly they were not, so she gave them the vapid smile reserved for nobodies who could not be completely ignored and said, "Do come in."

"Yes! Do!" Moolee ran his fingers through the curly chest hair crawling out of his half-buttoned Versace shirt. "The more girls, the merrier. Bungles, Darsee, Jaans, good to see you all. Hammy-Sammy, as usual—looking ready to mingle and tingle."

Moolee gave Hammy and Sammy lingering hugs. He turned to the Binats with thirsty eyes. "We look forward to mingling and tingling with you all, don't we, Fazool? Now, which one of you pretty sisters wants to hug me first?"

Before the Binat sisters could reply, Fazool laughed as if Moolee had cracked a great joke and then she adroitly turned her husband around, pushed him inside toward the party, and led everyone else indoors.

"What delights has Moolee been smoking?" Darsee asked Fazool as they entered the marble entrance with its winding staircase next to a piano with a vase full of blue twigs.

"Who knows?" Fazool said. She led them through the entrance and into a glass-paneled corridor alongside the garden and toward the music. "Since it's Happy New Year, I've let him off the leash a little." She smiled gallantly. "And he has let me off my leash too. Fun! Fun! Fun! For me, for him, for everyone. Anyway, he's harmless, Valoo, you know that!" Fazool linked arms with Darsee.

"Val, you've become way too somber," Jaans said tipsily, linking arms with Fazool. "You need to learn to live and let live."

Darsee shrugged. "Live and let live does not mean living conse-quence free."

Jaans sighed. "You used to be so much fun before you went to America, *behen chod*, sisterfucker."

"Mind your language, Jaans," Darsee said, as Bungles rested a calming hand on his shoulder. "I don't care how much you've had to drink."

"Ja-ans!" Sammy pouted. "How many times should I tell you not to not say *behen chod*, sisterfucker. It's so insulting to women. Use your own gender and say *bhai chod*, brotherfucker."

Alys glanced at her sisters. Lady was thrilled. Mari looked about to faint. Jena and Qitty looked shaken at how casually such exple-tives were being bandied about. Even Bungles was looking embar-rassed and Darsee's jaw was clenched.

"Come on now, people," Fazool said, laughing, "no fighting on New Year's. That's a rule. The party is in the living room, the drawing room, and out by the swimming pool."

Alys watched as Bungles whisked Jena away and Sammy, Jaans, Fazool, Moolee, and Hammy, pulling Darsee along, gamboled toward a room pulsing with disco lights. Lady and Qitty followed them, as did Mari, who'd only come in order to observe firsthand the misguided partiers of Pakistan, so that she would know exactly which preaching methods to employ in the future to return them to the *sirat-ul-mustaqim*, the path of the righteous.

Alys followed her sisters into the disco room. It was full of men and women lounging on settees. All nursed obese glasses of wine, cigarette smoke clouding every face. A few shimmied on the makeshift dance floor. Clusters of friends hung out by the bar, the bottles of scotch, vodka, gin, and wine twinkling under the bright bar lights.

The Binat sisters ordered orange juices from the bartender, a Punjab Club waiter in his white uniform with plumed turban. Once they got their drinks, Alys seated them on a sofa. Then she left to explore the other rooms, where it was all the same, except hip-hop played in the dimly lit drawing room, where billiards was in full swing, and techno pulsed by the aquamarine swimming pool, where the guests lolled under the starlit sky.

Alys looked for Jena but couldn't find her. She wished Sherry had agreed to tag along; they would have had a fine time deconstructing this social circus. Alys circled back to the disco room. Mari and Qitty were on the sofa, watching Lady dancing by herself to ABBA's "Money, Money, Money." After Alys decided Lady was in no harm or doing any harm, she went in search of a toilet. She passed by walls full of the most insipid art: pastoral paintings of mustard fields, watercolor sketches of rowdy-haired men on horses, and Quran calligraphy, which, according to Nona, was all the rage these days for both the pious and the not-so-pious art collector.

Alys passed by one young man instructing another young man on how to most effectively snort the cocaine he'd been guaranteed was going to be the time of his life. A young woman was complaining about how her bootlegger was charging her more for alcohol than her male friends *just* because she was a woman. A few steps on, a cricket star Alys had only seen on TV was politely listening to a mediocre but well-connected musician telling him that, though a dud at the game himself, he had advice for the cricketer's bowling.

Passing by two men, Alys realized that one was Qazi of Qazi-Kreations and the other was another fashion designer frequently featured in *Social Lights*. They were engaged in debate: "You're awesome, you're awesome," "No, you are, no, you are." Then she stumbled upon Sammy and Jaans in a passionate embrace, whispering urgent terms of endearment—"parasite," "upstart"—and Alys tapped Sammy on the shoulder: "Where's the toilet?"

On the way back, Alys passed by a room with the door half-open: a library. Curiosity overcame her. Which books graced Fazool and Moolee's shelves? She was skimming a cherrywood shelf of leather-bound classics, which she found were hollow—

"We meet again."

"Shit!" Alys spun around, a hollow book almost falling out of her hands.

It was Darsee. He was stretched out in a chaise longue, a tumbler of scotch by his side.

"You scared me," Alys said, annoyed. "What are you doing in here?"

"What do you think I'm doing?" Darsee held up a tome: *Betty and Veronica Double Digest*. "I just got back to the country, and I'm in no mood yet for Jaans and Moolee, et cetera. Their entire life's purpose has begun to boil down to 'drink until you drop, preferably daily,' while Sammy and Fazool, et cetera, are getting PhDs in congratulating themselves on being amazing. Ridiculous. Prefer it here, reading."

Alys gazed at him for a long second, then said, "Looks like you and I seem to share this preference, given that we're both in here instead of out there making fools of ourselves."

"I don't know if I'd say you could ever make a fool of yourself. As for me, I think definitely not."

Alys blurted, "I hear it's more your scene to force your relatives into becoming fools."

"Excuse me?"

"Jeorgeullah Wickaam. Your cousin. The cousin you've treated abominably."

"*I* treated abominably!" Darsee's face turned livid.

"Wickaam told me everything."

"I know you have a very high opinion of yourself," Darsee said, "but you don't know anything about Wickaam and, trust me, you don't want to know. My advice to you is stay far away from that guy. Far, far away."

"Why? Oh, but of course, because he didn't salute your highness and kiss your ass!"

"Salute me! Kiss my ass! I find such behavior repellent."

"How could you cheat your own cousin out of his inheritance? How could you betray someone who is like a brother to you?"

Darsee got up and strode out of the library.

After Alys regained her composure, she rejoined the party, keeping one eye out for Darsee in order to stay far, far away from him. In the disco room, Lady was dancing on a tabletop to Donna Summer's "Love to Love You Baby." She was dancing with Shosha Darling, who kept yelling to no one and everyone, "Be a winner, baby, don't be a loser."

Both Lady and Shosha were sandwiched between a geriatric socialite Alys recognized from *Social Lights* and the host Moolee. Fazool was clapping and encouraging her husband to give Lady all his tingling-mingling.

Alys yanked Lady off the table. Lady gave Alys a murderous look as Alys plonked her beside Qitty, who was browsing through a coffee-table book on Islamic art history.

Alys whispered furiously to Qitty, "Didn't you see how those men were dancing with your sister? Why didn't you stop her?"

"I tried," Qitty said crossly, "but she started calling me fat in front of everyone, and then that senior citizen looked me up and down and said, '*Mashallah, sehatmand* sister'—healthy sister."

"Tch!" Alys looked around. "Where's Mari?"

She spied Mari standing behind the refreshments table, nibbling on mini cheesecakes, her *dupatta* chastely spread over her chest, her smug expression suggesting she was witnessing hell to her heart's content.

Alys was about to go to Mari when Hammy came upon her.

"Alys," Hammy said, "may I speak to you for a second?"

Alys followed Hammy into the entrance, where it was a little quieter.

"Listen," Hammy said, "I just want to let you know that Valentine left the party in a huff. I know you brought up Wickaam, and so I say the following to you with the best of intentions: There is bad blood between the two cousins, and it is not Val's fault. I don't know the exact details, but I do know that Wickaam is a dishonorable man and that he's done something truly unforgivable to Val, and it's unfair that you should annoy Val like this. Of course, Val requires no defense, but still I thought it my duty to speak up for him."

"I'm sure you thought it your duty," Alys said.

"Wickaam is a scoundrel."

"According to whom?" Alys said.

"Valentine!" Hammy said. "Valentine!"

"I see," Alys said. "Darsee speaks and you believe."

Hammy squinted. "It seems to me that Wickaam speaks and you believe."

"Yes, I do," Alys said.

"Suit yourself." Hammy raised her brows. "Well, do enjoy the party, and see you around, I guess. Happy New Year."

Alys watched Hammy head toward the pool. She certainly didn't sound the way the sister of a man who was about to propose should sound to the sister of the girl he was going to propose to.

"Alys!" It was Jena. "I've been looking everywhere for you."

"I was looking for you," Alys said.

"I want to leave. We need to leave. Why did we even come?"

"What's wrong?" Alys frowned. "What's happened?"

Jena's eyes filled for a second, but she hardened her face. "Darsee dragged, and I mean dragged, Bungles out of here ten minutes ago. After which Sammy tells me that they're all so exhausted attending NadirFiede that she, Jaans, Hammy, Bungles, Darsee, and his sister, Jujeena, are going to the Maldives for rest and relaxation. She hopes to announce Bungles's engagement to Jujeena Darsee when they return, and she'll send me an invite."

"She's bluffing."

"He didn't propose, Alys." Jena's voice cracked. "All these days, all these opportunities. I want to go home. I'm so tired. I never thought I'd say this, but I want to return to grading papers and making lesson plans and not dreaming about more."

Alys and Jena quickly rounded up their sisters, despite Lady's objections to leaving minutes before the New Year was going to be rung in, and they wished each other a Happy New Year in the car, quietly, without knowing when the stroke of midnight officially arrived and when it officially passed.

Part Two

JANUARY–AUGUST 2001

Chapter 14

What Will People Say
Log Kya Kahenge

PARTY SEEN: *Fazool and Moolee Fazal of Cockatoo Interior Designs pulled off yet another rocking New Year's Partay for 151 of their closest friends. The hip and happening crowd reveled till dawn. Funtastic music and a poolside countdown under the stars made this the scene to be seen. Eat your hearts out, the rest of you.*

RIP MELODY QUEEN OF PAKISTAN: *A little bird tells us that tempers were high in some quarters over the televised tribute to the late and great Madame Noor Jehan, whose sonorous voice has been wooing hearts for over six decades. "It should not," said one wannabe songstress, whose voice routinely scares the alley cats, "have been scheduled at the same time as my live concert."*

BIRTH OF A STAR: *Demand is so high for up-and-coming designer Boobee Khan's Nangaparbat Lawn Collection, we hear two eager customers slapped each other to be first in line. Congrats, Boobee! Watch out, Qazi! There's yet another contender in town for the crown.*

CHARITY POLO MATCH: *Every lady should have a knight as gallant as eligible bachelor Fahad "Bungles" Bingla to come to her rescue. Wouldn't you agree, Jena Binat, damsel du jour?*

The long school day finally ended, and Alys sat in the school van between Jena and Sherry. Outside, a late January drizzle abated, and Alys wound down the window for fresh air, only to be assaulted by the stench of burning garbage. Jena was sitting with a hand to her head, her eyes shut tightly, and she barely shifted.

Principal Naheed had called Alys in today. Alys thought Rose-Nama's mother had lodged yet another grievance or was demanding yet another apology. Instead, to Alys's shock, Principal Naheed said she was getting complaints about Jena. Jena was zoning out during class, and, at times, leaving class altogether and not coming back.

Was Jena okay? Naheed had asked, her teeth gleaming. Did it have anything to do with that delicious fellow mentioned in *Social Lights*?

They'd been back in Dilipabad right after New Year's and Alys—in fact, all the Binats—had hoped that with the school semester starting and life returning to its usual routine, Jena's sadness would subside, but that had not been the case. Even worse, teachers would bring celebratory sweets to the staff room every day, and Alys wondered if, each time Jena was offered a *ladoo* or a *barfi* for a son's promotion or a grandchild's birth or some other happy occasion, it reminded her anew that, had things turned out differently, she'd also have been offering teachers celebratory sweets.

Jena had not cried or railed, at least not in front of them, but she'd been inordinately quiet on the subject, except to say that it was their mother who had promised that Bungles would propose and that he himself had never promised her anything. Mrs. Binat was one minute full of ill will for Bungles, who, she claimed, had toyed with Jena, and the next minute upset with Jena, who, she accused, had thoughtlessly let him slip off her hook.

The van went over a bump and Jena's eyes fluttered open. Alys gave her a big smile. Jena replied with a tiny smile. There were dark circles under her eyes and she looked beaten. Alys sighed as she recalled how Jena had blanched at seeing her name, fodder for a gossip column, in *Social Lights*. She wondered if girls from Jena's classes might be asking her invasive questions and if this was the reason for her erratic behavior. She glanced at Qitty and Lady. Had anyone said anything to them?

Alys caught Sherry's gaze. Sherry continued to insist that Jena should have asked Bungles point-blank: "Am I just a time pass or are you planning to marry me?" While Alys believed in being up-front, she was glad that Jena had not debased herself, and she was sure that Jena too was relieved to have not embarrassed herself.

The only bright spot in these bleak weeks was Wickaam's visits. The first had been on the pretext that Mr. Binat's signatures were required on the Fraudia Acre case papers and Wickaam did not trust the mail. He'd used a similar excuse for his second visit. But the third was simply the result of Mrs. Binat's open invitation to visit them anytime. In fact, she'd since urged him to stay the night, given how tiring a four-hour round trip from Lahore to Dilipabad could be, and he'd cheerfully accepted: a sleepover!

More time for Wickaam to captivate all with the story of his childhood, his becoming a full orphan, BeenaDeenaWeena, Valentine Darsee's betrayal. He'd been amused and appreciative when Lady began to call Darsee "Dracula," and before long, all the Binats were referring to the traitorous cousin as Dracula.

Wickaam was installed in the cozy guest room, and the only awkward moment was when Alys had to send Lady to change her night-suit, with the admonition that she was not allowed to wander around the house in such a sheer nightie when they were hosting a male guest.

"Jeorgeullah is no mullah," Mari had said gravely. "Be careful, Lady."

"You be careful, weirdo," Lady said. "Mullahs aren't all saints, and I know you have flutters for Fart Bhai."

Lady pronounced Kaleen's first name, Farhat, so fast she'd transformed it into "Fart."

"I do not." Two bright splotches appeared on Mari's face. "Alys is right about the negligee. It's obscene. Go and change."

Lady had gone weeping to their mother. Mrs. Binat told Alys and Mari to mind their own business. Lady wasn't naked. A nightgown was a nightgown. When Alys had appealed to her father, Mr. Binat had declared, red-faced, that he was gladly relegating all matters of nightwear and nighttime activities to Mrs. Binat's expertise.

The school van stopped outside the graveyard, and the Binat girls and Sherry got out and sprinted to their homes to avoid the sudden downpour. In the Binat living room, Hillima laid out steaming chai and deep-fried *pakoras,* always a staple comfort food on a rainy day. Mr. Binat rose from the crackling fireplace, where he'd been reading a book on ornamentals, and kissed each of his daughters on the forehead.

The girls kicked off their shoes and settled onto sofas. Alys climbed into the window seat, enjoying the dark bubble of a sky. For a long minute, there were few sounds but the rumble of thunder, the sipping of chai, and the chewing of piping-hot *pakoras.* Mari finished up her prayers in the corner of the room and blew blessings of prosperity and peace on each of her sisters, spending a few seconds longer on Jena.

Mrs. Binat came into the living room. She beamed as she replaced the cordless on its cradle. She hadn't beamed like this since they'd returned from Lahore. Sometimes she felt she'd never recover from Jena's failure to grab Bungles, and she was beginning to believe that truly of what use was beauty without a brain that could plot and scheme.

"We are to receive a special visitor," Mrs. Binat said. "He will be arriving tonight in time for dinner and plans to stay for a few days."

Everyone smiled.

"It's not Wickaam," Mrs. Binat said. "It's Farhat Kaleen."

Everyone's smile faded. Except Mari's. Her heart pattered at the thought of being under one roof with the good doctor. Perhaps, together, they could inject some righteousness into her sisters' heads. Then he would see how perfect she was for him, and he would propose to her, and they would live happily ever after. Mari shook herself and asked God to forgive her the Farhat fantasy, in case it was untoward of her. But, God, she bargained, if you make me the first sister married, then I swear to thank you by starting to wear a *hijab*.

"Fart *Bhai*!" Lady said. "Fart *Bhai* is the big surprise? Is this a joke?"

"What's there to joke about?" Mrs. Binat said. "He is an up-and-coming EIP, extremely important person."

"He's a purity pervert," Lady said. "He told me that I shouldn't wear skintight shirts."

"He's right," Mari said. "And don't dare insult pious men by labeling them purity perverts."

"Women like you are the biggest purity perverts of all."

"Now, Lady," Mrs. Binat said, "do not disrespect Kaleen in any way. He's coming to check Mari's asthma, as well as other patients in Dilipabad, and I would like all of you girls—and you too, Barkat—to make yourselves amenable to him."

"He is a popcorn-nosed yuck-*thoo*," Lady said. "I'm not even going to come downstairs while he's here."

"I will," Mari said.

"I bet," Lady said, "you're looking forward to Fart Bhai's stethoscope roaming all over your chest."

"Lady," Alys said, "have you lost all sense of decorum?"

"Aunty Alys, who made you the Superintendent of Virtue and

Vice? At the New Year's party I was dancing with Shosha Darling—
Shosha Darling!—and you dragged me off the table like a *paindu*, a
yokel. Bungles—"

Jena left the room.

"Thanks for bringing him up yet again," Alys said.

"I didn't mean to," Lady said. "You provoked me. You always do."

"Honestly, Lady," Qitty said. "You are so inconsiderate."

"Shut up, baby elephant."

"You shut up," Qitty said, "Miss See-Through Nightie You-You
Eyes while Wickaam was here."

"*Tauba,* you girls are too much for me," Mr. Binat said, also leaving the room.

"I wish," Mrs. Binat sighed, "that I too could be the sort of parent
who can walk away from my daughters. Alys, go see that the guest
room is ready for Kaleen. Why are you staring at me? Go. Do as you
are told."

Farhat Kaleen arrived at Binat House exactly on time. Punctuality
was a good habit no matter how un-Pakistani, he said, as he exited
his car and his driver took out his bags. He beamed at all the Binats
standing in the driveway to greet him, a gesture he found befitting
his stature. He gave Alys a once-over and approved of her white
wide-leg pants, white eyelet tunic, and the sunset shawl thrown
around her shoulders. His nose wrinkled at Lady's tight jeans and
tight T-shirt saying GALZ RULZ on her plump bosom. Ever since his
wife's death, his daughter's attire had begun to lapse for lack of
proper supervision, but—Kaleen smiled at Alys—that would soon
be remedied. He was pleased to see Alys avert her eyes from him and
proceed indoors. Such was indeed expected of a girl from a good
family, and it warmed his loins.

After Kaleen freshened up from his journey, he checked Mari,
recommending she continue her breathing exercises. As soon as that
formality was finished, he requested a tour of Binat House and, as-

sessing each room with the eyes of a future son-in-law looking to impress colleagues and clients—especially Begum Beena dey Bagh—he was pleased with what he saw.

Dinner was served after the Isha prayers, and Kaleen was delighted at the Binats' generous spread of mutton *karahi*, beef *seekh kebabs*, ginger chicken, eggplant in tomatoes, creamy black *dal*, potato cutlets, cucumber *raita*, and *kachumber* salad.

"You girls," Kaleen said as Mr. Binat invited him to begin, "must have spent all day in the kitchen."

"We have a full-time cook," Mrs. Binat said tersely. "And when he's on holiday, Hillima takes over. My girls never set foot in the kitchen unless they want to for fun."

"I meant no offense," Kaleen said. "My late wife was an exceptional cook, and I only wanted to pay my compliments to the chef of such delicious fare."

The cook, Maqsood, was called from the kitchen, and Kaleen, pressed into a corner to perform social obligations, tipped the fellow. Hillima appeared on the cook's heels, touting her contributions to the meal, and Kaleen delved back into his pocket with a forced smile.

Later, Maqsood and Hillima shared notes and concluded that Kaleen had not been as stingy as Wickaam but they prayed that the next visitor to grace Binat House would not only have money but also be bighearted.

Kaleen filled his plate to the maximum as Mrs. Binat handed him entrée after entrée. He was happy to see that Alys ate sparsely and with sophistication. By contrast, Lady had a robust appetite and kept licking her lips.

"My late wife," Kaleen said as he tore apart a *roghni naan*, "believed women who eat freely find it hard to control their desire in other matters too."

"What other matters?" Lady asked naughtily, her fleshy lips glistening with ghee.

Kaleen glanced at her distastefully. "Begum Beena dey Bagh also believes gluttony is unappetizing in a woman."

Alys wished she'd overfilled her plate like a glutton supposedly might, however she had little appetite. The phone had rung earlier that evening, and she'd seen Jena's face light up and then fall when it had turned out to be Mari's friend. Now Jena played with a tea-spoon's worth of food on her plate, and even though their mother had instructed the cook to prepare Jena's favorites round the clock—spaghetti *keema* and Kashmiri mustard greens with white rice—she barely ate.

"Beena dey Bagh was not at the NadirFiede wedding?" Mr. Binat asked.

"Rest assured," Kaleen said, "she was the first luminary to whom an invitation was sent. Unfortunately, Begum Beena dey Bagh has been unable to attend many functions this winter on account of Annie suffering a setback. Far be it from me to ever brag, but they are lucky to have discovered me—otherwise, who knows what state Annie may have been in by now. She could even be dead. In which case, I tell mother and daughter, I am not just a doctor but also a savior, Annie's hero."

"Is such self-praise," Mr. Binat asked with a straight face, "spon-taneous or practiced?"

"Both," Kaleen said. "For example, the food on this table deserves spontaneous praise, and so I gave it, but in homes where the food is tasteless, practiced praise is required. Same rule applies for the ac-complishments of men and the looks of ladies."

"The looks of ladies?" Mrs. Binat said.

"Yes," Kaleen said. "Praising plain and ugly girls makes their day, so they tell me. I now regard it as *sawab ka kaam,* God's own good work."

"What's wrong with Annie?" Alys asked, for she was curious about Wickaam's and Dracula's cousin.

"Sad story," Kaleen said, ladling a hefty amount of ginger chicken into his plate.

Annie was once a vibrant girl standing five foot eleven in her bare feet and studying at Berkeley, after which she'd planned to return to

Pakistan to join her mother's business. Along the way, Annie was discovered at an airport by a fashion designer, and next she knew it, she was walking runways. One weekend she'd gone on a camping trip, after which her health began to fail rapidly. She'd sought Kaleen out at a medical conference where he was a guest speaker on autoimmune afflictions. "I'm Pakistani," she said, "you're Pakistani. Please help me. Not too long ago, I was walking in stilettos, and now here I am with a walking stick. Nothing shows up in my blood work and doctors insist it's all in my head. Please help me."

"I helped her," Kaleen continued. "Within days, thanks to the guidance of Almighty God, she was better. But once the conference ended I returned to England, and next I know, Begum Beena dey Bagh is offering me a dream package to move to Pakistan, and here I am."

"*Inshallah*," Mari said, once Kaleen was done, "may Annie dey Bagh and every other human being suffering from disease and illness be fully restored to health."

"*Ameen*," everyone at the table said, cupping their palms and looking skyward.

"*Summa ameen*," Kaleen said, invoking a double blessing as he appraised Mari anew. His eyes lingered on the gold Allah-in-Arabic pendant nestling in her cleavage and visible beneath her muslin *dupatta*. Perfectly pious but, compared to Alys's striking looks, quite insipid.

Dessert was brought out—a vibrant beetroot *halwa* and chai, after which Kaleen asked to retire for the night. He gave Mrs. Binat a special look, which she rightly interpreted as his wanting to be fresh for the life-altering event the next day. After bidding him sweet dreams, she sent everyone to their rooms for an early night. They should all rest, she decided, for tomorrow would bring one long celebration.

Chapter 15

*F*arhat Kaleen came down for breakfast with his heart beating fast. He'd never thought in his wildest dreams that he'd have to propose twice in his lifetime, but this was obviously God's plan. He entered the dining room and was pleased to see that the Binat girls were still at breakfast. His eyes glanced at the food first—fried eggs, Pakistani omelet brimming with cumin and green chilies, potato *bhujia,* French toast, and cornflakes—and then at Alys, who was nibbling on a boiled egg and sipping black coffee.

She was reading the newspaper, which was all right by him—being a good woman did not mean being uninformed. But he frowned for a moment at her tracksuit bottoms and T-shirt that read NOT YOUR AVERAGE BEHEN JEE. Then he smiled. The casualness of her outfit at this most momentous of events for her would be but their first sweet memory.

Best, Kaleen decided as he looked for a place to sit, to do the deed on a full stomach. Mr. Binat was not present. Alys was at the foot of the table, flanked by Mari, drinking the herbal tea he'd prescribed, and Qitty and Lady, who sat in a nightie too flimsy for his comfort. He glanced at the empty chair beside Jena. Best not to sit next to her either, since she was getting engaged and so belonged to another man. He finally settled beside Pinkie Binat and took hefty servings of everything.

Mrs. Binat gave Kaleen an encouraging maternal smile, even as she wished he'd dressed differently. He was wearing a skintight red T-shirt and pale-gray pants. This ensemble may have looked snazzy on the K-pop musicians Lady and Qitty watched on MTV Asia, but on Kaleen it failed. For one, his nipples were pointedly on display through the fabric. Lady and Qitty were smirking and Mrs. Binat glowered at them to stop, as did Mari. Mrs. Binat wished Kaleen would hurry his breakfast before Alys left, and as soon as he swallowed his last bite, she scrambled up and ordered her daughters to come with her.

"Except you, Alys *meri jaan*, my darling, you stay," Mrs. Binat said. "Best daughter of mine, I've given my blessings to Kaleen, but it is only fitting that in this brave new world you get to say yes yourself."

Alys stared at her mother. Things fell into place. How could her mother believe that she and this man could be a match? Her sisters exited with sympathetic looks—even Lady looked sad—and, before Alys knew it, she was alone with Kaleen. She abruptly rose from her seat, and Kaleen rose too. He plucked a droopy gladiolus from the vase on the table and held it to his heart.

"Alys," he began, even though Alys raised her hands to stop him, "my sweet Alys, you are the sweetest creature. And believe me, my late wife would have agreed. Sweet chaste Alys, make me the happiest man in all of Pakistan, in the world, and marry this humble servant of yours?"

"No!"

"I know good girls are trained to say no at first, for eagerness does not become them—"

"Stop! Please stop! My no means no."

"Sweet, sweet Alys, unsullied Alys." Kaleen tried to hold her hand. "Demureness becomes you, my sweet!"

"I am not demure." Alys clasped her hands behind her back. "Trust me."

"Sweet, sweet Alys, with such sweet, sweet lips, from which emanates such sweet bashfulness, stop playing with my heart, my sweetheart, and agree to be my virtuous wife."

"Please stop proposing!"

"So coy. So coy. This was my late wife's reaction at first too."

"Kaleen Sahib"—Alys took one step toward the door—"I have no idea why your first wife changed her mind, but I'm not going to. We are incompatible, and I genuinely apologize if anyone in this family has led you to believe otherwise."

"Sweetest purest Alys." Kaleen took two steps toward her, thrusting the gladiolus at her. It fell to the floor. "Even your pretend denials are sending shivers through my heart and other regions. How dearly my late wife would have approved. Our union will be blessed by Begum Beena dey Bagh herself, and we will make a power couple the likes of which Pakistan has yet to see. Were I younger, indeed, sweet innocent queen of my heart, I would be proposing to you from astride a stallion, but—"

Alys burst out of the dining room, only to bump into her mother, whose ear had been glued to the door. Pinkie Binat reached out to seize Alys, but she dodged her mother and fled to her father's study. Mr. Binat was in his armchair. He was toasting his toes at an electric heater, the double rods glowing a fiery orange, and he glanced up at her from a compendium of Rumi's ruminations.

"Why are your feathers aflutter, Princess Alysba?" he said. "What's wrong?"

"Daddy, did you know *why* Mummy invited that odious *uncle* to our house? Did you know?"

"Know what?" Mr. Binat sat up at the distress in his favorite daughter's voice.

"She wants me to marry that buffoon."

"Not a buffoon," Mrs. Binat said, entering and banging shut the study door. "He's a first-rate catch for the likes of you!"

"He's hardly a first-rate catch for a clown, let alone for the likes of me," Alys said.

"What is going on?" Mr. Binat asked.

"Farhat Kaleen wants to marry this ungrateful fool," Mrs. Binat said, "and she is refusing."

"Daddy, how can I marry that man?"

"How can you not?" Mrs. Binat roared. Alys was nearly thirty-one years old. Soon her waist would thicken and she would grow stout. Her hair would thin and what would be left would turn to gray wires and she'd be dependent on hair dye for the rest of her life. Her skin would wrinkle, her neck would droop, and her eyes would go from being beautiful to just another pair of fine eyes. A woman's curse, Mrs. Binat reminded Alys, was to age, no matter what Alys believed.

"Barkat, you'd better make your daughter marry Farhat Kaleen, or I swear I'll never talk to her again."

"Alysba is not going to marry him," Mr. Binat said. "And perhaps, Pinkie, my love, it might be best for your nerves if you do stop talking to her."

Alys gave a sigh of relief. Her father had ended the matter, for had he sided with her mother, she would have faced a formidable battle. Alys turned victorious eyes on her mother and, fleeing to her bedroom, she cried in relief.

Mrs. Binat's heartbroken shrieks must have surely reverberated all the way to Sherry's house, for Sherry, who'd been preparing breakfast for her family, decided that she must pay the Binats a visit. Farhat Kaleen was visiting them, and she wanted to request he take a look at her diabetic mother's swollen feet.

As soon as breakfast was done and she'd washed and dried the utensils and fed her cat, Yaar, Sherry grabbed the translations Alys had requested of Manto's story "*Khol Do*" and Ghulam Abbas's "*Anandi*," and she hummed her way to Binat House.

Lady and Qitty opened the front door. Sherry thought she could hear shouting coming from inside the house.

"You're in for a treat," Lady said, pulling her in. "The house is in an uproar."

Sherry had never ever known the fifteen-year-old Lady to whisper.

"Has Bungles, thankfully, finally proposed to Jena?"

"Fart Bhai has proposed to Alys," Lady cut in.

Sherry blinked. Alysba and Farhat Kaleen?

"And Alys," Qitty said, "has point-blank refused. Our parents are yelling so loudly I'm sure Fart Bhai, who slunk into the guest room after Alys's rejection, can hear them too."

"I thought it was going to be yet another boring day Chez Binat," said Lady, linking arms with Sherry and Qitty as they walked to the living room. "But this is better than my wildest dreams. Fart Bhai and Alys up a tree, K-I-S-S-I-N-G. Fart Bhai told Alys that if he were younger, then he would have come for her on a stallion. Can you imagine that purity pervert on a horse? *Waise himmat dekho popcorn naak ganje ki, Alys se shaadi!* Imagine the popcorn-nosed baldy's boldness in proposing to Alys!"

"He's a decent catch, Lady," Sherry said, sighing.

"You and my mother always think alike," Lady said.

Sherry shrugged. A marriage was a marriage and Farhat Kaleen was no ordinary frog, and Mrs. Binat, poor woman, could see that, even if her daughters refused to.

They stepped into the living room. Mrs. Binat lay on the sofa while Mari gloomily applied headache balm to her mother's temples.

"*As-salaam alaikum,* Pinkie Khala," Sherry said, sitting beside her.

"*Walaikum-asalaam.*" Mrs. Binat managed an anguished smile. "Have you heard what your foolish friend has done? I ask you, if something was wrong with Kaleen, would I insist upon my daughter marrying him?"

Mrs. Binat took a moment to blow her nose into her *dupatta*—not a very classy thing to do, she knew, but given the circumstances who could blame her? Such a decent proposal, and Alys had broken her heart by not only snubbing it but also running to her father for protection. The same father whose family was the reason they were stuck in Dilipabad with no worthy proposals to begin with.

"Is not Farhat Kaleen marriageable material?" Mrs. Binat implored of Sherry. So what if she herself would never have considered him back in her day? That was then, and this is now.

Sherry nodded. "Any sensible girl would deem him a great grab."

"My daughters are not sensible." Mrs. Binat gazed with hurt eyes at Sherry. "You must make your friend see sense, Sherry. It is all up to you now. Promise me you will make your foolish friend marry him."

Before Sherry could promise anything, the living room door swung open and Jena and Alys entered.

"Sherry," Alys said. "I heard you'd come."

"Here she is!" Mrs. Binat flared her nostrils at Alys. "The most thankless daughter in the universe. God knows I love my daughters equally, but you, Alys, have always been my least favorite, for you put yourself before the well-being of this family. It's your father's fault. Always indulging you. What's your life plan now? To become Teacher of the Year and die an old maid? Oh God, better to remain barren than birth a disobedient child."

Sherry flinched at the word "barren." Alys shrugged an apology to Sherry for having landed at their house in the midst of this mess. Mrs. Binat continued telling Alys what she thought of her until the man of the match, Farhat Kaleen himself, entered the room.

Mrs. Binat quieted. "Girls," she said, adjusting her eyelet *chador* prettily over her shoulders, "be quiet now. Kaleen and I have important matters to discuss."

Kaleen pointedly ignored Mrs. Binat and turned to Sherry: How were her parents, brothers, sister, cat? Alys took the opportunity to slip out of the living room. Jena, Mari, and Qitty followed her, and though Qitty tried to pull Lady along, Lady would not move. Once Sherry satisfied Kaleen that her family and cat were well, she glided toward the window and pretended to busy herself checking the growth of the money plants on the sill. Like Lady, Sherry was tuned in to Mrs. Binat and Kaleen and so she was witness to Mrs. Binat's utterly doleful "*Hai*, Kaleen! Believe you me—"

"Pinkie, please." Kaleen pressed his palms together. "Let us forever be silent on the utter anarchy plaguing this house."

He settled ramrod straight on the Victorian chair adjacent to Mrs. Binat and proceeded to shatter the silence by assuring her that he did not resent Alysba. Why waste his time, he asked in a grave tone, resenting a woman whose favor he was beginning to be glad had been withheld after all? Obviously, Alysba would not have proved to be a perfect companion for him, let alone a good mother for his children, for he needed to marry a woman who knew her place, and Alysba had exercised displacement.

His first impulse had been to leave the Binats' home for a hotel, but in remaining, he hoped to protect the family's reputation from gossip. Pinkie was to rest assured that he did not hold her or Mr. Binat responsible for their daughter's behavior. He was a father and knew how hard it was to control one's children these days, although Alysba was no longer a child but a very aged woman. Alysba was lucky that he was not the sort of man who'd respond to her insult of a refusal by throwing acid on her. In fact, he was firmly against such retaliations.

Mrs. Binat felt faint as Kaleen's speech came to an end. Excusing herself, she fled to her bedroom and sobbed. Lady left the living room in order to give her sisters a rundown of Fart Bhai's speech—not the type to resort to an acid attack!—and she glanced down at him with horror before flouncing out.

Kaleen scowled at Lady's back and decided that this *behooda*—vulgar girl—not ending up his sister-in-law was a blessing in itself. And Alysba too, he decided, was no doubt pretending to be pure and pristine, for she was far too sexy to really be a good girl. As Sherry turned from the money plants, the midmorning sunshine bathed her in its golden glory and it suddenly occurred to Kaleen that Alysba's friend looked like a spotless sturdy sapling of some spotless sturdy tree. For the rest of the day, he paid great attention to Sherry, partly in order to pointedly ignore the Binats and partly, he hoped, to annoy Alysba.

The next day, Sherry arrived yet again to aid the Binats by keeping Kaleen occupied. Alys thanked her best friend for doing so, but Sherry had an ulterior motive. If Alys did not want Farhat Kaleen, then he was fair game for her. That evening, the Binats and Kaleen dined at the Loocluses', and Sherry was dismayed to hear Kaleen proclaim that his late wife believed women who smoked possessed loose morals.

"My late wife," Kaleen said, "God grant her a place in heaven, agreed with me that cigarettes are different from the hookahs our foremothers used to smoke, for hookahs do not possess the indecent shape of a cigarette."

"Your late wife," Mrs. Binat said spitefully, "seems to have missed the fact that tobacco is tobacco no matter the receptacle."

Mrs. Binat was most unhappy at Mr. Binat forcing her to attend this dinner at the Loocluses' when all she felt like doing was pining away in bed. She darted a poisonous eye at Alys, who seemed truly unaffected, and at Kaleen, who seemed to have recovered all too fast. Why was he praising Bobia Looclus's décor? Pinkie cast a baleful glance over Bobia's tiny drawing room, the discolored cheap lace curtains behind a sagging plastic-covered sofa, the wobbly coffee table, the fraying artificial flowers atop an outdated TV, which, gallingly enough, reminded Mrs. Binat of the fact that, growing up, her family had barely been able to afford such a one. The only redeeming feature of this entire evening, she granted, was the delicious dinner poor Sherry must have spent the entire day preparing.

At the dinner table Mrs. Binat flinched when, after a few bites of the feast, Kaleen exclaimed that it was by far the best meal he'd eaten for days.

"Compliments to your cook, Bobia *jee,*" Kaleen said, raising an appreciative eyebrow at the perfectly round puffed *chapatis* in the bread basket.

"Sherry is our cook, *mashallah,*" Bobia Looclus said. She pressed upon Kaleen the mutton *pulao* and *achaari* chicken. "There is magic in her hands."

"Indeed! Magic!" Kaleen liberally helped himself to these dishes as well as the *chapli kebabs* and *shahi korma.*

From across the table, Sherry refilled his glass with sweet *lassi.* The extravagance of the meal had cost them a good amount of her paycheck, but she was determined to show off her cooking skills.

Alys was dismayed when her mother rudely interrupted Kaleen's praise with the prayer that the Loocluses be able to hire a cook so that poor Sherry could see the last of the hot kitchen and stinky dishes.

"Pinkie," Bobia Looclus replied in a pinched voice, "I hope we never see the day where we can afford a cook if it means our daughters forgetting how to cook. Girls who cannot cook are destined to be divorced."

"Then," Mrs. Binat said, "all the upper-class women should be divorced."

"Trust me"—Bobia Looclus glanced keenly at Kaleen—"if husbands had to choose between wife or cook, cook would win hands down."

"Bobia"—Mrs. Binat glanced archly at Kaleen—"cooks may be irreplaceable for you, but for me wives are."

Kaleen was too busy eating to give either woman attention and, anyway, he wasn't in the business of giving the bickering of elderly housewives much thought. Instead, he complimented Sherry on her cooking again, much to Bobia Looclus's gratification and Pinkie Binat's chagrin, as the desserts—a green jelly trifle and a red carrot *gajar ka halwa*—were brought out. By the evening's end, Sherry was sure that if only Farhat Kaleen were to remain in Dilipabad long enough to eat her meals for a few days in a row, she might stand a chance.

The next morning, Sherry awakened for dawn prayers in the bedroom she shared with her younger sister. After praying, she stretched her arms in a yawn and, glancing out of her tiny window, she saw Farhat Kaleen shuffling up the lane. Sherry dressed as fast as she could and set out to meet him by accident.

Kaleen turned into Sherry's narrow lane. Though stirred by Alysba's spurning of him, he was not so shaken that he did not, the morning following Sherry's divine dinner, decide, after his prayers, to slip out of Binat House and make his way toward Looclus Lodge Bismillah. Stepping on weeds growing out of the dirt road, he continued rehearsing the very speech he had laid at Alysba Binat's feet. To his tremendous delight, Kaleen saw Sherry walking up the lane.

Sherry and Kaleen stood at the edge of the empty lane in the early morning under a mango tree that had grown not by design but due to littering. After exchanging shy *salaams,* Kaleen plunged straight into affairs of the heart. Sweating profusely, he hung his head and spoke of recently proposing to Alysba, of which Sherry was well aware.

"A terrible mistake," he exclaimed.

Sherry assured him that although she and Alys were friends, in too many respects she and Alys were opposites; one was not the company one kept. Minutes passed as Kaleen enumerated why Alys would not make an ideal wife. Sherry began to worry that Alys or one of the Binats would venture out to the lane and see them or the school van would arrive. Kaleen was assuring her he had lofty roots. His ancestors had owned carpet factories in Kashmir. When his side of the family had left the Kashmir Valley for the Punjab plains in order to further the family trade, they became known as simply *kaleen wallas,* carpet makers. Over time, the carpet trade had fallen away, and now all the connection that remained to their once-prestigious status in Kashmir was their name, Kaleen, "carpet."

Kaleen told Sherry that he'd grown up in a half-loving home, with a stern, unaffectionate father who owned a small handicraft shop and a stay-at-home mother who, amid constant hugs and kisses, never let him forget that he was the most handsome and intelligent son in the galaxy. His late wife, he informed Sherry, had held the same opinion. Sherry glanced at the rising sun as Kaleen branched off into the virtues of a good wife: cooking skills; a natural shyness combined with a cultivated modesty; could have opinions but must not voice those opinions, especially if they are in opposition to a husband's opinions; serve in-laws; cleanliness, punctuality, innocence; sacrificing self and career for children's well-being; sacrificing self for husband's well-being; sacrificing self for everything.

"I can be a good wife," Sherry blurted out. "The best."

It was out, and she was relieved. Let the likes of Jena Binat leave the likes of Fahad Bingla wondering whether she wanted to marry him. Sherry had meant it when she'd told Alys that a woman should not leave a man in doubt of her interest. If Kaleen laughed at her, she would survive. There were worse things in life than being laughed at, and one of them was being a poor spinster. She glanced at her cat slinking down the gutter along the sidewall, a large ball of gray fur. Why was Farhat Kaleen not saying anything? Was he appalled by her directness? She badly needed a cigarette. Two cigarettes.

"You can be a good wife," Kaleen repeated. He wasn't sure what to make of such straightforwardness. He'd promised his late wife that he'd remarry a woman as worthy as her, and just as she'd begun to instruct him on what exactly constituted worth, she'd taken her last breaths, which had sounded like a cat meowing. Now here was a gray cat meowing at him. Suddenly Kaleen knew this was the clue his pious wife had given him for recognizing a worthy woman; that it should be a cat's meow made perfect sense, because the Prophet Muhammad's favorite animal was the cat, and righteous people received signs in religious terms.

Kaleen would have fallen to his knees in a prayer of gratitude had the dirt road not been excessively strewn with stones. God had known Alys was the wrong woman for him all along and thus her shockingly unexpected refusal. Instead here was Sherry Looclus, the woman who was to be his wife, and God again had blessed him by making her reveal herself to him by her boldness, for there were certainly times when natural shyness needed to take a backseat. *Meow-meow* came again from behind him, and Kaleen took a giant step forward. Taking Sherry's hand in his, he declared:

"You, my sweet, will be *my* wife, for, trust me, it has been ordained."

Sherry's knees nearly buckled. She caught herself. Until a moment ago she'd been sure Kaleen was going to spurn her. Instead, the opposite. Would she truly never have to work again unless she wanted to, or fret about bills again, or worry about whether a sister-in-law would turn her into an unpaid maid? Best to get Kaleen inside and announce the unbelievable proposal to her parents and legitimize it before he had time to reconsider. As for smoking, she would try her best to quit. But the fact was, she had a bigger secret than smoking, and though she could have hidden it from him, Sherry did not want to dupe anyone into marriage.

"I have something to divulge," she said nervously.

"Tell me, sweet, sweet Sherry."

"I am unable to have children."

"Truly," Kaleen said, "God is showering me with blessings."

Her lack of a working uterus suited him perfectly. He wanted a mother for his children, he told her, but he did not want any more children.

Sherry hurried her beau into her house, where he proceeded to formally ask Haji Looclus for his daughter's hand. Sherry shivered the whole time. She could hardly believe that her spoiled uterus had not ruined her prospects, having constantly heard that grim verdict over the years, and now she promised God a gratitude Hajj, extra prayers for the rest of her life, and even more alms for the poor.

Her younger sister, Mareea, shed happy tears that no one could ever mock or dismiss her hardworking elder sister for being barren. As for Sherry's brothers, Mansoor and Manzoor, their delight was unparalleled: They loved their sister, but they were beyond relieved that someone was finally marrying her and that she was going to her "real" home.

Bobia Looclus chortled with pleasure—Bobia 1, Pinkie 0—as she retrieved her Quran and blessed the future couple by touching the holy book to their heads. Whatever his reasons for marrying her, she informed Sherry in the kitchen as they quickly prepared chai, Sherry was not to worry—*Allah nigehbaan,* God was watching over her. Sherry was going to prove to Farhat Kaleen that he'd made the best decision. Why should they care that Kaleen had only days ago proposed to Alys. Every man was allowed his blunders. Alys's loss was Sherry's gain. The Binat girls were spoiled, and their mother was to blame for always telling them that they deserved no less than princes and presidents.

"*Agar uski betiyan ghar behtee reh jayen*—if her daughters rot at home for the rest of their lives," Bobia muttered, "it will be Pinkie Binat's fault for giving them standards instead of teaching them to make do." Bobia kissed her daughter's forehead. "I cannot wait to tell snooty Pinkie our good news."

But Sherry made her family promise that they would keep this a secret until she told Alys herself. Everyone agreed, though Kaleen wished he could go straight to the Binats and inform them that he was marrying Alysba's friend. Instead, when he returned to the Binats' house, he packed his suitcase to immediately leave for Islamabad and surprised the Binats by his graciousness and promise to return very soon. As his car drove away, Mrs. Binat mentioned to Mr. Binat that she was sure Kaleen meant to turn his attentions to Mari, since she seemed to actually enjoy his sermons.

———

Sherry avoided telling Alys her big news during the school day on the pretext that it was the wrong venue but that evening, as they had their smoke in the graveyard, she could no longer stall.

"Alys," Sherry took a deep breath, "Alys, I'm engaged to Farhat Kaleen."

"What?"

"I'm engaged to Farhat Kaleen."

Alys had wondered whether Kaleen might be interested in Sherry, but she'd failed to imagine that Sherry would reciprocate.

Sherry lit a fresh cigarette with trembling fingers. "Stop looking at me like that."

"When did this happen?"

"This morning," Sherry said. "Before the school van came."

"I see."

"You see?" Sherry said. "That's all you're going to say?"

"Congratulations on a fine catch," Alys said. "If he could, he would come for you on a stallion, did he say?"

"Tch! Don't be like that! He doesn't care that I can't have children, and because he doesn't care, perhaps one day I *truly* won't care. Alys, the biggest attraction in marrying him is that his children will be mine. I will become a mother. I swear, his youngest already looks at me with so much trust and affection."

Alys wanted to tell Sherry yet again that she was more than a childbearing and child-rearing machine. But what was the use? Perhaps you truly could not make someone disbelieve what they'd been so thoroughly conditioned to believe.

"You know," Sherry said, "if you had accepted his proposal, you could have resigned from British School today without having to listen to Principal Naheed and Rose-Nama's mother's demands ever again."

"I'd rather be accused of imaginary crimes my entire life than become that man's wife."

"He has shortcomings. He's human! No one is perfect. Not even people like Darsee, or you."

"You're taller than him," Alys said feebly as she looked up at Sherry.

"I don't care, and he hasn't said anything," Sherry said. "And, anyway, only by one inch."

Alys took a deep breath. "Listen, Sherry, I'm happy for you if this is what you really want."

"I want." Sherry took a long puff. "Of course I want. Children. Hel-lo: S-E-X. Car, driver. And he's a British citizen because of which I will become a British citizen. And then I will be able to sponsor my parents, my brothers, and my sister. This will change our lives. Do you understand that?"

"Love? Like? Respect? Or do only the material things he can provide count?"

Sherry shook her head. "You want to call me a gold digger? Go ahead. But my name should be Budgeting, Saving, and Serving. I've been working outside the home ever since I can remember, as well as inside cooking and cleaning, and I want to be in a relationship where duties will be shared. My husband-to-be may say ridiculous things like 'Dignified women do not work outside the home' and 'Men who expect their wives to earn are losers,' but I am perfectly capable of being content in a traditional marriage. He will be an excellent provider and, I guarantee you, I will be the best mother and homemaker in the world."

Alys sighed. "Sherry, people marry for money, for security, for children, then get stuck in crappy financially dependent relationships."

"Alys, stop being dramatic. I'm not saying I won't ever work outside again and earn my own income. When I choose to, I will."

Alys raised a brow. "And you think your husband-to-be will give you that choice?"

Sherry took a moment to answer. "I am practical, Alys. I am not you. Please try to understand. Please. For me marriage is not a love story; it's a social contract. *Inshallah* you'll get your love story and never have to compromise, and I sincerely pray you find a man who'll respect and appreciate you exactly as you are, and you a man you respect exactly as he is. But let me tell you, if Farhat Kaleen talks about me half as affectionately and respectfully as he talks about his late wife, I will be a very lucky woman."

"Affection and respect," Alys said, "increase exponentially once one is dead."

Sherry spluttered on her smoke. Alys patted her on the back.

"I've said it before," Sherry said when she could speak, "and I'll say it to my dying day: There is no guarantee of happiness in any marriage, and being in love with your prospective partner is not going to solve that. People change, relationships change."

For the first time since their friendship had begun in this graveyard ten years ago, they walked out in an awkward silence. But it was done, thank God, and when Sherry returned home she told her parents that they were now free to spread the good news.

Duly, Bobia and Haji Looclus arrived at the Binats' with a box of heart-shaped *barfis*.

"*Wah jee wah*," Mrs. Binat said taking a *barfi*. "To what do we owe this celebration?"

Bobia Looclus spewed the news like water out of a high-pressure hose.

"Our Sherry and your Farhat Kaleen are getting married, *mashallah, inshallah*."

Mrs. Binat's *barfi* fell into her lap.

"Please, Aunty Bobia," Lady said. "*Itni bari gup*, such a tall tale. Don't you know Fart Bhai is madly in love with Alys and dying to marry her?"

Bobia Looclus sucked in her cheeks. Her husband gave her a calming look and she contented herself with huffily adjusting her *dupatta* over her head.

"They are marrying," Alys confirmed. "Sherry told me herself."

"Aunty, Uncle." Jena got up to hug them. "*Bohut mubarak*, my sincere congratulations. Congratulations from all of us."

"Yes, heartiest congratulations, Bobia Behen, Haji Sahib," Mr.

Binat said, even though he was surprised that poor Sherry had agreed to marry Alys's reject. Mari's, Qitty's, and Lady's congratulations followed, and, eventually, Mrs. Binat managed a congrats.

"*Oof Allah,*" Bobia Looclus informed her husband once they left Binat House and proceeded to another neighbor's, "if Pinkie Binat's looks could kill, Alys would be a dead girl." She let out a big happy sigh. "Dear God, protect my Sherry from *buri nazr,* the world's evil eyes and ill wills."

The very next day Sherry fulfilled a dream. She marched into Principal Naheed's office and handed in her resignation. Naheed was about to make a big stink about a week's notice when she looked at Sherry's form.

"You're marrying Beena dey Bagh's daughter Annie's doctor? That Farhat Kaleen?"

"*Jee,* Principal Madam."

Naheed's mouth fell open. How in God's good name had this gangly nobody managed to snag what was for her a stellar match, a doctor, despite the fact that Kaleen was a widower with three children? She had to tread carefully, for she did not know exactly how close Kaleen was to Beena dey Bagh, but it would not bode well if he informed Beena that Naheed had been rude to his wife-to-be. And so it was that Naheed accepted Sherry's resignation with courtesy and told her that she was not to worry about finding a replacement— Urdu teachers were a dime a dozen—and proclaimed that she looked forward to attending the wedding.

Sherry left Naheed's office stunned. She'd been expecting fury, and suddenly the full force of her coup hit her: She wasn't just getting married; she was marrying a *somebody.* A somebody who mattered so much that Principal Naheed had been forced into politeness. Sherry did not know why the universe had, after years of insult, decided to smile upon her now, but she went straight to the toilets, where she allowed herself a sob. She was late to her class but for the first time she didn't care.

———

The Loocluses fixed the wedding two weeks hence, *chut mangni pat biyah,* a quick engagement followed by a quicker marriage, lest Kaleen change his mind. There was not much to prepare because, per the teachings of Islam, Kaleen declared that he and Sherry were to have a simple wedding. Instead of weeks of *dholkis,* a *milad,* and a *mayun* leading up to the bankruptcy-inducing three main events of *mehndi, nikah,* and *walima,* Sherry would hold a Quran recital at her humble abode, Looclus Lodge Bismillah, where they would read the good book in order to begin the marriage auspiciously. The recital would be followed by the marriage vows, followed by a nice lunch for close family and a handful of friends, as well as sweet and savory *deyghs* prepared to feed the poor.

Once back in Islamabad, Kaleen would host a decent *walima* in a nice wedding hall, where Begum Beena dey Bagh and all his important clients would not hesitate to be seen. As for dowry, Kaleen hated the concept and would not hear of it. There was no dowry in Islam. Rather, the groom was required to give *haq mehr,* the mandatory monetary gift to the bride, and he planned to hand over to Sherry a generous amount on the very day of their nuptials. Sherry wanted to ask for the right of divorce, but her mother forbade it.

"An ill omen," Bobia stressed, "to begin a marriage with provisions for divorce. A good girl stays married for life no matter what, and only silly girls believe that making compromises toward lifelong commitment is old-fashioned. Sherry, if you want to be happy and successful in your marriage, then forget all the nonsense that bad influence Alys has been putting into your head." Sherry silently comforted herself with the thought of *khula,* no matter how much more difficult that method of procuring a divorce could be—not that, God forbid, the need for divorce would ever arise.

Bobia and Haji Looclus were overjoyed that Kaleen had not turned out to be one of those greedy men who expected his bride's family to fulfill material demands. Nevertheless, they could not stomach sending Sherry with zero dowry, lest anyone taunt her for arriving at her husband's house empty-handed, and so they prepared the minimum: a gold jewelry set, a bed and matching wardrobe plus dressing table, a wristwatch for Kaleen, and suit pieces for his children and close relatives. Thankfully, Sherry's *haq mehr*, which she would dutifully hand over to her parents, would defray the cost of the dowry. As for wedding outfits, Sherry was reluctant to spend a fortune on clothes that would never be worn again. Alys came up with the solution. Sherry could wear her mother's wedding clothes from back in the day.

"If someone asks," Alys instructed, "just say you're wearing them because of sentimental reasons and also: vintage."

Other than conferring over wedding outfits and *mehndi* designs for her hands and feet, Sherry did not spend much time with Alys. Visiting the Binat household meant enduring Mrs. Binat's comments about friends who stole their friends' paramours and, when Alys visited Sherry at her house, the chasm between them was palpable: Where before they had discussed every topic freely, now they skirted around the one topic they knew was futile to discuss. Sherry missed Alys, but she was growing increasingly excited as her wedding day approached, and she was loath to let Alys's silent reproach dampen her enthusiasm.

Then the wedding day was upon them. The guests proclaimed that Sherry was glowing in her pink *gota-kinari gharara*, and Farhat Kaleen, dressed in a white suit and green tie and looking like a Pakistani flag, was overjoyed at his lovely bride. They signed the wedding papers, and Sherry was married, and before she knew it an entourage was walking her to her husband's tinsel-decorated car, with her parents holding the Quran aloft over her head, and her siblings and Alys walking behind her.

The car door opened, the real moment of impending *rukhsati*, of bridal departure, and everyone started to cry. Sherry clung to her parents and siblings for a long minute, and then she hugged Alys farewell. "I truly wish you happiness," Alys said. "I know," Sherry said, and she made Alys promise that she would visit her in Islamabad. In fact, her family was planning to come during the summer holidays and Alys was to accompany them. Alys, overcome by this moment of transition from home to home that most every Pakistani girl dreams of and dreads in equal measures, agreed to the visit, *pukka* promise.

Chapter 16

The wedding was done, there was no undoing it; Sherry Looclus was Mrs. Syeda Shireen Kaleen, and Pinkie Binat came undone, stitch by stitch, and she was determined to unravel her daughters too. Always critical, in her despair she turned cruel: No one would marry Jena, because she was a guileless nincompoop. Qitty was a mustached walrus. Mari was asthmatic and dim—that's why she hadn't gotten into medical school—and she had no sex appeal. No one would marry Lady, because who would marry the youngest sister at the tail end of four unmarried sisters. As for Alys, total loser.

"You are alienating your daughters," Mr. Binat said. "You are losing your mind."

Trying to make sense of how Sherry had pulled off this victory under her watchful eyes had put Pinkie Binat's very identity in a tailspin. She was a failed mother. She was a useless mother. How could Alys have been replaced by Sherry, of all people? Were her daughters not special after all?

The month of Ramadan at the Binat House was a subdued cycle

of *sehris* and *iftaris,* with Mari leading her troubled family through mandatory prayers and plenty extra. The daily fasting and feasting were followed by a subdued *Chaand Raat,* the moon sighting leading into a quiet Eid lunch at which, to everyone's dismay, Mrs. Binat wanted to only lament Sherry's festive Eid as a new bride as per Bobia Looclus's boasts: Sherry's brand-new designer clothes for a gala Eid lunch, gold bangles and earrings and necklace set to match, three goats and three sheep sacrificed and the meat distributed to relatives, friends, and the poor. At each lament, Mrs. Binat eyed Alys with distraught rage. Alys's birthday came. She turned thirty-one. Mrs. Binat refused cake and wept. Jena turned thirty-three. Mrs. Binat wept even more and berated her daughters with new ferocity.

After weeks of their mother's haranguing, Alys grabbed Jena one afternoon and drove them to High Chai. They ordered cappuccinos. Jena was not hungry. Alys ordered baklava. The spring weather had turned warm and pleasant enough for High Chai to have opened their patio area, and the sisters sat outdoors. A vibrant fuchsia bougainvillea clambered over the red-brick boundary wall, and the scent of freshly mowed grass was in the air. Their mother was out of sight, though not out of mind.

"Mummy wants you to apologize," Jena said, poking a hole in the cappuccino's foam heart.

"Mummy, Principal Naheed, Rose-Nama's mother—is there anyone who doesn't want me to apologize?" Alys said. "Maybe I should tattoo a scarlet 'sorry' onto my forehead."

"Mummy just wants you to admit you made a mistake and that Sherry is a snake of a friend."

"I made no mistake and Sherry is no snake." Alys scraped a fork across the baklava's honey-soaked pistachio topping. "It's not as if I was about to walk down the aisle and she coiled herself around him. I had zero interest and Sherry knew that."

"I know," Jena said.

"Which is why I am never apologizing or accepting any of Mummy's unreasonable demands. I've grown up hearing, 'Who will marry you? Who will marry you?' Never once has she deigned to ask whom *I* will marry. She needs to apologize to me."

"You're both too headstrong."

"I swear," Alys said, "our mother would sell us off to the first bidder if she could. Who in their right mind abandons their daughter at a polo match so that she can be proposed to?"

"She's desperate to see us married, that's all," Jena said miserably. "It's not her fault, Alys. She's the product of her time and this system, and she can't see beyond it."

"She should try," Alys said. "She has a brain. And don't tell me that, no matter what, it's disrespectful to speak of one's parents like this."

Jena sighed. A sparrow hovered over one of the wrought-iron chairs. The sisters looked at it for a moment.

"We are," Alys said, "a society teeming with Austen's cruel Mrs. Norrises, snobby looks-obsessed Sir Walters, and conniving John Thorpes and Lady Susans."

"The whole world is full of these types," Jena said.

"Aren't you sick of everything, Jena?" Alys asked. "I'm sick of the hypocrisy and double standards. It's like they break your legs, then give you a wheelchair, then expect you to be grateful for the wheelchair for the rest of your life. How can you trust anyone? How could anyone be happy with a Farhat Kaleen?"

"Everyone's standard of happiness is different," Jena said. "Sherry's settling down and she'll be well settled."

"Settling down. Well settled." Alys laughed derisively. "That's the golden ticket."

"Can I tell you something?"

"What?"

"I keep thinking," Jena said, "that maybe if I'd worn something more flattering, something more alluring, he might have proposed."

"Oh please." Alys swallowed back tears. "Jena, it's not even just the men. We dress to impress other women. Everything is a competition, and the reward is the other women's envy. But Mummy is wrong about style and looks outweighing everything else. It doesn't work that way. It *can't* work that way. I won't let it."

"Maybe it's not my fault," Jena said. "If he was meant to get engaged to Jujeena Darsee—"

"Of course it's not your fault. And I'll bet Bungles has no idea he's engaged to Jujeena Darsee."

"Alys, stop it," Jena said. "His sisters were very clear that he and Jujeena Darsee are to be engaged."

"His sisters!" Alys stabbed apart the baklava layers. "Hammy *wishes* Bungles and Jujeena would get married. She thinks that will lead to Darsee marrying her."

"Alys, it makes complete sense to me that Hammy and Sammy would choose Jujeena Darsee for their sister-in-law. They've known her for a long time, and Bungles must want it too, for no grown man allows his sisters to impose their will on him. I was simply mistaken in his intentions. He thought of me as a good friend and that was all."

"You sound like a film star denying a love affair. 'We're good friends only, blah blah blah.'"

"I'd rather have mistaken his level of interest," Jena said, "than think he or his sisters are deceitful. Just let's change the subject." Moments later she said, "And, anyway, why would Hammy and Sammy try to sabotage their own brother's happiness?"

"Because," Alys said, "their own happiness is more important to them than his. They are selfish sisters, selfish girls, who manipulate their brother without any qualms. They hide their ugly hearts behind dressing well, and so manage to fool people like our mother, who believes clothes-style-accessories-grooming reflects character. Hammy and Sammy think we are beneath them and so couldn't care less how much their brother likes you. And he does like you. Very much."

"If he liked me that much, he'd call me. He'd show up. He—"

"I'll bet he wants to, but his dragon sisters and Dracula—"

"Have they tied him up and gagged him? He's not a puppet."

"The problem is that he trusts that they have his best interest at heart. No one wants to believe that relatives and friends can betray them for their own selfish reasons."

"I'm sure Aunty Tinkle said something to them about us," Jena said, "and you know how crucial good reputations—"

"Stop," Alys said. "If you truly love and like someone, then nothing you hear about them should matter. Bungles is weak willed."

"Don't say that." Jena pushed away her cappuccino.

"Okay. And Sherry and I were going to spend our old age together, by a seaside, eating scones and *samosas*, two bachelorettes bingeing on the sunset forever."

"Don't be silly," Jena said with a wan smile. "Who eats scones and *samosas* at the same time?"

Alys grabbed Jena's hand. "You'll be all right. You'll be perfectly all right and Bungles will be a footnote of a funny story."

"Maybe I should have cracked some jokes?" Jena said, sadness settling on her face. "I was just being myself. I would be reserved with any man who showed interest in me. At least I didn't give him the satisfaction of knowing I was in love with him. But should I have? A little bit?"

Jena's eyes filled with tears. She laid her head on the table. Alys stroked Jena's hair, and by and by Jena dried her eyes and they sat together as long as they could, until it was time to return home.

A week later, Falak and Nona arrived with tranquilizers Nisar had sent for his sister. Mrs. Binat gave them an earful concerning Sherry. "*Kitni chalaak nikli*—what a schemer she turned out to be." "*Aastheen ka saanp*, a snake in our backyard." "*Budhi ghodi lal lagam*, an old mare dressed in youngster's red." She was supposed to have made Alys marry him, instead she married him herself! Then Mrs. Binat began on Alys yet again. Jena was obviously suffering from someone's evil eye, which had prevented Bungles from performing as expected, but Alys had let an already netted fish escape. Kaleen should have been theirs. Instead, he now belonged to the Loocluses. Pinkie 0, Bobia 1.

Mrs. Binat picked up her shoe and threatened Alys with a beating. Nona, her arms spread out, rushed between mother and daughter.

"Pinkie, *pagal ho gai ho*?" Nona asked. "Have you gone mad?"

"Nona *jee*," Mrs. Binat yelled, "would it have killed her to marry Kaleen? Who will marry her now? Who will marry her?"

Alys strode toward her mother. Everyone froze. Then Alys hugged her mother tightly, not letting her go.

"Don't sell us short, Mummy," Alys implored. "Don't sell me short. I'm not useless or good for nothing. I don't want to get married just for the sake of it. I don't need to."

Mrs. Binat sobbed on her daughter's shoulder. Alys rocked her mother gently. Finally Mrs. Binat pushed Alys away, but it was not as rough a push at it could have been.

"Don't be so hard on the girls, Pinkie," Falak said, handing her sister a tranquilizer and a glass of water. "No matter what we do, kismet is the real decider of our fates."

"Kismet has nothing to do with anything," Mrs. Binat said. "It's all about looks."

"Kismet, fate, destiny," Falak said. "I was as beautiful as you, and look what became of me."

"You're still beautiful," Mrs. Binat said, because what else was one to say to a faded beauty.

"Good looks don't guarantee happiness or riches," Falak said. "Also, I've seen a thousand handsome and rich men marrying ugly women."

"True," Nona seconded.

"The only men who marry ugly women," Mrs. Binat said, "are men terrified someone else might find their wife attractive and tempt her into cheating. Proper men are proud to wear beauty on their sleeve. Look at Prince Chaarless and Lady Dayna."

"Charles," Lady corrected her mother. "Diana."

"Charles and Diana," Alys said, "are a perfect example of a mismatched arranged marriage."

"At least Dayna married a prince," said Mrs. Binat tearfully. "Tell me, Falak, how to flip my daughters' rotten kismets? How many more times should I read the Quran for their luck to change? How many more *wazeefays* must I pray? How many more fasts must I keep? How many more *manaats* must I make? Nothing is working."

Mrs. Binat turned to Nona's children, who'd been watching her with wide eyes. She kissed them and told them to go forth and play and make as much noise as they pleased. Indus, Buraaq, Miraage, and Khyber ran rampant through Binat House, their blissful laughter drowning out Mrs. Binat whenever she slipped back into a berating mood. The Binat girls began to unfurl. Lady gave Indus piggyback rides up and down the stairs. Mari bowled to Buraaq's bat. Qitty made paper planes with Miraage. Jena tossed Khyber up in the air and caught him, letting his mirth plant smiles on her face.

"The children have done wonders for Jena," Alys told Nona one morning as they sorted out gently used clothes to donate to charity. "I can't tell you how quiet and somber she'd become. I just know it's his sisters and that horrid Dracula that have kept Bungles away."

"In our culture," Nona said, "men flirt. They enjoy. They move on. They are brought up to believe that women are expendable. We are brought up to believe the opposite. One glance from a man and we readily give away our heart."

"Jena certainly did not mean to set herself up," Alys said. "It's all Mummy's fault. Dressing up Jena to be sold like a commodity. Convincing her that all she needs is the right outfit to get him to propose. Jena asked me if wearing something else might have made the difference. That's how insecure Mummy has made her feel. Did I tell you she keeps leaving her classes at school? Principal Naheed called me in again the other day to warn me that one more time and she'll have to ask Jena to take a leave of absence."

"A leave of absence?" Nona squinted. "Might Jena want to return to Lahore with us? A change of scenery may do her good."

"Being away from our mother will definitely do her good."

"I didn't want to put it like that." Nona smiled. "Lahore is Bungles's city too, but I'll make sure we have no reason to visit their part of town."

"I think being in the same city but with no contact will be good for her."

"Good. As for you, I want to talk to you about Jeorgeullah Wickaam. He's very popular in your household, I can see, and your mother is certain that he's going to marry Qitty, because he encouraged her to dance all of once, but I've heard the special way you speak of him."

"I don't speak of him in any special way." Alys folded a *dupatta* and added it to the keep pile.

"Sure." Nona flicked Alys on her nose. "Now, he's very handsome and magnetic, but I warn you, he's not marriageable material."

"How can you say that?"

"Believe me, I can tell. In my line of work, I come across all sorts of people, and Jeorgeullah Wickaam is a coaster. I would hate to see you end up with a coaster, Alys, and marriage has a way of turning coasters into burdens on their wives. Look at your Falak Khala."

"I have it on good authority," Alys laughed, "from Advocate Musarrat Jr. that Wickaam is a rising star."

"I'm serious, Alys," Nona said. "Wickaam's wife will be a star before he ever is. He'll be content at home, getting manicures, pedicures, facials, and massages all day long, a triumphant trophy husband."

"That's not true." Alys sat up. "Wickaam has faced much adversity, as you know—"

"Oh yes." Nona discarded a turmeric-stained sweater into the rags pile. "How could I not know? He is very eager to tell everyone all about his misfortunes. Look, Alys, it was my duty as your aunt to guide you, I have done my duty, and now I will keep quiet."

"Your duty is several hours too late!" Alys smiled at the alarm on

Nona's face. "Wickaam called me this morning. He's recently gotten engaged to one Miss Jahanara Ana Aan."

"Engaged!"

"He met Miss Jahanara Ana Aan during a work trip to Karachi. Miss Jahanara Ana Aan is her father's only daughter and stands to inherit his accounting firm, and Wickaam intends to inherit it with her. Obviously well-off-enough people for him to see a good match."

"I see," Nona said. "You're very forgiving when Wickaam grabs it, not so forgiving when Sherry does."

Alys flushed. "I'm sure Wickaam's fiancée is not an ass-kissing social-climbing buffoon."

"Poor Qitty. Does your mother know yet?"

Alys shook her head.

"And you, my treasure, are you all right?"

"Too all right." Alys shrugged. "I believe that if Wickaam had money, or I did, I would have been his first choice. In any case, Miss Jahanara Ana Aan sounds like a smart and nice girl. I wish them well. Qitty and Lady were crying, but I thought, What's there to cry about? I'm telling you, Aunty Nona, I'm truly not cut out for marriage, children, that sort of thing. I'm actually quite pleased that Miss Jahanara Ana Aan has inadvertently resolved this 'situation' for me."

Chapter 17

Jena readily accepted Nona's invitation to come to Lahore. Principal Naheed was not thrilled at Jena's wanting to take off the remaining two months of the semester, but Alys volunteered to teach Jena's classes and Mari would substitute as a teacher-in-training. Mari was disgusted with the change in her lifestyle but, since it was for Jena's sake, she didn't grumble too vehemently.

Mrs. Binat prayed that fate would bring Jena and Bungles together in Lahore, and the thought cheered her. Satisfied that she might yet have her coup through Jena, Mrs. Binat inquired after Wickaam. Where had he disappeared? She was informed of Miss Jahanara Ana Aan. Her heart sank, but, then, she'd never truly believed Qitty would be able to attract such a gorgeous man, and neither could she blame Wickaam for grabbing a moneyed woman, and so she searched for a silver lining. Of course! Her daughters would be invited to Wickaam's wedding.

Immediately she began to discuss what outfits would be best for the events. Alys, Jena, Qitty, Lady, and Mari shared a glance and then looked at their father, who wore the same expression of dazed relief. Was Pinkie Binat back to normal and all right in their world?

Nona, the children, Falak, and Jena packed to leave for Lahore, and it was a tearful parting as the remaining Binats stood watching them drive away. Alys turned to Sherry's house for a cigarette, then remembered that Sherry too was gone.

Alys was not restless for long. Her days began with a whirlwind of a schedule as she managed her own classes as well as the workload for Jena's. Mari was turning out to be of little help, because she was more interested in preaching religion than in teaching the syllabus. Then there were the underprivileged children whom she, Jena, Sherry, and Mari used to tutor together, and now Alys insisted that Qitty and Lady get involved too.

Sherry called Alys frequently, and no sooner would Alys hang up than Mrs. Binat would inquire, "And what does your *friend* have to say for herself today?"

Alys would tell her mother the truth. Sherry was having the time of her life. Sleeping in. Car and driver at her disposal to go wherever and whenever she wanted. She'd joined a gym and had developed a yen for yoga and power aerobics. She was making friends, whom she met for brunches and kitty parties. She and Kaleen had dined at Beena dey Bagh's; both mother and daughter thought highly of Kaleen. Kaleen's elder son was respectful to Sherry, while the seven-year-old son said the cutest things and clung to her like a duckling. Kaleen's daughter was as friendly as she needed to be. Sherry's cat had also settled into the new environment as if she'd always been living there. All in all, all was good and Kaleen had only one request, which Sherry was beyond delighted to fulfill: that she cook for him.

"Hah!" Mrs. Binat said. "Even he knows all Sherry is good for is the kitchen."

"They have a cook, Mummy," Alys said. "All Sherry says she does is add spices."

"Let's hope," Mrs. Binat said, "Kaleen gets food poisoning and drops dead. Then Sherry will be a widow and that'll teach her to steal men interested in other women."

"*Tauba!* Dear God!" Mr. Binat said. "What a thing to say!"

Alys did not share with her mother the prevailing awkwardness between Sherry and herself and how they had to force the closeness they'd once so easily shared.

It was Jena's phone calls Alys looked forward to. Jena called home daily to share news of her activities: shopping, films, restaurants, taking the children on outings. She would help Nona in the kitchen and they would make cake deliveries together. She visited Falak Khala once a week and was helping Babur prepare for an interview with a recruiter from Cornell.

Jena professed to be over Bungles. As proof, she planned to drop in to see Hammy and Sammy. No, she was not going to listen to Alys and stay far away from them. Bungles had been nothing more than a passing infatuation, pushed to extremes by their mother's pressure. Jena knew that now. She was merely going to visit Hammy and Sammy as she would any acquaintances of hers who lived in Lahore.

Jena dropped in one afternoon. Hammy and Sammy were at home. They were hosting a luncheon, and the maid, thinking Jena was one of the guests, led her into the drawing room where socialites were lining up to pose for a photograph. (The photo later appeared in *Social Lights;* Lady told Jena she'd seen it.) There'd been a hush when Jena entered the drawing room. Fazool said, "Ham, Sam, isn't that the damsel Bungs—"

Hammy and Sammy cut off Fazool. They hurried to Jena and hugged her and said what a nice surprise to see her and too bad it was not a good time but that they'd visit her in the next few days; they needed to see someone in Jamshed Colony anyway. She'd not asked about *him.* She'd not even looked for him at their house. The fact was, Hammy and Sammy had been very nice to her.

They were not very nice to you, Alys thought. They could have invited Jena to stay for lunch, a not-unusual courtesy in their part of the world; instead, she'd been sent off.

Three days later, Nona called Alys: "Jena needs to leave the house and stop waiting for them to visit. Who knows if they'll ever come?"

They came on the seventh day. Jena called home as soon as they left. For the first time, anger edged out her hurt.

"You were right, Alys," she said in a steely voice. "They are superficial and shallow and they never liked me. The person they were coming to see who lives in this part of town is their *dhobi*. They are attending a charity ball and need their gowns laundered according to specific instructions, which they didn't trust the driver to convey to the *dhobi*. I was the stop after the *dhobi*. They stayed for eight minutes and forty seconds and looked as if they expected spiders to descend on them the whole time. Basically they came to tell me that their brother knows I'm in town but he's busy with Jujeena Darsee and doesn't have a moment to spare on frivolities. I am a frivolity. They said they hoped I enjoy my visit to Lahore, and then they left. Good riddance to them. Hammy, Sammy, their brother—I will not let them spoil my mood for a single second more. You are right, Alys, I am too quick to believe people are nice. I am cured. I assure you."

The two months passed by. Alys set exams for her classes. She graded exams. She attended the staff meetings to discuss student promotions to the next grade level. She sat through end-of-term class parties, where students—who always discovered newfound love for teachers at the end of the school year—gave her gifts and handmade cards. Tahira hugged Alys and thanked her for the B-minus on her final exam. Rose-Nama thanked Alys for her A grade too. Alys nodded, for she was not one of those teachers who settled scores through grades. Unfortunately, though, after the summer break, Alys would see Rose-Nama in her tenth-grade literature class, while Tahira was leaving to getting married. *Best wishes for the future!* Alys wrote on Tahira's uniform as students scampered about, getting their uniforms signed for posterity. Finally, the last bell for home time rang and everyone, including Alys and her sisters, headed to the gates, where they boarded the school van for the summer holidays.

Alys was leaving the next day for Islamabad. Sherry's family had rented a minivan so that they could travel in comfort. On the way to Islamabad, they were going to stop over in Lahore for a night, a prospect that had cemented Alys's decision to go, for she would get to see Jena and Nona.

"Don't forget your old father despite your change of scenery," Mr. Binat said as he hugged Alys goodbye. Mrs. Binat, Mari, Qitty, and Lady waved glumly, because they wouldn't have minded a trip to Islamabad and a change of scenery too.

The journey to Lahore took a quick two hours. The Loocluses passed the time with singing competitions, eating the homemade lunch of *aloo paratha* and *cheeni roti,* and marveling at how wonderful it was that Sherry *ne itna bada haath maara*—that Sherry had managed to marry so well. The Loocluses were looking forward to eating in good restaurants and sightseeing in style, for Sherry had assured them that they did not have to worry about the expense. She was going to foot all the bills, thanks to the generosity of her husband.

In Lahore, the Loocluses dropped Alys at her uncle's house for the night. Jena, Nona, and Nisar were eagerly waiting for Alys, and they insisted the Loocluses at least have chai before heading off to spend the night with their own relatives. Since it was the polite thing to do, and also because who would refuse Nona's *naan khatai* cookies, the Loocluses obliged.

During tea, Bobia Looclus whispered to Alys that Jena looked much happier, *mashallah.* Alys was grateful she'd said so, for she'd thought it herself. Later, Nona said that on occasion a cloud would yet pass over Jena but that she was determined not to wallow in it.

Chapter 18

The remainder of the journey to Islamabad was just as merry as the trip the day before, if not merrier for Alys, since Jena was on the mend. Hours later, they drove off the motorway and into the pristine capital city with its wide leafy roads, and eventually the minivan turned off the main road and entered a nice upper-middle-class neighborhood. Everyone in the van held their breath in anticipation of seeing Sherry's marital home. It was just as Sherry had described: a large two-story house with a decent driveway set in the midst of a pretty lawn. Farhat Kaleen and Sherry stood on the stoop of their home, waiting to greet them, Sherry with open arms, and Kaleen with a satisfied face that seemed plumper, no doubt courtesy of Sherry's cooking.

Bobia Looclus could not help but burst out in pride, "Sherry, *tum tho sitar say guitar bun gayee ho.* Sherry, you've transformed from the local sitar into an international-level guitar."

"Nothing lesser about the sitar or other local instruments, Aunty Bobia," Alys said, because it was not in her nature to let anything go. Sherry was looking very nice. Gone was her thin braid. Her new chin-length style suited her bony angles. Her skin had cleared up. She was clad in a well-tailored lawn *shalwar kameez* from one of the better brands and black ballet flats. Amethyst drops shone in her ears.

"Ammi," Sherry giggled, "if I tell you how much my haircut alone cost, you will faint."

"It's got nothing to do with that," Bobia Looclus admonished her daughter, "and everything to do with inner happiness. You are glowing."

"Of course she is glowing," Kaleen said as he welcomed Sherry's parents and awestruck siblings to Islamabad. "Nothing but the best for my sweet blemish-free Sherry."

He gave Alys a wide smile. "Most welcome. Most welcome."

"You came," Sherry said, hugging Alys tightly.

"I came," Alys said, hugging her back, even as Kaleen urged them to part so that they could start the tour of his *gareeb khana*, his most humble abode.

Off they all went to tour the house. Like most standard upper-middle-class homes, it boasted multiple bedrooms—in this case five—with attached baths; a drawing-and-dining room looked out to the back garden, which was a haven for fruit trees. Bobia Looclus kept squeezing Sherry's hand. There were air conditioners in every room. Every room! And a backup generator to handle load-shedding. There was a cook, cleaner, driver, maid, gardener, gate guard, *dhobi*, tailor, and countless other amenities and luxuries at her daughter's disposal. Never had she imagined that her Sherry, whom everyone had written off, would be *so* well settled. This was proof that there was a God.

Alys noticed the glances Bobia kept giving her, which rivaled Kaleen's, signifying that all this could have been *hers*. Alys suppressed a smile and managed a suitably awed expression as they walked from the russet-tiled portico into a flourishing garden that also contained a large chicken coop and a milking goat lounging on lush grass.

Sherry's brothers, Mansoor and Manzoor, and her sister, Mareea, rushed to stroke the goat, and even Alys fell in love with its soft bleating and ebony eyes. The only goats she'd ever known were the ones inevitably sacrificed at Eid for meat, and it was blissful to see this goat living its life, even if tethered to the low water tap jutting from the boundary wall.

Kaleen began to lecture on the benefits of happy animals and fresh eggs and goat milk, until Sherry gently ushered the party back indoors to their bedrooms so they could freshen up.

Alys was given a comfy room that overlooked the back garden. She opened the windows to faraway goat bleats and a chikoo tree thick with brown ripe fruit.

"It's a lovely room," Alys said. She plucked a chikoo straight off the tree and inhaled its sweet scent before handing it to Isa, who was perpetually glued to Sherry's hip.

"It's a lovely life," Kaleen said jovially as Sherry's cat contently circled his legs. "It's a lovely house. Sherry couldn't be happier or healthier. Right, Sherry?"

Sherry nodded and, kissing Isa and promising to peel the chikoo for him, she herded everyone out of Alys's room.

Alys took a hot shower in, she had to admit, a cozy cobalt-tiled bathroom and then, as instructed, she returned to the living room. There, the maid, Ama Iqbal, was serving a high tea and Kaleen was breaking the great news: Tonight they dined at Begum Beena dey Bagh's.

"Tonight?" Alys said. She'd been looking forward to getting in bed with a good book. "What's the hurry?"

"Hurry!" Kaleen scowled. He was beyond flattered that Beena dey Bagh had insisted Sherry's family's first dinner in Islamabad be at her table. "There's no hurry except that she wishes to do me a great honor."

"If you don't mind," Alys said, "may I be excused?"

"Excused!"

"Please, Kaleen," Sherry said, "your blood pressure will go up. Calm down."

"Number one, no one excuses themselves when Begum Beena dey Bagh summons," Kaleen said, seething. "And number two, Alysba, I expected your parents to have instilled some manners in you and some sense of protocol."

"Kaleen Sahib," Alys said, "number one, I'm assuming that Beena dey Bagh will honor you by inviting us at least once more in these next three weeks. And, number two, at my age I should hope I've taught myself how to exercise good manners and protocol of my own free will."

"Alys," Bobia Looclus said in a tight voice, "Begum Beena is Kaleen's employer, and we must not give cause for complaint."

"You're right, Aunty Bobia." Alys smiled sweetly at Kaleen, who was clearly squirming at being categorized as a mere employee. "I should have thought of this technicality myself. I would not like to be the cause of Kaleen Sahib getting into trouble with his employer."

Kaleen spluttered as he looked for something to say that would restore his full glory in everyone's eyes. Sherry squinted at Alys, a playful request that she cut it out.

Later that evening, Alys was the first guest ready and waiting to leave for Beena dey Bagh's estate, which was a good forty minutes away. Sherry was dressed in a brand-name silk *shalwar kameez*, and she was wearing new gold earrings that Bobia and Mareea were swooning over. Mareea had to borrow a silk outfit from Sherry's closet. Sherry told her younger sister that they'd go shopping the very next morning to update her meager wardrobe. Mansoor and Manzoor were dressed in ill-fitting suits with clip-on ties; they reminded their elder sister that they too required an upgrading, and Sherry promised them a shopping spree as well.

Kaleen entered in brown pants and a purple shirt. He glanced at Alys's *zari* embroidered *khusse*, white capris paired with a green-and-red *ajrak kurta* and matching *dupatta*, and the gray pearls dangling from her ears. He assured his guests that they were all looking decent and that none of them should worry anyway, because everyone's taste and style fell short compared to Begum Beena dey Bagh's and that—such a kind soul she was—she readily imparted her sartorial advice, as Sherry could attest.

"True," Sherry said with a glimmer in her eyes. "Begum Beena is enormously generous with her opinion to better people as she thinks best."

"Yes, she is." Kaleen beamed at Sherry as they all squeezed into his car, for the Loocluses' rented minivan was a rather tacky vehicle and not one Begum Beena dey Bagh deserved in her driveway. "You're so perceptive, Sherry; you're able to see things exactly as I would like you to see them."

Sherry twitched a smile at Alys in the backseat. Alys nodded. If such a marriage was working for Sherry, then so be it. As they drove out of Islamabad, the city fell away to increasingly rural surroundings until they were passing acres of land between grand houses nestled behind walls. Kaleen stopped at imposing gates with gold lettering, VERSAILLES OF PAKISTAN, and he honked politely until a guard opened the gate. They drove down a long driveway with peepal trees on either side until they arrived at a massive house with a huge fountain, water gushing out of the beaks of black and white swans.

The butler led the guests over black marble floors strewn with hand-woven Kashmiri and Afghani rugs and into the main drawing room. An Amazonian woman in a blue *ajrak shalwar kameez* and matching *dupatta*, though in a different pattern from the one Alys had on, looked up from the candles she was lighting on the mantel over the fireplace.

So this was the aunt, Alys thought, who was instrumental, along with Darsee, in robbing Wickaam of his inheritance. Beena dey Bagh's thick salt-and-pepper hair fell to her broad shoulders in a blunt cut. She wore diamond studs, a diamond Allah pendant, and several obese diamonds on her large French-manicured fingers. Her coral lipstick bled into the creases around her mouth. Above the fireplace was a blown-up Warhol-style photograph of a very striking

girl. Kaleen had told Sherry, who had told Alys, that Annie was engaged to Darsee, and if it was Annie, Alys thought, then Darsee was
in luck, looks-wise at least.

"You are on time, good," Beena dey Bagh said as she handed the
candle lighter to the butler. Kaleen introduced everyone. Bobia and
Haji Looclus nearly fell over themselves as they thanked Beena dey
Bagh for her gracious invitation. Mareea, Mansoor and Manzoor
were tongue-tied as they looked from glass ashtrays to porcelain
vases to the myriad sculptures and figurines that adorned the coffee
tables, side tables, and consoles of the four separate seating areas in
the drawing room. Alys had grown up in a similar setting before
Uncle Goga and Aunty Tinkle had kicked them out of their ancestral house, and she was not intimidated by expensive décor no doubt
chosen by a costly interior designer.

Beena dey Bagh motioned to the sitting area with a minimalist
arrangement, its angularity softened with plush cushions and a Zen
tabletop waterfall with budding bamboos standing in black pebbles.
She settled her imposing frame into a curved chair with spindly legs
and invited them to seat themselves.

"My favorite corner," she said, peering at them one by one. "So
peaceful. No, Mr. Looclus? Wouldn't you say, Mrs. Looclus?"

Bobia, who'd been wishing she could free her inflamed feet from
the confines of her good shoes, managed a fawning, "*Jee, jee,* fuss
class, fuss class."

"It is A-one setting," Haji Looclus said. "We are very sorry to be
missing Lolly Sahib."

"Yes," Beena dey Bagh said. "My husband is in Frankfurt, attending a pen show, and then he heads to Switzerland for some skiing.
Such an adventurer."

"Such an adventurer," Kaleen echoed.

"I remind him that, Lolly, you are too old to be going skiing,
bungee-jumping, zip-lining but he informs me age is just a number
and he's not going to allow his knees, or me, to hold him back."

Haji Looclus threw in his trump card, for either you were rich or you elevated your status by claiming direct descent from the Prophet, which he did.

"We are Syeds, you know," he said with a magnanimous smile, "so we did not let age stop us from performing Hajj. Have you been for Hajj?"

"Hajj?" Beena dey Bagh said. "Seven, actually, and we're planning to go next year in order to give thanks for the miracle Kaleen here has managed with Annie."

Haji Looclus shrank into his chair. His single Hajj had left them all but bankrupt, and suddenly to have insisted on the title "Haji" on the basis of a lone pilgrimage seemed empty. Haji Looclus swallowed. To be a seven-time Hajjan! And still want more! Beena dey Bagh was a truly pious woman, and no wonder Almighty God had blessed her with so much.

Luckily for Haji Looclus, Beena dey Bagh was not interested in how many times anyone else had performed the holy pilgrimage and, instead, she pointed to the portrait above the fireplace and informed them that it was Annie at her best.

"And where is dear Annie?" Kaleen looked toward the archway that separated the drawing room from the large parquet foyer.

"As you know, Kaleen," Beena said, "if Annie cannot go to the salon, then the salon must come to Annie. She is so fond of mani-pedis, she gets them done as regularly as others brush their teeth. It so heartens me that my daughter remains interested in a few things."

A maid entered with a silver tray holding soft drinks. Mareea, Mansoor, and Manzoor excitedly chose from the array of colas. Alys took a glass of lemon squash.

"Ice, Alysba?" Beena said, and before Alys could answer, Beena had signaled to the maid, who whisked Alys's glass out of her hand, topped it with ice, and set it back down on a cut-crystal coaster. "Sherry has told me so much about you. Also I have Naheed's reports. I will say that the Dilipabad English-literature exam scores are consistently admirable."

"Thank you," Alys said, as she signaled to the maid to remove the ice.

Beena dey Bagh's eyes narrowed. "I hear other things too, Alysba. I'm not averse to progress, within reason, but I hear you like shocking students."

"I believe—"

"You teachers," Beena dey Bagh cut Alys off, "are such ardent believers in this, that, or the other." She looked up at a woman who entered. "Yes?"

"Madam," the woman said, "we're done with Madam Annie. Payment, Madam."

"Where is Nurse Jenkinudin?"

"Don't know, Madam."

Beena dey Bagh picked a walkie-talkie off the coffee table. Within minutes a woman in a starched white *shalwar kurta* came running in, apologized, and glared at the salon woman as she shepherded her out.

"I had such an efficient Filipina nurse for Annie." Beena dey Bagh threw up her hands. "Unfortunately her mother also got a visa to work in Pakistan and off mine went to join her in Lahore. A replacement is in the works, but visas can take time. Nurse Jenkinudin is my third local. The local domestics are shoddy compared to the foreign domestics. No work ethic. Of course, you pay through the nose for foreigners, but then you get the best."

Everyone nodded. Kaleen remarked that staffing his clinic with hardworking locals was a challenge too.

"Might you say," Alys said, looking at Beena dey Bagh even as everyone turned to look at her, "that if one were to pay the local servants the same wages one paid the foreign, then the local would be just as good?"

"Begum Beena dey Bagh," Kaleen said, grimacing at Alys as if she'd farted in public, "prefers the term 'domestics' to 'servants.' She believes it gives them an air of respectability that the term 'servant' lacks."

"Right you are, Kaleen," Beena dey Bagh said. "That is exactly how I feel."

"Of course, everyone deserves dignity," Alys said.

"Precisely," Beena dey Bagh said.

"But," Alys said, "were I a servant, I might be compelled to say, 'Call me by whichever term you want—"domestics" or "the help" is fine—but please pay me the same exorbitant salary as you would foreign servants.'"

"Are you a communist?" Beena dey Bagh hissed. "Surely you do not believe that everyone deserves the same salary if they have unequal qualifications. The foreign come trained, while I have to train the domestic. Anyway, inequality is ordained by God. Jew, Christian, Muslim, Hindu, Sikh, Buddhist—show me any religion or philosophy that does not speak of rich and poor. It is the rich's job to take care of the poor in their own way, often via charity, and it is the poor's job to take care of the rich in their own way, often through serving."

"But charity," Alys said, "is dependent on goodwill, and serving is a job that should be highly paid. If you ask me, even teachers' salaries should go way up."

Kaleen spluttered on his juice. Sherry gave a hint of a smile. Beena dey Bagh cackled.

"Everyone," she said, "ultimately thinks of their own skin."

"Yes," Alys said. "Everyone does perhaps think of their own coffers and comforts. But some people deserve and others simply hoard and exploit."

"Such confidence. How old are you?"

"I believe girls are not supposed to be asked, or expected to divulge, their ages. However, I recently turned thirty-one."

"And the other teacher, your older sister?"

"Jena is thirty-three."

"And neither one of you is married yet, I hear." Beena dey Bagh gave an all-knowing smile. "Must be hard on your mother."

"It is," Alys said. "But I believe that as hard as it may be on our mother, it seems to be even harder on absolute strangers."

Beena dey Bagh geared up for a choice reply but, at that very moment, everyone turned to see Nurse Jenkinudin helping Annie walk in and sit down. Annie's tall frame wore well a white silk blouse and bottle-green jeans and gold Dior sandals, from which shone ten long toenails in pearly glittery crimson. The color rendered her complexion even sallower, Alys thought, but her hair was glossy and fell in a blue-black curtain to her waist and was cut in bangs above her pallid eyes.

"Sorry to have kept everyone waiting," Annie said, breathing heavily.

"My love, never any need for sorry from you," Beena dey Bagh said, as she signaled to the maid to set dinner. "How was this new mani-pedi team?"

"Fine, Ammi." Annie smiled at everyone. "Sherry, you must be so excited your family is finally here. So pleased to meet you all. And your best friend, it is Alys, right? Good to meet you. Sherry mentions you at least a hundred times each visit."

"All good mentions, I hope," Alys said, smiling.

"So far," Annie said, laughing. Alys laughed too.

Kaleen joined in the laughter, though he was miffed that Sherry would mention Alys at all. The maid announced that dinner was served, and they all rose and proceeded to the fourteen-seater dining table, where servers waited with three main dishes—*paya, nihari,* and *haleem*—and the many accompaniments that went with each of the delicacies—fresh coriander, chilies, lemons, julienned ginger, and crisp fried onions.

Beena dey Bagh asked Mr. and Mrs. Looclus to please begin. *Paya* was Haji Looclus's favorite dish, and he ladled the gummy hoof soup into the fine china bowl and sprinkled ginger and coriander on it. Bobia Looclus helped herself to choice chunks of meat from the *nihari*. Once they were done, the servers moved on to Beena dey

Bagh and then around the table. Alys poured a little *haleem* into a bowl and squeezed lemon over the meat-and-lentil stew and topped it off with sliced green chilies. She dipped her buttered *tandoori* bread into it. Delicious.

Alys complimented the food, and Annie said that their cook should be declared a national asset.

"I do so miss being able to eat anything I want," Annie said as Nurse Jenkinudin placed a bowl of steaming chicken broth before her and cracked a fresh egg into it. "Did you know that in order to enjoy food one must smell it? So at least through smell, I get to eat. I had a friend back in college who developed anosmia—couldn't smell a thing—and lost all interest in eating. Once I fell ill, we'd compare notes about which was worse: no smell or not being able to keep anything down."

"Annie, you'll be eating everything you want in no time," Beena dey Bagh said. "Right, Kaleen?"

"Why not?" Kaleen said. "If God wills it."

"Life," Sherry said, "can change from good to bad so fast, and it follows that just as fast it can change from bad to good."

"You're so wise, Sherry. An angel to Dr. Kaleen's saint." Annie turned to Mr. and Mrs. Looclus. "Your daughter is an angel. Ever since she's arrived, she regularly reads the Quran to me, with excellent Arabic pronunciation. Neither of us understands the language, but just the rhythm is such a balm to my soul."

"It is very good," Beena dey Bagh said to Mr. and Mrs. Looclus, "that you people teach your children to recite the Quran by rote in Arabic regardless of whether they understand it or not. Of course, the best thing would be to learn Arabic, and if I ever had the time and inclination, I would be as fluent as any native speaker, possibly even better. Sherry has such a soothing voice and it brings such peace to Annie. In fact, Sherry, I'd like you to record the Quran for Annie so she has access to your voice at her convenience."

"Sherry does have a soothing voice," Alys said. "Sherry, you should sell the recordings."

"*Astagfiruallah,* God forbid," Kaleen said. "Selling the word of God!"

"Aren't Qurans sold?" Alys said.

Kaleen bristled. "There's no need for Sherry to earn a single penny. She's merely doing me a favor by helping me heal Annie through oral-to-aural therapy."

"I think every woman should have her own income," Alys said to Kaleen, "even married women."

"I agree," Annie said.

"Every woman should have the ability," Kaleen said, smiling at Annie and Sherry, "to earn her own income, but what will we husbands do if you women start to earn comparable incomes *and* have the babies? The lucky woman is one whose husband can provide well for her in his lifetime as well as after his death."

"We agree," Bobia and Haji Looclus said. "Sherry agrees too."

Sherry nodded politely.

"Alys," Annie said, "Sherry told me that you'd be the perfect person to ask: Can you recommend any stories with characters who are chronically ill and yet rise above it? But no *becharis,* no pitiable creatures."

"Have you read the short story 'Good Country People' by Flannery O' Connor? The main character, Hulga, is a non-*bechari.* Also there's Anne de Bourgh in Jane Austen's *Pride and Prejudice.*"

"I've read *P and P,*" Annie said. "It was helpful in an unexpected way. Anne doesn't say a single word the entire novel, she just sits there, sickly and voiceless, and I decided that, no matter how ill I got, I'd never turn or be turned into Anne de Bourgh."

On the ride back, Kaleen wanted everyone to tell him their exact impressions of Versailles of Pakistan as well as of Beena dey Bagh and Annie. Was Versailles not sophisticated? Was Annie not marvelous? Was Beena dey Bagh not majestic?

Bobia and Haji Looclus praised the estate and the pious Hajjan

mother and her daughter to Kaleen's satisfaction, as did Sherry's siblings, their tongues loosening as soon as they left Versailles.

Alys, however, was not as forthcoming as Kaleen would have preferred. He did not like her tone at all when she said, "Beena dey
Bagh certainly enjoys praise and compliments."

"Why shouldn't she?" he snapped, thanking his lucky stars yet
again that he'd avoided marrying her, and he took over the exalta-
tions until they were parked in his driveway.

Once Sherry settled everyone in for the night, she tiptoed to
Alys's bedroom. Alys opened the door, her smile matching Sherry's.
Sherry went straight to the almirah and extracted a pack of cigarettes
from under a pile of spare quilts.

"This used to be Kaleen's daughter's bedroom before she returned
to England, and now it's my smoking room." Sherry opened up the
pack. "It's also the most remote room in the house, and I thought
you'd like that."

Alys cranked open the window. A heady scent of night-blooming
jasmine wafted in. The two friends discussed Beena dey Bagh and
Annie. Annie seemed a nice-enough girl, they decided. Alys mentioned that Darsee would not be as miserable with her as she'd like
him to be.

Alys informed Sherry about Wickaam and Miss Jahanara Ana
Aan and assured her, as she had Nona, that she was quite the opposite of heartbroken. She entertained Sherry with tales from school
and of Principal Naheed constantly gloating about how Gin and
Rum had both been proposed to on account of looking irresistible in
their QaziKreations outfits.

"I have a good mind," Alys said, "to tell her that maybe the proposals should be directed to the outfits. Anyway, Rose-Nama's
mother is still demanding that I apologize for saying the desire for
sex can lead to early marriages. You know better than most, Sherry,
that legal sex is a big reason people in Pakistan get married."

Sherry told Alys that she was quite enjoying the conjugal duties
of being Mrs. Kaleen, even though they slept in separate bedrooms.

"Kaleen snores like a truck, and apparently I snore too; thus he very shyly suggested that we should try separate rooms for sleeping purposes. I jumped on the offer. I've been sleeping alone for too many years to suddenly be comfortable with someone else in bed. Of course, I hop, skip, and jump to his bedroom for a visit when he asks, which is often, and I always return very satisfied. Since I don't have anyone else to compare my husband to, I'm quite sure it's as good as it can get. In fact, it is everything I'd dreamed of and more. I'm married, and yet I have my own space."

"I'm happy you are happy," Alys said simply.

"And how is Jena? Better?"

"Much better," Alys said.

"My mother was saying the same thing." Sherry dropped her cigarette butt into a bottle with water. "*Allah ka shukur hai,* thanks be to God. I was worried about her. No man is worth losing one's heart or one's looks over, especially if one looks like Jena."

"A lot of good her looks have done her."

"Kismet," Sherry said. "Look at me."

"You've always sold yourself too short."

"Now that Kaleen has bought me, I quite realize my worth."

"Yuck," Alys said, smacking Sherry on the arm. "What a way to put it!"

Sherry opened the cabinet and took out a spray deodorizer. "This thing is so expensive. But I can afford it."

"Which reminds me," Alys said, "I would like to spend my morning in bed, lazing away, without being hauled off anywhere if that's all right with you."

"Fine by me." Sherry showed Alys how to buzz through to the kitchen. "If your majesty wants tea, breakfast, et cetera, in bed."

"I want," Alys said.

"Imagine," Sherry said. "This buzzer could have been yours, and I could have been visiting you."

"Be quiet," Alys said as she climbed into bed, "and good night and sweet dreams, before I remind you of my views on that."

Chapter 19

The following week was spent sightseeing and picnicking at Faisal Mosque, Daman-e-Koh, Rawal Lake, and shopping in Jinnah Supermarket. During the evenings, they would gather around a TV drama or a romance or action film before bedtime. Alys and Sherry would catch a quick midnight smoke and chitchat. Sherry hosted a luncheon for her new friends, who were the wives of Kaleen's friends. They were nice enough women, interested in being skinny, holidays and shopping, throwing costume parties, outdoing each other through their children's accomplishments, and bonding over the incompetence of their servants. When Alys teased her about her new best friends, Sherry was a good sport.

"Rather happy dimwits than a cynical crab like you," Sherry said, smiling. "Anyway, I have my translation projects to keep my brain oiled and, honestly, Kaleen encourages me to buy all the books I want."

That evening, when Alys made her routine phone call to Jena, she acknowledged that while Farhat Kaleen could be faulted for many a thing, being a miserly husband was not one of them, and both sisters were pleased for Sherry.

Alys sensed a returning melancholy in Jena's voice. Nona confirmed that Jena was certainly less lively than she'd been the previous week, and Nona suspected the cause. Had Alys seen the current issue of *Social Lights*?

"I recommend you suffer through this issue," Nona said. "Bungles, Hammy-Sammy, and gang are prominently featured."

After Alys hung up, she sent Sherry's cook to the market to buy the issue. The issue had a special section devoted to the luxe and snazzy vacations enjoyed by Pakistan's VIPs. The gang's week of rest and relaxation in the Maldives had a full page to itself. There they were, all smiles and sun and sunglasses and aqua, as if clueless that they'd left a heartbroken girl in their wake. Hammy, Sammy, Jaans, posing on a yacht. Darsee and his sister, Jujeena, in scuba gear. In another photo, Bungles in a pool with his arm around Jujeena, who was in a hot-pink bikini top with a gigantic waxy flower behind her ear.

Alys tossed the magazine into the trash. Nothing in life was fair. Nothing. Horrible people prospered and good, kind people did not, and there was no rhyme or reason to it. And for consolation, one attributed it to destiny.

Alys woke up the next morning still feeling dismal. She went for her morning walk-jog in the pretty park not five minutes away, determined not to let "Social Blights" ruin her day. She returned hot and sweaty. She bathed and changed into leggings and a T-shirt saying NOT YOUR AVERAGE BAJI. Then she proceeded to the dining room, where a late brunch was being enjoyed by all.

"*As-salaam-alaikum,*" Alys greeted everyone. Taking a seat opposite Sherry, she poured herself a mug of instant coffee and cracked a boiled egg against her plate. She grabbed the newspaper no one had opened yet and flipped through the usual news of honor killings, dowry burnings, rapes, blasphemy accusations, sectarian violence, corruption scandals, tax evasions, and the never-ending promises by vote-grubbing politicians to fix the country.

Alys was on her second coffee when the doorbell rang and, moments later, two men entered the dining room. Kaleen jumped up.

"*Aiye, aiye,* welcome, welcome," Kaleen said, his voice shaking as he led Darsee and his friend to chairs at the head of the table. "An honor! An honor! Sherry, have the cook brew a fresh pot of chai and fry up another batch of your superb *shami kebabs.*"

Darsee's companion was a friend from India, Raghav Kumar. He and Darsee had been in college together in Atlanta for their undergraduate degrees. No, he was not a vegetarian, Raghav said, as the cook brought in the piping-hot kebabs. Yes, many Hindus ate beef. Yes, he would very much like a cup of chai, with three teaspoons of sugar and plenty of milk.

Raghav was here on a twofold mission, one personal and the other a lifelong dream of climbing Pakistan's—nay, the world's—impossible mountain, K2. Last year he'd made it quite far up Everest. There were congratulations all around. Mansoor and Manzoor began to ask him questions about mountaineering, which was his hobby, and film editing, which was his job. Yes, he'd met quite a few superstars. No, he wasn't married. Yes, he was in a relationship.

"There's a lovely park just around the corner from here," Alys said, "with a really nice jogging track but also an indoor climbing wall if you're interested."

"Interested. Thank you."

"And," Alys added, "just in case it's as big an issue for you as it might be for some people, a warning: It's not some fancy gym or exclusive climbing club but part of a public park."

"Exclusivity," Raghav said, "is a silly problem for silly people, for the most part."

Alys laughed. "Every segment of society here prides itself on being exclusive in some way."

"Such pride is a worldwide epidemic," Raghav said.

Darsee finally spoke. "How long are you here for, Alys?"

"A few weeks," she said a little curtly. "When did you come to Islamabad?"

"Last night," Darsee said. "We drove in from Lahore. Annie mentioned that you were all here. . . ."

"Did you happen to see my sister Jena in Lahore?" Alys asked. "She's been there these past few months."

Darsee cleared his throat. "No. Have you read the novel I gave you yet?"

"No. How was your time in the Maldives?" Alys asked.

"The usual."

"And what is the usual, for those of us not privy to your usual or to the Maldives' usual?"

"Hot and too commercial."

"Your party was featured in *Social Lights*. You seemed not too bothered by the heat and commerce."

Darsee scowled. "Hammy and Sammy had no right to release my sister's or my photos for public consumption."

"Some people," Alys said, "think it a great badge of social currency to be featured in social pages. I believe the term used is 'making it.'"

"Good for some people," Darsee said. "I find it crass. We're private people, not celebrities."

Alys groaned. "Please don't tell me you're one of those people who both love the exposure and complain about it."

Raghav raised his cup of chai to Alys. "If nothing else, *Social Lights* has catapulted Val into the role of even-more-eligible bachelor."

"Every mother, father, and daughter," said Alys, "has him in their sights now. There is no escape, thanks to his holiday in Maldives, drinking piña coladas at pools with bars."

Darsee rose abruptly. "Let's go, Raghav. Thank you, Dr. Kaleen. Good to meet your family, Mrs. Kaleen. We actually came to invite you all to dinner tonight at Beena Aunty's, but I understand you must be unavailable at such a short notice, so—"

"Not at all. Not at all," Kaleen said. "For your 'unty I would break an engagement with the Queen of England. We'll be there."

After Darsee and Raghav drove away in a gleaming Pajero, Kaleen dropped into a chair with a self-satisfied look.

"That man, Valentine Darsee, has never thought it made sense to stop by my house, let alone exchange a word with me, in all this time. Yet here he was, come himself, drinking my chai, eating my kebabs. Clearly my importance for Annie is on the rise."

After Kaleen left for work, Sherry dragged Alys to the back of the garden in order to feed the goat and gather eggs. She duly informed Alys that her husband must be forgiven his flights of fancy for, clearly, dear Valentine Darsee had come for Alys.

"Don't be stupid," Alys said, flushing.

"He's aching to discuss the novel he gave you. Aching!"

"Shut up."

"Such an ache." Sherry lifted a squawking chicken and swayed it obscenely. "Such a deep ache."

"Too deep!" Alys said, laughing. "I thought you'd become all goody-goody once you married, and your sexual innuendos would end, but how nice that you've added flapping gestures to your repertoire. I don't know what Darsee's motive was for coming here. Last I saw him was at Fazool and Moolee's New Year's party, where we quarreled and he stormed out."

"And now he's stormed back in," Sherry said, and, singing "*Kabootar Ja Ja Ja*, pigeon fly, fly, fly," she impishly thrust the protesting chicken at a shrieking Alys before letting it loose.

The guests duly arrived at Versailles of Pakistan at the designated time and were once again ushered into the drawing room. Raghav and Annie were delighted to see them. Darsee was politely formal. Beena dey Bagh was, it seemed, a little put out. She was grumbling about her masseuse not showing up this morning for her daily rise-and-shine massage. However, it soon became evident to Alys that, when Darsee was present, Beena dey Bagh wanted him all to herself and had patience for no one else. Annie looked much healthier this evening. Her cheeks were flushed and her general mien vibrant, and Alys concluded it was on account of Darsee's presence. Although, since they'd arrived and been seated, Alys hadn't seen Darsee pay Annie any attention. If she ever got engaged, Alys thought, and her fiancé ignored her, she wouldn't put up with it.

"I loved Flannery O'Connor's short story 'Good Country People,'" Annie was saying. "Alys, the one you recommended."

The wretched mother, the gossiping neighbor, the angry daughter, the dreadful Bible salesman, the wooden leg. Annie could easily see this story set in Pakistan, and that made Flannery O'Connor an honorary Pakistani.

Alys laughed. "O'Connor, Austen, Alcott, Wharton. Characters' emotions and situations are universally applicable across cultures, whether you're wearing an empire dress, *shalwar kurta,* or kimono."

She recalled that Darsee had also said as much at the clinic and glanced at him at the bar, fixing a scotch for himself.

"I'm so glad you recommended her," Annie said. "Sherry, have you read it?"

"I've translated it into Urdu for a collection I'm putting together."

"How divine," Annie said.

Sherry smiled. "I've always wanted to work on such projects but I've never had the time before, and now I have all the time in the world."

"Time for?" Raghav joined them with his freshened vodka. "You all look like you've been anointed. Tell, tell."

Alys told him about Sherry's undertaking and Annie's new love and that he should read it.

"It's not too long, is it?" Raghav said. "I'm more of a haiku person, short and punchy."

Alys shook her head. "You sound like a student asking how many pages an essay must be. You'll survive reading a short story. Imagine you're climbing a mental mountain."

"Yes, ma'am," Raghav said, giving her a mock salute. "Anything else, ma'am?"

Alys laughed. She was having a glorious time with Sherry, Raghav, and even Annie. Now if only Darsee would stop gazing at them from across the room as if they were worms. There was that look again, this time aimed at her.

"Instead of plotting our demise," Alys called out, "you may join us."

"I would," Darsee said, "but your figures look best from here."

"I'm sure they do." Raghav performed a pirouette. "Especially mine."

"Yes," Darsee said, "most especially yours."

"Oh, look," Alys said, "it has a sense of humor when it wants."

"It certainly does," Raghav said. They all laughed.

Beena dey Bagh, who'd been informing Kaleen and the rather baffled Mr. and Mrs. Looclus of the benefits of sashimi compared to sushi—*kachi machi,* raw fish, the Loocluses would exclaim for months—insisted that they share the joke. They did. Beena was not amused.

"Would any of you like to be referred to as 'it'?" she asked.

"Only," Alys said, much to Kaleen's consternation, "if I was being referred to as the 'It' Girl."

Beena clenched her fists. She would have forbidden them their laughter, except she was thrilled to see Annie enjoying herself. However, Beena was not happy with Alys. She clearly had no respect for Beena or her esteemed family. Perhaps time to seriously look into the parental complaints against her. Swearing. Promoting premarital sex. Her claims of marriage's being legal prostitution. Or some such nonsense, which Beena had so far ignored, at Principal Naheed's behest. Not that such views and impropriety were a surprising trait coming from a woman like Alysba Binat. Beena had heard all about Alysba's mother's family background. *Khandan* was *khandan,* after all, and sooner or later your pedigree showed. With the satisfying thought that no one could ultimately hide where they came from, Beena pressed the buzzer to the kitchen and ordered that the *khow suey* dinner be served.

Annie's entertainment being paramount to Beena dey Bagh, she saw no reason not to invite the Loocluses and, to her disgust, Alys—for there was no way to exclude her—night after night for dinner. Besides, Darsee and Raghav were also keen to have company over.

For his part, Kaleen felt he would explode at this nightly honor. Mareea, Mansoor, and Manzoor were thrilled to dress up and eat from such a splendid table in such luxurious surroundings and happiest when Kaleen's children joined too. Bobia and Haji Looclus compared, nonstop, the menus from the dinners as well as the sitting areas into which they'd been led. They felt that so much gracious chitchat with Beena dey Bagh must surely elevate their own social standing and that this change in their status must be reflected once they returned to Dilipabad. Perhaps a photo with Beena dey Bagh, which they would display prominently? And if a guest did not know who she was, well, then, that would prove the guest's insignificance.

Alys seemed the only one run a bit ragged by having to attend daily dinners, but it was nice to see Raghav and Annie. Darsee was tolerable enough given that, thankfully, they hardly interacted.

One morning, Alys found herself being joined on the jogging track in the park by Raghav.

"Hello, hello," Raghav said warmly.

"Hello!" Alys said, very pleasantly surprised.

"I checked out the climbing gym," Raghav said. "Thanks for the recommendation. Are you still walking? Join you?"

"Of course. So nice to see you."

"I also had to pick up some gear in town. I'm leaving tomorrow, earlier than scheduled. Big expedition going to K2, and my sherpa advises we should join."

Alys made a sad face.

"But let's do keep in touch," Raghav said. "And if you come to India, my home is your home."

"Thank you," Alys said. "Likewise, if you ever come to my hometown, Dilipabad, my home is your home."

"Dilipabad." Raghav squinted. "Sounds familiar."

"Trust me," Alys laughed, "if you'd come to Dilipabad, you'd know. It's a tiny town."

"I did visit one small town, where my mother was born before partition. Last year, my mother passed away—"

"My condolences."

"Thank you, and she wanted me to spread some of her ashes in her childhood home here."

"So this trip is no ordinary visit for you, then," Alys said.

"Not at all. Valentine was instrumental in my getting a visa to come here as well as helping me locate my mother's childhood house. I am so grateful to him. My boyfriend couldn't make it. He's a photographer. He would have loved it here. Hold on! I know where I've heard of Dilipabad. I believe Darsee was there recently, for a wedding. Are you aware of any recent weddings that took place there?"

"Please," Alys said as nonchalantly as she could, "this is Pakistan. The home of the marriage-industrial complex. Always a wedding taking place everywhere. Weddings are our nation's bread and butter and foundation and flag."

"I believe Valentine recently saved a friend of ours, Bungles, from making a bad marriage or some such in Dilipabad."

"Saved?" Alys stumbled. "What do you mean 'saved'?"

"I think Bungles really liked some girl there, but Valentine didn't think it a good match."

"Who's Darsee to decide that? How do you know him and trust him so much?"

"Valentine and I were in college together in the U.S. for our undergrad degrees. He was serious back then too, the sort of person who feels compelled to tell someone to turn off a running water tap because waste-not–want-not. That's how he met Bungles. Bungles was a year junior and in our dorm. Bungles was brushing his teeth one morning and he'd left the water running, and Valentine descended upon him in the name of environmental enlightenment."

Raghav grinned. "I only met Bungles twice before I graduated— both times at a club, where Valentine was keeping a strict eye on him. Bungles is a decent but fun-loving guy and, if I recall correctly, Darsee steered him away from many a Miss Trouble back in college. Obviously he continues at it—hence the Dilipabad wedding rescue. Apparently the girl's mother is a mega–gold digger and kept flinging her daughter at Bungles, while the daughter herself showed zero interest. Valentine told me he was able to convince Bungles of her disinterest with concrete examples, until even Bungles could no longer deny that she'd probably even smiled at him only because her mother forced her to."

"Perhaps Darsee is interested in him for his sister?"

"No way! Val thinks women should be independent and know their minds before they get married. If Darsee has his way, Jujeena will be a double PhD, have solved world hunger, fixed the environment, brought wars to an end, and found the cure for at least three diseases before he recommends she marry."

"How nice for Jujeena."

"The fact is, Valentine is a good and sincere man and has been a great friend to Bungles and me."

A few steps on, Alys pled a sudden migraine. She assured Raghav she'd be fine and headed back to Sherry's as fast as she could. She was shaking when she got to her bedroom. By dinnertime, her head was pounding. Sherry gave her three painkillers, a strong cup of chai, and a plate of stomach-settling *khichiri* with homemade yogurt.

Alys did not eat. She stared at the plain ceiling and plotted Darsee's downfall. She abhorred him. He was singlehandedly responsible for Jena's misery. She would never forgive him, no matter how much he begged, were he ever to do so, which she prayed to God that by some miracle he would.

———

That evening Alys insisted she be excused from dining at Beena dey Bagh's. Kaleen, seeing how drained she looked, decided it was just as well that she stay behind. If she was coming down with something, he did not want her around Annie's immune system. When everyone left, Alys went to the living room, wrapped herself in a quilt, and switched on one of her favorite films, *The Terminator*. She tucked into a plate of her soul-settling comfort food—yellow lentils and white rice topped with cucumbers—and hoped that the machine-versus-man movie would at least soothe her for the duration of its running time. Oh, how she despised Darsee. If she ever saw him again she'd—

"Alys *baji*," the maid, Ama Iqbal, poked her head into the living room. "There's a man to see you. Shall I bring him in?"

"A man?" Alys said.

"He came here once before. Ate all the *shami kebabs*."

Alys nodded. Raghav. How sweet of him to come see if she was all right and to say goodbye before he left in the morning for K2. At least he wouldn't care that she was in her tatty pajamas and had oiled her hair. Perhaps she should tell him the whole tale and trust that he might tell Bungles the truth about Jena's feelings.

The door opened. Alys's smile disappeared.

"Hello," Darsee said.

"Is everyone all right?" Alys said. "Isn't there a dinner at your aunt's place?"

"All fine. No need to panic." Darsee glanced at the plate of half-eaten *dal chawal*. "I came to see how you were doing."

"How I'm doing?"

"Sherry said you've had a bad headache since this morning. Raghav said he and you had jogged together and it was humid. Could it be heat stroke? Is that oil in your hair?"

"Yes, it is. I was not expecting the Crown Prince of Pakistan to visit."

"I was worried." Darsee sat down. "You're watching *Terminator*. Is this your first time?"

"No," Alys said rudely.

"This is one of the only films with an even-better sequel. Have you seen it?"

"Listen," Alys said, "where does your aunt think you are?"

"Picking up emergency mountain stuff for Raghav. He leaves to-morrow morning."

Darsee rose. Then he sat back down. Then he rose again. He cleared his throat.

"What?" Alys said, as he looked down at her. "What's wrong with you?"

"Will you marry me?"

Alys stared at him.

"I *love* you."

This was so preposterous, Alys let out a hearty laugh.

"My admission is a joke to you?"

"Is this a prank?" Alys looked around. "Is there a hidden camera somewhere?"

"Don't be absurd." Darsee crossed the room. "I've tried to get you out of my head. I've tried so hard. I think about you all the time. Of how I want your opinion on this book and that film and this work of art and that play. I respect your opinions."

"*You* respect *my* opinions."

"Will you, Alys? Marry me? It's not the wisest of matches," Dar-see said dolefully. "In fact, it's a disadvantageous match for me in all respects—well, except that you're smart, fun, and have a quirky per-sonal style, which I like. And *you* are not a gold digger. This is the biggest plus of all."

"It is, is it?" Alys said.

"Beena Aunty will take some convincing, of course, but I'm sure I'll be able to win her over. Annie will help me too. I'm hoping that, once we're married, you'll agree with me that we need not meet your family with any regularity."

Alys had been in a daze this whole time. Now she stood up. Did Darsee think she'd agree to marry him? No doubt he'd been brought up to believe that he was a prince and all the girls everywhere were eager to be his princess and locked away in his castle.

"Aren't you engaged to Annie?" Alys flushed. She had not meant to ask this.

"Beena Khala would like that—consolidate property and the British School Group and all that—but Annie and I have grown up like siblings. It's gross. Anyway, Beena Khala's upset these days because Annie is refusing to break up with her Nigerian boyfriend. They began dating before she got sick. I like him. But why are you asking about Annie when I've asked you to marry me?"

"Marry you!" Alys said, even as she took in everything he'd told her. "Here's to bursting your bubble—I don't know what gave you the impression that I would marry you. I would never marry you under any circumstances. You are unmarriageable."

"I see." Darsee folded his arms. "I see. And why would you never marry me under any circumstances? Why am I unmarriageable? Do I stink or something?"

"Yes," Alys said. "You do stink. Of hubris. You are a pompous ass."

Darsee swallowed.

"You insult my family, tell me to seldom meet them, and then expect me to kneel in gratitude for the chance at being your wife? You think a way to a woman's heart is by calling her family coarse and crude?"

"I didn't use those terms, you did." Darsee scowled. "But they certainly are champions of what is called *ultee seeday harkatein,* bizarre behavior. You and I are both truth-tellers, and the truth is your family behaves disgracefully in public."

"*You* are uncouth," Alys said, "and unfeeling to expect me to not see my family. And if that's not bad enough, my sister Jena is in deep depression because of your interference between her and Bungles. That's why she left Dilipabad for Lahore. She was so upset she had to take time off from work to recover. She *really* liked Bungles and I know he *really* liked her, but you ruined it for them."

Darsee reddened. "She certainly didn't act as if she liked him."

"How stupid are you? My sister's reputation has taken a beating because of Bungles. She was even a gossip item in that stupid *Social Lights* column 'What Will People Say—*Log Kya Kahenge.*' Had Jena dared to openly encourage him, have you any idea what people would be saying about her then? Don't you know how people in this country talk? Show interest in a man and be called a slut. Don't show interest in a man and be called a tease or a prude or, as you'd say, disinterested. What's a girl to do?"

"It seemed to me that your mother was far more interested in Bungles than your sister was."

"Just come out and say it," Alys said. "You believe my mother is a gold digger. If we women decide to marry according to standards, then we are gold diggers, but when you weigh us in matters of looks and chasteness, then you're just being smart. I can't stand these double standards."

"Look," Darsee said, "it's terrible your sister is depressed, but based on what I saw, I was protecting my friend. Wouldn't you have protected your sister if it were the other way around? Have you any idea how many girls, how many women, throw themselves at Bungles all day long? At me?"

"It's not exactly you they're throwing themselves at," Alys said, "so don't unduly flatter yourself."

"Oh, I know," Darsee said grimly. "I was disillusioned ages ago. It's not me. It's my money, my family name, or both. Do you have any idea how hard it is to find someone who likes you for who you are? Marries you for yourself and not your assets?"

"Poor little rich boy Valentine Darsee. Such a hard life. Valued for what he has to offer rather than who he is. Welcome to a woman's world, where we are valued for tits, ass, womb, sometimes earning capacity, but above all else being servile brainless twits. Have you any idea what it feels like to want to be liked for your brains and instead be coveted for your body?"

"I like you for your brains."

"I don't like you for anything," Alys said. "I've refused your be-nevolent offer of marriage. Why are you still here?"

"So you've made up your mind."

"My God! You have more hubris than a Disney prince. I don't like you. At all. We have nothing in common. Nothing."

Darsee looked Alys up and down. "Yes we do. We like reading and we have growing up abroad in common. We both grew up mul-ticultural kids. We know no one person represents a group or a coun-try in things good or bad. We know how to plant roots where there are none. We know that friends can be made anywhere and every-where, regardless of race or religion. We know how to uproot. We know how to move on from memories, or at least not let memories bury us. Most of all, neither of us is a hypocrite, Alys. Neither of us would call an ugly baby cute."

"Even if we did have all this in common, I would never marry you," Alys said. "And you *are* a hypocrite. Or have you forgotten Jeorgeullah Wickaam?"

"Wickaam again!"

"Wickaam forever! You cheated your cousin out of an inheritance so that you could get it all for yourself. My father's elder brother did the same, and it damaged my family. Don't you think for a second that a betrayal of this type is something that I can ever forget or forgive. If you aren't a decent person, then your money and lineage mean nothing to me. Loyalty means everything to me, and you, Val-entine Darsee, are not loyal to family or friends. You may have fooled the whole world into thinking otherwise, but you'll never fool me."

"I see." Darsee nodded. "You've spent time with me and with Wickaam, and your conclusion is that he is a saint and I am a mate-rialistic disloyal villain. A good thing, then, that you have rejected me. Saves me from being with a person who has such a low opinion of me. I'm so sorry to have wasted your time, as well as my own. Goodbye, then, and best wishes."

After Darsee left, Alys did not move for a long while. She stared at the TV screen without hearing a word. The film credits rolled and the film turned off and the DVD self-ejected and she sat there still. Valentine Darsee said he loved her. That he valued her opinions. Valentine Darsee proposed to her despite all his objections toward her family.

He proposed.

She refused.

Alys heard honking at the gate. The party was back from dinner. Sherry would take one look at her and know something had happened. Alys did not want to discuss anything with anyone, not yet. She rushed to her bedroom, got into bed, turned off the lights, pulled the covers over her head, and fell into a deep and restful sleep.

Chapter 20

Alys woke the next morning and instantly recalled Darsee's proposal. She took a deep breath and decided that there was no need to tell anyone. Her mother would faint at her having turned down an offer of this magnitude. Sherry would tell her that she'd made a bad decision. Even Jena, she suspected, would scold her for having been too quick to refuse. But Alys was more than satisfied with her decision. The next order of business was to go about her day exactly as she would any other day, and what was so shocking now would in time turn ordinary.

Alys slipped on running clothes and left the house for the park. Not bad, Alys, she thought to herself as she embarked on her first lap. You must be doing something right for two proposals in one year, all the way from Kaleen to Darsee.

Suddenly Darsee appeared before her on the path, holding out a letter.

"I didn't want this delivered at Kaleen's house, in case anyone else opened it, so I waited here, hoping you'd show up. Please read this and then, as I said last night, goodbye and best wishes."

Alys took it and watched Darsee disappear out of sight. She made
her way to the nearest bench and slit open the sealed envelope.

Alys,

*You made two accusations against me and I deserve a chance to
explain. The first is about your sister. I've known Bungles for a
long time, and he's always falling "in love." This time I did sense
gravity in his feelings, but I honestly did not see those feelings re-
ciprocated by Jena. I understand that in our society women play it
safe until they get a proposal; however, there is a difference between showing restraint and showing indifference. I was beyond
convinced your sister was showing indifference.*

*And then, your family. Look, you can't deny that your mother
and Lady display no propriety. Even if a guy acted in private the
way Lady does in public, I'd call him out. Lady and Qitty quarrel
in public like they're hired entertainment. Your sister Mari is
Muslim fire and brimstone, and your father seems unable, or unwilling, to discipline anyone. Then there is the matter of your maternal ancestry. Alys, you must see that no true friend would
recommend marrying into your family regardless of whether the
girl showed great interest, which Jena did not.*

*I accept one wrongdoing. I did know Jena was in Lahore. I'm
sorry I lied to you. I am not a liar. Bungles had no idea, because
his sisters and I didn't tell him.*

*The second accusation concerns my cousin Jeorgeullah Wickaam.
Wickaam gives everyone the sob story he gave you. My father and
both his parents did pass away in the Ojhri arms-depot explosion;
that much of Wickaam's story is true. We were all traumatized.*

*Wickaam became extremely clingy. No one blamed him given
his circumstances. He needed love and stability. He could not sleep
alone, so he and I shared a bedroom. When my mother, sister, and I
moved to England, he came with us.*

*After a string of unsuccessful relationships, my mother remar-
ried and we moved to Bangkok. It was Wickaam who decided to*

stay back with his father's family. As it turned out, he'd befriended an older woman; so began his philandering. When Wickaam's father's family found out about his "affairs," they didn't know how to handle it. My mother had divorced by then and so, after three years in Bangkok, we'd returned to Lahore, and my mother requested that Wickaam be sent back to us.

When he arrived at Lahore Airport, Wickaam was seventeen years old and turning every head. He targeted that most vulnerable of people, the adolescent maid. One, two, three maids came forward: Wickaam Sahib had seduced them by promising them marriage, money, gold earrings, etc. My mother was appalled. She tried to protect these young girls by sending them back to their villages and away from Wickaam's urges. And then one of the maids got pregnant. Mahira was adamant that Wickaam marry her and legitimize their child. Wickaam said she had no proof that he was the father.

Thanks to my mother and Beena Aunty, Mahira delivered a healthy baby boy. We paid for her and the baby's upkeep for life as well as his education. My mother and Beena Aunty requested Mahira not disclose the arrangement to anyone but, next we know, another pregnant maid shows up.

My mother had recently been diagnosed with a late-stage cancer, and all this stress made her sicker. She felt she'd failed her late sister's son, and she worried about what would become of these poor maids, their children, and Wickaam with his inability to keep his pants zipped.

My mother and Beena Aunty decided to use Wickaam's inheritance to set up a school for underprivileged children, in which Wickaam's offspring would also study for free, as well as a facility for taking in abandoned infants who may otherwise be victims of infanticide. Wickaam was livid at his inheritance being taken away. He blamed me. Instead of taking his side like a "brother," I was some bleeding heart who'd sided with the maids.

After Wickaam visited my mother on her deathbed, my mother decided that he should receive tuition money for a college abroad, and Beena Aunty agreed. But what does Wickaam do? He uses the funds to travel the world of lechery in luxury.

My sister, Juju, is ten years younger than him, Annie, and me. Annie and I decided that Juju didn't need to know about Wickaam's sexual exploits. However, the minute I left for my MBA, that asshole began to prey on my sister, convincing her they were in love. Beena Aunty didn't even know the two were meeting, let alone what was going on. No one did.

One day I received a phone call from Juju. She was pregnant and Wickaam was insisting they elope. But she wanted me to be at the wedding. I booked the first flight back from Atlanta to Lahore. I told my sister to tell him they could marry but that I was going to cut off her inheritance and there'd be no money. Wickaam called my bluff. Next I took Juju to the charity school, where she saw Wickaam's children and had to believe what I'd been telling her. She was distraught. I told Juju to convince Wickaam she'd given up her inheritance to be with him. His response was to abandon my pregnant sixteen-year-old sister. Next I hear, he's in New York, where, while having a good time, he has purchased a fake law degree and is now going around telling people he went to a college in New York. He did—he literally walked through a college campus in New York City.

I told Juju I would support her no matter what she chose to do. After much agonizing, she opted for an abortion. I was unwilling to trust my unmarried sister's secret to doctors and nurses in Pakistan, and so I took her to Europe. She suffered so much, and all I could do was feel like shit.

Wickaam thinks Juju miscarried. Only she and I—and now you—know she had an abortion. I wish I could tell the world the truth, but I cannot without risking my sister's reputation as well as the reputations of others Wickaam has seduced.

He is my cousin, my blood relative, I'm sorry to say, but he is not my friend. He is no one's friend and does not know what the word "loyalty" means. Weena Aunty and Uncle Hassan, his parents, were so gentle, kind, and upright—they would be shocked to see how their son has turned out.

I'm sharing all this with you to tell you that Wickaam is not the victim here nor we conniving relatives, and I would advise you and yours to stay far away from him.

Alys, I wanted you to have a signed statement from me to prove that I trust you.

Valentine Darsee

Alys looked up. The sun was still shining. Bees buzzed over a bed of petunias. A group of elderly ladies power-walked past her. She could not believe what she'd just read. His explanation for his interference with Bungles and Jena had not appeased her, and she was furious that he'd kept Jena's presence in Lahore from Bungles. But he'd told her the truth. And if he'd told her the truth about that, then how could she doubt his account about Wickaam? But if Darsee was telling the truth, then Wickaam had lied.

Alys recalled Wickaam's face as they'd sat in Pak Tea House and he'd related his tale. He'd sounded so sincere. And yet here was this letter from Darsee. A letter in which he'd confessed to his sister having premarital sex that had ended in an abortion. In Pakistan, no one in their right mind would make up such a thing, let alone a brother about his sister.

It occurred to Alys that when Wickaam had smiled at Darsee at the Wagah border, it had been a sheepish smile. That it was Wickaam who'd decided to back out of attending NadirFiede's *walima*. Wickaam who was always keen to demean Darsee.

Poor Juju! Poor maids! Should she warn Miss Jahanara Ana Aan that her fiancé was a heinous man and a father of children whom he did not acknowledge? "Father" was the wrong word. Wickaam was not a father. He was just a man who'd sired children. But what concrete proof could she offer without betraying Darsee's confidence?

Alys reread Wickaam's section. She read it several times. After she was done, she marched on the jogging path, trying to regain composure. She felt dizzy and sick. Wickaam must have seen the Binat name on the Fraudia Acre case papers and assumed they had money. Upon realizing they had none, he'd perhaps decided that if not marriage for money, then he could attain something else from one of them. He'd never tried anything untoward with her, but Alys recalled his attentions to Qitty, and she shuddered at the memory of Wickaam sleeping over while Lady pranced around in her nightie. Shame on their society, where maintaining unsoiled reputations was considered more vital than exposing scoundrels, for such secrets only allowed the scoundrels to continue causing harm.

Alys stopped walking and read the letter again. And then again. Each time, she felt a fresh pinch at "maternal ancestry," and anger that Darsee had believed this rumor as readily as everyone else seemed to. She also felt nauseous over his allegations about her family's crude behavior. The truth, as much as it stung, was that his charges were valid. And hadn't Sherry also feared that Jena's guardedness could be read as blatant indifference? But Alys was not going to blame Jena. She'd told Darsee that women were stuck in a bind, and they were.

Darsee had apologized for withholding word of Jena's presence in Lahore from Bungles. He'd written, *I'm sorry I lied to you. I am not a liar.* And from everything she could see, Darsee was a doting brother. Why had she so readily believed Wickaam?

Because she'd wanted to believe him. Alys swallowed her disappointment in herself. In Wickaam's case, she'd been favorably biased, and in Darsee's unfavorably prejudiced. She'd been flattered by Wickaam's attentions and offended by Darsee's initial dismissive assessment of her looks and her intellect. She'd readily welcomed Wickaam's—a total stranger's—derision of Darsee, and, even worse, she'd added to it.

Alys groaned as she recalled how she'd compared Wickaam to

Darsee and told him he could never be loyal. His proposal had been conceited, there was no denying that, but she'd been petty in her rejection.

Alys wasn't sure how she was going to react when she saw Darsee next, but when she finally ended her walk and returned to Sherry's house, the Loocluses were discussing the day's events: Raghav had left this morning as scheduled for K2, and Darsee had suddenly decided to return to Lahore. Beena dey Bagh had telephoned to cancel dinner.

By and by, Kaleen decided that the cancellation was a stroke of good luck, since the Loocluses and Alys were scheduled to leave three days from now and this would allow them time to wrap up things. Three days later, the Looclus family and Alys set off for Lahore and from there to Dilipabad. As had been the case before, the Loocluses dropped Alys off at Nisar and Nona's and popped in for chai before heading to their relatives' house. They would pick up Alys and Jena the next morning.

Alys had hoped to have a few moments alone with Jena, but she quickly realized that a few moments would not be enough for what she'd decided to share with her sister and that, once they got home, privacy would be a dream. Consequently, she told the Loocluses that she and Jena had decided to stay an extra day in Lahore and that they'd take the Daewoo bus back to Dilipabad.

Two days later, Alys and Jena boarded a deluxe bus. The bus hostess introduced herself as Qandeel Baloch and, with a striking smile, distributed the boxed lunches and pointed out the toilets at the back. Once the bus started moving, Alys told Jena to brace herself for all she was about to hear.

"What?" Jena opened the box lunch to a chicken-salad sandwich, potato chips, and an apple. "What great secret has required us to spend money on bus tickets so we can get privacy?"

"Darsee proposed to me."

Jena's hands stilled on the apple.

"Darsee sought me out one evening when I was alone at Sherry's and informed me that he loves me and respects my opinions and wants to marry me."

"Dear God!" Jena said. "Oh my dear God!"

"I said no."

"Valentine Darsee proposed to you and you said *no*?"

"And that's not even the real explosive secret."

Alys took out Darsee's letter from her bag.

"Read from here." She tapped at the beginning of Wickaam's section.

"What's this above?" Jena said.

"You know what"—Alys bit her lip—"read the whole thing, except it's about you and Bungles."

Jena read it slowly, her expression going from wounded, to hurt, to puzzled, to resolute.

"Are you all right?" Alys asked gently as Jena came to the end of the part on Bungles.

"Yes and no." Jena shook her head. The fact was that of course friends asked friends for advice all the time, but Bungles should have trusted his own intuition about her rather than what his friend or sisters told him. They had not seen her looking into Bungles's eyes; he had. They had not seen her ensuring that his plate was always full of food; he had. They had not heard the tenderness in her voice for him when they were alone; he had. He should have trusted what he was seeing rather than what they were seeing.

He was weak willed and, the fact was, she did not want a weak-willed man.

Jena returned to the letter. As she got deeper into Wickaam's section, she began to fidget. Often she glanced at Alys in agitation. When she was done, she folded the letter and handed it back to Alys.

"Can Wickaam truly be so two-faced? Can he hide his double nature so well?"

"Yes," Alys said, "and yes."

"But there's got to be some misunderstanding between Darsee and Wickaam. What Darsee relates here is just terrible."

"Doesn't make it untrue."

"My God, Alys, Wickaam spending nights, our mother offering any of us up to him for marriage, Lady in her nightie!" Jena's hand flew to her chest. "My God, do you think—"

"Lady is not that stupid," Alys said. "She's *zinda dil,* full of life, but even she knows the limits."

"Poor Jujeena. Do you think Bungles knows about this?"

"Darsee's clearly written that only he, Juju, and now I know."

"And now I know," Jena said. "Are you going to tell him you showed me?"

"No. Not yet. I don't know. I trust you."

"As he trusted you," Jena said, sighing. "I honestly don't know what to believe."

"I believe Darsee. I do. He's not the villain after all."

"I always told you not to judge so quickly."

Alys looked out the window at the orange grove they were passing.

"Jena," she said, turning to her, "ever since I read the letter, I knew you were right. And Sherry was right too. I was being unreasonable in my dislike for him, a dislike that started because he wounded my vanity and I let his judgment cloud my judgment. He's such a snob— you should have heard the dismal way he proposed to me—but surely snobbery is not equal to evil. I'm not saying he's suddenly turned into a saint, but I am cringing at all the times I agreed with Wickaam that Darsee was horrid. Cringing at all the times I defended Wickaam to Darsee."

"You didn't know any better." Jena squeezed Alys's hand. "You didn't have all the facts."

"Had Wickaam told me Darsee kidnapped babies and ate them for breakfast, I would have believed him."

"Oh, Alys."

"Darsee was right. I like to tell others the truth about themselves, but I'm not so keen to hear truths about me and mine. I'm ashamed that I'm not the person I thought I was."

"You should be proud that you possess the ability to revise your opinion and want to develop qualities you lack."

"Yes," Alys said wryly, "I plan to be very proud at being able to call myself out on my own prejudice. But, seriously, Jena, what should I do? Should I warn Miss Jahanara Ana Aan? Should we tell others about Wickaam?"

"It's not our secret to divulge," Jena said, truly troubled.

"Doesn't Wickaam need to be exposed so he can't dupe other girls? But this could truly ruin Jujeena Darsee's reputation for the rest of her life."

"Not just her life." Jena's voice was steel. "It would affect her children's reputations and her grandchildren's reputations. Is this not what we face? Thanks to Aunty Tinkle's slander concerning our grandmother's supposed profession, people malign us even though no one can furnish a shred of proof toward that rumor."

"I dare not imagine," Alys said, "what will happen to Jujeena's story in the hands of people like Rose-Nama and her mother and Naheed and Hammy and Sammy."

"I can," Jena said softly. "These people could be having premarital sex and abortions left, right, and center, but they'll put on such self-righteous airs you'll think they are the world's greatest *naik parveens*, pious women."

"Internal misogyny has made a mockery of female solidarity," Alys said, forlorn. "It's not even as if abortion is the issue. Married women here use it as birth control. It's all about premarital sex. Are you a virgin or not?"

"And these pigeon problems," Jena said in despair, "are only meant to preoccupy us while the men are free to focus their energies on the important things in life."

"Can you imagine the schadenfreude?" Alys said. "How gleeful people will be to hear of Jujeena and Darsee's scandal? In front of

Jujeena they'll say, 'Poor Jujeena this, poor Jujeena that,' but behind her back they will call her a slut and blame her for becoming pregnant. All the while, even as they condemn Wickaam for being vile, women will try to reform him with their own true love, while men will slap him on his back for being such a manly man. This is the society we live in."

The sisters were still talking in hushed whispers when the bus reached Dilipabad, where they were met by their family, amid a cacophony of greetings.

"Missed you both so much," Mr. Binat said, hugging his eldest daughters.

"He did," Mrs. Binat said, giving Jena and Alys pecks on their cheeks. "Your father wants to discuss his beloved flora and fauna, and no one else has the patience to hear him blather on about aeration and lime content. You look so relaxed and refreshed, Jena."

"Do I look like I've lost any weight?" Qitty tightened her *kurta* around her waist. "I've lost ten pounds since you left."

"You do look trimmer," Jena said.

"Shut up about your ten pounds, Qitty," Lady said. "It's not visible on your body, so it has to be your brains getting lighter."

"Lady! Behave!" Alys said as she hugged Qitty.

"Great," Lady said. "Aunty Alys is back."

"Qitty," Alys said, "I've brought you a bundle of used magazines I found, called *Mode,* for plus-size women."

"Did you get the things on my list?" Lady said.

"Yes," Alys said. "Such a long list of nothing but beauty products. Let me remind you: books over looks."

"I didn't have a single beauty product on my list," Mari said proudly. "I do not care about outer looks but rather the inner beauty of the soul."

"Inner beauty of the soul," Lady repeated, mimicking Mari in a squeaky voice. "Jena, Alys, this is her new thing. Inner beauty of the soul. Mari, you have little outer beauty, so of course you are going to lecture on inner beauty. God, I want a long holiday away from this town and my family. We're dying of heat here. Jena, Alys, I went to see Mareea Looclus yesterday. She said Fart Bhai has air-conditioning everywhere and she was freezing all the time. I wish we could afford to freeze."

"We can't, thanks to Goga and Tinkle," Mrs. Binat said. "May God sprout warts on their privates."

"Pinkie, shhh!" Mr. Binat glanced around to see if anyone at the bus stop had overheard. "Your curses become more colorful with each passing day."

"Mareea also said," Lady grumbled, "that Sherry bought her everything she wanted and then some."

Mrs. Binat snorted. "I'm telling you, she must have bought clearance."

"No, Mummy," Lady said, "I told you I saw the full-price stickers. Also, she was crowing about how Fart Bhai has said that, as soon as she finishes college, she can move in with them. I say, good riddance. If Fart Bhai wants his fish-faced sister-in-law around, good for him. But, Jena, Alys, is it true? Did he really invite her to live with them? It's so unfair. Even Mareea will leave Dilipabad, while I will languish here and die."

"*Hai!*" Mrs. Binat said. "Why will you die? *Die karein tumhare dushman.* May your enemies die."

"They are not dying. They are prospering. Mareea said Fart Bhai is going to replace their shitty motorbike with a car, a very good car. Mummy, imagine those flamingo-faced Mansoor and Manzoor going from being motorbike boys to having a better car than ours. I can't stand it. Alys, it's not even as if they worked for it themselves, but you keep saying that us girls must earn everything for ourselves."

"Don't you listen to Alys. *Yeh tho pagal hai.* She's mad." Mrs. Binat's nostrils fluttered in her despair at Bobia Looclus's coup after coup. "Alys has done nothing for her family, while all that snake Sherry does is elevate hers via her husband's fat wallet. God only knows what spell she has put on that wife-worshipping Kaleen. Lady, my love, you watch—you will make the best marriage in all of Pakistan and have a million good cars."

"At this point," Lady said, "I won't settle for less than a private plane or two."

Mrs. Binat sighed helplessly. "Jena, Alys, is Useless Uterus Sherry still giving herself airs and graces? How eager she was to call herself 'Mrs. Shireen Kaleen' as soon as she got married."

"But, Mummy," Jena said, "what else would she call herself?"

"Mareea swears," Lady said, "that Fart Bhai really does let Sherry sleep in for as long as she likes and that he insists she go to the beauty parlor daily and spend as much as she wants. Imagine! Before Sherry's marriage, visiting the 'porler,' as they pronounce it, was such a big deal for those two sisters, and now Mareea claims she's been so many times, she's tired of the very word 'porler.'"

"Lady," Mrs. Binat said, gently, "don't make fun of anyone's accent."

"I will!" Lady said. "Mareea Looclus is a show-off, and I hate her."

"You should not hate anyone," Mari said, "for hate will come back to haunt you, and envy will eat you alive."

Qitty added, "Don't be petty, Lady. Be happy for your friend."

"Mummy, High Priestess and Behemoth are ganging up on me again," Lady said.

"You're being very spiteful, Lady," Alys said as Jena nodded in agreement.

"Leave Lady alone, Alys," Mrs. Binat said, frowning, as they walked to the parking lot. "It is thanks to your refusal of Kaleen that Mareea Looclus is in a position to preen in front of Lady."

"I just wish Mareea would remember," Lady said, "that, had Alys bothered to marry Fart Bhai, then I'd be the one going to the 'parlor,' but what's the use? No one cares about what could have been, and the fact is, Sherry grabbed Fart Bhai, and Mareea has lucked out. Jena, Alys, please, for the sake of my soul, please find someone outstanding to marry you. You've already reached your sell-by dates, and before you completely expire, I also want to see what it feels like to have a benevolent brother-in-law."

"Is Sherry hoity-toity all the time?" Mrs. Binat asked as they climbed into the car and proceeded homeward. "Or does she retain the good sense to remember where she comes from and to never forget her *phateecher* wretched home?"

Alys and Jena exchanged a look. They were home.

Chapter 21

Every year Nisar and Nona left their children with her parents while the two of them went on a holiday. This year they were supposed to have gone to New Zealand, but Nisar discovered his passport had expired too late to get it renewed, so they decided instead to retour Pakistan's Northern Areas. Alys had always been eager to see the breathtaking Lake Saiful-Muluk, Gilgit, Naran, Kaghan, Skardu, Hunza, Chitral. They weren't sure which lakes and valleys and peaks they would visit, but they would love for Alys and Jena to accompany them.

Alys agreed immediately. Jena declined. Their father's face had fallen at the invite and Jena decided that, having so recently spent so much time away from home, she would stay back. Everyone else's face fell too: Mrs. Binat, Qitty, Mari, Lady. There were shrieks and tears. Couldn't they have also been invited? In fact, Mrs. Binat and her three younger daughters would have happily invited themselves, had they considered hiking and staring at night stars the least bit fun. If only, Mrs. Binat kept lamenting, they could all afford a holi-

day the way they used to. How she longed to return to London! *Hai,*
Lundhun! *Hai,* Oxford Street! *Hai,* Hyde Park!

Lady joined in her mother's longings. Holiday! Holiday! She'd
been a toddler when they used to go abroad, and she didn't even remember these destinations everyone else had such fond memories
of. Holiday! Holiday! It was all she would talk about, until even Mrs.
Binat regretted mentioning the word "holiday."

"We have no money for even a week's getaway to a decent place,"
Mrs. Binat said. "We spent a fortune on clothes for the NadirFiede
wedding, and for what—nothing! Now, had Alys married Kaleen,
we'd have spent the entire summer in Islamabad. And had Bungles
married . . ."

But Mrs. Binat silenced herself. It was evident to all that no matter which smile Jena plastered on her face, she was still hurting, for
she'd fallen in love and was now being forced to fall out of it. Even
Mr. Binat had stopped cracking jokes about "eating shoes" in order
to not cause Jena further pain.

Alys's holiday news was scarcely digested when the phone rang
again. It was Lady's friend Hijab. Hijab's family had just this year
relocated from Dilipabad to Karachi, and she was missing her friends
so much that her mother had relented and allowed her to invite a
close friend to visit for the remaining two weeks of the summer holidays. Hijab came from a good family—meaning, in local parlance,
they were well off. Her mother fancied herself a journalist, having
written a couple of recipes and New Year resolutions lists for *Social
Lights,* and her father was in an executive position with the national
airline, which meant Lady's ticket would be complimentary and all
she would have to bring with her was shopping money.

"No," Alys said, as soon as Lady got off the phone and waltzed
into the living room to inform everyone that she was going to Karachi. "You are not going anywhere by yourself, let alone to a different
city hours away by plane."

Why couldn't she go? Lady screamed. Was Alys the only one in the family who deserved holidays? She'd barely returned from Sherry's in Islamabad and was now packing for Nona's and the Northern Areas. Alys hadn't even had to ask for permission, so why should she? Hijab had made plans for every day. Her family belonged to the Marina Club, and they were going to go sailing and crabbing and have bonfires on the beach! Her ticket was free! There was no force on earth that was going to stop Lady from going!

Alys did not even bother to appeal to her mother, who was already beginning to make a list of things Lady must pack. Instead, she marched to her father. Mr. Binat was in the garden, picking tomatoes off the vines. He smiled when he saw Alys and straightened up and stretched his lower back.

"These will make the best *red salan* yet," he said, pointing to the jute basket full of ruby fruit, which would be used to make one of the Binats' favorite dishes: tomatoes stewed in oil and spiced with turmeric, salt, and red chilies and topped off with hard-boiled eggs.

"Daddy," Alys said, "Lady's friend who moved to Karachi has invited her to stay with them for the rest of the summer. I don't think she should go."

"Here." Mr. Binat handed Alys a pair of gardening gloves. "Help me bag some for the few neighbors who remain in your mother's good graces."

"Daddy, did you hear me?" Alys slipped on the gloves and stepped into the vegetable patch.

"I heard you," Mr. Binat said, "and I've been hearing Lady's shouting all the way out here. Why can't she go? You know she'll make our lives miserable if she doesn't and, frankly, your mother is enough to make life miserable already."

"Daddy, please be serious for a second," Alys said. She couldn't help think of Darsee's letter, which she never stopped thinking about anyway: *Your father seems unable, or unwilling, to discipline anyone.*

"I am being serious." Mr. Binat plucked another tomato. "I could not be any more serious if I was being paid."

"I don't think Lady should be sent anywhere by herself," Alys said.

"I'm sorry to say this to you, Daddy, but she makes you-you eyes at everyone. I think the only man she's not made you-you eyes at is Farhat Kaleen."

Mr. Binat looked discomfited, as would any *ghairatmand*—principled—Pakistani father, but he was not one to pretend that girls did not go through puberty or did not have feelings for the opposite sex; his wife had made sure he was most comfortable around them while they discussed bra sizes and menstruation and, as a result, as far as he was concerned, making you-you eyes was just another thing women did.

"Princess Alysba," Mr. Binat said, lifting a green tomato to check its color on the other side, "let Lady have her fun and get it out of her system. She's just like your mother, a bit propriety-challenged, but neither means any harm."

"But harm is already done," Alys said.

Mr. Binat handed Alys a tomato for the basket. "Don't tell me Lady frightened away some suitor of yours? None of you girls need men like that in your lives. You've been given a lot of liberties in this home, which most Pakistani girls can only dream of, and a controlling man will suffocate you. Even Mari, though she may not think so, will not be happy with anyone who expects his to be the final word."

"I'm afraid for Lady," Alys said. She thought of Lady at the New Year's party, blissfully sandwiched between Moolee and his geriatric friend, and mocking Qitty in front of them. "I admire her high spirits, but she has no self-control over her actions, or her tongue."

"Alys, you're surprising me, *beta*. You are the last person on earth I expect to worry about *log kya kahenge*."

"I don't care what people say," Alys said. "But I do care that Lady's carelessness could put her in a situation she can't handle. Please listen to me, Daddy—Lady is impulsive, too trusting, and lacks all sense of consequences."

"With such fine qualities, I think being away from us all will be excellent practice for Lady to learn self-discipline instead of always relying on us to provide it."

"She needs us."

"And we need some respite from her, especially Qitty, who could do with two weeks of no one making fun of her being fat." Mr. Binat stepped out of the tomato bed. "I think we're getting a bargain, Alys, with someone else paying for Lady's ticket to Karachi, which, may I remind you, is not cheap. Hijab comes from a good family. Hijab's mother will make sure that everyone behaves. In fact, if she reprimands Lady, it may have more of an effect than our doing so."

"Perhaps," Alys said, even as she shook her head, unconvinced.

"Perhaps we should have Wickaam keep an eye on her?" Mr. Binat said. "Now that he has moved to Kar—"

"No!" Alys stared at her father in horror. Wickaam had telephoned them a week ago and spoken to her. He'd left Musarrat Sr. & Sons Advocates and was instead planning to remain in Karachi and seek new prospects. Frankly, he told her, law wasn't for him after all. Furthermore, he and Miss Jahanara Ana Aan had decided to break their engagement. He'd realized that she wasn't for him either. Her family had sent the distraught girl to Cairo, where she had relatives, in order to recover from a broken engagement.

"Is that so?" Alys had asked in a cold tone. "That's why her family has sent her away?"

Perhaps Wickaam had sensed her sardonic tone, because he asked her how her trip to Islamabad had been. Was not his aunt, Beena dey Bagh, a tyrant? And had Dracula been there?

Alys replied that Beena dey Bagh was who she was and that Darsee was who he was too but that, upon spending more time with him, she didn't think he seemed such a monster.

"Is that so?" Wickaam repeated.

Alys replied, "That is exactly so."

He'd wished her and her family well and, within seconds, he'd hung up.

"No," Alys said forcefully. "No, Daddy, there is absolutely zero need for Wickaam to know that Lady will even be in Karachi."

"Oh dear," Mr. Binat said, "still upset Wickaam-of-the-rising-star left you for Miss Jahanara Ana Aan. He's free of her now and can return to you."

"God forbid," Alys said. "And I was never upset over anything. Simply put, Aunty Nona thinks Wickaam is a wastrel, and I believe her. As such, there is absolutely no need to socialize with the likes of him."

Mr. Binat shrugged. "Whatever you think is best, my princess. He's moved to Karachi anyway and we're in no danger of your mother inviting him to stay the night. Honestly, I think she's too generous with the guest room, but she means no harm and just wants to entertain herself."

Her father winked at her and, for the first time, Alys recognized her own complicity in her family's dynamics. She was her father's favorite daughter. His princess Alysba. And because she enjoyed her status as first daughter, Alys had chosen to overlook her father's ridiculing her mother. It was not that her father was wrong, but he should not have turned Pinkie Binat into a joke between them. Should not the husband-and-wife bond be more sacrosanct than that between a parent and child?

Part Three

AUGUST–DECEMBER 2001

Chapter 22

$\mathcal{A}$lys and Lady boarded the bus from Dilipabad to Lahore, where Alys would meet Nona and Lady would fly on to Karachi. Mari waved goodbye with glee. She was looking forward to making some inroads into her Quran studies without Lady's taunts of purity perverts, high priestesses, and *hojabis*. Qitty also waved contentedly, for she was looking forward to poring over the *Mode* magazines Alys had given her, without Lady insulting every voluptuous body. Mr. Binat and Jena were looking forward to some quarrel-free peace and quiet, and they too waved gaily at Lady. Only Mrs. Binat moaned about how she would miss her youngest daughter as she blew kiss after kiss to Lady, seated in the bus by the window.

"I'll bet they are all so jealous of me," Lady said to Alys. "Are they going to stand here until the bus leaves?"

"Yes," Alys said, and she was right.

Once the bus left Dilipabad station, Lady immediately opened the box lunch, unwrapped the chicken-salad sandwich, and took a messy bite.

"Yum-yum," she said to Alys. "Are you going to have your sand-wich?"

"Yes, I am," Alys said. "And for God's sake, try not to be greedy at Hijab's house. Display your best manners. Don't get overexcited about anything. Don't speak out of turn. Don't talk back to Hijab's parents. Say please and thank you to the servants. Remember to tip them when it's time to return. Do not use that tip money on yourself, Lady, I mean it. Imagine I'm right behind you, watching you the whole time."

"So creepy."

"Every minute my eyes will be on you," Alys said. "Did you hear me?"

"What do you think I'm going to do?" Lady said. "Run away with someone?"

"The fact that you'd even joke about such a thing scares me."

"Aunty Alys, I'd warn you not to run away too, except you're such a party pooper, I don't know who'd want to run away with you."

"*Khuda ke liye,* for God's sake, just don't make you-you eyes at anyone, okay?"

"What if someone makes you-you eyes at me?" Lady finished her sandwich, opened Alys's box, and took out her sandwich.

"I'm serious, Lady." Alys eyed her rapidly disappearing sandwich. "Please remember that the actions of one family member have reper-cussions for all family members."

"Oh, I know." Lady licked mayonnaise off her fingers. "Do you know how many girls at school saw Jena's name in *Social Lights*? Do you know how many asked me and even Qitty if we planned to allow guys to sweep us up in their arms?"

Alys looked at Lady in dismay.

"Qitty and I don't say anything, because we don't want to upset Jena but, trust me, we're suffering too."

Having gobbled up Alys's sandwich, Lady turned to her fashion magazine and a quiz on finding Mr. Right. Alys opened up *Sunlight on a Broken Column.* She'd started reading it after Darsee's proposal, curious suddenly about his "favorite partition novel" and his claim that it had allowed him a "Pakistani identity inclusive of an English-speaking tongue." So far, she was enthralled by the tussles between Laila, the headstrong, unconventional protagonist, and her cousin, Zahra, who wanted to marry well and enjoy her life.

Alys took out a pen and underlined a quote: *Do you know what is wrong with you, Laila? All those books you read. You just talk like a book now, with no sense of reality.*

She wondered what Darsee had thought about this line and whether he believed books led to an escape from reality or were windows into it. She recalled the animated look in his eyes when they'd discussed literature at the clinic, how he'd sought her out at the wedding to give her *Sunlight,* the feel of his fingers on hers, how he'd said he wanted her opinion on things. It was a truth universally acknowledged, Alys suddenly thought with a smile, that people enter our lives in order to recommend reads.

Such pleasant thoughts occupied Alys as the bus drove into the Lahore Daewoo station, where Nisar and Nona were waiting for her and Lady. They had good news and bad news. The good news was that Nona was being awarded a prestigious Indus Civilization Award for Women Who Make a Difference. Alys and Lady squealed in delight as they hugged their aunt. The bad news was that the award ceremony prevented them from visiting Pakistan's Northern Areas.

"I hope you're not too disappointed," Nona said to Alys.

"Of course not, given the reason," Alys said. Some of the other women being honored were a commercial pilot, a police officer, a comedienne, a CEO of a multinational company, an NGO health-care worker, a human-rights advocate, and an environmental activist. Nona's award was for a home-based business entrepreneur, and Alys was extremely proud.

Nisar was saying they would remain in Lahore and visit heritage sites close by. Shalimar Gardens, Badshahi Mosque, Lahore Fort,

Wazir Khan Mosque, Lahore Museum. He was also trying to get tickets for the Naseeruddin Shah–Ratna Pathak play at the Alhamra Art Center.

"Hijab's parents," Lady gloated, "already have tickets for when the play comes to Karachi."

"Good for you, my dear," Nona said. "Now, remember to behave there."

"Goodness, Aunty Nona, you're as boring as Aunty Alys. What are our plans for tonight?"

They went out to dinner at a new Thai restaurant, after which they picked up the latest Indian movie, *Dil Chahta Hai*. Alys declared it excellent for its blend of a serious topic with commercial flair, though her three seminal films remained *Dhool Ka Phool*, *Umrao Jaan*, and *Insaf Ka Tarazu*, all judged by Lady to be much too gloomy to do anyone any good.

Overall, Alys decided that night, as she slipped into bed, she was glad she'd come to Lahore, though she wished Lady was not going to Karachi or that Jena was not sitting depressed in Dilipabad. Opening up *Sunlight*, Alys read a chapter on the protagonist, torn between a duty-bound life and her own desires, and gradually drifted to sleep.

The next morning, Nona and Alys dropped off a deliriously excited Lady at the airport. Once they returned home, they saw her note stating she'd "borrowed" Nona's designer sunglasses and blow-dryer but that she really, really needed them in Karachi. Together, Nona and Alys shook their heads at Lady's audacity and wished Karachi well.

They began to plan their excursions for the next two weeks. The first week passed in relaxation and merriment. Upon Nisar's insistence, each day was begun with a leisurely breakfast at home after which they'd visit the site of the day, enjoy dinner out, and end their evening back at home chatting over chai and a boardgame.

At the start of the second week, Nona had two final cake deliveries, after which, she assured Alys, she was truly all hers. Alys joined her in the kitchen to help prepare the cakes, a dark-chocolate globe and a rose-flavored rose garden. The cakes were ready to be delivered by late afternoon. Nisar, Nona, and Alys all got into the car because, after the deliveries, they planned to go for an early dinner. Alys volunteered to go into the houses, and she delivered the globe cake to the mother of an excited birthday girl. The second house was in a very posh area of town, and Nona read from the address, "Get ready for this, Alys: Buckingham Palace."

Alys chuckled. "Did I tell you Beena dey Bagh's humble abode is named Versailles of Pakistan?"

They arrived at Buckingham Palace, with its towering metal gates topped with ornamental spears and boundary walls lined with shards of glass glinting like the broken bones of crystal birds. A sleepy-eyed guard opened the gate to their honking, and they proceeded up the long driveway lined with sculpted conifers alongside a vast landscaped garden. Her father would love it, Alys thought as she got out of the car.

Alys carefully balanced the cake box in her hands and made her way up marble stairs to an elaborately carved front door. She elbow-rang the doorbell. When no one answered, she tried the handle and entered an airy foyer with bright-yellow walls covered with black-and-white sketches of whirling dervishes.

"Hello?" Alys called out. She walked in farther, finally arriving at stained-glass double doors, and stepped into a large room. Sunlight poured in from a paneled skylight, and floor-to-ceiling windows looked out to a rock plunge pool with a waterfall. A broad-shouldered girl sat cross-legged on the marble floor with her back to the double doors. She was playing a sitar. Her music teacher, Alys presumed, sat before her, bobbing her head to the girl's strumming. The teacher stopped when she saw Alys. The girl turned around.

"So sorry to have barged in," Alys said, "but I'm here to deliver the rose garden cake from Nona's Nices. I rang the doorbell several times."

"I'm so sorry," the girl said. "My teacher, Rani-ul-Nissa *jee,* and I get so engrossed in practice, we hardly hear anything else."

The girl got up, her smile shy but warm as she asked Alys to set the cake on the octagonal coffee table. Alys had seen the girl's face before. But where? Dear God. She nearly dropped the cake. It was Jujeena Darsee. Not in a bathing suit in a Maldives resort pool with Bungles's arm around her but towering over Alys in simple cotton culottes and *kurti,* her hair cut in waves that framed her square chin, her wide feet clad in plush Gucci mules. Jujeena Darsee in the flesh.

"Do you have the receipt?" Jujeena asked.

Alys crammed it into Jujeena's hand. Was Darsee here? She needed to leave as soon as possible.

"Let me get my wallet," Jujeena said.

"Juju *beta,*" Rani-ul-Nissa said, slipping on her *chappals,* "I think enough for today. Also, I was hoping to see your brother. I wanted to thank him again for his tremendous help toward my husband's treatment and wheelchair purchase. The generosity has saved his life. A lot of people have money but do not have giving hearts. Your brother is a saint. God bless him."

"I'll tell him," Juju said. "But you know he'll only be embarrassed."

"I've yet to meet a man," Rani-ul-Nissa said, strapping on her motorbike helmet, "who's been blessed with so much and yet is so humble."

Alys was taken aback at this appraisal of Darsee. She tried to reconcile "Darsee" and "humble" in the same sentence. She couldn't. Still, this praise was unsolicited and, she could tell, heartfelt. Alys watched Juju and the music teacher exit the room, and then she looked frantically for an escape route in case Darsee appeared. She wished Juju would hurry up with the payment.

Alys's eyes flicked over the expensive rugs on the floor, the decadent black-crystal chandelier, the ebony-and-silver floor lamps flanking ivory sofas arranged in semicircles on either side of the room, the forest green silk cushions, and glass vases with white gladioli everywhere. She looked at the huge sepia watercolor of two young women gossiping in what looked like the Thar Desert, the only dashes of color their ocher *dupattas,* and, on the opposite wall, the large abstract with swirls and shadows of coppers and russets suggesting a figure on a divan.

Jujeena returned with the remaining payment. Alys took it, sighing with relief that Darsee had not found her in his house. And then there he was, coming through the doors, dragging in a huge cardboard package.

"Juju, guess—" Darsee's voice faded.

"I didn't know this was your house. I came to deliver the cake. Rose garden. Nona's Nices. She's my aunt. Nona is. I didn't know this was your house. I'm leaving, though, so, bye, thank you."

Alys was halfway to the car when she heard footsteps behind her.

"Wait, Alys," Darsee called. "Come back. I'd like you to meet my sister."

"I can't," Alys said. "My uncle and aunt are in the car and—"

"Ask them to come in too," Darsee said, "please. You can't come all the way here and then leave like this."

Why not? Alys thought as she tapped on the car window and apprised Nona and Nisar of the situation. Suddenly there was Darsee next to her, inviting them in, using a tone of voice she'd never heard, a tone in direct opposition to the cold tone in which he'd spoken when he'd handed her his letter in the park. While the contents of the letter had certainly softened her assessment of him, Alys wondered what was causing him to so respectfully invite her family members inside for chai. It was always polite, of course, to offer guests, invited or uninvited, a cup of tea, but Darsee was insistent. He was holding open Nisar's car door and leading him and Nona indoors and introducing them to Juju, who was putting away her sitar in a corner between two decorative tablas.

"Juju," Darsee said, "this is Alys Binat and her uncle and aunt."

"Nona and Nisar Gardenaar," Alys said. "My uncle Nisar is my mother's brother, the pulmonologist you may remember us mentioning when my sister twisted her ankle."

Darsee's blink was so rapid that no one save Alys noticed. And she only did because she was on the lookout for his disdain the second her mother and anyone related to her mother were mentioned. Instead, Darsee smiled at Nisar and Nona.

Alys was glad her aunt and uncle were doing her proud. They were not ones to be impressed by money and social status, and thus, instead of fawning over Darsee, they were treating him like an equal. Juju asked her to sit down. Alys sat down. Juju sat beside her and kept giving her shy glances.

Alys smiled at her. So this was the nervous young girl who'd been taken in by Wickaam and become pregnant and opted to have an abortion. Seeing Juju with her slumped shoulders and trusting smile and her gentle demeanor, Alys couldn't help but feel protective. Shame on Wickaam for duping this girl. And shame on him for duping the maids who hadn't even Juju's privileges. But, then, Alys fully knew that the lure of a handsome face and flirtatious manners was one that could easily bridge class and prove equally irresistible to maid and mistress.

"I love your *kurti*," Alys said to Juju. "The color suits you."

"Really?" Juju said. "Everyone always tells me that I look good in baby pink, so I wear it a lot. I like your T-shirt so much."

Alys was wearing white linen pants and a black T-shirt saying NOT YOUR AVERAGE AUNTY.

"Thanks. My sister Qitty makes these for fun. How long have you been playing the sitar?"

"A year," Juju said. "I'm not very good."

"I thought you were playing beautifully."

"Was I? I do try to practice every day. I wanted to learn the guitar, but my brother said first sitar and then the guitar, and I thought, why not listen to him for once?"

"How very kind of you!" Darsee smiled indulgently at Juju.

Alys looked from brother to sister and concluded that Darsee was most definitely not the envious sibling Wickaam had branded him.

"You live in Lahore, right?" Darsee said, turning to Nisar and Nona.

Alys braced herself for his grimace at the answer, Jamshed Colony. Instead, Darsee mentioned a *dhaba* in Jamshed Colony that made the best chicken *karahi* in town.

"Don't tell our cook that, though," Darsee said. "Hussein is quite sensitive."

"We'll try not to," Nona joked. "In fact, that *dhaba* is one of the reasons we're reluctant to move from Jamshed Colony. We've been living there forever. I'm happy with the schools and my children are well settled, and to dislocate them for a bigger house in a more prestigious area makes little sense."

"I understand," Darsee said. "It's hard to let go of geography. Although—and I've told Alys this several times—I believe people like her and me have an advantage having grown up for a time period without any set roots, and so we are quite comfortable letting go of places. We're the sort of people who believe home is where you make it, and borders are ridiculous, and airports are the most harmonious places on earth."

Alys smiled. "You make the nomad's lifestyle sound so ideal, but depending on your personality, it can be really hard to get up and move, physically as well as emotionally."

"True," Darsee said. "What are you doing in Lahore? Is your family here too?"

Alys stared at him. He was asking about her family? With such congeniality?

"My family is in Dilipabad, except for my sister Lady, who's visiting a friend in Karachi. I'm here to tour Lahore with my uncle and aunt."

"Hoping to get tickets to the Naseeruddin Shah–Ratna Pathak play in town," Nisar said. "I had a friend who was supposed to purchase them, but by the time he got around to it, they were all pretty much gone."

"*Ismat Apa Kay Naam?*" Darsee asked. "In the Name of Ismat Apa?"

Nisar nodded.

"We're going to see that tomorrow evening," Darsee said. "Are you free? Were you looking for three tickets?"

"Four," Nona said. "Me, Alys, Nisar, and our nephew, Babur."

Darsee phoned someone named Pacman to ask if four more tickets for the play could be arranged. He was put on hold for a moment before being told yes. Darsee refused to take ticket money from Nisar. Next time it could be Nisar's treat, he said. Alys blinked. When exactly had Darsee learned good manners? And why was he going out of his way for them? Alys avoided Nona's glance: This is the rogue who robbed Wickaam of his inheritance?

"Alys," Darsee said, "Bungles and party are coming to the play tomorrow too."

Alys nodded as casually as she could. She turned all her attention to the maid rolling in a tea trolley with silver spoons resting on bone-china platters holding potato cutlets, chicken sandwiches, savory *dahi baray,* and the rose garden cake, which, it turned out, had not been ordered for a special occasion but because Juju was craving it.

"*Daane daane pe likha hai khane wale ka naam,*" Nona said, grandly reciting the proverb—on every grain is written the eater's name—and she laughed as she took a sliver of her very own concoction. Juju rose to serve everyone tea and snacks.

How well mannered Juju was, Alys thought, as she accepted a delicate bowl and helped herself to the *dahi baray,* topping it with deep-fried crackers and fresh chopped coriander. After one bite, Alys declared the mashed white-lentil balls in cumin yogurt sauce superb.

"I have a friend Sherry who is an excellent cook," Alys said. "But your cook would give her a run for her money."

"Are you talking about the Sherry who recently married Farhat Kaleen, my cousin Annie's doctor?" Juju asked.

Alys nodded. She wondered how ridiculous Kaleen had been in front of Juju.

"I met Sherry at my aunt Beena's house. Sherry is so good-natured and kind."

Alys was delighted to hear the compliments.

"And Dr. Kaleen is so nice too," Juju said. "He takes such good care of Annie. A friend of mine tore his ACL, and he also sings Dr. Kaleen's praises."

Alys was pleased to see that Juju Darsee, far from being stuck up, instead shared Jena's propensity for finding good in everyone. The thought of Jena back in Dilipabad saddened Alys. She glanced at Darsee. He looked at ease, perhaps because he was home. But perhaps this persona was the real him, and that other persona, which had earned him the nickname Dracula, was someone else; he sounded nice and friendly, and certainly not like some busybody who would interfere in his friend's life. Dr. Jekyll and Mr. Hyde.

Darsee and Nona were talking about the paintings above the sofa sets. Nona admired both the geometric abstract and the women in the desert. She was familiar with the artists, she told Darsee, and she congratulated him on buying art that spoke to him.

"Aunty Nona's pet peeve," Alys said, "is people who buy art to match the décor."

Upon discovering that Nona had attended the National College of Arts, Darsee had a question for her. He went to the cardboard package he'd dragged in. Nisar helped him open it and they took out a huge pastel in beiges and pale pinks of Lahore's inner-city rooftops and children flying kites.

"I either got it for a steal," Darsee said, "or I've been robbed."

"Why?" Nisar asked.

"Because," Nona said, smiling, "it's either real or an imitation. I wish I'd invested in a few of Iqbal Hussain's paintings back in the day before they became so expensive. Where did you find this?"

"Gallery," Darsee said. "Owner's private collection. He said it's authentic. Except the only art I've ever seen by this artist is of women from the red-light area. There is a signature at the back." Darsee tilted the painting so Nona could look at it.

"It's genuine," she said. "One of his earlier works. Iqbal Hussain was my professor at NCA; if you're interested, we can visit him and he can confirm it for you."

"I'd love that," Darsee said. "In fact, I'd love to meet him."

"I'll arrange it, then," Nona said. "I believe he's out of the country at the moment, at a conference, but as soon as he's back."

"Thank you," Darsee said.

"Can I come too?" Juju piped up. "He's a brilliant artist, the world knows that, but for me, it's that . . ." She stared into her lap. "It's that he doesn't shy away from who he is and where he comes from. He celebrates his origins. Actually, he thrusts them in the faces of society and says, 'Deal with my inconvenient truths.' And he's getting the last laugh, as his stock goes up and respectable women purchase his red-light-area paintings to hang in their drawing rooms, and so it is that women they wouldn't deign to sit with perpetually look down at them from their walls. I wish . . . I wish we could all find the courage to tell our truths."

Alys's and Darsee's eyes connected.

"Of course you can come too, Juju," Alys said. "You don't have to ask. In fact, that will be the first step in finding your courage."

Juju smiled shyly. Alys caught Darsee's grateful look, and she hurriedly looked away.

"Please stay for dinner," Darsee said, inviting them all.

"We were actually headed to the inner-city Food Street," Nisar said, "as part of our Tour Lahore. Alys is very fond of Lahori fried fish. Please, you and Juju must join us. But I warn you, this is my treat."

Darsee did not hesitate to accept, and they left, only to reconvene on a bustling street lined with open-air eateries, some established as far back as pre–1947 partition. They managed to find a table for their large party in front of a *tandoor* lit with a string of naked light bulbs and proceeded to order mango *lassi* and items on a menu they could smell long before they appeared—grilled meats marinated in spicy yogurts, freshly baked *naans* glazed with white butter, and onion, ginger, garlic frying in cauldrons, the sizzle and crackle and pop in the open air.

Soon their order was served, and Alys passed Juju the chickpea-batter deep-fried fish. She asked Juju her interests and hobbies besides music, even as she kept one ear on Darsee, Nisar, and Nona, who were munching away as they discussed the demand for bottled clean air given the rise in pollution worldwide—"Laugh, laugh," Nisar said, "people laughed at bottled water too, but I would advise investing in bottled air; fortunes to be made"—and the future of Pakistani art and music and its growing popularity internationally.

Alys could not recall a more pleasant evening, and she was sad when dinner was over. She went to bed happy. Darsee's stellar behavior had surprised her and it also thrilled her, and she knew, suddenly, that had he always behaved like a gentleman, things might have been different. She snuggled under the quilt and caressed the spot on her hand where his fingers had so briefly touched hers at the NadirFiede wedding. She flushed. She thought of how he'd come running after her at his home, insisted he wanted his sister to meet her, how graciously he'd welcomed her aunt and uncle, how he'd gone out of his way for tickets, how animated he'd been at dinner, how carefully he'd heard everyone's views, especially hers, and how respectfully he'd disagreed if he had to, and, when dinner ended, how sincere he'd sounded when he told them that he was looking forward to seeing them the next day. Alys caught her breath as she recalled how he'd glanced at her at that moment.

A tremendously lovely day it had been, and tomorrow they were going to a play she'd been eager to watch, and she would see Darsee again, and she was not going to let anything spoil her evening, not even the addition of Bungles and party.

———

The next morning at breakfast, Nisar and Nona were still marveling over how Darsee was not the snob they'd been led to believe he was.

"Lady calls him Dracula," Nisar said as he poured milk into his oatmeal. "And Pinkie painted such a Frankenstein picture of him, I expected him to push us over a cliff for being middle-class professionals. Even Jena, who defends everyone, never defends him. Why you women insist on maligning perfectly first-rate men, I don't know."

Nona flicked a raisin at him. "Let's not canonize Valentine Darsee just yet. There is still the matter of Wickaam's accusations. However, I must say, even I was surprised by how nice he seems."

"It's my fault," Alys said unhappily. "I've always said one's opinion regarding anyone is only as good as how one is treated, but I confess, I'm to blame for the generally unfavorable impression of Darsee. I was biased after hearing him say mean things about me in private to Bungles. That, in turn, affected everyone's perception of him."

"But Wickaam?" Nona said. "Darsee certainly does not seem the type to go around stealing inheritances. But, then, Goga didn't seem the type either."

"In Darsee's case," Alys said, blushing, "I have it on good authority that Wickaam is lying about the whole inheritance thing."

"What!" Nona and Nisar cried out simultaneously.

"I can't tell you how I know," Alys added wretchedly, "but trust me when I say that Wickaam is a liar and a deceiver and Darsee is innocent."

"We trust you," Nona and Nisar said. "But are you positive?"

Alys nodded.

Nisar whistled.

"Well, well," Nona said, raising her brows. "Alys, the *innocent* Darsee's attentiveness to us is due to you. He certainly seems to like you."

Alys stared at the black pepper sprinkled on her scrambled eggs. "He just likes that we've both lived abroad and that I actually read and don't just pretend to in order to come across as intellectual or unique. That's all it is, Aunty Nona. No need to give me that look."

Alys and Nona spent the afternoon at Liberty Market, going from boutique to boutique and checking out what new designs people were spending good money on. They also visited Redmon Book Gallery, where Alys spent her own good money. In fact, throwing guilt aside, she splurged. She leapt on a fresh copy of Jamaica Kincaid's *A Small Place* and also bought Leila Ahmed's *A Border Passage,* Jessie Fauset's *Plum Bun,* Rohinton Mistry's *A Fine Balance,* and Marjane Satrapi's graphic novel, *Persepolis,* which she knew Qitty would love to read too, and Mari would appreciate the pretty arabesque booklet with all of God's ninety-nine names explained.

They returned home well in time to get dressed for the play. Even fussing over attire was fun. Nisar settled on a smart *shalwar kurta.* Nona wore slacks and a floral blouse with a lapis necklace. Alys decided on a black *peshwas* with a black paisley print and mirrored bodice, matching *dupatta* and *thang pajamas,* black heels and accessories from Nona's silver jewelry, which she preferred to her mother's gold and precious stones.

Ajmer dropped them off at the main entrance to the Alhamra Art Center and then drove to the parking lot to wait. The play was in Hall One. Darsee was waiting for them in the entrance with their tickets. He looked good, Alys couldn't help noting, in charcoal pants and a slim-fit black shirt. He greeted them as if they'd all been best friends forever, even Babur, who, upon Darsee's inquiry, informed him that he'd gotten into Cornell University and been offered a scholarship. Alys had not thought she could be any prouder of her cousin, but the look on Darsee's face proved her wrong.

They climbed up the circular stairs to the vast auditorium and stepped inside the carpeted amphitheater. Their seats were near the stage, and as they wound their way down the aisles, Darsee, Nona, and Nisar stopped to greet friends. When they finally reached their row, Alys saw that Bungles and his sisters were already seated. Bungles jumped up as soon as he saw Alys, his entire face a smile. He stepped over many toes to meet her and greeted her with such warmth that Alys almost forgot his weak will. She was delighted to see Hammy and Sammy looking ready to faint at her reappearance in their lives.

In order to annoy the sisters further, Alys hailed Bungles with jubilant camaraderie, even as she merely waved from the aisle at the sisters and Jaans, who was complaining loudly about being dragged here when he would have much preferred the invite to a weekend of boar hunting.

Alys was thrilled to see Juju stepping over shoes to welcome her with a giant hug. As Alys hugged her back, she caught Hammy squinting at Sammy. Good. Let her fret. Alys was also very happy to hear Juju use the tag "bhai"—brother—when she addressed Bungles. It was clear that the two shared nothing but a sibling-like camaraderie.

Darsee introduced Nona as the proprietress of Nona's Nices. Sammy shrieked. She loved Nona's Nices cakes! She congratulated Nona on the upcoming Indus Civilization Award. She and Hammy had received an award last year for their sanitary-napkins company, and this year they were presenters and had been sent the list of recipients. Hammy advised Nona not to be nervous during her thank-you speech, despite how prestigious an award the Indus Civilization was. After all, wonderful women like them deserved every accolade they received.

The second Hammy and Sammy became cognizant of Nisar and Nona's relationship to Alys, their expressions soured. Alys was sure that the prestige of the Indus Civilization Award must have fallen accordingly. Neither Nona nor Nisar missed the dynamics, and they were most bemused by the fluctuations in their social status. Babur too was mistaken for a somebody at first, and then his star also fell, only to be back on the rise at the mention of Cornell, though Hammy and Sammy looked as if they were about to ask to see his acceptance letter.

"Alys, it is so good to see you," Bungles said yet again. "How are you? How is your family?"

"Everyone is well," Alys said. "I'm in Lahore for a holiday with my uncle and aunt."

"Jena didn't come?"

"She was here for a few months a little while back."

"Jena was here?" Bungles frowned. "In Lahore? Why didn't she contact us?"

Before Alys could answer, Hammy asked, "Alys, how long are you in Lahore? You must visit us."

"But," Bungles interrupted Hammy, "wasn't Jena supposed to be teaching?"

"She was," Alys said, "but she wasn't feeling well and took some time off from work."

"Is it her ankle?" Bungles asked, alarmed.

"She's fine now," Alys said.

"How is Cherry?" Hammy called out in a thick Pakistani accent.

"Hammy," Darsee said, "have you changed your accent?"

"No," Hammy said.

"Then are you deliberately mocking Sherry's?"

"No," Hammy said, turning pink.

"Good," Darsee said.

Alys looked at him with yet-new eyes.

"Alys," Sammy said in a conciliatory tone, "are you the only fortunate one of your family to be getting a proper holiday?"

"No," Alys said, "my sister Lady is in Karachi."

Hammy said, "How very exciting for her. Lady's first time in K-chi?"

"First time staying with a friend in Karachi," Alys said.

"And who is that lucky friend?" Hammy said. "Jeorgeullah Wick-aam? He's a close friend of yours, isn't he?"

Juju winced and Alys quickly replied, "Actually, that man is no friend of mine. And please, Hammy, do not be absurd. Of course my sister has not gone to stay with any man."

The lights began to dim, and Bungles returned to his seat and Alys slipped into hers. Next she knew it, Darsee was sitting beside her. Alys could smell his cologne.

"Thank you," he whispered, leaning into her. "Hammy has no idea about . . . how upset Juju gets at Wickaam's mention."

Alys kept her eyes straight ahead and muttered, "No problem."

The play began, and for the next couple of hours, she concentrated as best as she could on the three Urdu short stories by Ismat Chughtai that the three actors had chosen to recite as monologues. The first, "Touch Me Not," contrasted the pregnancy experiences of a prostitute versus a girl from a good family. The second, "Mughal Child," was about a dark-complexioned man married to a fair-complexioned lady and the effect on his self-esteem. And the third, "Housewife," explored class-based sexuality and domestic violence. When the lights turned on, the actors received a standing ovation and Alys glanced in Darsee's direction, sad that the evening was ending.

They exited the theater, chattering about their favorite stories. Jaans was boasting about napping through the play, and Darsee and Alys inadvertently exchanged a wry glance.

In the parking lot, Nisar and Nona thanked Darsee yet again for the excellent evening.

"Dinner?" Darsee suggested eagerly, but unfortunately Hammy complained of a bad headache and, since they'd all come in his car, Darsee called it a night.

In the car, Hammy's headache became bearable enough for her to hold forth on what a snob Alys Binat was about her aunt's award and Cornell-Babur, and didn't Juju agree that Alys was overly tanned and *junglee*, wild-looking?

Juju glanced at her brother and then said softly that she thought Alys was so nice and that she liked her tan and thought her unusually pretty.

Hammy laughed. Juju had no need to be civil about Alys for Valentine's sake.

"Remember, babes?" Hammy said to Darsee. "When you first met Alys you thought she was the most ratty thing you'd ever seen, and then, after she came stomping in from a walk in a public park without a *dupatta,* you generously decided her eyes were nice enough. I wonder where you stand now."

"No need to wonder," Darsee said. "Since then I've come to the conclusion that Alysba Binat is one of the most good-looking women, if not the most good-looking woman, I have ever set eyes on."

Chapter 23

The next morning Alys was curled up in an armchair in Nona and Nisar's living room, holding *Sunlight on a Broken Column* to her heart, when there was a knock on the door and a servant let in Darsee.

"Hello," he said. "I came to thank you again for diverting the conversation away from Wickaam last night."

"I'm glad I was able to," Alys said, slipping the book in her lap. She wished she'd bathed and that she wasn't in her peacock pajamas. She buzzed the kitchen and asked Ama Iqbal to bring chai.

"Where are your uncle and aunt?" Darsee perched on the armchair opposite her.

"We had so much to discuss about the play that we stayed up all night and then went for a *halwa puri* breakfast this morning. When we came back, they finally went to sleep."

"Why are you still up?"

"Life is short," Alys said joyfully. "I'm not sleepy."

"Lack of sleep is not good for your health," Darsee said. Then he flushed as if he'd said something he shouldn't have.

Alys felt a nervous flutter in her stomach. "I've been meaning to ask, how is Raghav? Did he conquer K2?"

Darsee smiled. "As much as K2 allows itself to be conquered."

"And how is Annie?"

"Trying to convince her mother to let her Nigerian boyfriend visit; otherwise she will pack up and move to Nigeria, which she just might do if Farhat Kaleen would agree to move with her."

Alys laughed. The book slid to the floor.

"So you are reading *Sunlight*." Darsee picked it up. "I thought you might not read it after . . ."

They were silent for a second, each thinking of Islamabad and what had transpired there, his patronizing proposal, her condescending rejection.

"I just finished it," Alys said. "I was rereading the ending. What a beautiful meditation on memory and place. It so perfectly captures the nuance of the difference between houses and homes."

"You liked it, then?" Darsee said.

"I loved it."

"Me too. What exactly did you love?"

"Everything. The way Laila struggles between the secular and the religious, the way Abida and Nandi embody class and gender issues. The way Laila is forbidden to love a poor man."

Darsee's smile faltered. "Yes, the love sto—"

The door opened and Ama Iqbal brought in the cordless phone. It was for Alys. It was Jena.

"Jena," Alys said, "I'll call you back. What? Slow down. What do you mean she's run away? With whom? Of course I'll leave for Dilipabad immediately. Uncle and Aunty too. Have you called Falak Khala? We'll all be there soon."

Alys hung up. Tears dripped off her chin. When had she started to cry? Darsee was kneeling before her with a box of tissues.

"Is everyone all right?" he said.

"No one is all right." Alys took out a bunch of tissues. "My sister Lady has run away with Jeorgeullah Wickaam."

The color drained from Darsee's face.

"She was in Karachi, staying with a school friend, very respectable family. She left a letter saying she and Wickaam were eloping. I think you know what that means. They've been together for four days, and if they were married I know Lady would've called home to show off. She just turned sixteen. She probably believes he loves her and will marry her. She will get pregnant, he will abandon her, and I don't know what we will do. My father left for Karachi as soon as he heard this morning. But what can he do? Why didn't I warn my family about Wickaam? Why?"

Darsee stood up abruptly. "I'm sure you want me gone."

Alys's heart sank, and after a moment she simply said, "Yes. Go."

As she watched him leave, Alys realized the depth of her feelings. She loved him. More important, she liked and respected him. As the fact of that admission settled within her, Darsee closed the door behind him and Alys knew that, had there been even a smidgen of a chance between them, it was gone forever. To be connected to a family ruined by Wickaam in the same way Juju herself had nearly come to ruin was not something Valentine Darsee would ever inflict on his beloved sister, and Alys was sure Darsee, at this very moment even, was thanking his lucky stars that she'd previously spurned his proposal.

Chapter 24

Alys, Nona, Nisar, and Falak arrived in Dilipabad by mid evening. Nona was going to miss the Indus Civilization Awards ceremony, but no honor any of them brought to the family could ever compensate for the dishonor Lady had dealt them. As they entered the front door, they could hear Mrs. Binat wailing. She was in the living room, laid out on the sofa, a thermometer by her side. Jena was wrapping up a blood-pressure monitor. Mari held a cold compress to her mother's head. Hillima rubbed the soles of Mrs. Binat's feet. Qitty was huddled in a corner.

"I keep getting panic attacks," Mrs. Binat said with a great sob when she saw her brother and sister. Nisar and Falak hurried to their baby sister's side with cries of not to worry, God would fix everything.

"I keep asking God, What did I do to deserve this? You should've seen Barkat's face when he found out. The last time he looked that way was when he discovered Goga had cheated him." Mrs. Binat clutched Falak's hands. She wouldn't let go of her big sister's grip.

"My poor Lady. My poor Lady. Kidnapped by that *ganda aadmi*, dirty man."

"He did not kidnap her," Alys said. "She eloped."

"Oh, be quiet," Mrs. Binat said. "Oh, Lady, Lady, my innocent baby, where are you! Imagine that man, Wickaam, a python let loose in my den of bunnies, and now he is squeezing to death our *bachee*, our baby bunny, which would be perfectly fine if only he marries her."

"He's never going to marry her," Alys said. She tried not to think of Darsee and how fast he'd fled. "Wickaam is a fortune hunter and Lady has zero fortune."

Mrs. Binat's eyes welled up. "You were the one who brought Jeorgeullah Wickaam into our house."

"He was the lawyer assigned to us, remember?" Alys said guiltily. "For the Fraudia Acre case."

"The case is over, con man has run off again, not a penny will we ever see from that *manhoos*—accursed—land, and now Lady is being plundered for free. Someone hand me my tranquilizers. I want to be tranquil. Better yet, I want to be dead."

"Don't say that," Falak and Nisar said in distress.

"God has abandoned us," Mari said, gripping her inhaler. "If you ask me, we should all kill ourselves. Better that than endure society's taunts for the rest of our lives."

"Oh, Mari," Nona said. "Let us have faith that this will come to a good end."

"Nona *jee*," Mrs. Binat said, "my sweet sister-in-law, someone has done *bura jadoo*—ill-will magic—on us. Useless Uterus Sherry married so well. Jena dumped by Bungles. Alys a failure. And now my Lady. Ill-will magic. No other explanation."

"The explanation," Alys said, "is that he targeted Lady and she likes to make you-you eyes at everyone, and this time she went too far."

"Alys," Mrs. Binat said, sitting up, "not everyone is content to live the life of an unmarried failure. Lady is bright and beautiful and soulful, and that is why that handsome devil targeted her. If I were him, I'd have done the same. Your father will find them and make them marry. That is what we should pray for."

"What we should be praying for," Alys said furiously, "are mothers who do not preach marriage all day every day until—"

"Come, Alys," Hillima interrupted her. "Come help me make chai."

Hillima took Alys by the hand and pulled her into the kitchen. This was hardly the time for daughter and mother to have one of their fights. Alys sank into a chair at the kitchen table. Hillima gave Alys two painkillers. Minutes later Jena joined them. She sent Maqsood, the cook, out of the kitchen and to his room—he had a tendency to gossip.

Once Maqsood left, Alys asked Jena, "Does Mummy really believe Wickaam kidnapped Lady?"

"I don't know what she believes," Jena said. "Her beliefs keep changing every minute. If it wasn't for Hillima, the rest of us would have gone mad by now."

Hijab's mother had phoned that morning. Hillima had brought the cordless into the dining room, where the family was at breakfast. She'd given the phone to Mrs. Binat. Seconds later, Mrs. Binat had tossed the phone at her husband and proceeded to wail. Hijab's parents were distraught at their house being the launching pad for such a thing. They'd thought Lady belonged to a good family. Girls from good families did not do such things. She was a *Binat*. Otherwise they would have never allowed Hijab to invite her. Hijab was traumatized by this turn of events and completely innocent of any complicity. How dare Mr. and Mrs. Binat send an *awara badchalan*, a sex-crazed daughter, to their home.

After Hijab's mother hung up, a bewildered Mr. Binat informed them that Lady had run away with Jeorgeullah Wickaam. Only Qitty seemed unsurprised. In fact, she'd said, "I can't believe Lady actually went ahead with it. She always wanted romance."

Qitty had known this was going to happen and she'd said nothing. Mr. Binat looked as if he was going to hit one of his children for the first time in his life, and he told Qitty so.

Qitty had begun to cry. Lady had telephoned her to share her secret and had been so nice to her for once. Like a good sister. Lady had said there was a beach bonfire and Wickaam was there and everyone thought he was gorgeous but he had eyes only for her. Lady had also said that it wasn't as if Mummy and Daddy could ever afford to get any of them married with *phoon phaan*—a splash like NadirFiede—and she wanted an unforgettable splash of her own. Eloping was her way of getting it.

Hillima set mugs of chai in front of Jena and Alys.

"At least," Alys said, wrapping her hands around her mug and drawing as much solace as she could from its warmth, "we know Lady believed Wickaam was going to marry her. But you and I know he's not going to. That would take a miracle."

"Miracles don't happen to people like us," Jena said, her head in her hands. "We don't have the kind of money that can buy miracles."

It was decided that Nisar and Nona would join Mr. Binat in Karachi. Nona's parents could keep the children for another few days, and Nisar would take emergency family leave from work, because this was a family emergency. Alys would have liked to accompany them, but the school year was about to start and if she and Jena didn't return to work, their absence would confirm the rumors that were already circulating about Lady.

Alys had told her mother to please not entertain the neighbors or anyone with the details of what had happened, but Mrs. Binat required more of an attentive audience for her grief than just Falak, and to the delight of a neighbor who stopped by for a chat, she related the whole sordid tale.

The news spread overnight, and the next day throngs of neighbors arrived with their great concern. Bobia Looclus came armed with a platter of chicken *pulao* because, though grieving, one must eat. Mrs. Binat ate and held court, howling loudly about her ill luck, her poor

Lady, that python Wickaam, and how this was all Hijab's parents' fault.

"People worry about servants gossiping," Mari said morosely to her sisters, "and here our mother is doing the job."

The next day, Nisar and Nona left for Karachi. Back in Dilipabad, everyone hovered around the phone. Mr. Binat called late at night. Nisar and Nona had arrived. To what good, though? Karachi was a sprawling metropolis; the couple, if that was what one must call them, could literally be hiding anywhere. The fact that they were hiding terrified him. Should they not have strutted back into society by now as Mr. and Mrs. Jeorgeullah Wickaam?

Nona got on the phone and assured Alys that her father was tired and dazed but otherwise all right and that, come tomorrow, they would go to every hospital, in case there'd been an accident. The hospital search proved futile and, the very next day, Nona took over and sent Mr. Binat back to Dilipabad.

A despondent Mr. Binat took himself into his study and crept into his armchair. Jena brought him a strong cup of chai and Alys laid her head in his lap and he stroked her hair.

"You were right, Alys," he said. "You told me not to let her go. That she was immature and had no sense of right or wrong. But I was more worried about peace and quiet in this house, and now, because of it, we will never have any peace or quiet. This scandal will ruin Lady's prospects forever, but Wickaam may yet find himself an heiress. Today, for the first time, I am feeling the full fire of patriarchy."

"Women are never forgiven in our society, but men can be," Alys said.

"That seems to be the rule." Mr. Binat sighed. "Lady may get what she deserves, but I'm heartbroken for what that means for the rest of you girls. No, Alys, don't tell me not to be harsh on myself. Let me

stew in my regrets. But have no fear. The Chinese proverb teaches us
'This too shall pass,' and make no mistake, it shall. I weathered my
brother's betrayal and now I will weather my daughter's, and you
girls will learn to weather it as well. It is your mother who will never
learn to see what is what and what is not. Claiming Lady was kidnapped. That it is Hijab's parents' fault. Such preposterousness bog-
gles the mind, but of course this too shall pass."

Farhat Kaleen's letter arrived the next morning at the breakfast table,
where Qitty, Mari, Falak, and Mrs. Binat were tucking away while
the rest stared at the food. Mr. Binat read the letter, then passed it on
to his wife, who dissolved into hysterics. Falak told Alys to read it
out loud.

> *My Dear Binats,*
>
> *What I have to say concerns all of you and deserves the staying
> power of a letter rather than the ephemeral nature of a phone call,
> which, in my vast experience, often means in one ear and out the
> other, an affliction I strongly believe Lady suffers from to a great
> extent, as per Sherry's assessment of her. I am of course writing in
> regard to this elopement business. Is there even an elopement? Or
> is Lady living in sin?*
>
> *I unfortunately had to break the news to Begum Beena
> dey Bagh—better she hear it from me rather than from
> rumormongers—and what she told me about Jeorgeullah Wick-
> aam was shocking. He is her nephew, but he is a disgrace. He was
> disinherited years ago. He has no money and, God help us, his law
> degree is fake! I ask again if Lady is living in sin? What will be-
> come of her when this scoundrel tires of her?*
>
> *A woman is nothing and no one without her virtue. Her vir-
> tue is the jewelry of her soul. But this is forgotten by modern
> women, who march around in their* patloons *under the impres-
> sion that wearing trousers means they are now men. A woman*

is a woman no matter what she wears and must behave like a lady.

Of course, this terrible business will affect all of you. Had I any doubts, then let me tell you that Begum Beena dey Bagh corrected me. I still pray that Jena, Alys, Qitty, and Mari may find someone to marry them, but Lady has permanently dimmed her sisters' prospects.

I heard that Lady is to set up shop and Wickaam to be the shopkeeper in charge of determining her price. God forbid this be true. One should pray for Lady's death before we should have to suffer such humiliation.

Given the situation, I'm sure you'll understand why I think it unwise to visit each other at this time. I will also be most obliged if Sherry is not contacted and, if she contacts you, to please ignore her.

I wish you all the best in these trying circumstances.

I will pray for all your souls.

Fi amanillah, *May God go with you,*

Farhat Kaleen

"A loose woman is a flower every man wants to pluck and chuck," Mari said desolately. "That's what his letter means. I always said Jeorgeullah is no mullah, but none of you ever listen to me. And Lady is no lady. Lady *nay humari naak kaat dhi.* Lady has cut off our noses for shame. We, as a family, have no nose left."

"Should we write back?" Qitty asked in a tiny voice.

"What's there to say?" Alys said. She felt a persistent melancholy at how she and Darsee had parted without a friendly look or word, and she could only imagine Beena dey Bagh and Darsee's mutual congratulations over escaping any association with this strain of the Binat family.

"How can I show my face at the religious-club meetings?" Mari said, drowning her grief in buttered toast. "What will the members say? One sister so pious and the other practically a prostitute."

"Yes, Mari," Alys said. "We all sympathize that this situation has disrupted your social life. Believe me, we are all irrevocably impacted."

Alys expected Principal Naheed to fire her and Jena. She could well imagine parents up in arms at their daughters being taught by teachers whose sister had, as Farhat Kaleen put it, "set up shop." And so it was that Alys and Jena were fully prepared to be terminated on the first day of the new school year. The staff room was a hush and they were glad no one asked them if the rumors regarding Lady were true. In fact, the teachers were extra-sweet. That Lady was absent, coupled with Alys's and Jena's long faces, was proof enough to all that some disaster had occurred.

For the first time, Alys felt no joy as she gazed at her new batch of ninth-graders and gave them an overview of the semester and the books they would read. The students in Alys's and Jena's classes did not say a word. Later that day, Principal Naheed did summon them into her office. She shook her head and pursed her lips and remarked that teenage years could be very trying and that they were to keep her posted on the fragile situation.

Jena was grateful for Naheed's support and Alys was too, but she told Jena she would not be surprised if Naheed was frantically searching for teachers to replace them in case Lady returned home in disgrace, unwed and pregnant, even. Perhaps the Dilipabad Gymkhana would break its die-hard rule of "once a member, always a member" in order to expel the Binats. Such were the questions that, Alys was positive, entertained all Dilipabad.

Nona called daily for the next few days with an update to say there was no update. And then: They were found. They were staying at a cheap hotel in a cheap part of town. They were fine. Lady was glowing. Wickaam looked bemused. He had no answer for why they were not yet married, which, come to think of it, was his answer. And, brace yourself, Lady did not care that they were still unmarried. She said they'd be married soon enough and were having too much fun to break the "honeymoon."

Nona was sorry to report it, but Lady seemed incapable of seeing she'd done something wrong and that her decision was going to negatively impact her family. Nisar had prevailed upon Wickaam to tell him whether or not he meant to do the honorable thing, and Wickaam voiced his demand: one hundred thousand dollars.

It was an exorbitant sum. Nisar and Nona had some savings, as did Falak for sending Babur abroad. But even after they pooled their resources, their savings amounted to a pittance, for what was a grain of sugar to one who demands a cup?

Alys paced in front of her father in his study.

"We must give them the Lahore shop," Mr. Binat said. "The rent is always steady."

"That rent is the bulk of our livelihood," Alys said in horror.

"And it still won't be enough for that greedy fellow," Mr. Binat said. "We must sell the car, this house. What else have we got?"

"Where will we live?" Alys asked. "How will we make ends meet?"

Mr. Binat wrung his hands. "What a failure of a father I am."

"Don't say that," Alys said.

"An utter failure of a parent. My one job was to provide financial security to you girls and your mother, and I could not even do that. I should invest in a cart and sell the flowers and vegetables I grow. But wait—with house gone, flowers and vegetables gone too."

"So we are to lose everything," Alys said, "to buy Lady her respectability, and thereby ours, whatever little respectability it will be."

A bleak evening it was at Binat House, with everyone mourning their lot and looking into the future with trepidation. Only Hillima reminded them that, ten years ago, they'd landed in this house with hardly a penny to their names and, look, they'd survived.

"We had this house," Mrs. Binat wept. "We had a roof over our heads."

"And now," Hillima said, "we have educated girls who can earn."

"This is true," Jena said. "We will never starve."

"We may never starve," said Mrs. Binat, hopeless at the thought of having to start over yet again, "but even on a full stomach one can lose the will to live. We will be forever hungry for better things."

"And dignity," Mari added. "And dignity."

And then, a reprieve. Nona called late that night. Such news could not wait for the morning. Must not wait when it would bring so much respite to all. Wickaam had agreed to marry Lady. No one was quite sure what had happened to change his mind. Perhaps Lady had wept and cried and begged. Perhaps Wickaam had decided he loved her after all. Perhaps—but who cared? They were to be married in the morning, as soon as four male witnesses were rounded up to take to the mosque. Nisar and three more men were needed; even strangers who were willing to sign their names to the marriage certificate would do.

And that was what was done, and Nona called to say: "They are married."

"Joy" would be too strong a feeling for what followed at Binat House. "Relief" was more appropriate. Only Mrs. Binat reveled as she put away the thermometer and blood-pressure cuff and began to plan a proper wedding for her favorite daughter, who was now married: Mrs. Lady Wickaam! *Oof* their children would be beautiful. Angels!

Mr. Binat put his hands over his heart and Alys, Jena, Qitty, and Mari panicked, but he told his daughters that he was perfectly fine. He couldn't be finer. At no financial cost to him, respectability and dignity had been restored.

"Wickaam must truly love her," Jena said.

"Don't be so gullible all the time, Jena," Mr. Binat said. "You think a greedy fellow like Wickaam will settle for a girl who loves him? I fear Nona has given him a huge share in her business and Nisar may have taken on debt. I dare not ask, because I can never repay them a hundred thousand dollars. All I know is that I am forever indebted."

"He is my brother," Mrs. Binat said proudly, "and this is how a loving brother comes to the rescue."

"Nisar and Nona have gone above and beyond loving," Mr. Binat said.

"Barkat," Mrs. Binat chirped, "at the very least we must throw the Wickaams a *mehndi* ceremony and a reception at the first available date open at the gymkhana. *Hai,* what will Lady wear? What will you girls wear? *Hai,* how exciting to have a daughter married! Finally! Finally!"

But Mr. Binat crushed Mrs. Binat's plans when he roared that, let alone throwing a *mehndi* or a reception, he was forbidding Lady and that *ganda aadmi* dirty man from setting foot anywhere near their home. If they dared show their faces in Dilipabad, he would shoot them.

Mrs. Binat began to cry. "You always begrudge me every happiness."

Mr. Binat was unmoved. He meant to keep this resolution, and he turned around and went into the moonlit garden, where he began to pull out weeds in order to calm his heart. This afternoon he had thought all was lost: shop, car, house, garden, jewelry, reputation. And now all was miraculously restored. He began to weep.

Alys and Jena found their father in the garden, weeding and weeping. They'd been sent by their mother to make him see sense, and he ordered them to return to her and make *her* see sense: Lady was dead to him, and Wickaam had never been alive.

"Daddy, she's not dead, God forbid," Alys said, "and she'll always be your daughter. You have to allow them to visit us at least once. If we abandon Lady, that man will treat her as shabbily as he wants, without any fear of consequences. Also, by inviting them here, by your making a show of accepting the situation, it will go from a big scandal to merely a messy situation and will put an end to much malicious gossip."

And so it was Mr. and Mrs. Wickaam arrived at Binat House for a week's visit, Wickaam driving a brand-new car and Lady, waving madly, decked out in a new designer outfit, Nona's "borrowed" sunglasses, and a fire-engine-red mouth.

"Your lipstick is *thabahi,* deadly," Mrs. Binat said, welcoming her married daughter with exhilaration. She held a Quran over Lady and Wickaam's heads for blessing. "Enter, Husband and Wife. May God keep you forever sane, safe, and satisfied."

Mr. Binat tersely shook hands with Wickaam and barely acknowledged Lady. Alys, Jena, and Mari smiled as congenially at the couple as their natures allowed. Qitty hugged Lady.

"*Moti,* Fatty, you're crushing my clothes," Lady said as she hugged Qitty back. "Qitty, I wish you'd come to Karachi too. I wish you'd all come. So many hot men. Not like the losers in Dilipabad. Karachi is for winners, and, look, I won myself a husband."

"Not won exactly," Wickaam said, "but *phasaoed,* lassoed."

"Hahaha. How Wick wishes he was funny," Lady said adoringly. "But he is handsome! Could any of you have guessed that, out of all of us, I would end up Mrs. Jeorgeullah Wickaam?"

"And I, Mr. Lady Binat?" Wickaam said, scratching his head.

Lady basked and chattered nonstop. Wickaam smiled his usual smile. Both behaved as if nothing was out of place. Perhaps, Alys remarked to Jena, they believed it. Lady was awfully sorry to hear that the Dilipabad Gymkhana had no dates for a reception and neither did Lotus, Burger Palace, or Pizza Palace, and not even High Chai. But it was understandable because of such short notice. She wouldn't have minded a big dinner thrown for them at the house, but next time.

This time she was going to visit each and every neighbor, school friend, and acquaintance, with Wick in tow. First she'd stop by and show off Wick to Mareea Looclus. That would put an end to fishface Mareea's showing off about Sherry and Fart Bhai. Should she take Wick to the British School? Display him to former classmates and to Principal Naheed?

"No!" said Alys and Jena, and Lady was too giddy to argue.

Thankfully, Lady stayed true to her plans, and she and Wickaam were hardly ever home. Mrs. Binat, the proud mother, accompanied them on their visits, her arms linked between her beloved daughter and her dashing son-in-law. Dilipabad wasn't quite sure what to think. On the one hand, Lady had run away. On the other hand, she was home with *her lawfully wedded husband.* To the chagrin of gossipmongers, the vilest of the gossip was dying down.

On their last evening, Mr. and Mrs. Wickaam insisted on dining at home, and Mrs. Binat made sure Lady and Wickaam's favorite dishes were prepared.

"I wish you would settle down in Dilipabad," Mrs. Binat said, thoroughly upset that they were leaving the next day.

"That would be a death sentence, Mummy," Lady said. She and Wick wanted to travel. She'd been dying to go to Disneyland, and now they would go there for their honeymoon. And they planned to settle in Karachi when they came back to Pakistan. Wick had of late come into some money—Mr. Binat spluttered on his rice—and he wanted to invest in some business or other, maybe a bowling alley or a highly exclusive restaurant. Law was so blah, *naa.*

Wickaam looked up from his *koftas.* "Hated law. Long, boring, tedious."

"What is long, boring, tedious?" Alys said, unable to resist. "Walking through a college campus in New York?"

Wickaam gave her a slow, grudging smile. Alys returned it with a nod, and turned.

After dinner, which Mr. Binat gulped down as fast as he could, he went to bed, completely unable to stomach being in the same room as these two equally *bagaireth,* shameless, newlyweds. Neither one had shown one iota of embarrassment, and Lady especially was acting as if hers was a love story to equal Romeo-Juliet and Layla-Majnun and Heer-Ranjha, except, of course, Lady and Wickaam were not star-crossed lovers who died. Mr. Binat expected no heartfelt apologies from Lady to them, but how he wished she had apologized properly to Nona for making her miss the Indus Civilization Award ceremony. Instead, the shameless girl told Nona that no doubt there was a reason God had not wanted her to attend and therefore found a way to prevent her from going.

Alys watched her father hurry out of the dining room. She very much wanted to follow him, except that all the sisters had promised Lady that, since it was her last night with them for who knew how long, they would stay up like old times and snack on pine nuts and chat. Thankfully, Wickaam declared he was tired and went to bed.

The Binat sisters and mother and Hillima traipsed into the living room and settled down. Lady wanted to know all the gossip at school.

"*Mashallah,* you were the gossip for a long while," Mari said dourly. "And with this visit you're the gossip again. You are notorious."

Lady clapped her hands. Better notoriety than invisibility. Who'd said what? And who was dying of jealousy that she'd married a man who looked like a movie star? In fact, Wick might star in a movie. A friend of his was making a movie and he'd asked Wick to be the hero, and Wick was seriously considering it.

"I thought 'Wick,'" Alys said, "was planning to write an earth-shattering novel."

"Oh, he will," Lady said. "He's just looking for the right person to write it for him."

Alys shook her head at Jena.

"I see you, Alys," Lady said. "You can make faces all you want, but I promise you, one day Wick and I are going to be rich-and-famous celebrities and socialites who appear in *Social Lights* all the time, and then you'll regret not believing in us."

"I hope so," Alys said. "For your sake."

"And I'm going to say I told you so," Lady said as she flipped through an issue of *Mode,* pausing at the pages where Qitty had turned the corners on obese models she thought resembled her. "I have so many people I'm dying to say I told you so to. And the number-one person is that yuck-*thoo* Dracula."

At Darsee's mention, Alys felt her stomach drop. She hated that it did.

"Don't mention that man's name on this perfect evening," Mrs. Binat said. She was dozing on the sofa, enjoying the voices of all her daughters drifting over her: If there was a heaven on earth, then being surrounded by one's grown children was it.

"I swear," Lady said, "Dracula nearly ruined my marriage. He spent the whole time standing on top of Wick's head as if Wick was planning to flee. If he wasn't Wick's first cousin, I swear I'd forbid Wick from seeing him ever again. I certainly don't want to see him again."

"Darsee was at your *nikah*?" Alys sat up.

"Oh Crapistan!" Lady said. "I promised Wick and Dracula I wouldn't tell. All of us promised Dracula we'd keep our mouths shut."

"All? Who 'all'?" Alys said.

"Me, Uncle Nisar, Aunty Nona. It was a stupid promise."

"What was Darsee doing there?" Alys glanced at an equally perplexed Jena.

Lady shrugged. "He was one of the witnesses. He frowned the whole time. *Bhalla*—imagine. Frowning at someone's nuptials. Such an ill omen. I hope his nose turns into a popcorn, just like Fart Bhai's. Qitty told me about the letter Fart Bhai sent, in which he said I should die of shame. That purity pervert married the best friend of the woman who rejected him—he should be the shameful one. What have I got to be ashamed of? Falling in love? Having a love marriage? *Lo jee!* I swear, all these men are so pompous, except Wick. He's a real catch. So down to earth. When I settle in Karachi, all of you visit me and I'll help you grab husbands. It'll be so much fun."

"Spare us," Alys said as she tried to make sense of Lady's revelation.

"I'd rather die a virgin," Mari said, "than resort to your tactics."

"Suit yourselves, then," Lady said, yawning. "But, seriously, my stupid sisters, think about the fact that I'm the only one married out of us. And on that note, I'm going to bed and to my husband, who is always Mr. Lonely Pants for me. Signing off for the night is your baby sister, Lady Binat, now also starring as Mrs. Lady Jeorgeullah Wickaam."

———

The next morning, Wickaam and Lady drove away from Binat House, but not before Alys pulled Lady aside once more to confirm that Darsee had been at her marriage ceremony, after which she wasted no time calling Nona. Nona was surprised that Alys did not already know. She'd thought Darsee was swearing secrecy because he wanted to tell her the sensitive news himself.

"Sensitive news?" Alys said.

"Alys," Nona said, "Darsee is the one who paid Wickaam a hundred thousand dollars to marry Lady. Of course, we shielded Lady from Wickaam's demand. Why break her heart? Darsee was at the marriage because he wanted to make sure Wickaam went through with it and didn't run off with the money. I'm so glad we've cleared this up. I would hate to think that any of you thought Nisar and I bailed Lady out. I mean, we gladly would have if we had that type of money. But who does? Well, Darsee obviously does, but you know what I mean. I wonder why he hasn't told you yet."

Alys hung up the phone. She headed toward the graveyard for some privacy. She paced the lanes between the graves. She walked by the grave of a Pakistani soldier who at the time of his death in World War II had been an Indian soldier; geography had converted his citizenship from one country during life to another after death. Darsee, with his romantic notions of being rootless, would have appreciated this observation.

Throughout her walk, Alys thought back to the last time she and Darsee had been together, in Nona's living room, about how they'd been talking about *Sunlight* until Jena's call had come, then Darsee had left abruptly, and she'd been convinced he'd have nothing to do with them ever again. Yet *he* was the one who'd paid off Wickaam to marry Lady. It was in all likelihood, Alys told herself, because he'd felt guilty. By asking her to keep Wickaam's sordid past a secret, he'd enabled Wickaam to manage yet another conquest, this time in the form of Lady. Perhaps, Alys also thought, Darsee believed that by marrying Wickaam off he would curb his cousin's carnal appetite once and for all.

The truth was, Alys had no idea why exactly Darsee had decided to spend a fortune on the cousin he despised. She would like to ask him, of course, but who knew if she'd ever see him again? Their paths were unlikely to cross; they had no reason to cross.

When Alys returned home, Binat House was in an uproar.

"You won't believe it, Alys!" Qitty said. "He just drove up and rang the doorbell and asked for her as if it was the most natural thing in the world. I said, 'Yes, she's home, in the living room,' and he went straight in and then he took her straight out and it's been over an hour since they left. But where have you been?"

"Who came in and who took who out?" Alys hurried to the living room, where both her mother and Mari were on prayer mats. "What happened?"

"Jena happened!" Mari looked up from the Quran she was frantically reading on Jena's behalf. "Bungles came and took Jena out. Mummy and I are praying for them."

"We are praying," Mrs. Binat said, "that this time the silly man gets it right."

"Oh my God," Alys said, and she rushed to find her father.

Mr. Binat was in the garden, transferring sprouting seeds from a pot into a flower bed. He was most amused at this turn of events but also had fingers crossed that this time Jena's heart would not be broken all over again.

Chapter 25

Jena had the shock of her life when Bungles came into the living room. She'd been sitting in the window seat, threading her mustache. Mari was holding up a magnifying mirror for her. When Bungles walked in, Jena stared for a long second and then hid the threading thread behind her back. Was her mustache area red? Then she decided, to hell with embarrassment. If anyone should be embarrassed, it should be Mr. Weak Will.

In fact, when Bungles asked her if she would please go on a drive with him, she agreed just so that she could tell him he was a weak-willed person and shame on him. Jena got into the car and hardened herself against the way his hair flopped over his forehead and the way he was nervously pursing his lips. They'd hardly turned the corner when Bungles parked under the mango tree that had grown not by design but due to littering. He turned to her and said, "Jena, will you marry me?"

"Are you here," Jena said, "because you've been given permission by your sisters and your friend?"

"What do you mean?" Bungles said.

Jena told him she knew that Hammy-Sammy and Darsee had previously been opposed to their match.

"They were," Bungles said slowly, "but the truth is, I honestly didn't know the difference between a crush and like and love. And when Hammy, Sammy, and Darsee kept telling me you were not interested, it was easier to accept that than to sort out my feelings. I'm so sorry to have hurt you. No, it wasn't a matter of a weak will, not at all. No, I'm not unduly influenced by others. I swear I'm not. Jena, I truly did not trust my own feelings. Jaans was the only one who always said he knew what I felt was true love. But Jaans. You know. Who listens to Jaans?

"But I didn't stop thinking about you for a single moment, and I finally admitted to myself that these feelings I have for you are it for me. As for my sisters and Darsee, while I value their opinions, this is my decision. I want to marry you. I hope you want to marry me. They told me that they'd known you were in Lahore and that they hid it from me. I was furious with them. They've apologized, profusely, and I hope you won't hold it against me that I've forgiven them. I hope you forgive them too, but if you can't, I'll understand.

"I told my parents of my decision to propose to you, and they flew in on the first flight out of California so that, if you say yes, there are no further delays for them to visit your house with a formal proposal. They came in last night, and here I am today to ask you if you will please marry me."

Jena returned home carrying a box of cream rolls from High Chai. She told everyone to sweeten their mouths, and then she broke into an ugly cry.

"I'm getting married to Bungles!" Jena said. "Mummy, you were right all along. He did propose."

"I told you so." Mrs. Binat chortled with joy. "I guaranteed he would propose, only none of you girls have any faith in me, not to mention your father prancing around insisting I eat my shoe."

———

Bungles's family was due to visit the Binats the next day with a formal proposal in order to ask for Jena's hand in marriage, as well as give her an engagement ring and set a wedding date. There was a great flurry of activity as residents of Binat House prepared for this event. In the morning, Mrs. Binat sent Jena to Susan's Beauty Parlor for a facial and to get her hair blow-dried. She was going to wear a simple pale-yellow cotton *shalwar kameez,* Jena had decided, and just lip gloss and her garnet earrings. This time she was getting dressed up for herself and not for anyone else.

Mr. Binat was dispatched to the *mithai* shop to order several kilos of *motichoor ladoos,* which would be distributed to the neighborhood and sent to the gymkhana and taken to school by Jena; oh, they were going to send celebratory sweets into every home in Dilipabad, such that no one would ever forget, cost be damned.

Bungles's parents turned out to be lovely. His mother kept kissing Jena's hands and telling her tales of Bungles's childhood and how naughty he'd been. For the first time in her life, Mrs. Binat did not have much to say, because she was so full of joy. She kept looking at the glorious diamond on Jena's hand and thinking it was exactly as she'd predicted: big and sparkling.

The Binglas had also given Jena a beautiful set of solid gold and diamond bracelets, as well as gifts and suit pieces to the rest of the Binats. Bungles's father and Mr. Binat got along well. They talked about politics and gardening and life in Dilipabad and life in California. Jena was very sweet to Hammy and Sammy. She was always sweet to everyone, but this time she was fully aware of her sisters-in-laws' duplicitous, cunning and manipulative capabilities.

Hammy and Sammy acted as if they'd always been madly in love with Jena and it was Bungles who'd been stalling. The fact was, they adored their baby brother, and if he wanted to ruin his life and marry 'senior citizen' Jena Binat despite their objections, then so be it. Such was their change of heart that they even declared D-bad a most charming and quaint town and High Chai hip and happening. Jaans behaved as best as he could and reminded everyone, every so often, that he'd predicted this coupling at first sight.

Darsee had accompanied them too. Alys watched him offer enthusiastic congratulations when Bungles slid the ring onto Jena's finger and Jena the engagement band the Binats had hurriedly procured for Bungles from a thrilled Ganju *jee*. Darsee discussed sports and politics with Mr. Binat. He ignored Mrs. Binat just as resolutely as she ignored him. He and Alys nodded hello to each other as if they were strangers. Alys wished she could thank him for paying Wickaam to marry Lady, but this crowded drawing room was neither the time nor the place.

After her future in-laws left Dilipabad to return to Lahore, Jena kept bursting into blissful tears. She'd truly given up hope of reconciliation with Bungles, for she'd believed that, even if he did reappear in her life, there was nothing he could say that would win her over or excuse his previous display of a weak will. But he had won her over and Jena's happiness knew no bounds, for herself as well as the fact that she was giving her family so much pleasure.

However, Jena supposed her favorite moment would be walking into the staff room the next morning with celebratory sweets and a ring on her finger. And it was. There was not a dry eye in the school or a moment of ill will; everyone loved Jena, and they hoped she would live happily ever after.

Alys was still smiling over the loving reception Jena had received in the staff room when Bashir, the peon, knocked on the classroom door. She turned to him with a knowing glimmer in her eyes.

"Let me guess," Alys said. "Principal Naheed wants to see me."

"Immediately," Bashir said, looking very scared. "There is someone here to see you."

It was Beena dey Bagh. When she saw Alys, she ordered Naheed to leave the office. Naheed had never been kicked out of anywhere, let alone her own office, but she walked out wordlessly onto the veranda. When the door banged shut, Naheed and Bashir crouched together by the keyhole.

"A pretty penny," Beena dey Bagh was saying, "your parents and relatives must have collected in order to buy my disastrous nephew Jeorgeullah for your sister, who, from all reports, is a girl of a disastrously loose character. As for this mess Bungles has gotten himself into by getting engaged to your sister Jena, well, he will face the consequences of such a rash decision. But that is not why I have come here."

"Why have you come?" Alys stood in the confines of the principal's office, matching, gaze for gaze, the towering Beena dey Bagh.

"You dare speak to me, an elder, in such a tone?"

"And your tone is justified because I'm younger?"

"I don't have time for your nonsense. I'm here to ask only one question, and the only answer I'd better hear is a no."

"What is your question?" Alys said. "I have a class to return to."

"I'll see how long you last in the teaching profession," Beena dey Bagh snarled. "My question to you, you rude, arrogant woman: Are you engaged to Valentine?"

"Engaged to Valentine?"

"It is a well-known fact that you Binat sisters are well versed in the art of bad magic and love spells. First you tried to grab Valentine's friend Raghav—"

"Raghav is gay," Alys said. "You know that."

"Nothing a nice girl can't fix, except you are not a nice girl."

"You can't 'fix' gay. It's a biological—"

"*Chup.* Silence. I was watching you at Versailles flirting with Raghav, and when you couldn't seduce him, you turned your attentions to my nephew. Girls of your class know exactly how to use their ways and wiles to grab men."

"Girls of my class!" Alys squinted. "I am happy to burst your bubble, but 'grab-it' transcends all classes. Class is immaterial to—"

"*Chup.* Silence," Beena dey Bagh said again. "Don't you dare lecture me on class. Have you lost all sense of your place in the world?"

"What place would that be?"

"A place where you should not be able to open your mouth in front of me, let alone dream of being engaged to a dey Bagh. Who are you? Nothing and no one."

"I'm a Binat," Alys said, "from my father's side of the family, and in your worldview that is not nothing or no one."

"Yes, you're a Binat. Albeit a poor lowly Binat, pseudo-gentry," Beena dey Bagh sneered. "But your mother's family. Your grandmother. Let me be absolutely crass about it: Your maternal grandmother was a prostitute."

"There is no proof."

"Your sister Lady's actions have proved this genetic link beyond any doubt."

"You know what?" Alys said. "Maybe my grandmother was indeed a prostitute. Maybe she was the biggest, baddest, busiest prostitute in all of history. Hear me: I'm very proud of my prostitute grandmother. She was a working woman putting food on the table and a roof over heads, unlike women such as yourself who are born into an inheritance or luck out into marrying one."

"You have the audacity to compare me to a prostitute!"

"I'm sorry you cannot celebrate all women and must denigrate some in order to feel good about where you come from. As a fellow educator, I find your sense of entitlement appalling, especially given that it stems from the hubris of inherited wealth and not one you've earned, not that self-made riches would make entitlement any more acceptable."

Beena dey Bagh had never in her life been spoken to this way.

"You dark-complexioned snake of girl," she said. "You're *no* girl. You're a woman. A *baigaireth aurat*, a shameless woman at that! You are *my* employee! A teacher in a backwater town! You slut! Who has allowed you the temerity to call yourself an educator? To put yourself on the same rung as me? Do you know who I am? I am Beena dey Bagh! I have founded an entire school system in Pakistan, English-medium no less. You *badtameez,* belligerent, bitch of a woman. If my nephew insists on marrying you, I will disown him. I will never speak to him again. He will rue the day."

"We'll see," Alys said.

"So you are engaged?"

"I'm not telling you."

"You are not engaged. Otherwise, a woman from a whore background would readily admit to grabbing respectability. If he asks you, promise me you will refuse him."

"Let me tell you what I will promise," Alys said. "I promise that I'm only going to do what is best for me and not what is best for you or anyone else."

"*Chup.* Silence. You classless hussy."

"You *chup.* You silence," Alys said, and she walked out of the office and into Principal Naheed and Bashir and half the school gathered in the veranda.

"Hussy, how dare you turn your back on me?" Beena dey Bagh roared as she followed Alys. "How dare *you* walk away from *me?* Do you know who I am? I am Beena dey Bagh, descendant of royal gardeners and a luminary of this land."

Alys walked even faster while Principal Naheed's voice beseeched Beena dey Bagh to calm down and return to the office and she sent Bashir to *futafut*—instantly—bring chai.

For the rest of the school day, Alys could think of nothing but Beena dey Bagh's visit. Had Jena's and Bungles's engagement scared Beena dey Bagh into believing she'd "grabbed" Darsee? Had Beena dey Bagh any idea what her showing up at school would do to the rumor mill?

After Beena dey Bagh left Principal Naheed's office, Alys was called back in.

"Oh dear," Naheed said. "This is a right muddle. Beena dey Bagh wants you fired, but I reminded her that, as per franchise contracts, firing a teacher is largely my decision, and frankly, Alys, I have no desire to. You're a good teacher despite everything and, more important, thanks to you, students are able to bring their English accents up to standard. But now that I have chosen sides and Beena's wrath, please tell me it is true. Are you to be Mrs. Valentine Darsee?"

When the bell rang for home time, Alys gladly settled into the school van and shut her eyes, willing herself to relax. All day long she'd been bombarded by concerned students gawking at her (Rose-Nama was agape) and teachers asking her if she was okay, if there was any truth to the rumor. When the van stopped in front of the graveyard, she was dismayed to see a Pajero standing outside Binat House. Had Beena dey Bagh come to terrorize her parents?

Mr. and Mrs. Binat were in the foyer, anxiously awaiting her.

"Alys," Mr. Binat said, "what is going on?"

"It's Dracula," Mrs. Binat said. "He said he'd wait for you in the garden."

Alys went straight to the garden. Darsee was by a pretty little wilderness with a tangle of fruit trees—orange, custard apple, tamarind—Alys's favorite area, not that he knew it.

"Hello, Alys," Darsee said. "Your mother called me Dracula."

"Oh." Alys looked sheepish. "My entire family calls you Dracula. It's a nickname from way back."

"I like it. Dracula."

"Good," Alys said. "They'll be so pleased to hear. Listen—"

"What?"

"I've been meaning to thank you," Alys said. "I must thank you."

"For what?"

"You know for what. I can only imagine how difficult it must have been for you to be in the same room with that man, let alone negotiate terms with him."

"I did it for you." Darsee cleared his throat. "I kept hearing you say how your sister's action had ruined the rest of you. I kept wondering what would have happened had I not had the resources to take my sister to Europe for a secret abortion. Also, writing that letter to you woke me up to several things. You see, Alys, you were right, I am a pompous ass"—Darsee smiled awkwardly—"but I'm a pompous ass with a heart of gold. Since birth I've been catered to by my parents, my aunts, by the help, everyone. When everyone pampers you, it takes superhuman effort to remain levelheaded, and yet how much I abhor sycophancy, which is status elevation by association. What can I do for someone? How can my friendship benefit them? Could I put in a good word even though it's undeserved? Zero unaffectedness. Zero authenticity. Zero sincerity. Flattery will get you nowhere with me, but at first I thought you were playing the 'I'm not interested' grab-it tactic. But your disinterest couldn't have been more genuine. Never in my life had I thought anyone would refuse to marry me. Never had I imagined that what I was bringing to the table would not outweigh my flaws. Time had turned me into that person, but that is not who I want to be. Sometimes we lose sight of ourselves, but you see me, Alys, and you force me to see myself."

"You force me to see myself too," Alys said. "When I think of the things I said about you and your loyalty, I'm so mortified. You're the most loyal person I know. You're always courteous to Sherry—the way you called out Hammy for belittling her accent. You gave me a book that meant so much to you, and then you genuinely wanted to hear my views on it. You were so hospitable to my aunt and uncle. Juju's music teacher called you humble. All these things may have been enough for me to revise my opinion of you, but the way you dealt with your sister's predicament, the way you expressed sorrow for her situation without blaming or castigating her for it, the way you acknowledged your mother's sexuality without judging her harshly, as too many other sons would have, I came to admire you even more."

Darsee pulled Alys close as they walked deeper into the fruit grove.

"The things I said," he said, "about your family. Right or wrong, I shouldn't have said them, or at least not like that. And how ashamed I've been over suggesting you not meet them as much as you might want."

"You should be ashamed," Alys said, smiling sweetly, "but I accept your apology."

"So very kind of you," Darsee said playfully.

"You didn't give me any signal at Jena's and Bungles's engagement that you still had feelings for me."

"You didn't give *me* any signal," Darsee said. "The last I talked to you in Lahore in Nona's living room, you brought up Laila from *Sunlight* and how she was in love with a poor man. I imagined you were trying to tell me that you loved some poor man. Clearly I am not poor."

"Clearly you are not poor." Alys laughed. "A nice bonus for me. I'm joking."

"I have something for you," Darsee said. "It was my mother's."

Darsee slipped a small sapphire ring onto Alys's finger. It was perfect. It was full of heart.

"I love you," Darsee said shyly. "I'm madly in like with you."

"I love you and I'm madly in like with you too," Alys said, equally shy. "When did you know you liked me?"

"From the very first look, and even more when you spoke."

Alys laughed. "I overheard you telling Bungles I was unattractive and not smart."

Darsee gave a guilty smile. "I was merely trying to get him to leave me alone and stop setting me up with anyone. I had no intentions of falling in love, and I resisted you as long as I could."

"Your Beena Aunty is going to have conniptions," Alys said.

"She's the reason I'm here," Darsee said. "She called me. She said she'd had words with you but, rude girl that you are, you refused to refuse marrying me if I asked you. I took that as my sign, and here I am."

Alys did not suppress her smile. "But why would she think we're engaged?"

Darsee reddened. "I may have inadvertently praised you one too many times."

"I see. Well, how very delighted Beena Aunty will be when she discovers she's played Cupid in our love story."

"She'll be thrilled." Darsee grinned.

"My Aunty Nona too," Alys said, "has, unbeknownst to her, played a role in our love story, as has Juju. If Aunty Nona didn't make cakes and Juju hadn't ordered a cake, I would never have turned up at your house—although, had I known it was for your house, I would never have even sat in the car, let alone delivered it."

"I know," Darsee said. "I'm so glad you didn't know it was my house and that you came, because, clearly, ignorance made all the difference. Although, in any case, I would have sought you out."

"It should have occurred to me that since your aunt's house is Versailles of Pakistan, then yours could very well be Buckingham Palace. What was your other aunt's house named, the White House?"

"Bingo." Darsee blushed. He took hold of Alys's hands and he kissed them. "You win a lifetime's supply of anything you want."

"I have everything," Alys said. She loved her hands in Darsee's grip. She thought back to the all-too-brief moment when their fingers had connected, and now she finally allowed herself to fall into the full luxury of a touch she'd dreamed about but had thought impossible. "I don't think my life could be any more perfect than it is at this moment."

Chapter 26

"Dracula proposed and you accepted?" Mr. Binat said. "But you detest him."

"Over time, I've come to like Dracula very much."

"Alysba, my princess." Mr. Binat peered at her. "I don't have to say this to you, but I will. If you are feeling forced to accept this offer because of his assets, which I agree are hard to ignore, please do not. You of all my daughters will not thrive on money and prestige alone."

"Will you feel better if I tell you I respect him?"

"Respect Dracula!"

"We must stop calling him Dracula." Alys laughed. "I have discovered that he has the humility to admit to a mistake and the ability to change."

"Humility! That man?"

"Yes," Alys said. "That man."

The family was called in. Mr. Binat told them all to sit down. Alys had an announcement.

"I'm getting married," Alys said.

"What!" Mrs. Binat yelped.

"To Valentine Darsee."

Mrs. Binat nearly fainted, and Jena rushed to the kitchen to get her water. She too was shocked. Everyone was shocked. Everyone said, "To Dracula! But! How!"

"When," Jena demanded to know, "did you first decide you even liked him enough to marry him?"

"Easy," Alys said. "When Aunty Nona told me how much he paid for the original artwork in his house. I thought, if he can pay that much to decorate his walls, imagine how much he'll spend to decorate his wife."

"Be serious, Alys," Jena said. "Marriage is not some joking matter. He disgusts you."

"You loathe him," Qitty said.

"Despise him," Mari said.

"*Nafreth si,*" Hillima said. "You hate him."

"We all hate him," Mrs. Binat said feebly.

It was time, Alys decided, to tell her family that their Dracula was responsible for Wickaam marrying Lady. Mr. Binat could not have been more grateful. Long hours he'd spent contemplating how he was going to repay Nisar and Nona. He would offer to repay Darsee, of course, but Darsee, smitten by love for Alys and filthy rich, would, thankfully, be sure to decline repayment.

"Princess Alysba," Mr. Binat said. "Get ready for people to detest you. People can tolerate a woman being intelligent or pretty, and you are both. To be intelligent, pretty, and rich is an open invitation to enviable envy."

Mrs. Binat told Mr. Binat to stop cracking silly jokes at such a momentous time. Alys was not intelligent. Intelligent girls grew their hair long and did not sit in the sun. Clearly, Darsee lacked intelligence too, but his stupidity was their gain. Begum Valentine Darsee! Mrs. Valentine Darsee! *Hai!* Mrs. Binat kissed Alys on the forehead and proclaimed she'd always known in her mother's heart that God would not abandon her strange naïve frump of a daughter and that Alys would be able to grab it, and, look, she'd grabbed a prize.

"I told you to stay away from him," Mrs. Binat said, beaming. "Luckily, you never listen to me."

Alys listened with amusement, her mother recasting Darsee from ugly duckling to stellar swan and her sisters turning him from Dracula to Darsee Bhai.

The phone rang. Hillima left to answer. She returned and handed the cordless to Mr. Binat. "*Fart Sahib da foon si.* It's Fart Sahib's phone call."

Mr. Binat literally took a step back as Farhat Kaleen blared an earful of congratulations. Was it true? Beena dey Bagh was livid. He'd called to warn his beloved family—Mr. Binat mouthed to his family, "We are beloved family today"—warn his beloved family that her wrath would be terrible and that perhaps Alys should reconsider, but, was it true, was she to be Mrs. Valentine Darsee? Was Alys there? Sherry wanted to speak to her.

Mr. Binat handed Alys the phone.

"Alys!" Sherry shrieked. "Is it true?"

Alys took a deep breath. "Yes."

"I told you," Sherry said. "I told you he was making mammoth you-you eyes at you. I also told you that you needed to grab him, and you did."

"Yes," Alys said. "Grabbing him has been my life's sole purpose this past year, as per your and Mummy's instructions."

But Alys's heart was doing funny things at the love in Sherry's voice. Their friendship had been in trouble for a moment, but now it was back on course. Sherry said she was leaving for Dilipabad—these were not celebrations she was planning to forgo. Kaleen could tend to Beena dey Bagh if he wanted, but tonight she and Alys had a date at the graveyard, where they would share a celebratory smoke.

Chapter 27

As per Mrs. Binat's fantasy, it was decided that Alys and Darsee and Jena and Bungles would have double *mehndi* and *nikah* ceremonies at the Dilipabad Gymkhana, while their *walima* ceremonies would take place separately in Lahore. Both the grooms-to-be were adamant that they were going to foot the bill for everything, and Jena and Alys had, after much deliberation, decided, Why not? It was going to be their money anyway once they married. They'd suggested a preposterous amount of *haq mehr*, but both men could afford it and they happily paid up. Also, the sisters insisted on the right of divorce being added to their marriage certificates, despite Mrs. Binat's protest that such a caveat was an ill omen.

"Life continues beyond happily ever after," Alys said. "Better safe than sorry."

People in the know were convinced that the eldest Binat girls practiced magic spells, for not only had the two grabbed eligible bachelors younger than themselves, but Bungles and Darsee also obeyed their every command. It was widely whispered that Alys did

not want children; the scandalized concluded that Darsee's acceptance of this proved that she was a highly accomplished witch. Beena
dey Bagh was very unhappy at what was transpiring, but after Annie
reminded her that Jeorgeullah was a catastrophe and to please not
alienate Valentine, she accepted that he was marrying Alys, and she
managed to find solace in the fact that a stellar educator was entering the family. Sherry was, of course, overjoyed, and Farhat Kaleen
said no one could be happier than he and that no one could have
prayed harder than he had for the Binat sisters to prosper. Ganju *jee*
was ecstatic: The Binats were going from fake to real jewelry. The
only person peeved was über-designer Qazi of QaziKreations, because Alys and Jena were not ordering their bridal outfits from him.
Instead, they were going to have their mother design them, because
Mrs. Binat had decided to give fashion designing a try: Pinkie Heirlooms, with an ecstatic tailor Shawkat at the helm. Still, Qazi was
dressing their sisters, so there was yet a holiday or two for him in that.

One evening, as the Binats were discussing the wedding menu,
the phone rang and Mrs. Binat went to answer it. When she returned, she was pale and Hillima was leading her by the elbow and
seating her on the sofa.

"You won't believe who was on the phone," Mrs. Binat said.

"You're scaring me," said Mr. Binat. "Who?"

"Tinkle," Mrs. Binat said. "Tinkle was congratulating us on JenaBungles and AlysDarsee. She said she'd always had full faith that
the girls would do the Binat name proud. She said she was looking
forward to their weddings. She said she wanted to host a big *milad*
and *dholki f*or each girl at"—Pinkie's voice trembled—"at the old
house. She said: 'We will invite the whole of Pakistan. We will show
them that nothing and no one can divide the Binat clan.'"

"No," Mr. Binat said loudly. Mrs. Binat, Jena, Alys, Mari, and
Qitty jumped.

Mr. Binat cleared his throat. "I did not tell you, but when I was
desperately looking for money to pay Mr. Jeorgeullah Wickaam to

SONIAH KAMAL

marry my daughter, I had no option left but to arrive at Goga and Tinkle's door."

Mrs. Binat gasped. So did the girls.

"It was not their meanness of spirit," Mr. Binat said slowly, "that was displayed in those stale biscuits they served me, or that Tinkle did not even bother to appear, or that Goga took his time appearing. Rather, it was the smile that spread on my brother's face when I told him why I was there. Goga said he'd heard that one of my daughters had run away. He said he did not have money to spare on marrying off wayward girls. 'Bark,' he said, 'you obviously don't have the brains to make money, for men fall on their faces all the time and yet manage to get right back up. In business you are a known failure, but I did not expect you to be a failure of a father too.'

"I wanted to tell him about my kind and generous Jena, my fearless Alys, my artist Qitty, who holds her head up high no matter what anyone says to her, and my Mari, who just wants everyone to go to heaven. Even my silly, selfish Lady, who doesn't know what is good for her and just wants to have a good time all the time. But I didn't tell him about any one of my daughters. He doesn't deserve to know a single thing about my precious girls.

"As I was leaving that house, Pinkie, I realized that I'd spent this past decade there, if not physically, then in my heart by missing it and longing for it. But there was nothing there. It should have ceased to be home the minute we arrived in Dilipabad and you began to scrub clean this house. I should have rolled up my sleeves and joined you. They say blood is thicker than water. I say to hell with that. If blood mistreats you, better water. And if friends prove false, no matter, find better or be alone and be your own best friend."

"But, Barkat," Pinkie said carefully, "you have always dreamed of patching up with your brother. I know it."

"Goga is my brother biologically and Tinkle my cousin biologically, but in no other way have they earned those relationships. And the time for chances is over." Mr. Binat raised his hand. "I'm not retaliating, Pinkie. It is not a matter of retaliation. It is a matter of principle. They've treated us shabbily, as if we were enemies and not blood. I realized that you are correct: Our failure is their success. Since they broke the blood bond, I have no interest reviving it. We will not be inviting them to Jena's or Alys's wedding. We will not be holding any functions in their home. They are not welcome in my home or in my heart. My only regret is that I was unable to develop a relationship with my nephews and nieces or give my own children the gift of close cousins. But so be it. Not my fault. Not my problem.

"Pinkie, my love, I apologize to you for all the times I ignored your complaints about them, told you to get over their insults, to tolerate it, to compromise, to let it go. It was callous of me. It is not how a spouse should treat a spouse. Not how I, your husband, should have treated you, my wife, when I'd vowed to love and protect you. Forgive me."

Khushboo "Pinkie" Binat instantly forgave her husband everything, for this was every Pakistani wife's dream come true, that her husband should sincerely apologize on behalf of his family.

"And Jena, Alys, the rest of you," Mr. Binat said, "if your husband ever mistreats you, know that you have parents who support you and a home to return to here in Dilipabad, to rest and recover before you go back out into the world."

What Will People Say
Log Kya Kahenge

PRINCIPAL NAHEED: *You know Alys and Jena were British School of Dilipabad teachers. In fact, I was the one who introduced Alys Binat to Valentine Darsee, at the NadirFiede wedding. So sad—Nadir's and Fiede's divorce. My daughters, Gin and Rum, are so excited for Jena and Alys, who will surely be among their first clients when my daughters begin their designer-clothing line. Expect brilliant things from all BSD brands. I mean girls.*

LADY: Hai, *my only regret in eloping was that I didn't get to wear QaziKreations at my wedding. But I will be wearing Qazi only at JenaBungles and AlysDarsee. Oh God, not this question again! Who cares if Wick was paid to marry me? Think of it this way: Instead of a man buying a woman, here is a woman who bought a man.*

MARI: *Shakespeare says "All's well that ends well." God says that too. So you know what that means? Shakespeare was Muslim.*

QITTY: *My sister Alys gave me the magazines.* Mode's *last issue was published in October 2001. They were forced to close down. It wasn't circulation. They had plenty of subscribers and were growing by the day. They were forced to shut doors because of lack of advertisements. Top designers only wanted to design for skeletons. Their Loss. Fat Stocky Short Squat Women Are Here. We Exist. We Are Visible.*

HAMMY: *Marrying Jaans was Sammy's choice, and staying with him is her choice too. My ring? Two-carat solitaire. Yes, he is one of Jaans's good friends but nothing like him. My fiancé is a gem of a person. No, I was never interested in Valentine Darsee. Who is spreading this rumor? What will my fiancé think if he finds out? For God's sake, Valentine is one of my baby brother's best friends. I've always seen him as just another brother.*

JAANS: Shaadi *equals* barbaadi, *marriage equals misery, a socially constructed battleground. My wife, Sammy, agrees with me.* Chalo, *what to do,* bale bale.

BEENA DEY BAGH: Jab mian biwi razee tho kya karey qazi. *When the bride and groom are willing, nothing the priest can do to stop the wedding.*

JUJU DARSEE: *My brother couldn't have found anyone better than Alysba Binat.*

ANNIE DEY BAGH: *I'm so excited that my boyfriend is coming to attend the weddings. Yes, he's Nigerian. Why the face? What's bothering you? That I have a boyfriend? That he's black? Both?*

MRS. SYEDA SHIREEN KALEEN NEE SHERRY LOOCLUS: *Of course it is necessary to have an income of one's own beyond pocket money. I have never believed otherwise. But what a pity that homemakers are unpaid and so undervalued. Yes, Alys and I are planning to open a bookstore, and I will be in charge of translations. We are very excited. If my husband objects, my secret weapon, Annie dey Bagh, will have a word with him. That always works.*

ROSE-NAMA: *Miss Alys was always my favorite teacher, and I was one of her teacher's pets. My mother switched my schools because she didn't like the alternating uniform/free-clothes days. Or the new British School Group motto: "Home Is Everywhere on Earth. Be Honest. Be Kind." Or the introduction of a mandatory comparative-religion class. Or, as per new guidelines, a class on the history of marriage and sex.*

TAHIRA: *I'm so thrilled for Miss Alys and of course Miss Jena. Next on the list of duties is the good news that they are expecting. Thank you! My baby is due soon.*

RAGHAV KUMAR: *I knew something was up between those two.*

HIJAB'S MOTHER: *Of course my daughter is best friends with Mrs. Lady Wickaam. Did you know Jeorgeullah Wickaam is Valentine Darsee's and Annie dey Bagh's first cousin? Wickaam is such a humble boy. Wants to make it on his own merit, so prefers to keep a distance from his relatives.*

HILLIMA: *My girls. They are like family.*

MOTHERS IN DILIPABAD AND OTHER "-ABADS," "-PURS," AND "-ISTANS" ACROSS PAKISTAN, TO THEIR DAUGHTERS: *If Alys Binat and Jena Binat at their advanced ages can grab such catches, then you have no excuses.*

DILIPABAD GYMKHANA VIPS: *Pinkie Binat has exceeded expectations in training her daughters in the art of hook, reel, grab. All in favor of acknowledging her now and then? Done! Let's buy an outfit or two from her debut collection.*

SOCIALITES IN SOCIAL LIGHTS: *Congrats to AlysDarsee and JenaBungles. Wishing them all the best on their Happily Ever After.*

Epilogue

One Year Later

Lady stood at the window in the Dubai apartment, looking at Jumeirah Beach in the moonlight. The glass was not as clean as she liked, and Wick did not take kindly either to smudges. They'd paid a pretty penny for this place, one of the finest in town, but you had to spend money to make money. You had to look the part. She would have an extra-sharp word with the maid about the windows. Lady patted her lips, pleased with the Botox, wondering if she should go plumper, bigger always being better.

"I'm bored," she said to Wick's reflection in the window. He was lifting weights. What a handsome man she'd managed to marry, Lady thought for the millionth time. Dracula and Bungles did not come close. But. Then. Their money. Wick had turned out to be an even bigger flop with finances than her father. Alys and Jena had sent her some money to spend as she pleased and she was not going to tell Wick, because, unfortunately, he had the annoying habit of thinking the money her sisters and mother sent her was meant for him. She could make money modeling, but Wick, like her father, did not want her to model. However, while her father was controlling,

Wick loved and respected her too much to bear the thought of other men doing the dirty with her pinups.

They'd had a rough patch for a while there, when she'd found out about his children, but that part of his life was behind him now. It wasn't even as if it was his fault alone—he was irresistible to women. They would have to learn to resist him, because there was only one lady for him now, she always reminded him, and that lady was Mrs. Lady Wickaam.

In fact, more than being upset with Wick, Lady was still annoyed with her family for barring him from Alys's and Jena's weddings. She would have boycotted in protest, except they really had been weddings of the year and Wick had encouraged her to attend. Best, he'd said, to stay in her sisters' good books.

"Let's go watch a movie," Lady said as she turned away from the window. "Or eat out."

Wickaam mumbled something about their budget.

"Not to worry, Wick," Lady said, "we'll be rich and famous yet—this time our business idea is foolproof. Touch wood." And she touched the granite counter in the kitchen.

They were going to open up a lingerie boutique, Pakeezah Passions. Pure Passions. Their logo would be peacock feathers rising majestically out of what anyone with half a brain would be able to see was cleavage. Their tagline was "No more Mr. Lonely Pants. No more Ms. Lonely Panty." Pakeezah Passions would be the hottest lingerie ever, with a Pakistani twist. So Sindhi *ajrak* teddies and Baluchi mirror-work baby dolls and Punjabi leather bra sets and Pathan pom-pom panties. Also, on a separate note, Lady had insisted on a line devoted to brassieres of cotton and lace for those blessed with big busts. Wick was terribly excited. He was sure this business was the one to turn them from Wannabes to VIPs, and he grabbed his wife and she grabbed him back.

———

Mr. and Mrs. Binat lounged in bed, enjoying chai and *samosas* prepared on this Dilipabad evening by Hillima, who was still elated at having received generous amounts of cash and gold earrings from both Alys's and Jena's bridegrooms, unlike Lady's useless husband—looks, *ka aachar dalna hai,* was one supposed to pickle and preserve his good looks!—who had asked her what wedding present she was giving him.

"I still can't believe it," Mrs. Binat said to Mr. Binat, her eyes perpetually shining. "Three daughters married in one year, and so well, *duniya dekhti reh gayi*—the whole world watched in envy. Barkat, did I not always tell you I would only give birth to marriageable material?"

Mr. Binat looked up from his book on Mullah Nasruddin's sagely antics. The miracle was Alys and Jena finding the rarest of husbands: supportive, decent, rich, smart, caring, faithful, uncontrolling, kind, good-looking, healthy, funny, generous, polite, affectionate, respectful. Such men simply did not exist except in novels. Pinkie had her eye on Cornell-Babur for Qitty or Mari, whichever he preferred, but she was not as bothered as she would have been a year ago, because she had more-pressing issues to keep herself busy-busy.

Pinkie Heirlooms had taken off, thanks to demand from gymkhana patrons, and she was adding a bridal line called Binat Bridals, and she had dreams of a vast empire under the umbrella House of Binat. Mr. Binat threw *samosa* crumbs to Dog and Kutta, new additions to the family. The puppies leapt off the rug, barking madly, happy to receive scraps.

Mari sat on the bed by her parents' feet. She'd been beaming so hard for the last year, her teeth ached. She was convinced each day anew that her sisters' outrageously good fortunes were the result of her piety and prayers. In giving thanks to the Almighty, Mari had taken to wearing a *burqa,* and whether Lady called her Ninja, or her mother called her Nut Case, or that brother in High Chai hissed, "Move it, Crow," she couldn't care less. The entire world was losing its way.

Mari flipped through brochures of the advanced Quran courses offered at the Red Mosque in Islamabad as well as of Harvard's comparative-religion courses. She'd apply to both. Though, really, going to Harvard would mean returning with prestige enough to set up her own Islamic school to rival all Islamic schools—*Al-Hira*, she would call it, after the cave in which the Prophet Muhammad had hidden from the baddies who wanted to kill him. She would come back and she would rule and she would make people like Fazool and Moolee give up their New Year's parties—God willing, of course.

Qitty glanced at Mari browsing through the brochures. She returned to the drawing she was shading. She'd met a guy at Alys's and Jena's weddings, and it had been a perfect courtship. Then he'd said, "Jumbo, I'll marry you if you lose fifty pounds and promise to maintain the weight loss forever." When people would ask Qitty what it was about that particular moment, all she knew to say was that, suddenly, she was fed up. She'd yelled at him with all her might: "*Daffa ho,* get lost. If I'm happy loving myself just the way I am, then who are you to put conditions on accepting and loving me?"

That day, a lifetime of rage was unleashed at Lady, her mother, people who compared her to globular fruit, people who used "health" as an excuse to mock her; her anger poured out of her and onto paper. She'd sent her words to a national newspaper: She was not just fat; she was fat and intelligent, fat and funny, fat and kind, fat and fun, fat and beautiful, fat and a good friend, fat and creative, fat plus every lovely attribute in the world. She was fat and happy and did not care about being thin—imagine that.

Next Qitty knew, she'd been offered a weekly column on self-acceptance and talks all over the place. How she'd reveled in Lady's stunned shriek: "What! You've become *famous* for being *fat.* A fashion and beauty blogger." How she'd relished showing a silent Lady the thank-you letters she was continuously receiving for talking about living large and celebrating *all* of oneself. Never in her dreams had Qitty thought that she'd be called a role model or an inspiration. ("Never in my dreams either," Lady had said in a pinched voice as she'd wondered if Pakeezah Passions should design lingerie for fatties.) But it had been a dream of Qitty's to pen a graphic novel about a fat sister surrounded by four not-fat sisters and how the fat sister was the one who triumphed. And dreams came true, Qitty knew, as she inked in the final panel for *Unmarriageable.*

In Lahore, Jena was wrapping up a meeting with potential financiers to discuss funding for her dream organization—TWS, Together We Stand—which would provide educational scholarships to underprivileged girls in Pakistan. On the way home, she had the driver stop at Nona's Nices, Nona's flagship bakery, recently opened in Lahore, where she purchased her daily cravings, cream rolls. Bungles would monitor her gestational diabetes and they'd enjoy the dessert together in front of their wood fire as they debated girls' names.

Alys Binat—she'd chosen to keep her maiden name postmarriage—and Valentine Darsee walked hand in hand in Jane Austen's House Museum, in Chawton village, on their holiday in England. It was the cottage that Jane's elder brother had given his widowed mother and two sisters, Jane and Cassandra, to live in, and where Jane had written and revised many of her novels.

Alys ran her hand over the outside walls, the main door, the guest book, which she signed. She would never forget that Darsee had arranged this surprise visit for her birthday. Next they were going to Bath, Lyme Regis, Steventon, Winchester, and other Austen stops. Alys made a mental note to pick up souvenirs from each place, for her and Sherry's thriving bookstore.

Alys squeezed Darsee's hand and he smiled at her as they moved from room to room. She thought of her favorite line in *Pride and Prejudice:* "For what do we live, but to make sport for our neighbours, and laugh at them in our turn?" She thought of Jane's mother and elder sister, both named Cassandra, outliving their beloved Jane, her father, George Austen, her brothers, James, George, Edward, Henry, Frank, and Charles, cousin Eliza, and of Martha and Mary Lloyd and Anne Sharp, Jane's friends. Of Harris Bigg-Wither, whose claim to fame was to be Jane Austen's fiancé of one night. She thought of Jane dead at forty-one and yet so very much alive in novel after novel.

Alys thought of the fictional Bennet daughters: Jane, Elizabeth, Kitty, Mary, and Lydia. She thought of Mrs. Bennet and Mr. Bennet. Mr. Fitzwilliam Darcy. Mrs. Lucas and Mr. Lucas and Maria and—her favorite character—Charlotte. Mr. Collins. Mrs. and Mr. Gardiner. Aunt Phillips. Of Charles Bingley. Caroline Bingley. Mrs. Hurst and her husband. Catherine de Bourgh and Anne de Bourgh. Colonel Fitzwilliam. She thought of the servants: Mrs. Hill and Mrs. Jenkinson and Mrs. Reynolds, the housekeeper at Pemberley, whose high praise of Mr. Darcy had made all the difference.

Alys thought of Jane Austen in this living room, at this small round wooden table, her inkpot, her paper, the gliding of her fingers, her mind conjuring up lives, story after story, smiling, laughing even, at something Mrs. Bennet said, something she'd made Mrs. Bennet say. Mrs. Bennet, the world's worst mother but also perhaps the best mother because all she wanted was for her daughters to live happy, successful lives according to her times.

Alys looked up at Darsee and she wondered how this had happened, how he had gotten so lucky to have her marry him (oh, how lucky was she). Then they were in front of the cabinet displaying different editions of Jane Austen's novels. Her gaze rested on the first page of the universally beloved novel *Pride and Prejudice*. Alys took Darsee's hand and together their fingers traced over that most famous of first lines, the one she still assigned students in her literature classes to reimagine as they saw fit:

> *It is a truth universally acknowledged, that a single man in posses-sion of a good fortune, must be in want of a wife.*

Pride and Prejudice and Me

I first immersed myself in Jane Austen's *Pride and Prejudice* when I was sixteen years old. As interesting as its marriage plot was, I was spellbound, rather, by Austen's social criticism and how it was conveyed through her pithy wit. Here was a centuries-old English writer who may as well have been writing about contemporary Pakistani society. As a postcolonial child who grew up in the 1980s and was educated in Pakistan's English medium system, I was well versed in classic English poets and novelists. For fun, I read Enid Blyton, and because I studied for some years in an international school in Saudi Arabia, American authors such as Judy Blume. While these storytellers spoke of boarding-school midnight feasts and bras and busts, it was Jane Austen's wit and wisdom that first encouraged me to think critically about patriarchal society; a woman's traditional role; the ties of family, friends, and frenemies; and the cost of keeping up appearances. As her stories skewered pretentious hypocrites, Austen's sharp pen drew a map for what marriage and compromise, silence and speaking up, meant, and her satirical insights on how to acknowledge drawing-room duplicity while still finding a way to laugh afforded comfort and solace.

Mrs. Bennet was like too many mothers I'd grown up around, those obsessed with getting their daughters married off because that was what "good mothers" did. As for "good girls," they obeyed their mothers, regardless of what they themselves wanted. But Elizabeth Bennet was a girl we wanted to be like, to arrive at a Netherfield Park in a muddy gown without a care for Pakistani society's quintessential cry of *Log kya kahenge?*, "What will people say?" In a country where marriages continue to be arranged on the basis of convenience, pedigrees, and bank balances, Elizabeth's spurning of the self-righteous Mr. Collins and the pompous Mr. Darcy were defiant acts we could look up to. According to Pakistani society, both "boys" would have made very suitable matches for Elizabeth, but—*gasp*—she said no, because *she* didn't believe they were right for her. Yes, Austen's novels end in the happily-ever-after of marriage, but these were marriages of the heroine's own choosing, after the hero had earned her respect, and they were based on both bride and groom *liking* each other. The marriages in Austen's novels gave me *hope* that there were good men to be found, and I wanted to pay tribute to that.

There were also other characters and situations in *Pride and Prejudice* that leapt out as mirroring Pakistani society. There was Lydia, who'd run off with Mr. Wickham, and whose whole family was terrified that if he didn't marry her, she'd be ruined and so would they. Was there any worry more Pakistani than the concern about what might bring a family honor or dishonor? There was sensible Charlotte Lucas, who made an expedient marriage for every reason but love. Was there anything more Pakistani than her calculated, "arranged" marriage? And there was Caroline Bingley, a snob disdainful of anyone who was not landed gentry or who hadn't inherited money—never mind that she herself was not landed gentry, since her wealth came via trade. Was there anything more apropos to Pakistan than class issues, snootiness, and double standards?

As I read and reread *Pride and Prejudice,* Elizabeth Bennet and every other character ceased to be English—to me, they were Pakistani. That I was imagining characters and scenarios in a Pakistani setting was nothing extraordinary. Ever since I could remember, I'd been engaging in literary transference/transplantation/translation from one culture to another. Growing up on English literature, I taught myself to see my daily reality reflected in my reading material, while plumbing its universal truths in search of particulars. Not just particulars in food and clothing, which were easily recast—*dupattas* instead of bonnets, *samosas* instead of scones—but rather in thematic content and characters' emotions. Thus Jane Bennet became just another Pakistani girl watching out for her reputation by being reticent instead of flirtatious, and her sadness at being spurned is no different from anyone's anywhere. In reading English literature through a Pakistani lens, it seemed to me that all cultures were concerned with the same eternal questions and that people were more similar to one another than they were different. As Alys Binat says in *Unmarriageable,* "Reading widely can lead to an appreciation of the universalities across cultures."

But Valentine Darsee says, "We've been forced to seek ourselves in the literature of others for too long." In Pakistan there are seventy-four living languages, and Urdu and English are both official state languages. However, English, and a good accent, remains the lingua franca of privilege and opportunity. As an adult, I came across Thomas Babington Macaulay's "Minute on Education" (1835), in which he sets the colonized Subcontinent linguistic policy for creating "a person brown in color but white in sensibilities." It was then that I realized what the origins were of the emphasis in the Pakistani educational system on learning English and English literature at the cost of exploring our indigenous languages and literatures. History has made it such that my mother tongue, for all intents and purposes, is the English language. I wanted to write a novel that paid homage to Jane Austen and *Pride and Prejudice,* as well as combined my braided identification with English-language and Pakistani culture, so that the "literature of others" became the literature of everyone. Therefore, *Unmarriageable.*

Notes and Resources

Dilipabad is a fictional town in Punjab, Pakistan, created by the author.

The play *Ismat Apa Kay Naam,* "In Ismat Apa's Name," was performed in Lahore in 2012. The author's setting it in 2001 is intentional.

For a list of books, authors, films, and people mentioned in *Unmarriageable,* go to the author's website, soniahkamal.com.

Charity Organizations in the Novel for Which Nona Bakes

Edhi Foundation (Edhi.org/usa/): A social welfare organization which also saves abandoned infants by placing "cradles" outside their offices for the babies to be put in.

Darul-ul-Sukun (Darulsukun.com): A welfare organization for people with disabilities.

Depilex Smileagain Foundation (us.depilexsmileagain.com): An organization that provides acid-attack survivors with medical care, rehabilitation, and opportunities.

Literacy Organizations Mirroring Jena's Venture

Developments in Literacy (dil.org): An organization that educates and empowers underprivileged students, especially girls.

The Citizens Foundation (tcfusa.org): A charity group that educates and empowers underprivileged students.

Jane Austen Literacy Foundation (JALF) (janeaustenlf.org): A foundation that supports literacy through volunteer programs, and funds libraries for communities in need across the world.

Acknowledgments

To Jane Austen, for the stories you wrote that speak across centuries, for being blunt, impolite, funny, and honest. For skewering "good society."

To my husband, Mansoor Wasti, thank you for your support in every way. I simply would not be here without you.

Shikha Malaviya, kindred spirit, for chai-scones-*samosas,* old age on a beach, for reading this novel, email by email, as it was being written, all original 160,000 words of it, and then helping me see the trees for the forest. Your friendship is everything in every language.

My parents, Musarrat Kamal Qureshi and Naheed Kamal, née Pandit, whose joy and pride is everything.

My children: Indus, who has been reading my work and giving feedback since she was eleven years old; Buraaq, Indus, Miraage, my heartbeats, who really, at the end of it all, just want to know, Mom, what's for dinner? To the One who should have stayed but even went Unnamed, and to Khyber, and all lost to miscarriages—not a day goes by when your mother doesn't think about you: You are in this book, my babies, because you live in me.

My literary agent, Al Zuckerman: truly your belief in my writing has meant the world and is why I am still writing. Thank you for keeping faith and restoring mine; for loving and championing *An Isolated Incident* as ferociously as you do; you are my blessing. Thank you also, Samantha Wekstein at Writers House.

Anne Speyer, my wonderful editor, from your very first email I knew you got what I was trying to write with *Unmarriageable.* A billion *shukriyas* for making my vision possible and, in acquiring this novel, making my big fat dream come true, and for loving all these characters, and for your wisdom and guidance. Thank you, Jennifer Heuer, for a gorgeous cover. Thank you with all my heart to Janet Wygal, Melissa Sanford, Allison Schuster, Kara Welsh, Kim Hovey, Jennifer Hershey, Marietta Anastassatos, Kathy Lord, and everyone at Penguin Random House–Ballantine.

My niece Jahanara, thank you for being my very first reader. I was so scared to hand it to you, and then you got back to me to say you'd read it twice, back-to-back, and it was your favorite novel in the world—there are no words to ever tell you what your words meant to me. My sister, Sarah, for literally letting me take your copy of *Pride and Prejudice* out of your hands because I needed to make notes that very moment, for your Iqbal Hussain painting story, and fact-check responses. My brother, Fahad, for grace under frantic fact-check emails, for your unwavering belief in my writing and this novel. Sobia, sister-in-law, also first reader of the epilogue and then the novel; your laughter at the characters, the situations; your encouragement—gifts that kept me going. Nephew Samir, you are my lucky star, born on the very day the cover was finalized and the launch date decided—your birth will be forever linked to this book. To my niece Ana for your input on the cover and for the cute—"but Soniah Khala, it's so long, I promise I'll read it when it's published." My Khalas and Mamoos—Tahira, Haseena, Mahira, Nisar, Mushtaq, you are in this book because you live in my heart, one way or another. My aunt Helen for giving me books as gifts, including my first *Pride and Prejudice.*

When I joined Georgia State University to embark on a four-year full-time academic MFA with closed-book exams, with three kids at home, I really did not know what I was getting myself into. This novel became my MFA thesis and was written in two months, and I truly believe that if it wasn't for that MFA-induced time crunch, I may still (perhaps forever) have been dreaming of writing it. Sometimes you can't help but believe that there is rhyme and reason behind every hard thing. To my inspirational creative writing professors: Josh Russell for your class on flash fiction, Sheri Joseph for your emphasis on novels; John Holman for your class on radical revision. Thank you all for your belief that this novel would sell. To Megan Sexton for being the best boss ever at *Five Points: A Journal of Literature and Arts* and for our fun conversations. My literature professors: Marilynn Richtarik for teaching me to write, which has made *all* the difference, and for William Trevor's *Felicia's Journey.* Jay Rajiva for postcolonial discussions and my soul text, Attia Hosain's *Sunlight on a Broken Column.* Tania Caldwell for talks on memory and Jill Ker Conway's *The Road from Coorain.* Scott Heath for *Harlem* and Jessie Redmon Fauset's *Plum Bun.* To the admin staff at GSU, for all you do.

To *all* my well-wishers—you know who you are—too many to name, who repeatedly cheered me on and kept asking when the novel was coming out. Hira Mariam for my beautiful website, so many jokes and laughs, and your love for *An Isolated Incident.* Meeta Kaur for your hospitality, passion, and encouragement. Zari Nauman for your feedback and giggles over Lahore. Manju Shringarpure, for your valuable texts: Get off Facebook and finish your novel! Sharbari Zohra Ahmed and Sadia Ashraf for weighing in on the cover and so much more. Kataryna Jakubiak for being the first to read the opening chapter and for your feedback. Devoney Looser for all your support and enthusiasm. Sonya Rehman for hope and more. Thrity Umrigar for hope and more. Sonali Dev for hope and more. To Pratima Malaviya for her delicious sketches of my Binat girls and more. Thank you: Kathleen A. Flynn. Jennifer S. Brown. Jessica

Handler. Nandita Godbole. Dipika Mukherjee. Maheen Baqai. Rebecca Kumar. Nina Gangadharan. Saadia Faruqi. Kwan Holloway. Swati Narayan. Missale Ayele. Priya Nair. Connie Buchanan. Laurel Phenix. Reema Khan.

To Janeites the world over and Jane Austen Society members everywhere, especially Jane Austen Society of North America (JASNA), where I first discovered fellow Austen fans and scholars. To JASNA Georgia Janeites: Erin Elwood. Renata Dennis. Kristen Miller Zone and everyone. To the Jane Austen Literacy Foundation, where I serve as a literacy ambassador.

To libraries everywhere, who are such a blessing, and especially to Fulton County libraries and Northeast/Spruill Oaks Branch, Georgia, for so much, and for weighing in on the cover: Laura Hoefner, Jayshree Sheth, Stephanie Gokey, Karen Swenson, Eva Mcguigan, and Gillian Hill.

To the baristas at Starbucks (store # 8202, Georgia), where much of this novel was so frantically written: Elise Watts, Brandon Ross, Emma Denney, Brittany Meekan, John London, Amberley Ferguson, and Beatrice—for keeping this immigrant writer in coffee (which is chai away from home), ice-cold water, and bright smiles daily for those two frightening, exhilarating months (for mothering me).

Thank you to all the following in Georgia and everywhere: independent bookstores and all others, literary organizations, book festivals, arts and culture magazines and websites for all you do for writers and for welcoming me into your fold.

Because there is always the kindness of strangers, to all in Georgia who I literally stopped on roads and in stores, who so willingly gave this author the time of day to weigh in on the cover: Thank you—we went with the teal one.

To: Sultan Golden, who makes his appearance in this novel as Dog and Kutta, and to Yaar, our cat, who made it to year nineteen.

To: Pakistan. Jeddah. England. America.

ABOUT THE AUTHOR

SONIAH KAMAL's debut novel, *An Isolated Incident,* was a finalist for the Townsend Prize for Fiction and the Karachi Literature Festival–Embassy of France Prize. Her TEDx Talk is about regrets and second chances. Kamal's award-winning work has appeared in numerous publications, including *The New York Times, The Guardian, BuzzFeed, Catapult,* and *Literary Hub.*

soniahkamal.com
Twitter: @SoniahKamal
Instagram: @SoniahKamal